D1023862

Conlan Brown's *The Firstborn* is a bullet train of suspense and supernatural visions. With brisk prose and razor-sharp action, *The Firstborn* satisfies any Christian fan of TV's *Heroes*. Brown has written a taut thriller of secret societies and Muslim terrorists in a story of Byzantine complexity. A nail-biting first novel from a rising star in Christian speculative fiction.

—Jefferson Scott
Author of *Fatal Defect* and *Operation: Firebrand*

Conlan Brown bursts onto the scene with a story that's every bit as intriguing as it is intense. Secret orders, superhuman gifts, and a deadly plot dot the landscape of *The Firstborn*. Brown's voice is unique and captivating and will draw you in on the first page. Don't miss this book!

—Mike Dellosso
Author of *The Hunted* and *Scream*

Fans of suspense will be delighted with *The Firstborn*. Conlan Brown weaves a wonderful tale of courage, forgiveness, and love.

—Larry J. Leech II
President of Word Weavers Writers Group

THE
FIRSTBORN

CONLAN BROWN

ReAlms
A Strang Company

Most STRANG COMMUNICATIONS BOOK GROUP products are available at special quantity discounts for bulk purchase for sales promotions, premiums, fund-raising, and educational needs. For details, write Strang Communications Book Group, 600 Rinehart Road, Lake Mary, Florida 32746, or telephone (407) 333-0600.

THE FIRSTBORN by Conlan Brown
Published by Realms
A Strang Company
600 Rinehart Road
Lake Mary, Florida 32746
www.strangbookgroup.com

The characters portrayed in this book are fictitious unless they are historical figures explicitly named. Otherwise, any resemblance to actual people, whether living or dead, is coincidental.

Design Director: Bill Johnson
Cover design by Justin Evans

Library of Congress Cataloging-in-Publication Data:

Brown, Conlan, 1984-
    The firstborn / Conlan Brown. -- 1st ed.
        p. cm.
    ISBN 978-1-59979-607-9
    I. Title.
    PS3602.R689F57 2009
    813'.6--dc22
                                        2009007002

09 10 11 12 13 — 9 8 7 6 5 4 3 2
Printed in the United States of America

For my late grandmother, Linanell Cecil—the woman who taught me to read and write.

And for the great-grandchildren she never got to meet: Canon and Allanna, Sam and Evelyn . . .

The legacy of the past. The joy of the present. The hope of the future.

The Triquetra

This ancient symbol was first seen in Europe in the form of Norse and Germanic runes. A recurring motif through Celtic art and a symbol of religious significance to pagans and Christians alike, the triquetra is a geometrically perfect depiction of three distinct parts, intertwined into a inextricable whole.

Over the centuries it has carried many different meanings, most notably that of the Christian Trinity: Father, Son, and Holy Spirit, but has historically carried other meanings, including: maiden, mother, and crone...land, sea, and air...life, death, and rebirth...

Past. Present. Future.

Prologue

DEATH CAME DOWN WITH the snow.

Devin Bathurst stood in the dawn flurry, unmoving, revealing none of the slicing chill that cut through to his bones.

Then he felt something. It always felt different for him. Sometimes it was a smell; other times it was a taste or a haze of color. He knew others with his gift who felt the same thing every time—a single feeling heralding the coming of—

Snow.

House.

Captors.

Anger.

Argument.

Rage.

Violence.

The girl, late teens or early twenties—

Crying.

Shouting.

Screaming.

BLAM!

The girl's body on the floor, grisly and broken, bored through by the bullet, lying in an expanding pool of red.

Devin's mind snapped back to the moment. The girl—he had to find the girl. He took a long, deep breath, letting it out with a puff of thick vapor. He had to stay focused. He had to stay placid, calm, icy. He reminded himself that none of it had actually happened—

—yet.

Chapter 1

THE DOOR TO THE gas station opened with a tinny *gling*, the antiquated bell chiming as Devin entered the store. The sound was a testament to the essence of the small backwoods town. At best it was quaint; at worst it was a sign of dilapidation in the middle of snowy nowhere.

As he entered he picked up one of the newspapers by the door, reading the headline: *Holy Man Murdered Outside of Ohio Mosque— Imam Basam Al Nassar Shot to Death in Car.*

The person behind the counter was a young man. He was too old to be a boy, but he hardly exuded an aura of maturity. He was blond, with shaggy hair that hung in his eyes. Lips, nose, eyebrows, and ears were all pierced. The Virgin Mary was tattooed on the side of his neck. He didn't seem to notice Devin's approach at first, until the clipping sound of expensive shoe heels were within feet of the counter. The checker looked up, face startled.

Devin was used to it. His skin was black, which meant he looked different from the locals. The result was distrust. He didn't like it, but he didn't sink to showing it—no sign of weakness. Instead he advanced with purpose, stopping at the counter.

"Can I help you?" the checker asked, eyes darting over the new face.

Devin said nothing, simply sliding a crisp fifty-dollar bill across the glass.

The checker nodded through his unsettled demeanor. "Just the gas?" he asked.

"And the newspaper," Devin said, voice articulate and commanding. Then something changed. He felt it in his stomach this time. No images, just the sinking feeling of finality and irreversible death:

Soon. Too soon.

Not days or hours.

Now.

His cellular phone came open with a snap.

—no signal—

Devin reached into his wallet, swiftly removing and writing on a business card before sliding it across the glass countertop. He tapped his index finger on the card, indicating the neatly written script across its back. He tightened his vocal cords, voice intense.

"I need you to call the police. Tell them to send a car to this address. A woman's life is in danger. Do you understand?"

Devin was looked over skeptically. "That all depends on what you have in mind. What's your business here?"

Small towns, Devin thought cynically. People always talked about the joys of small town living, but he personally found it infuriating—nosy people who didn't trust you if they hadn't grown up with you. At least in the city you had a reason not to trust each other.

"Do it," he said with a commanding edge, "and do it now." He left the store, pushing through the curtain of early-spring snow.

The young man behind the counter looked over the letters, taking a moment to let the information sink in. He brushed his thumb anxiously across his lower lip, shifting a piercing. "Hey…" His voice dragged inarticulately. "Hey, Gary." The checker lifted his head, calling to the far end of the gas station near the refrigerators on the back wall.

"Yeah?" a voice called back.

"Come here."

A gruff-looking man with a craggy face approached the counter. "What is it?"

"That guy just told me to have the cops sent here," the checker said, handing over the business card.

Gary looked it over, thinking for a second. "I know this place," he said with a nod. "Outsiders trying to tell us how to run our own town," he growled, then crumpled the card in his fist.

The eggs were burning.

Brett cursed quietly under his breath as he reached for the skillet, trying to keep breakfast from turning to coal.

The kitchen phone rang.

He lifted it from the cradle, positioning it snugly between his shoulder and cheek as he fought with the eggs, waving smoke away with a towel.

"Yeah?" he said through a cough.

"This is Gary."

"Hi, Gary; how can I help you?"

"Some guy just came by the gas station. Black fella, nice suit, fancy coat—looked like he might work for the IRS or something."

Brett paused. "Did he say what he wanted?"

"He wanted somebody to send the cops over."

"Why?" Brett stammered, eyes moving toward the CCTV monitor on the countertop.

"Didn't say."

"Do you think he's headed here now?"

"Don't know."

Brett continued to stare into the monitor. "How long ago did he leave?"

"Just a second ago."

He watched as the black-and-white screen flickered: it showed the image of the girl as she sat tied to her chair in the dark basement room below, hair hanging across her bowed face, morose from her captivity. "I can't talk right now," Brett said shortly, then hung up.

This was a problem.

Hannah's head hung, long brown hair in her eyes.

Her face felt pasty with cold, fatigue, and pain. Dark lumps covered her body, swelling bruises on her cheek and forehead from rough treatment. Arms behind her back, she sat in a chair, wrists and ankles tied to the wooden frame, chair legs bolted to the floor.

The room was dark. Mattresses and foam padding lined the walls and windows to soundproof the basement room. Tan foam lined the seams between sound-buffering pads, rippling in imperfect bubbles and waves, frozen solid in time as it had been spewed from an aerosol canister. A tiny security camera was fixed in an upper corner.

Time stood still for her. One long unbroken moment of darkness and fear was all that filled her memory. Hours? Days? Weeks? She had no perception of how long she had been there. They had turned on lights at moments, brilliantly hot and bright, stabbing at her eyes, then extinguished them for what could have been days on end.

Every time she fell asleep they woke her. Feedings were sporadic— two meals she knew could have only been forty-five minutes apart. Judging time had been easier when they were still playing music— something they had done to make sure she couldn't hear them until they realized how well they had soundproofed her room. The length of the songs had given her a perception of time, but now that measure was gone, and her sanity was going with it.

Hannah had been raised in a conservative Christian home. It was something she had taken at varying degrees of seriousness throughout the phases of her life, but here, now, in the abyss, in her hour of dark- ness, she clung to it.

At first her prayers had been specific, personal, and directed to God as if He were standing right in front of her. Now she was tired, her mind swimming. Her lips mumbled out a tiny incoherent appeal, begging for rescue, pleading for light, imploring for continued safety, hoping upon terrified hope that the sanctity of her body would not be violated. Through her pleas she felt God draw closer and her sanity slip further away.

She was hallucinating. She had to be, seeing things that had happened long ago or not at all—and she felt it coming on again. It had been different each time, but she always felt it coming. This time it was a taste, like the bright tang of a penny in her mouth.

Then she began to see things that weren't there—

A cold car.

An Islamic holy man praying for forgiveness that Allah, the merciful and just, would have pity on him. He had recruited young, innocent Palestinian men to bind explosives to themselves—to walk into crowds of Israelis—to kill—and to die.

He had failed for years to free Palestine from Israel.

He was an American now, the imam of a small Ohio mosque. A man of peace.

Sitting in the car, waiting for it to warm up.

Thoughts of his sons—wanting to kiss them before they went to sleep.

A pedestrian in a heavy coat walking in the direction of his car.

Eye contact.

The man reached into his jacket.

—a gun—

Panic.

Clawing at the car door—trying to escape. The first bullet punching through the glass.

Pain. Skin breaking. Muscle splitting. Bone shattering.

Horror. Pain. Grief. Screaming.

The windshield blistering with holes.

Thoughts of his wife—of his children.

Body torn to pieces by the striking of lead.

Darkness.

Minutes later a jogger in the middle of the street, stammering into his cell phone. "The windshield is filled with bullet holes and there's blood…everywhere!"

It all came over her like a flood, a pouring out of pictures in her mind. But then there was one more thing. Not an image, but a feeling—that half a continent away someone else had felt it all happening too.

The sedan thundered down the wet, snowy dirt road. White snow, brown mud, and ashen gravel kicked up and out from the sides of the vehicle. The silver automobile cut through the road's debris like a blade as the surrounding world blurred into fleeting streaks.

A midsize luxury sedan with a manual transmission—as always, the vehicle of choice the rental company had in his file. Devin had rented it at the airport expecting to have more time, but he didn't. He hadn't expected to cut it so close, but there was no reasoning with it now. All he could do was drive, hands gripping the wheel as if he had to wrestle the sedan to the ground like a beast.

The snow had stopped falling for the moment, and that helped—a little. But what a horrid frozen wasteland to be trapped in. Back home in New York, spring had already begun—sunshine all over. But he had to be called here: to the only place in the entire continental United States to have a blizzard, where snow had fallen in buckets and the sun hadn't been seen in days.

To his right Devin saw the house appear over the horizon as the silver car glided up the hill. Five minutes at the most. He was almost there. He checked his phone again and snarled—too far from any kind of cell tower—a snowy wasteland.

Somewhere in the back of his mind he focused himself, aligning his will and his strength in faith. Some would call it a prayer. Devin resisted that word *prayer*. To him it was a necessary requisitioning of needed resources—spiritual or otherwise, it didn't matter.

It was his thoughts narrowing into a finely focused, single-minded bolt of mental force, preparing for imminent havoc.

Hannah's mind swam.

She saw him as her world dissolved to white.

Tall, handsome, dark skin.

Sitting at a dinner party.

Pausing. Something changing.

A thought or epiphany.

The man boarding a plane.

Searching for…

Her.

Strikingly handsome in an olive-colored suit that seemed to radiate class, money, and power. His frame stood strong in the midst of the frozen breeze, his tight muscular body accented by the hang of the trench coat over his strong shoulders.

He had been afraid for her, more than just for her captivity; for something far more treacherous. She paused. How afraid should she be for herself?

Brett growled in anger. It was really fear, but he denied it by letting it bubble out in a swell of wrath.

"I should never have let you use my home!" He was frantic, nearly wringing his hands. "This can't be happening!"

Snider and Jimmy stared at him, unmoved. They didn't take him seriously. They thought he was prone to panic, that was all.

"Calm down," Jimmy said sarcastically.

"Calm down? Calm *down*?" His face burned. "We've got a girl in the basement. That's kidnapping! And this fella's gonna bring the cops!"

Snider, middle-aged and dressed in black, stepped forward. "And what if he's not?" He was the leader, the one who had approached Brett, offered him money for the use of his home. Brett knew he had a reputation for being somewhat shady, but Brett liked money. And now things were getting serious.

"If you don't settle down, you're going to look suspicious," Snider continued. "And then what will you do when he really does bring the cops?"

Brett waved his hands nervously. "This has gotten out of hand. We can't do this anymore."

"What do you suggest?" Snider asked. "That we dispose of her?"

There was a long silence as they all looked at one another; then Brett turned sharply, heading for his room.

"Where are you going?" Snider asked.

Brett called back, "I'll deal with this!"

The turn was a blind corner, covered by snow. Devin slammed on the brakes, and the car lost control.

The back end of the car swung wide, losing traction in the slick of white. The tires left wide swaths of grime as the side of the car crunched into a pack of snow. Devin worked the sedan into gear and eased into the gas—the engine revved, the vehicle rocked, but he didn't move forward. He gave the pedal a futile stomp, but he knew all he was doing was chopping ground into snowy pulp.

His eyes lifted, mind calculating the distance—maybe a hundred or so meters. He shoved the door open and climbed out into the snow. Cold ran up his foot, into his throat. It wasn't the cold of the snow; it was—

Panic. Anger. Desperation.

Blam. Blam. BLAM!

The killer's face, covered with relief.

His foot slipped, his body nearly going down. It had snowed again the night before, and the snow was as deep as three feet in some places. Devin lifted his burning legs, body heaving forward through the thick mass beneath him.

He'd done forced marches before. Ten years of military life had provided him with everything he needed in this moment, everything he'd ever needed to live this life.

Devin looked up.

Almost there.

Beretta 9mm.

Shimmering blue steel nestled in a form-fitting glove of padding. The scent of gun oil wafted from the case, sweet and lethal. Brett lifted the firearm, felt its weight as he removed a magazine swelling with a full allowance of rounds and thrust it into the grip's base.

"What are you doing?" Snider demanded from behind as he cursed in exasperation.

Brett snapped the safety off, shoving past Snider toward the door. Snider shoved back, slamming Brett's shoulder blades into the wall.

"Let go!"

"*Answer me!*" Snider shouted, face filled with wrath. "What do you think you're going to do with that?"

Brett's face burned with reckless emotion. "This is *my* house. I'm going to protect myself *my* way!" He stared into furious, unforgiving eyes.

"I swear if you do anything stupid I will put you in the ground!"

Brett shoved back to no avail. A third voice called from the hall.

"Hey, guys. There's somebody coming."

Snider moved to the window, betraying none of his worry. To his left Brett leaned, hand resting against the window frame, twitching with near-frantic energy.

The man outside was coming up the snowy drive, drawing closer and closer.

"This is bad," Brett said again. "This is very bad."

"Calm down," Snider ordered. "I'll deal with this."

"We've got to get rid of the girl."

Snider shook his head. "Do you want him to find the girl or a dead body?"

Brett groaned, agonized.

"That's not the answer."

"Then what do you suggest?"

Snider went calm, looking at the other two men. "Let our visitor in—"

Brett tried to protest.

"—then kill him."

Devin reached out to the door with an ebony hand.

Frantic whispers slipped through the door. They were stalling.

The door opened, and a middle-aged man in black jeans, a black button-up shirt, and a tan undershirt looked back at Devin.

Devin smiled disarmingly. "Good morning, sir. I hate to say it, but it looks like I might have been driving too fast for the conditions. I seem to have slipped into the snow." Devin pointed back over his shoulder to the sedan's front end consumed by a drift. "My cell phone isn't getting a signal, and I was wondering if I could use your phone."

The man looked past Devin, examining the buried vehicle in the distance. "We can help you dig that out." He gestured toward a younger man standing behind him.

"Thank you."

The man stepped aside welcomingly. "My name's Snider. You look completely frozen—why don't you come in and warm up? I'll pour you a cup of coffee. There's a fireplace in the next room if you want to sit there for a few minutes before we dig out your car."

"Thank you, sir." Devin stepped across the threshold, knocking the snow from an expensive shoe. The interior carpet was factory standard beige, the walls white. Devin's eyes scanned the room, looking for any hint of the girl. He remembered what he'd seen. She had to be in the basement, but for now he was just going to have to see what he was up against.

Snider squared up to Devin. "Jimmy here can take that wet jacket of yours and put it in front of the fire to dry it out."

Jimmy reached for Devin's trench coat.

"Thank you," Devin said, as he felt strong arms grab his own—restraining him from behind.

He threw his weight back, shoving against Jimmy. Fighting. Struggling. Lashing out.

Throwing his weight back he lifted his legs, heel landing in Snider's chest with a thud, sending the man crashing back. The man behind him spun him and the world blurred. Devin kicked backward, going for the knee—

Something jammed into his neck, hard.

He tried to fight. Tried to knock it away. A repetitive, electric clicking.

Too late.

Brett heard the fighting and the sound of dead weight hitting the floor as he ran back up the stairs, Beretta in hand. The intruder lay on the floor, limp. Brett's hands began to shake.

"We've been found," he said, voice anxious and wavering.

Jimmy groaned. "Shut up, Brett."

Brett's face flushed, his ears turning bright pink. "No. I'm not going to shut up," he shouted, gripping his pistol. "This is bad. This is very, very bad, and we're neck-deep in it."

"Knock it off."

"No. We're all going to go to prison. Do you understand that?"

"It was just one guy—"

"—who's now lying limp on my floor!" Brett's tone raised an octave.

Snider knelt over the intruder's slumped form. "Take him to the lake in his car. Make it look like he lost control and went in."

"Like an accident?" Jimmy clarified.

Snider nodded. "These roads can be treacherous in snowy conditions."

Brett watched as Jimmy hoisted the intruder over his shoulder, heaving him out the front door. "You know the police are going to tie this back to me."

"Calm down," Snider snapped.

"Stop telling me to calm down. They're not going to tie this to you. They're going to tie this to me."

Snider ran a hand through his hair wearily. "Where's breakfast?"

"Don't try to change the subject. This is serious!"

"Finish breakfast," Snider ordered as he moved down the hall, back turned.

"Don't you walk away from me!" Brett blustered as he stomped after him, gun in hand. "I'm talking to you!" He reached out, putting a hand on the black-clad shoulder, then felt it twist as Snider spun.

Brett doubled over with his arm cocked violently in the air, wrist screwed in an unnatural direction, a strong hand shoving his shoulder down like a fulcrum. A knee to his stomach and the pistol hit the carpet.

Snider came close to Brett's ear. "You do not talk to me that way"—his tone was soft but ferocious—"or so help me you'll find yourself in the lake next to our uninvited guest here. Got it?"

Brett felt like his arm was about to be torn from its socket.

"*Got it?*"

Brett didn't say anything; he only groaned in agony. A whimper escaped him; then he felt the force of the floor as Snider gave a brutal shove. He lay there, groaning, carpet pressed to his cheek as he watched Snider scoop up the pistol and walk away.

Jimmy came back in the front door and Snider handed off the Beretta, then looked back at Brett.

"Finish breakfast. I'm hungry."

Brett sat up, leaning his aching body against the wall, seething. He touched his nose. Blood.

His shaking hands clenched.

Hannah listened intently. They'd done a good job of soundproofing the room, but there was only so much foam and mattresses could keep out. She held her breath, trying to hear more.

It had sounded like fighting. Shouting mostly, but things hit the walls, shaking the beams down to her shadowy basement.

There wasn't much time for her, she supposed. They were getting desperate. What little she could make out from the tone of the shouting told her that. They weren't going to keep her around much longer. That was certain.

What was the point? Two decades of living. She was nineteen years old and alone. A college freshman, living in the dorms, failing to adapt. Her roommate liked to drink and liked guys even more—Hannah had come home to find a "do not disturb" sign hanging from her own door at least once a week all semester, forcing her to sleep on a couch in the downstairs commons. The food in the dining halls was bad, the company worse. All she had wanted was to go home.

She didn't want to be a college graduate with a career. All she wanted was to meet a nice man and love him, feed him, raise his children. It was an old-fashioned and naïve desire, all her professors and friends had told her that, but still it was the life she wanted.

She wanted peace and quiet and love and cookies made for her children—not an education or a life in the fast lane, but her grandfather had made her go, wanting her to get a degree in business so she could make the family business more profitable.

The sensation was in her temples this time—soft images blending one to another.

Her eighth birthday party.

She wore a cowgirl hat and boots.

A chocolate cake with sprinkles.

The number eight embedded in frosting, a single flame rising from the wick.

Her friends smiling.

Her childhood dog, Max, licking her face.

Bees.

The stinging all over her.

Crying in her grandfather's arms.

—her grandfather's arms.

Hannah lifted her head. She wanted to live.

Snider dialed the phone.

"Yes?" his employer said across the line.

"It's me."

There was a pause. "What do you need?"

"Some guy started snooping around."

Silence.

"I think it's time you told me exactly why you hired us to kidnap the girl."

"I'm sorry, but I can't—"

"I swear, we'll kill her now."

There was another pause.

"Are you watching the news?"

"Do you mean the murdered imam?"

"Yes."

"Are you guys responsible for that?"

"We need control of our situation."

"And the girl's kidnapping provides you with that?"

"We'll double your money."

Snider sneered. "We're now connected to a politically charged killing. You'll triple our money, and you'll have the rest of it for us tonight, because after that we're sending her back in a garbage bag!"

Devin's thoughts floated.

Confused—in the front seat of the car. The car hood breaking the ice, plunging into the water.

The windshield cracking—leaking. Breaking. Cold water spilling in.

Body seizing from the shock. Lungs filling with ice water.

Devin's eyes opened—darkness everywhere. His whole world shook as his head slammed into something. How had he gotten here? On his back, in some dark, confined place.

His world shook again with a jarring slam as he heard the engine rev.

He was in the trunk of a car.

It smelled new or at least freshly detailed—like his rental car. He shivered in the chilled trunk as his mind put it all together. It was his rental car. He remembered what had flashed through his mind. They were going to send the car into a lake with him in it, make it look like an accident. But it wouldn't look like an accident if he was in the trunk. He remembered what he'd seen—

They weren't going to leave him in the trunk. How had they gotten him here in the first place?

Something had pinched him in the neck, hard. There had been some sort of ticking sound and—

They'd hit him with a Taser, an electrical stun gun. Police and military used them for restraint purposes. He'd had to use one himself on several occasions when he was with intelligence. They were available to private citizens too for self-defense, and he'd been hit with one of those.

They weren't going to take any chances. They were going to stun him again for good measure, put him in the front seat, and send him into the lake. He wouldn't even have to drown. The water was cold enough that the chill would get him first. The shock of it alone would be enough to suck the air from his lungs, cause his muscles to seize. The impact would batter his body, and the breaking glass would slash him to ribbons. The water would cut off his air, choking him to death.

And if he survived all that, his lungs would fill and burst.

Brett moved into the living room, his body still sore. The TV was on—the morning news—all about this murdered imam in Ohio.

Brett watched for a moment and thought.

They were going to have to get rid of the girl, no matter what Snider said. It was going to have to happen.

He looked on the ottoman.

The Beretta.

Devin fumbled in the dark. He couldn't find what he was looking for.

Just the previous summer he'd been led to the trunk of an older-model car where a four-year-old boy had accidentally trapped himself on a sweltering day. He read up on it afterward. He'd learned of the eleven children who had died in the summer of 1998, trapped in the trunks of automobiles. As a result, new standards required the auto manufacturers to have interior release handles inside every trunk manufactured after 2000. Most glowed in the dark with pictographic instructions inscribed on them. Devin saw nothing.

He searched with his eyes and his fingertips. He couldn't find the latch. This wasn't right. The rental was a brand-new car with all the latest safety requirements. They must have removed the safety latch somehow in the fear that he might come to and search for it, exactly as he was doing now.

There was another option—he could kick out the backseat and find himself face-to-face with his captor, a fight he would have to win against a man who was almost certainly armed.

He turned back to the trunk latch, feeling with his fingertips.

Snider stood in the kitchen, touching his forehead. It all gave him a headache—the logistics of it all. It was supposed to be a simple job, not this. The news was playing in the background—some Muslim had been murdered. He rubbed his temples.

He trusted Jimmy, but it still bothered him to delegate something like ditching a body to him. Why hadn't he done it himself? Why hadn't he made sure it was flawless?

Because, he reminded himself, Brett was the biggest problem they had. Someone needed to keep an eye on that trigger-happy...

Where was Brett, anyway?

Snider stepped out of the kitchen and looked around. Then his eyes fell on the ottoman.

The pistol was gone.

Devin's fingers glided across the plastic surface of the trunk's latch cover and found the edges. He worked at the plastic, but his short, manicured fingernails couldn't work their way underneath.

He traced the cover farther up. The cover was the size of his hand, roughly the shape of an egg, and at the top he felt two small indentations, one on each side of the release. His fingers worked their way in and the cover came loose. He felt blindly at the mechanism, working at it with his fingers.

Cold metal and a long, thick wire running the length of the mechanism.

That's it, he thought. He pulled. The trunk popped and white light exploded off of the snow, flooding Devin's eyes.

An old country road. Trees streaming away on each side.

He hurled himself out into the snow, rolling with the impact.

Brett moved to the door, unlocked it, and pushed it open gently.

There was the girl. She looked up and saw his face. His heart skipped as he tightened his stranglehold on the pistol's grip behind his back. She'd seen his face. She could identify him.

Now there was no changing his mind.

He stepped in, closing the door.

Jimmy slammed on the brakes as he saw the trunk burst open in his rearview mirror. To the left he saw the man lift himself out of the snow and dash for the trees at the edge of the road.

The vehicle came to a sliding stop in the snow. He lunged at the passenger's seat, clawing at a pile of things he'd brought along for cleanup. He snatched the Glock pistol with his rubber-gloved hand and glanced back at the escaping figure in the mirror.

He launched out of the car door, spinning in a single fluid motion, the handgun resting on the roof of the car as he braced himself to fire.

Only time for one shot before the man slipped into the trees…

The gun sounded like thunder.

Snow exploded off the burdened branches of an evergreen, sending white scattering through the air like a starburst. Devin hit the ground and rolled, then quickly scrambled back to his feet and sprinted into the trees.

Hannah stared at the man. He stared back, hand hiding something behind him.

He stood there, not moving, as if he were trying to work up the courage to do something. Her mind skimmed across the surface of possibilities. There were only a few options of things he had come for: her body or her life—or both.

The doorknob at the far end of the room turned, and someone pushed on the door. The man in front of her flinched, then turned around quickly, showing her his back—and the pistol he was holding.

The door opened.

"What are you doing?" Another man, dressed in black, looked around the room.

"Nothing. I was just…"

Hannah stared at the pistol. She wanted to scream, to tell the second man what she saw, but she couldn't. She tried to speak, but her voice held in her throat.

"You don't belong in here," the second man announced.

The first man nodded. "You're right." As he spoke he tucked the firearm discreetly in his belt and moved toward the door, following the other man.

Jimmy moved into the trees, lowering his head beneath a branch—eyes sharp and attentive, handgun at the ready. The tracks were clear and distinct in the deep snow.

Just beyond, the world was darker, the ground shadowed by the canopy of trees. He looked for blood—there was none, but there were gaping tracks in the snow. He pushed on toward his quarry.

Silence.

That was all Hannah heard for several moments. Then she heard it, even through the padding—

Her captors.

Arguing. Yelling. Shouting.

Violence?

She held her breath for a moment then threw her head up, attentive to the noise—

The gunshot was deafening.

Devin pressed his back against the tree, his stalker so close he could hear the crunch of snow. He took a long, deep breath—and held it. He had to be completely undetectable, or he was dead.

Jimmy squinted. Just ahead he saw it—the cloth of a trench coat peeking out from behind a small tree. He took in a breath and stepped gently.

Carefully. Silently. Agonizing as he placed his feet in the packed snow at the bottom of each track he followed.

He was getting closer. Rounding the tree. Then his moment—

Jimmy threw himself forward, the pistol in his hand blasting.

One—two—three rounds.

He stopped.

The coat was empty. Riddled with bullets, it hung from a branch, limp and vacant. Cursing to himself he looked around frantically.

Something rammed between his shoulder blades, and he went face-first into the snow, pain stabbing at the base of his skull, chest slamming into the icy cold. His vision only went black for a moment.

He pushed up with a fist then felt an arm swoop around his neck, his chin locking in the cleft of the man's elbow. Jimmy fought to bite the other man's arm as he struggled to gain hold with his clawing fingertips. A hand pressed expertly against the base of his skull.

He threw elbows to the side, punches to the face. He clawed, scratched, and tried to jam a thumb under the man's eye to put it out. The choke hold only tightened. Jimmy felt his body being thrown as he was fought deeper into submission, forced to his knees, his vision swinging hard to the right—

He saw it.

In the snow.

The pistol.

He snatched the cold metal, swinging it upward toward the black man's face.

One bullet would do—

The pistol bucked in Jimmy's hand as a round exploded from the muzzle, firing off into the air as a well-placed strike knocked the weapon away. The other arm continued squeezing, and Jimmy reprised violently.

Sweat ran down his back, sweet and slick.

His face burned. Muscles flaming.

Frustration. Burning rage.

He fought to bring his restrained arm to bear—the pistol going off again and again and again, blasting away at the snow near their feet.

He screamed in anger.

The man he would have murdered was quiet, calculated.

Jimmy snarled as the weapon was stripped from his hand, tumbling into the snow.

They both went back, slamming into snow. The air left Jimmy's lungs and he gasped. The other man's legs wrapped around his own, holding him down tightly. Trapped.

How did this happen? He was going to kill this man. In cold blood. But he was losing control, body locked in an expertly executed choke hold.

He gasped for air. Gray crept into his vision. Sight blurred. Consciousness slipped.

His world went dark.

Hannah was bleeding from her wrists, the ropes cutting deep into her soft flesh as she tried to work her way free. Her bruised wrists twisted under the stinging strain of the ropes that bit into her. A trickle of her own warm blood slithered down her finger. It hurt so much, but she just kept working.

She wanted to live. She wanted to see the sun.

Footsteps down the hall. Nearing.

Her work became more rapid, trying harder to free herself from the expertly tied fetters.

The door opened. She saw a man dressed all in black. He came close, leaning by her ear. Hannah went stiff—except for her lip, which quivered uncontrollably.

Devin climbed into the silver rental car and looked around. The keys were still in the ignition. He turned them and heard the rush of air—

The woods. The girl.

Snider, aiming his pistol deliberately.

"Please don't kill me. Please!"

The girl, back turned, walking away.

Death.

Devin set the sedan into reverse, easing into the gas. He felt the tires grip and begin to slowly roll out of the snow—couldn't rush it or he'd get stuck. He turned the car around, working the wheel to the left.

Devin pushed the gearshift forward, locking it in place, and fed the gas. The car began to move forward, gaining speed, then took off, blazing down the snowy road. His eyes glanced at the dashboard—a mile ticked over faster than it should have for the conditions. Then another. And another.

"Please don't kill me. Please!"

The words played over again in his mind, frantic and desperate.

He was driving much, much too fast for the conditions. The back end slipped, and he adjusted the gearshift. The car was fishtailing. Too fast, he thought again, but he had no choice now. No other option. Not now. Not with the future racing toward him.

He recognized the landscape. From the other side, but this was it: his turn was just ahead, where he'd hit the drift before.

Devin's fist wrenched the emergency brake skyward.

He spun the wheel.

The car snapped to a ninety-degree angle, sliding to a stop—right in front of the long drive.

First gear. The sedan leapt into action.

The engine snarled.

Second gear. He laid into the gas.

Over a small hill.

The house ahead.

Like the chiming of a bell announcing the drawing of midnight, the words repeated in his mind:

"Please don't kill me. Please!"

No more time. The future was becoming the present.

The gas pedal touched the floor. The car began to fishtail, the front end nosing to the right. Devin overcorrected as control of the car slipped away from him. He fought the vehicle as he felt it tipping inexorably out of control. Something slipped beneath the car, the tires losing all traction—he was completely out of control, the car swerving perpendicular to the long drive. His foot pumped the brake, but the wheels were no longer propelling the car, only the force of gravity pulling him down the incline—screaming across a layer of slippery packed snow—careening toward a tall embankment at the end of the drive.

Devin braced for impact, and his entire body shuddered as the silver sedan plowed into the drift. The seat belt snapped tight, constricting against his chest as the force of the blow threatened to throw him out the far side of the car. The shock wave subsided, and he reached for the door handle with a disoriented hand.

Devin threw the door open and got out, Glock pistol in hand—raised in anticipation of trouble.

He stared down the iron sights at the front door of the house, only feet away. Devin moved from the car with purpose and speed, eyes locked on the front door, weapon held out in front of him as he moved up the steps.

Devin turned the door handle and gave a hearty kick, sending the door flinging in. He charged across the threshold and paused, weapon ready, arms locked in place, body turning with the pistol. He moved in.

Left turn—one sharp movement as he glared down the iron sights.

Nothing.

To the right—same.

Devin moved into the kitchen. On the counter was a black and white monitor—a room. Chair, bonds—that was where he'd seen the girl—but the room was empty.

Then he saw it—something more shocking. Next to the monitor was a lapel pin. A royal crest—he recognized the symbol. The Trinity knot—a triquetra—under a crenulated label: the sign of the Firstborn.

No color—simply the symbol itself. It didn't have any of the distinctive colors: the red of the Domani, the gold of the Ora, or the blue of the Prima. But it was the symbol of the Firstborn—that was simple enough to see. And more disturbing than anything else he could consider.

A cool draft played against his cheek, and he turned. The sliding glass door was slightly ajar. Devin moved forward, looked through the glass at the distant trees—

And saw them.

Hannah screamed again.

Snider shoved her into the trees. She fell down, and he reached for her, grabbing her hair roughly with a fist.

"Do *not* make my life more difficult than it has to be. Do you understand?"

She quavered.

"*Do you understand?*"

Hannah nodded, and he pulled her to her feet. They kept walking, deeper and deeper into the trees.

Snider stopped in a clearing, a hundred yards beyond the tree line. She went to her knees. He lowered himself down to her ear, whispering.

"That way," he said, pointing deeper into the trees. "Start walking that way, and don't look back."

She turned and looked at him. Her first thought was that he was letting her go, then she looked him in the eye and felt—

He'd killed before—

A deal gone bad.

A job gone wrong.

Intimidation gone too far.

To survive in prison.

To repay a debt.

For money.

For safety.

For revenge.

For convenience...

She saw it all—

He was going to kill her too.

"Get up." His voice soft but stern.

She stood and looked into his face. "Please don't. Please don't kill me. I won't tell anyone. I promise."

"Start walking," he said flatly, "and don't turn around."

She held for a moment.

"Now."

Hannah turned slowly, facing the snowy trees ahead of her, and began to walk. One foot in front of another, waiting expectantly for it to happen any moment. She turned her head, saw the man in the corner of her eye still standing there, pistol in hand.

"Keep going," he instructed.

Another step. Another moment of life.

Another step—

Crack!

Her entire body went stiff and she looked down—she'd stepped on a twig.

"That's good."

She stopped, turning back to Snider.

"I didn't tell you to turn around," he reprimanded, as if she were a child. As she looked back into the trees she sucked air, slowly.

She looked at the trees. So beautiful. The snow and the early-morning sun. Her heart slowed. Her muscles relaxed. If this was going to be the last thing she ever saw, she was going to embrace it.

Days in a dark basement had driven her back to the faith of her childhood; now it filled her entire heart and mind.

She was coming home.

The gunshot was loud, hammering in her temples as if a hole had been punched in her eardrums. A single round fired in the stillness of the snow, echoing endlessly through the trees.

Snow dropped from branches. Birds took off into flight. And the blast rolled through the world.

She stood for a moment, waiting to feel it, but all she felt was the chill in her feet and in her lungs. Hannah looked down. No wound.

Slowly she turned around and saw Snider clutching his chest, bleeding from a steaming wound. He coughed, face confused, and a trickle of blood ran down his lip. The man hit his knees and went face-first into the snow.

The body lay there, steam rising from the hot wound. Beyond stood a man—tall, handsome, black skin—a pistol in hand raised expertly, face blank, a single twist of smoke rising from the muzzle of the weapon.

He approached Snider's body, weapon pointed down, kicking the Beretta pistol away. Kneeling down, he checked for a pulse. When he was satisfied, he put his own weapon on safety and looked up at Hannah.

"Are you hurt?"

She shook her head.

"Good." Then he took her by the arm and led her away.

Chapter 2

HANNAH STARED OUT THE window, the world passing by. Her forehead was cold as it pressed against the glass. She curled up in the seat, pulling her rescuer's olive-green sport coat close.

Her rescuer didn't speak. He sat at the wheel, eyes forward, hands set precisely at two o'clock and ten o'clock. His grip loose but obviously in control. His breaths were long and deliberate.

"Who are you?" she asked slowly.

"Pardon, miss?" he said. "I'm afraid you're going to have to speak up."

"Who are you?" she asked again.

His eyes remained on the road as he reached into his wallet, pulled out a business card, and handed it to her.

She scanned the card. "Devin Bathurst?"

He nodded. "Correct."

"Financial planner and advisor?"

"Yes, ma'am."

She paused as her eyes met a familiar design. "What's this?"

"Pardon?"

"This." She pointed, and he glanced from the corner of his eye.

"Family crest."

"It looks like a symbol my grandfather uses."

"Much of heraldry looks similar to the untrained eye."

She shook her head. "No, this is identical. Except my grandfather's is blue."

He was quiet for a moment. "What did you say your name was again?"

"My name's Hannah. Hannah Rice."

He turned his head, looking at her. She felt as if he were seeing her for the first time.

"Did you say *Rice*?"

Henry Rice ripped the phone from the hook mid-ring, hand trembling.

"Yes?" he said into the receiver.

"Mr. Rice?"

"This is he."

"This is Devin Bathurst."

Henry paused, heart skipping. "How can I help you, Mr. Bathurst?"

"You have a granddaughter named Hannah, correct?"

The old man gripped the phone with all his arthritic might. "What's this about?" he said, trying not to shout in anger. "What do you want?"

"I'm taking her to the hospital to be examined."

"She's safe?"

"Yes."

Henry sat, relief washing over him. "Where are you?"

"Colorado."

"Colorado?" Henry asked, eye lifted. "She's here in Colorado?"

"Yes," Devin announced. "Once she's given her statement I'll bring her to you."

"No," Henry insisted. "Tell me what hospital you're taking her to, and I'll come pick her up."

"Good," Devin said in his typical flat, heartless tone. "Because we need to talk."

The carpet in the hospital's chapel was cranberry red and soft to the touch.

Devin lowered to his knees, hand steadying himself against the floor. Back straight, hands clasped—the way his grandmother had taught him to pray. Head bowed, eyes closed. He took in air and held it, releasing it slowly—then let his mind begin to work.

The Lord's Prayer.

Nothing fancy, but it was like fresh air for his soul. Behind him he heard the door creak open softly. Someone stepped in. He raised a finger gently, indicating his desire for a moment.

He finished then stood.

"Devin?"

Henry Rice stood just in the door, a worn old rancher—white hair, stocky build.

Devin took a place at one of the pews, gesturing. "Have a seat."

Henry sat down. "What's going on, Devin? Who took my granddaughter?"

"I don't know," Devin said, reaching into his sport coat. "I was called to her; I can't help that, you know that. But I found this..." He revealed the lapel pin.

Henry looked the artifact over. "Where'd you get that?"

"It was in the house where they were keeping her."

Henry went quiet.

"Is there any reason one of the Firstborn would want to abduct your granddaughter?"

A sigh escaped from the old man's heaving body. "Overseer," he said, shaking his head.

"The leadership proposal?"

"Yes. I've been opposed to any kind of central leadership since the beginning. I'm hardly comfortable with it within the orders..."

"And you're opposed to a governing body between the orders?"

Henry shook his head. "I don't know. I'm just not ready for that kind of change, but to go so far as to kidnap my granddaughter?"

"You think someone is trying to coerce you into changing your mind?"

He nodded. "I received a message the other day explaining that I would receive assistance in finding my granddaughter if I would agree to change my stance on Overseer."

"Were you going to change your stance?" Devin asked bluntly.

The old man bowed his head. "I didn't have a choice."

"Yes, you did."

"They had my granddaughter; I'd have done anything."

Devin considered for a moment. "Do you have any idea who did this?"

"No."

"Do you have any hunches?"

"No."

Devin stood. "Contact me if you come across any leads."

Henry's head lifted. "You know it's forbidden for us to talk. I shouldn't be talking to you now." The old man groaned. "Who knows what our own people might do to us if they found out we were talking."

"Well…" Devin opened the chapel door and paused. "You said it yourself: you'd have done anything for your granddaughter." He paused a moment longer, then pushed through the door.

Outside the chapel, he scanned the corridor for a bathroom. He felt grimy. He'd been in his suit all day, a day that had included a flight, a long drive, two major physical altercations, travel through snow, being shut in a car trunk, and shooting a man in the chest. Sweat had soaked his undershirt, and now faint dampness clung to his body with every step.

He loosened his tie and headed down the hospital corridor.

"Devin," a voice said from behind.

Devin stopped. He knew that voice. "Blake," he said without turning, "how can I help you?"

"We need to talk."

Devin turned around and tightened his tie again. "OK."

Blake Jackson looked as competent as Devin knew him to be. Blue jeans, work boots, down jacket, strong body. He was Henry Rice's right-hand man, and he took the job seriously.

"Look," Blake said, tone already dropping a register, "I really appreciate what you did, coming to his granddaughter's rescue—"

"But?" Devin interjected, knowing the statement was conditional.

"But you have to be more careful. Got it?"

Devin nodded slowly.

"It's against the rules for you two to be talking," he continued. "You know that."

"I do."

A male nurse walked their direction and the two of them stopped talking for a moment, staring into one another. A moment later the nurse was gone.

"Normal contact between the orders will get you both into trouble. What you've done today will earn the Domani some respect, but people aren't going to put up with you being around for very long."

They stood for a moment, neither saying anything. Devin looked both directions, scanning for anyone who might be watching them.

"We shouldn't be talking in the open," Devin said. "We could be seen."

Blake nodded. "We'll talk in San Antonio," he said with a casual nod.

Devin watched Blake turn around. "Just one thing."

Blake stopped, looking back. "Yeah?"

"What have you heard about that murdered imam in Ohio?"

"The Muslim guy?" Blake shrugged. "Not much, why?"

"Some people think all Muslims are terrorists. I just wondered what your thoughts were."

Blake didn't respond for a moment, studying Devin's face. "I guess they can't all be terrorists. But if this one was, then somebody did the world a service." Blake looked at his watch. "Any other questions?"

Devin shook his head. "That's all."

Blake dipped his head and walked away. Devin watched until Blake was gone, then did the same, pretending their conversation had never taken place.

Henry pushed Hannah in a wheelchair out of the front door of the hospital. She had a clean bill of health, a few bumps and bruises, some dehydration, but mostly she was unscathed.

Hannah stared forward, unspeaking, unmoving. They'd said that she would need counseling. Henry believed them. They'd explained that victims of kidnap and abduction frequently had serious changes in personality and demeanor, but she'd always been so quiet it was hard to tell.

Henry squeezed the handles tightly as his blood pressure began to increase. They had abducted his granddaughter—that was heinous. But the thought that they had robbed who she was—that was despicable.

"How are you feeling?" he asked, probing for some sign of her old self.

No reply.

"The doctors said that you were going to be just fine."

She remained silent.

The glass doors parted in front of them and he stopped, helping her out of the wheelchair.

"Who was he?" she asked.

"Do you mean Mr. Bathurst?"

"Yes. He said he knew you. How?"

Henry offered his granddaughter his arm as they moved down the steps. Blake waited in the car, engine running. "He and I belong to different branches of the same organization."

"What kind of organization?"

He thought for a moment, trying to skirt any details regarding the Firstborn. "It's a religious organization. We deal with needs that God brings to us."

"What kinds of needs?"

"Whatever needs to be done," he said, "past, present, or future."

She was quiet for a minute. "Are those the people who come to the house for meetings sometimes?"

His heart skipped and his hands felt numb. "You knew about that?"

"I've always known," she said softly. "I just assumed it was business."

"Well," he said, trying to be diplomatic, "it might be for the best if you didn't mention Mr. Bathurst to any of those people."

"Why?" she asked without a moment's hesitation. They stopped at the car and held for a moment.

"Sometimes people in this world are different, and when people are different, other people don't like them very much."

"Is this because he's an African American?"

"No," he said with a smile, "nothing that simple. It's just a matter of seeing different things."

He opened the car door for her. "Now let's take you home."

Chapter 3

HOLY MAN MURDERED OUTSIDE of Ohio Mosque—Imam Basam Al Nassar Shot to Death in Car.

Clay Goldstein threw the newspaper down with a heavy smack. He stood, seething.

The roomful of people stared back at him. He knew full well that he was being dramatic—a career in the film industry gave him that edge—but this moment deserved it.

"The Prima did this," he said with a snarl, voice echoing through the office of his sunny Napa Valley mansion. It was way too early for this garbage. He'd only been out of his bathrobe for twenty minutes and had barely had a chance to pull on one of his trademark Hawaiian shirts and blue jeans before everything had come crashing down. At this rate he was lucky he'd gotten his glasses on before the universe had imploded.

"Do you know for sure?" Vincent Sobel asked, trying to be tactful. "I mean, you could be mistaken."

He stared at Vince, sitting on the couch in his smarmy Italian suit and sculpted hair. "I felt it as it happened," Clay sneered. "It was one of Henry Rice's people. I know it."

"Well," Vincent continued, "you've been pretty skeptical about the other orders for a while and—"

"Don't patronize me. I know I've made speculations before, but now we have a smoking gun."

The room remained silent.

Clay put a pensive hand to his beard, thinking as he spoke. "Nobody likes the Ora—never have. We see people where they are—nobody likes to be that vulnerable. We're the least respected of the three orders, and now we're sitting on evidence that the Prima are killers. That's only going to make us less popular."

A woman spoke. "You don't have to share with the other orders what you think you saw—"

"I know what I saw!" he shouted. "I saw it, plain as day—as it happened."

The room went quiet again. He looked them over.

"This is why Overseer is so important. If we unite the orders, then lone gunmen could be stopped. And since they've already started killing others, how long will it be before they start killing us again too?"

"Do we contact Henry Rice?" someone asked. "We could use this to put pressure on him—to force unification."

Clay nodded. "But if we do, then we'd have to stay out of San Antonio."

"Why?"

"Because if his cronies have killed before, they'll kill us too—especially if they find out what we know."

Vincent spoke up. "This strikes me as a very dangerous game."

"It is."

"We still need people to represent us at the meeting."

"Agreed. Whoever goes stands a good chance of getting killed." Clay scanned the room. "Any volunteers?"

He watched every set of eyes in the room turn down.

"Come on, people," he snorted sarcastically, "there's got to be somebody we're willing to lose."

There was a moment's consideration.

"What about that guy who had a fling with Morris Childs's niece?" someone offered.

Vincent laughed. "Do you mean John Temple?"

Clay considered for a moment. "He embarrassed the Ora and the Domani. He's a loose cannon and annoyance."

He thought a moment longer.

"He's perfect."

John Temple hammered his last nail for the day. He sat back, mopping the drench of sweat from his brow with a red paisley handkerchief. The Central American heat was still draining by his American standards. Six weeks, after all, was hardly enough time to acclimate to the rain forest. He took a few deep breaths and lay back against the roof he had been working on.

"Johnny Temple," a voice shouted, "wake up; I have water for you."

John sat up, looking down from the roof to see the boy calling up to him. Paolo, seven years old, stood with a smiling face. "Come down," he shouted again, smile getting bigger.

"Just a second," John replied and in a moment descended the ladder. On the ground the boy handed him water in a jug. John threw back the container and chugged. It wasn't very cool water, but it kept him hydrated. He finished the water, using the last of it to wash his face and hands. He passed the jug back to Paolo, mussing the boy's hair.

Thunder growled in the distance.

"Do you think it's going to rain?" John asked rhetorically. Paolo shrugged, and they started walking up the road to the temporary building where he'd been living.

Paolo followed like a baby goose in a gaggle. "Johnny Temple, can I ask you a question?"

"Sure," John replied warmly, still walking.

"Why are you going back to America?"

"Because my visit was only for six weeks," he said.

"As a missionary?"

"That's right."

"Are you sure you have to leave tomorrow?"

John put a hand on the boy's shoulder as they walked. "Yes, I'm afraid I do. Now wait here while I change."

He entered a small, bare room that held only a cot and his duffle bag. His shirt didn't come off—it peeled from his skin, soaked with sweat. He tossed it on his cot and dug out a new white cotton shirt. He buttoned it most of the way up, still allowing it to breathe, then rolled up his sleeves. Next, he changed his wet socks, soaked from heat, and considered putting on a new pair of khaki cargo pants before replacing his work boots on his feet. He put his elephant-hair bracelet on his wrist, a souvenir he'd picked up while doing missions work with farmers in Kenya. He pulled out a small mirror, looking at his stubble.

Shaving was probably a good idea, but he liked the scruffy look. It was his hair that bothered him. Normally he kept it short, but it was starting to get longer, blond strands tickling his ears. He brushed them away. At least his tan was coming along nicely.

He reached down, next to his bed, and picked up his Bible and prayer journal. Books in hand, he stepped out of the temp building. There Paolo stood, waiting patiently.

"Where are you going?" Paolo asked.

"I'm going to go spend some time alone with God," John replied, squeezing the boy's shoulder. "When I get back we'll play some catch, OK?"

"OK," the boy replied cheerily.

John headed down a narrow pathway toward the river. When he reached a grassy clearing, he took a seat near the river and opened his Bible.

He stopped for a minute and looked at the photograph tucked in the front cover. It was a picture of him and a beautiful young woman. He kept meaning to get rid of the old photo, but he just couldn't bring himself to do it.

John flipped through some pages. He was in Psalms again. It was his favorite book in the Bible—the poetry, the rapture, the joy of walking personally with God. It was reading Psalms that had led him into a life of consistent, short-term missions work.

He read, prayed, and wrote in his leather-bound journal for nearly an hour before the first droplet of rain landed on the Bible page with a smack, leaving a ragged circular blotch on the paper. Above, the clouds were dark and gray, moving in front of the sun.

John felt it—this storm was serious.

Andy stomped into the temp building.

"Where's John?"

Judah, a fellow missionary, lay on his cot. He looked up from his Bible. "I don't know. He was working the last I saw him, but after we finished he disappeared."

"He better get back here quick," Andy announced, peering out the front door. "The rain is getting bad. Nobody should be out in this."

Judah shrugged. "Maybe Paolo knows."

Andy nodded. The boy certainly admired John, and the two of them had spent a lot of time together. If John was around, Paolo would either be with him or know where he'd gone.

"I'll go ask."

He stepped outside, pulling a jacket over his head for shelter. The sky was dark now and the rain heavier. Water poured down from the trees above, and tiny, muddy tributaries began running downhill toward the river. To his relief he spotted Paolo right away, playing in the rain, hopping from puddle to puddle, kicking and splashing.

"Hey, Paolo," Andy shouted. Paolo looked up. "Have you seen Mr. Temple?"

Paolo ran up. "He said he was going to talk with God. Why?"

Andy shook his head. "He's not back yet, and I'm starting to worry."

Paolo flashed a big smile. "I'll look for him."

"You don't have to—" Andy started to say, but the boy was already running, disappearing into the trees.

Andy shrugged and headed back inside.

"I'm so sick of John running off like this," Andy announced as he plopped on his cot. "He's so reckless."

Judah looked up from his own cot again. "But his heart's in the right place."

Andy groaned. "He's an irresponsible showboat."

Judah turned a page in his Bible. "He leaves tomorrow, so I wouldn't worry too much."

Andy nodded. "I suppose I should be thankful for that."

Just ahead John saw the village through the thick curtain of rain.

Between the buildings the ground had turned to mud again, boiling with the relentless downpour, chubby drops of water bursting like mortar shells as they hit the ground. John trudged forward, heading for the temp building when his vision began to blur, filling with a greenish haze—

Paolo in the trees.

The constant deluge.

The boy slipping, falling to the ground.

Sliding toward—the river.

John dropped his Bible beneath a tree and ran into the forest.

Paolo tried to stand—but his world was thrown to the ground.

Shock overtook him. How was he on the ground? He'd slipped in the mud and rushing runoff.

Reaching out with his hands for—

He slipped, body crashing into the mud. Paolo began to cry. He wanted to get home, to be with his parents, to see John. All he knew was that he didn't want to be in the rain anymore.

Looking back, he realized he was sliding down the steep embankment—

—into the river.

The boy grasped at leaves, roots, and rocks.

Something came loose in his hand, and he fell backward, body slamming into soggy earth, air escaping from his lungs as he rolled and tumbled—his view disintegrating into a swirling kaleidoscope of mud, fronds, and rain.

Then he crashed through the river's surface.

A cascade of water burst off a frond as John knocked it out of his way, smashing through the foliage, running as fast as his legs would carry him. He hacked at the leaves that obscured his path, striking at them with open palms as he sprinted through the torrential downpour.

A clearing. He stopped, looked around—*lost*, he thought, furious with himself for not keeping track of the boy. Nothing but trees all around—every direction was wrong.

Round and round he turned, hands working through his sopping hair, trying to think what direction he was going.

"God," he shouted into the rain, mouth filling with water, then dropped to his knees, head bowed. Water spilled down his back and face, drenching every inch of him.

He needed a sign, a signal, a vision. Something to save the boy—and he needed it now.

Then he felt it—not images—sensations, soaking him to the bone—

The boiling river. Water—rushing fast.

Hacking. Choking.

Exploding to the rainy surface. Clawing at rocks.

Hands slipping. Plunging back into the dark.

Fear. Panic. Pain.

Kicking. Thrashing. Clawing.

The knowledge of inexorable drowning.

Slipping farther down the river.

John stood, looking around. He knew it in his gut now, like a compass in his soul. He spun in the right direction—

And ran.

John Temple smashed through the foliage like a juggernaut.

The boy was being pulled downstream by the current, grasping at everything in sight, unable to gain a hold—John could feel that now.

He felt the panic of a seven-year-old boy—the thrashing that drained the boy's strength as he tried to save himself, only wearing out his tiny body. Only hastening drowning.

The river was ahead.

John surged, rushing through trees to—

A steep embankment yawned wide out in front of him, and he grabbed hold of a tangle of vines, his weight teetering out over the precipice. He held on, looking down. Far to his right, slipping down the river he saw—no, felt, the boy—his thoughts screaming in horror.

Throwing himself back he snatched a handful of branches, dragging himself back into the forest.

Parallel, he thought as he tore a swath through the jungle, he had to run parallel to the river if he was ever going to get ahead of the boy. That was his only hope—to get ahead of the boy.

It was impossible, every bit of sense he had knew it was impossible, he couldn't outrun the river's current through the tangle of the trees— but there was something else, another voice, the same voice that had shown him where Paolo was. It goaded him on.

John surged.

Paolo felt his body plunge beneath the surface again, trying to hold his breath, air escaping from his lungs like frightened birds from a tree, spilling out in a billowing froth. He fought to the surface again, sucking air into his burning lungs, hands trying to force himself upward—but there was only water.

The river consumed him.

Then his body hit something hard.

John ran.

His attention was divided between the world ahead of him— rippling with green—and the river beside him where the boy bobbed. He couldn't see him or feel him anymore. John stopped at the steep embankment and looked out. The boy wasn't downriver.

Maybe Paolo had hit a fast current.

Maybe he was too far down the river to catch.

Maybe he'd already drowned.

Then he heard shouting. His head snapped to the left—he saw something. Paolo had hit a rock, a big one, and was holding on for dear life.

The boy was slipping fast. He couldn't see it, but he could feel it in his own hands, the jagged edges of the sharp rock slicing in. Paolo wasn't going to be able to hold on long.

But it was a delay—that was what John needed.

Somewhere in the back of his head he thanked God and continued his crash forward.

Then he felt it—Paolo couldn't hold on any longer. The boy slipped.

Ahead the river forked, one branch cutting a hard right, the other branch cutting equally hard to the left. If the boy was pulled to the right, he'd be able to cut the corner and grab him. If he was pulled left, he'd be pulled off and away—lost forever.

John had faith. Not in his own ability. It was beyond that now. He couldn't control which way the boy slipped. What he had was the faith that the river would pull him to the right—that the God of the universe, who had created everything in six days, could catch one seven-year-old boy in the right current to carry him to the right.

It was blind faith, he knew that, but it was his.

Ahead of him he saw the river turn perpendicular to his path.

There was another embankment, not as steep, but slick with mud and runoff. He threw himself over the edge, legs first, careening down the mudslide. Roots punched at his sides and rocks clawed at his arms. His heels tried to dig in, but his boots didn't catch, his clothes soaking up mud like a sponge.

He caught a root with a battered hand.

Holding on, he took stock of his surroundings. The ground beneath his feet gave way, sinking into the river. His boot skipped over the surface of the rushing torrent.

He cursed out loud at the top of his lungs, hoping Paolo couldn't somehow hear.

Where was Paolo? He should have been able to see the boy by now—if the river had pulled him to the right.

All around the embankment was giving way. This had been a very bad idea. He should have taken a closer look before he'd jumped over the edge.

To his right he saw a fallen tree that had been dislodged by the disintegrating embankment, its trunk stretching out over the water. Good, he thought.

To his left there was still no Paolo. Bad, he reassessed.

He worked his way to the fallen tree, boots sinking into the mud as he walked laterally across the hazardous slope. A moment later he was there. He looked back—

Still no Paolo.

John positioned himself so he could reach down and grab the boy. His legs gripped the wet trunk. He looked up—

There was nothing in the river except for loose chunks of debris.

He prayed, heart searching for answers. Why didn't he see the boy? God wouldn't allow that—wouldn't permit it.

Or maybe, John thought, he was mistaken.

Then he saw something.

Bobbing and dark, the size of a boy, it drew closer and closer—

A chunk of loose bark. Debris.

His heart sank. This was unbelievable. Unacceptable. He sat upright, putting a hand to his forehead. How could this happen?

He looked upriver—and saw Paolo.

Reaching out, he caught the boy by the back of the shirt and pulled him up, changing his grip to haul the child out of the water. A moment later Paolo was out of the water, but he wasn't moving.

"Oh no," John said to himself.

John found a flat place on the embankment and laid the boy out, checking his pulse.

Weak.

He tipped the boy's head back, cleared the airway, and placed his ear close to the boy's nose and mouth.

He didn't hear any air.

He didn't feel any breath.

John fished in the boy's mouth to see if anything was clogging the esophagus.

Clear.

He listened again.

Nothing.

Pinching Paolo's nose, he held the boy's chin and formed a solid, airtight seal over the boy's mouth with his own. One puff of air, then a second. He listened again. No air.

Another two breaths. No air.

He tried again.

The boy was getting cold.

"Come on!" John growled, feeling like a character in a bad medical drama.

Moments passed, repetitions blurred together, one to another. Breaths—then listening, one after another.

Tears mixed with rainwater. Prayer mixed with profanity. The boy grew colder; his pulse grew weaker. Soon he'd have to begin chest compressions just to keep Paolo's heart beating.

He gave another breath, then another, then stopped—he heard something. A hacking gurgle.

The boy's body lurched, shoulders bucking, stomach churning, his mouth turning into a fountain as the first of it came up.

Water. Bile. The contents of his stomach.

He spewed them all up in a nauseating eruption of vomit that spilled over his cheeks and chest. John turned the boy on his side, letting it all drain out onto the mud, preventing him from choking on his own vomit.

The boy curled into a ball, moaning.

He was alive.

The rain had stopped.

Andy was standing on the front porch of the temp building when he saw John approaching with Paolo in his arms, the boy's head resting on John's shoulder. The missionary's body sagged with obvious fatigue.

Andy approached. "Where did you run off to?"

"I was reading my Bible when it started to—"

"Why didn't you tell anybody where you were going?" Andy demanded, trying not to let his anger show.

"I was only gone—"

"That's not the point," Andy interjected again, fists clenching in his pockets. "You could have gotten yourself killed, or Paolo for that matter."

John nodded. "He fell in the river."

"What?"

"We almost lost him."

Andy felt livid rage bubble up inside him. "How did you find him?"

"That's not important."

"Why didn't you come for help?"

"There wasn't time," he said, still walking. "Now, if you don't mind, I'm taking this boy to his parents."

What an arrogant punk, Andy thought. Always the rebel, always on the outside.

Andy prayed for forgiveness for the things he had just thought, then went back to the temp building, glad John would be leaving the next day.

Chapter 4

EVIN BATHURST TURNED THE key in the door and stepped into his penthouse apartment. The walls were red. He hadn't chosen the colors, but it worked for him.

There were few pictures, mostly those that had been given to him as gifts. The majority were landscapes or foreign architecture.

Out the window he could see down into the Manhattan skyline, millions of tiny lights shining like stars across the landscape.

He sighed and approached the stereo, picking up the remote control. He keyed the command to start the CD player, and a long, melancholy trumpet note lifted warmly from the speakers. The dissonant notes of a jazz piano joined, and the jagged rhythms of the drums filled out the ensemble.

He liked jazz—it was calming, sophisticated, and not overly decorative in its sounds. It was good for filling the silence that otherwise hung from the walls in long, tedious stretches.

Devin loosened his tie, moved to the phone, and pressed the button on the answering machine.

"You have no new messages," a cold, mechanical voice announced.

He nodded to himself and moved to the refrigerator. Frozen leftovers sat stacked in Tupperware containers, like bricks in a fortress wall. Masking tape with black marker scrawled along their sides announced what each container held:

Meatloaf. Mushroom stroganoff. Spaghetti. Lasagna. All frozen and cold, prepared by a woman named Bonnie who came and cleaned for him twice a week, making him meals while she was at it.

He reached in and removed the first container on the top right—just like always. Working his way across and down kept the refrigerator organized. He looked at the container to see what tonight's selection was.

Swedish meatballs. He opened the container and put it in the microwave, setting the cooking time for exactly five minutes and thirty-five seconds—precisely the amount of time needed, a fact he had deduced from exact experimentation for each of the seven meals that Bonnie knew how to cook.

He stood, waiting for the microwave to finish its work, listening casually to the somber tones of the music from the next room. His fingers felt like tapping on the counter, but he refrained.

Living alone was easy. Didn't have to cook or clean. More income could be freed up for personal interests, and you didn't have to worry about someone nagging you about how your day had been.

The microwave continued its pedantic, tinny whine. The music continued its unpredictable, meandering rhythms.

His lifestyle gave him more time for work. He reached for the phone. Maybe someone was in the office and needed help with something. Devin dialed and waited a moment.

"You have reached the offices of Domani Financial. No one is currently in our offices; however, normal business hours are—"

He hung up, staring out the window into the night sky.

The microwave beeped, announcing that his food was finished warming. Devin scraped the contents onto a plate and set it on the dining room table.

He sat, bowing his head over the plate and folding his hands the way his grandmother had taught him and his brothers and sisters those many nights she had looked after them while their father worked extra hours driving a bus.

The Lord's Prayer, muttered quietly under his breath. He concluded softly and reached for his utensils.

Devin Bathurst ate alone.

He was trying to decide if washers or screws would kill more people. At first he'd thought that screws would be the better choice—it was a simple conclusion to come to. Screws were sharp, like barbs. If he packed enough of them in front of the explosives they would make for truly lethal shrapnel. The washers, on the other hand, were flat, and he would be able to pack more of them on top of the explosives. It was a tough call.

He spent forty-five minutes arranging the tiny metallic objects in geometric patterns before finally deciding on an arrangement laid over the explosives, bound together in plastic shrink-wrap.

The next step would be to fasten them to the vest, then to wire the explosives. A detonator with a safety trigger, which would have to be held down for arming, and a detonating button on top to discharge the explosives would have to be set up for the vest to work properly.

He looked over the plans he had drawn up, partly inspired by what he had found on the Internet and partly inspired by what he had devised himself. But he knew, in the proper place, with the proper crowd, he could kill dozens.

It was too bad he didn't live in Palestine—Hamas would have made sure that his family was taken care of for the rest of their lives for this. But the fact that they weren't here didn't stop him. Nothing would stop him.

Soon he would make a video recording, telling who he was and why he had chosen to die in jihad.

Joy filled his heart—soon American blood would be spilled on American soil.

They would pay for the murder of the imam.

Morris Childs staggered, nearly falling over as he braced himself against his desk.

"Are you OK?" Trista asked. He looked at his niece. She was blonde and strikingly beautiful. Morris sat in his chair. "Did you see it again?" she asked.

He nodded slowly.

She approached, holding a glass of water. He took a sip and felt the cool, refreshing liquid slide down his throat.

He sat for a moment. "I'm moving forward as planned," he said with a sigh.

She put a hand on his shoulder to comfort him. "Are you certain it's the only way?"

He sat for a moment, then nodded. "It's the only way."

Devin drove his car through the city. He was glad to be out of the snow, back in the real world, where spring had already set in.

His phone rang, chirping pedantically from the center console. He placed his wireless headset in his ear and activated the phone.

"This is Bathurst."

"Stay away," a garbled voice said through the headset.

"Pardon?"

"The doctrine of isolation was created for a reason—"

Not the doctrine of isolation again, he groaned inwardly. "Look, I'm afraid—"

"You drive," the voice said calmly, "and I'll do the talking."

Devin frowned.

"Have you been keeping track of the news?"

"The murdered imam?" Devin asked, thoughts racing.

"That was the beginning. Now things are going to get worse. Much worse."

"I'm afraid you're going to have to clarify."

"The Firstborn are in danger. Something is coming, something more terrible than anything we've seen in generations. Brother will turn against brother, order against order."

"Who are you?"

"It's more important now than ever," the voice continued. "Stay away from the other orders. Stay away from the old man and his granddaughter. You don't belong around them."

There was a long pause.

"Do you understand?"

Devin sat for a moment, eyes focusing sharply on the street ahead. "Who are you?" he asked again.

"That doesn't matter," the voice said calmly.

"Why?" he asked, trying to understand. "Why doesn't it matter?"

The stoplight ahead blinked to red. The car slowed to a stop.

"Because," the voice said firmly, "you can't trust any of us."

Then the line went dead.

Domani Financial had several offices. Chief amongst them was in Manhattan, thirty floors from the street below.

The elevator doors rolled open, and Devin stepped into his old familiar office, latte in hand. Devin liked the office. It was starkly furnished with a bold contrasting of black and white. Everyone was well dressed, well behaved, and things happened on time. It was his day job, and it made sense to him.

"Good morning, Mr. Bathurst," the receptionist said from behind the counter.

"Good morning, Sharon," he replied and opened a glass door set in a clear wall, leading to the main offices.

The floor was hardwood with offices lining the halls, all with glass walls where all activity could be seen. Financial planning and advising was what they did here. Venture capitalism, to be more precise. Putting people with money with people who needed investors. There was money to be made—if you knew what was coming.

"Devin," a voice said from just down the hall.

He looked up from his copy of the *Wall Street Journal* and saw her.

"Follow me," Trista Brightling said crisply. "Mr. Childs would like to see you." Morris Childs was actually her uncle, but Trista believed in maintaining clear boundaries between family and professional relationships in the workplace. Devin followed her to his boss's office.

She was blonde and thin, beautiful by most standards. In fact, it had been said on more than one occasion that she could have been a model if she had chosen. No wonder that punk had taken such an interest in her—a debacle she was still recovering from.

Her face was fixed in a continual look of command and authority— nearly a scowl. She wore burgundy as was typical with her—a color that expressed both vitality and professionalism.

"Can I have Cynthia bring you anything?" she asked flatly, leading him to the office down the hall.

"No, thank you, ma'am."

"Very well."

"Is your uncle expecting me?"

She stopped, looking at Devin. "Something has happened. Morris hasn't left his office in days. Something has him scared."

Trista's face almost looked concerned—an expression she rarely had. In fact, she rarely ever gave any sign of emotion at all.

Something was very wrong.

Devin stepped into the big office and the door closed behind him, cutting off most of the room's light with it. All the lights had been turned off, and the only source of illumination came from the tall window where the older gentleman stood, staring at the city beyond, back turned.

Morris Childs was tall, thin, bald as a billiard ball, and sharp as a tack. He always wore glasses and a crisp suit.

"How did your trip go?" Morris asked with his deep, commanding baritone voice.

"I killed someone," Devin reported.

Morris nodded. "Was it unavoidable?"

Devin looked at the model F-4 Phantom on Morris's desk—the craft he'd flown during the Vietnam War. Morris knew what it meant to kill or be killed.

"I believe it was."

"What about the girl?"

"Recovered," Devin said, considering if he should mention that it was Henry Rice's granddaughter.

He looked at his superior again, examining the anguish that seemed to lift from his hunched shoulders. "What's wrong?"

The older man looked down at the street, more than thirty stories below. "Something is coming," he said soberly.

Devin joined him at the window.

Morris shook his head. "What God has shown me of the future is too little. There's only so much I can do."

"What do you mean?" Devin asked, "What's coming?"

Morris stared out the window across the Manhattan cityscape. Devin followed the older man's view to where there once stood—

"America is under attack," he said with a sigh. "We have been for years. People who hate us because we're different—because we value freedom." He stopped, waited a moment.

Devin remained quiet.

"I lost friends in the World Trade Center attack," Morris declared.

"So did I."

"Then you understand," Morris said with a nod. "I know you do. That's why I gave you this job, chose to mentor you. That's why I introduced you into the Firstborn as I did."

Morris's face became expressionless, nearly hypnotic as he stared out.

"We are a Christian nation, founded on the principles of mercy, love, and tolerance. But these jihadist extremists? They don't understand that. All they know how to do is kill."

"I don't understand."

Morris moved back to his desk, shoulders stooping as he braced himself against the edge. "There's an attack coming," he said, shaking his head. "Children," he declared flatly. "They're going to kill hundreds of innocent children. And I don't know how to stop it."

Devin moved to the side, looking the man over in profile.

"Where's it going to be?"

"The attack? An elementary school, but other than that I have no idea."

"Who are the suspects?"

"I don't know."

"What have you seen?"

Morris stood, turning around. He buried his forehead in a palm. "One man. He prays at a mosque, then enters a school wearing a bomb—"

"And kills people."

Morris nodded. "Children. All in the name of his god."

"Do you know who the man is?"

"I never see his face. He could be anyone."

"Do you know where the bomb is supposed to go off?"

"No."

"You said he prays. Can you find this mosque?"

The phone rang. Morris picked it up.

"Yes?" A moment. "Put her through." He looked up at Devin from the receiver. "It's Audrey."

Devin turned to go. "I'll let myself out."

"No, no," Morris said, waving a hand, "this should only take a—hello, darling."

Devin sat.

"Good," he said with an obviously forced smile, "the grandchildren will love it." He listened for a few more minutes. "Good," he said again, "and Audrey—I love you."

Morris set the phone back in the cradle.

"It's my granddaughter Angela's tenth birthday this weekend, and we're throwing her a party. You're invited, of course, as always."

"Thank you, sir."

There was a moment's silence; then Devin leaned forward. "When is this attack supposed to take place?"

"I don't know," Morris said, polishing his glasses with his tie, "but soon."

"Weeks?"

"Maybe."

"Days?"

"Probably."

"Do you think we can stop it?"

"I'm afraid this may be too much for just the Domani," Morris said with a sigh.

"Then what do you suggest?"

The older man shook his head slowly. "If we don't learn how to stand united, free of isolation, I'm afraid for the future of the Firstborn. We have to stand together or children will die."

"Agreed."

"Devin," Morris smiled, "you are the future. You are the one who must lead us all to unity when the moment comes. All of the Firstborn know you and respect you."

"Thank you, sir."

"And thank the Lord you're not that blasted John Temple."

Chapter 5

THE CAB SLITHERED UP the road to the top of the giant hill.

John Temple stepped out and paid the driver, hoisting his single duffel bag onto his shoulder as the car drove off. He approached the big house's gate and pressed the buzzer.

A moment.

"Yes?" a voice asked through the intercom.

"It's John," he said loudly into the speaker, then made a deliberate look up into the camera above.

"Just a second."

There was another loud buzzing and the massive wrought-iron gate snapped open. He stepped through into the driveway. Cobbled stones led up to the big, Mediterranean-style house. The place was worth millions.

When he made it to the front door he knocked.

"Be right there," someone shouted from the other side. The door cracked open.

Vincent Sobel was an athletic-looking middle-aged man with a trendy appearance. He looked John over.

"You look horrible," he said with a smile. "Come on in."

The interior was white stucco with statuary placed intermittently.

John stared at the tall ceilings. "I like the new place, Vince," he said with a nod. "I take it business is good?"

Vincent shrugged. "High-end stuff just isn't selling right now. I'm only living here until I can sell it."

"How long will that take?"

"It's been six months already—can I get you something to drink?"

"Sure."

Vincent poured two sodas then led John to a balcony overlooking the steep drop down the backside of the hill. In the distance John could barely make out the skyline of San Francisco against the setting sun.

Vincent took a sip of his drink. "Clay and I talked."

"What did he have to say?"

"He's not going to San Antonio."

John shrugged. "I'm not surprised—he's thought the rest of the Firstborn were out to get him for years. How long has it been since he left that fortress-mansion of his?"

"Two years," Vincent said with a nod.

"Has it really been that long?"

"Yes, it has. And he's still convinced that someone is trying to kill him."

"Does he still think it was the Domani who killed his sons?"

Vincent shrugged. "He never said the Domani—he just thought it was the Firstborn."

"That's ridiculous," John said, shaking his head. "This amount of distrust? It doesn't even make sense."

Vincent shrugged. "D'Angelo warned about traitors—those who were not of the Firstborn living among them."

"That warning is a thousand years old and was probably a metaphor to begin with."

Vincent leaned his back against the balcony rail. "All I know is that nobody likes the Ora, never have. We see people where they are—and nobody likes to be transparent."

"Is he paranoid?"

"Of course he's paranoid. He's one of the most powerful producers in Hollywood. Privilege leads to the fear of loss—"

"And that leads to paranoia?"

"Exactly."

John looked around at the balcony, resting his hand on the marbled railing. "Of course you wouldn't know anything about possession."

"You don't have to be sarcastic," Vincent groaned. "How many of your mission trips have I funded now?"

John furrowed his brow skeptically. "What are you getting at, V?"

"I'm just saying you haven't held a real job in, what? Six years? You're in a new country every eight weeks or so."

"Making the world a better place," John interjected, trying not to sound defensive.

"Whatever," Vincent shrugged. "I'm just saying that you owe me."

"I'm sure that statement earns you treasure in heaven."

Vincent groaned again.

"I guess you're right," John said. "What do you want?"

"San Antonio," he replied flatly. "We want you to go to San Antonio to help represent the Ora."

John blinked. "You and I both know that I have a really bad reputation through the entire Firstborn, ever since Trista—"

"That doesn't matter."

"Clay doesn't even like me. Why would he send me as a representative of the Ora?"

Vincent spread his hands calmingly. "Don't ask me, but pretty much everybody else is afraid to go."

"Why?"

"Something scary is going on."

"What do you mean?"

"Did you hear about that imam who was murdered?"

John shook his head. "I just got back from Central America this morning."

"Somebody murdered an Islamic holy man, and Clay thinks it was one of the Firstborn who did it."

"What?" John asked, confused. "Why would any of the Firstborn do something like that?"

"Don't ask me, but he's scared," Vincent said intently. "That's why we need strong, centralized leadership. Lone gunmen are dangerous for everybody—especially the Ora. The Firstborn have got to come together."

"Do you mean Overseer?"

"Yes," Vincent said with a nod. "Overseer will bring an end to the factions and to murder."

"That's still speculation."

"Either way, we're pretty sure it's the only way to ensure the continued safety of the Ora."

John sighed. "So he needs somebody to show up because Clay's paranoid?"

"Pretty much."

John fumed inwardly. "OK," he said after a moment. "When do I go?"

"Next week."

John considered. "Do you think Trista will be there?"

"Get over her, John," Vincent rebuked. "She belongs to the Domani. It was never meant to be."

John took another sip of his drink. "I guess you're right."

The guest bedroom was bigger than any John had ever stayed in. It was also nicer than what most Americans were used to, and a monumental leap over the conditions he'd grown accustomed to in Central America for the last six weeks.

He sat on the edge of the bed and felt his body sink into the soft cushion. A wave of comfort moved up his body. John lay back, the tense muscles feeling as if they were popping as they released against the soft fabric.

John lay for a moment, staring at the ceiling. He needed to call his mother.

"Hey, Vince?" he called down the hall.

"Yeah?" a voice called back.

"Can I make a long-distance phone call?"

"Sure. There's a phone next to the bed in there," Vincent called back.

"Thanks."

John sat up, his softening back protesting as it lifted from the comfortable mattress. He lifted the receiver from the cradle and dialed the number by heart. His mother always wanted to hear from him when he got back into the country. Sometimes it was to hear about his trip; other times it was simply to make sure he was safe.

John had resented the thought that he was a mama's boy for a long time, but now that he was older, he seemed to understand her more.

She had grown up in a small California town, a small-town beauty queen. The belle of the ball. Beauty of the backwoods. She'd broken more hearts than any girl had a right to and was known as the catch of the county. Prom queen, homecoming queen, hometown pageant winner—all by the age of seventeen. She dated the quarterback—and was three months pregnant with his child at graduation.

What had started out a fairy tale had become a nightmare. The child's father married her but was hardly an equal partner—he was a drunk, mean, and hardly able to keep a job. It fell on her to serve as breadwinner. When he finally beat her so badly that she thought she might lose the baby, she fled. She gave birth to her son, Jonathan Temple, in Reno, Nevada, while she was working as a waitress.

As a result John had been raised on the road, moving up and down the coast and along Route 66, never staying long in any one place. Despite her stunning looks and striking figure, she declined every one of the many men who approached her. John was the only man in her life, and he was not going to take a backseat to another user.

When John was eighteen, he moved on to college, paying his tuition with the hefty nest egg his mother had saved for him in her many years of waiting tables throughout the American West. And the moment she was done raising and taking care of her little man, she went looking for a man to take care of her.

It took five years before she met Barry, a doughy, bald accountant from Sacramento. He was hardly a thing of glamour, but he genuinely, desperately loved John's mother. He was good to her and spent every spare moment he had with her.

The phone rang for a moment, then the answering machine picked up: "Hi, you've reached Barry and Marcia Parson. We're not able to come to the phone right now..."

John set the phone down and lay back again. It was for the best; she'd only ask if he'd seen Trista, and that wasn't a conversation he wanted to have again.

He wondered if he'd see Trista in San Antonio, then heaved a sigh, reprimanding himself.

"Let her go, John."

Chapter 6

ANNAH STEPPED OUT OF the car and looked around.

The ranch was home. It was where she spent her summers growing up. She didn't say anything. Too much of herself still felt more comfortable nestled in her mind, away from the world, for her to share her feelings. The blizzard had passed, and in true Colorado form, nearly a foot of snow had melted to slush in less than a week. Colorado could be like that, a foot of snow one day, spring the next. There was a stinging chill to the air, even though the sun was shining.

"Come on," her grandfather said, offering her an arm.

She took it, silently, and followed him into the house.

Hannah leaned against the fence, watching the cattle.

Blake walked and leaned next to her.

Hannah had known him most of her life. He was tall, blond, handsome, and strong. Blake was a tough man who had never lost a fight and was an expert marksman. As a result, her grandfather had kept him around like a bodyguard. She didn't understand, but she had come to accept him. In fact, in her young teens she'd been madly in love with him, a crush that had soon passed.

"How do you feel?" he asked.

She didn't reply. She felt sickly, nauseous. She felt—

Cold night. A man in a car. Another man—she couldn't make out his face—approaching. Glass blistering with jagged bullet holes.

She felt death crawl up her skin.

"I'm sorry," Hannah said, turning to walk away. "I feel sick. I'm going inside."

She wandered through the dark halls of the house, the same as she had done every day for the past two weeks, running her hand along the coarse wallpaper in the dim light. Rows of pictures adorned the wall, hung in patterns that made little to no sense.

Then she saw herself, her reflection, tired and distant, floating in the glassy sheet that covered a picture frame. Her hair was a mess and she wasn't wearing any makeup. She didn't touch her hair, not even to displace the tangled strand that hung in her face.

She took in a long breath of air, held it, then let it out slowly, as if to feel the substance of her own body with her lungs. Instead she felt hollow.

Her eyes focused on the picture in front of her. It was of her, a little girl in a blue dress on the Fourth of July, sparkler in hand, twirling for her parents.

She missed her parents, even though she knew she shouldn't.

Her father had been a truck driver and was gone too much. Her mother was a lonely woman who passed her time with too many male friends while her husband was away. When Hannah was five, her father came home a day early and found her mother with one of her "uncles." Her father left and never came back, and Hannah's mother went shopping. She found men and ran off with them, leaving Hannah with her grandfather for long stretches of time, only to come back and sweep her away at a moment's notice to go live with the man of the week.

When Hannah was fourteen, her grandfather had put his foot down, refusing to let his daughter drag Hannah all over the world to live with unseemly men. That was the last she would see her mother for two years, and only sporadically after that.

Hannah sighed. Last she knew her mother was living in Black Hawk with a man named Robert, but that was all she really knew. She looked at a picture of her grandfather and his late bride and smiled. They were her real parents.

Something in her lungs ached and she felt it again—

Bullets punching through a car's windshield, a holy man's body being punctured with lead—

"Hannah?"

She snapped back to the moment and looked at her grandfather standing at the end of the hall.

"Hannah?" he said again. "Dinner's ready."

She nodded, glanced at the picture one last time, then followed him into the next room.

Henry Rice sat at the dinner table, shaking salt onto his potatoes, eyes fixed on Hannah. She sat, shoulders stooped, hair in her face, staring at her plate.

"How are you feeling?" he asked, putting a hand on her shoulder.

She didn't reply.

"You need to eat," he said with a concerned smile. "Do you think you could eat?"

After a moment she nodded, reached down, and picked up a knife and fork. She took a bite of food and chewed silently.

"Maybe we should do something tomorrow," he said, trying to be helpful. "Would you like that?"

She shrugged dispassionately.

"You know," he said, groping for the right words, "when your grandmother passed away, I didn't leave the house for a month. I was miserable."

Hannah dabbed at her plate.

"Then, one day my granddaughter showed up," he said with a smile, "and she took me out of the house and we went for a drive through the mountains."

She stopped.

"Do you remember that?" he asked.

She nodded. "It was fall."

"Yes, it was," he said warmly. "You got me out of the house and you helped me see the world again."

"I'm just not ready," she said in a small voice.

"You will be," he said, confidently, "and when you are, I'll be right there to take you to see the world again."

She smiled weakly and went back to her plate.

They finished their meal in silence.

Hannah sat in her room in an old rocking chair, a stuffed bear in her arms. Back and forth she rocked, staring at her bed, pajamas laid out neatly on the soft, tight sheets.

Outside the world was dark. It was time for bed. She was tired, but she couldn't bring herself to crawl into bed. All she could think about was the way they had grabbed her as she left her home in the morning, throwing her roughly into a van.

Hannah felt scared, unwilling to go to bed. She'd slept with the light on every night for two weeks now, fighting sleep. She knew better than to be afraid of the dark, but she felt it anyway. The thought of going to bed scared her, not with blind terror but a kind of unsettling knot that twisted and clawed at the inside of her stomach.

She got up to get herself a drink of juice. On the way to the kitchen she heard her grandfather's voice coming from his office. The door was nearly shut, a single sliver of bright light slicing through the blackness.

He was a gentle man who didn't lose his temper, but he was nearly shouting into the phone.

"I don't care if Al Nassar did recruit suicide bombers. If I find out one of our people is responsible, I will be not kindhearted."

She paused, certain she must have heard wrong. Then, changing direction, she slipped out the front door and headed for the horse stalls.

Her grandfather had always owned horses as long as she could remember. The smell of hay and livestock hung in the air, sweet and homey. This was where she'd come to think when she was a little girl, away from the world.

She sighed and crawled over the fence, making sure not to touch the electrified wire that ran across the top.

Ahead was one of her favorite horses—Dante, black as the night itself. She reached down, tugged at a handful of tall grass, and approached the big animal.

The horse seemed spooked for a moment, drawing back.

"Hey, boy," Hannah said in a soothing tone. "Do you want something to eat?" She reached out with her hand, offering the grass with an open palm, making sure not to let her fingers get in the way of chomping horse teeth. Dante bowed his head and bit into the wad of grass, smacking loudly as he chewed.

"Good boy," she said with a small voice, patting him on the neck.

Hannah still didn't care for the dark, chilly and mysterious, but she felt safer near the hulking black horse. She hugged his neck, and the horse gave an accepting grunt, clopping in place with his hooves.

She smiled for a moment then felt her face sag. How was she supposed to go home? To live alone? To spend her days fearful of strangers?

Her face buried in Dante's mane, she breathed in the smell of the horse. Then she felt it—like a ringing in her ears that seemed to echo through her head. And then—

Beatings—punching and kicking.

A man on the ground.

They spit on Him—screaming in His face.

The cross He carried up the hill.

The crown of thorns.

The cuts—weeping red.

The flesh, tearing from His body.

The sweat—the blood—running down His arms and legs.

Crying women.

Blackened sky.

Thunder.

Lightning.

—It is finished.

Silence.

Immutable, impregnable silence.

CRASH!

The sky splitting. The earth shaking. Buildings tumbling. Soldiers falling to the ground. The curtain tearing.

The tombs—stone coverings—breaking open—

The dead—rising—

Hannah was huddled in the corner of the barn, petting the kittens, when her grandfather entered, a single yellow lightbulb hanging from a wire above.

He stood in the doorway for a moment, not speaking.

She looked up at him. "I'm seeing things."

He nodded. "I always wondered if you were one of us." Henry approached her and sat on a bale of hay. "There's something we need to discuss."

Her head drooped as she ran her fingers through the kitten's short fur.

"Tell me what you saw," he said.

"I saw the death of Christ."

"And?"

"I saw... tombs breaking open. Dead people came back to life."

Her grandfather nodded. "'The tombs broke open and the bodies of many holy people who had died were raised to life.' The Book of St. Matthew, chapter 27, verse 52."

She shook her head. "I don't understand."

"Those who were raised from the dead at the death of Christ went back to their lives, as best they could. But they had seen the other side—they had seen eternity, and when they were returned to Earth they continued to see the world free of time and space. It was their gift, enhanced by the Holy Spirit that would come at Pentecost. They were the first to be born in the grace of Christ—the Firstborn. It was their charge to serve Christ with their gifts of the Spirit, like any other. Theirs was a kind of prophetic gift that followed them through their lives—they and only they were gifted like this, they and their offspring."

"Their descendents?"

"Yes. But it wasn't simply a matter of lineage, but faith. As the Firstborn reached out to Christ, He reached back and shared with them each their own unique charge—their own calling to fulfill. To some He gave the gift of foresight, to see things that had yet to come. To others He gave the gift of insight, to see the truth of the moment, and to others still He gave the gift of hindsight—"

"The ability to see things that have been," she said, piecing it all together.

"You," her grandfather said, leaning close, "are a descendant of that ancient line. In your blood you carry that same gift, and in deeper faith it has been made manifest."

She looked his face over, skeptically. "And you're one of these—Firstborn?"

"Yes," he said with a nod. "In fact, I am the patriarch of the Prima."

"The Prima?"

"Yes, those who are gifted with the ability to see events from the past. *Prima.* The word is Italian; it means what has come before. There are also the *Domani*, a word that means 'tomorrow.' They are given the gift of foresight—the ability to see into the future. And there are also the *Ora*, a word that means 'now.' They are blessed with insight—the ability to see the truth of the moment. I look over our brothers and sisters of the Prima and keep them together so that we can use our gifts together to serve our purpose in Christ."

Her mind raced, trying to understand better.

"And Devin Bathurst?"

"He is a member of the Domani—those who see the future. Using his gifts he was able to prevent any harm from coming to you."

"Then why don't people like him?"

"Devin is highly regarded throughout our community. All the Firstborn know about Devin Bathurst and his many successful callings—but long ago the Firstborn turned against one another and began to kill one another. Every order turned against the others, and so the Firstborn agreed that the orders would never mingle. The Prima do not interact with either the Domani or the Ora, and vice versa. Only on special occasions do the Firstborn ever talk with other orders."

"I don't get it."

Her grandfather nodded his head understandingly. "When people are gifted with very different forms of knowledge, they begin to see the world very differently—and if there is one thing that people can't abide, it's people who see the world differently from them."

"And people stop talking about those differences?"

"People will kill over those differences."

She thought about all the things she wanted for her life. A house. A husband. Children. But an ancient order of prophets? This was not what she had ever dreamed of.

"I don't want to be one of the Firstborn," she said in a small voice. "This was never what I wanted."

His look was gentle as he laid a hand on her shoulder. "But this is your life now."

She pulled away from him, standing. "This isn't the life I want." She left the barn and her grandfather behind.

Chapter 7

CLAY WAS MEETING WITH his people when his cell rang. He lifted his index finger to request a moment from the others.

"This is Clay."

"Have you seen the news?"

"No."

He stood, walked toward the television, and pressed the button on the remote control.

"It's the Al Nassar thing."

"What about it?"

"There's been a copycat shooting in Florida, and it looks like a couple of retaliatory attacks—a guy got on a bus this morning and knifed the driver to avenge Al Nassar. There was nearly a riot at Al Nassar's funeral."

Clay turned up the volume on the television, watching the broadcast intently.

"Clay—this is all getting out of hand."

"Yes," Clay said, mind focused on the television, "it is."

"It's time to do something about this."

"Yes, it is."

The phone sat in the middle of Clay's office on a coffee table. A half dozen other members of the Ora gathered around as the speakerphone dialed.

There was a clicking sound on the other end.

"Yes?"

"Henry Rice," Clay said, taking a seat on his leather couch as he leaned close to the phone, "we need to talk."

There was a long break.

Clay looked around the room at the others. Several eyebrows raised.

"What would you like to discuss?"

Clay nodded to himself. "I'd like to talk about a man named Basam Al Nassar."

"Yes?"

"I felt the murder as it happened—I know who did it."

"Good. Who?"

Clay pursed his lips. Not the reaction he was hoping for. "I think you know who it was."

"I don't know what you're talking about."

Subtlety was getting him nowhere. Clay squeezed his hands together, working them into red knots. He'd been losing his temper more and more lately, and his doctor said it was bad for his heart.

Clay took a deep breath. "Then I suggest keeping a handle on your people, or"—he paused, clicking his tongue—"we might have to do it for you."

Dead air.

"Are you suggesting it was one of the Prima who killed that man?"

Clay stood and looked around the room smugly as he prepared for his big finish. "I don't know, Henry. You tell me."

"I'm sorry," he came back, sounding defensive, "but if you want to discuss this matter, you'll have to take it up with me in San Antonio."

They said their good-byes and ended the conversation.

The room sat in consideration for a moment.

Clay nodded to himself. "Let's see if that ruffles some feathers."

"And then?" Vincent Sobel asked, arching a brow.

He shrugged. "Let's get Overseer established. It's the only way to stop people like this."

"And how do you plan on doing that?"

"Get me a flight to San Antonio. I'm blowing this thing open—in front of everybody."

It was midmorning, and Hannah was still in bed. She lay on her side, facing the wall, studying the wallpaper border. She heard her grandfather's steps near the door—there was no mistaking them with anyone else.

"Hannah?" he said softly. "Are you awake?"

She didn't reply.

"Things are getting bad among the Firstborn."

She remained quiet. If other people wanted to waste their lives fighting over their petty differences and chasing after visions, that was fine, but she wanted no part of it.

"We're having a meeting in San Antonio," he said calmly, "and I need someone there whom I can trust."

She felt like telling him to go away, but it wasn't good to be rude to your elders.

"I need you there, Hannah. I need your help."

Hannah didn't want to reply. She knew what she would do for her grandfather, and she knew that no matter how hard she fought, there was only one choice she would come to.

Henry Rice sighed. "Think about it," he said, "and let me know."

Then his footsteps moved away.

Hannah curled into a ball. She was going to San Antonio, and there was no questioning it now.

Devin Bathurst moved through the airport to the car rental desk. He filled out the paperwork and handed over his credit card, signing with a crisp snap of his wrist, then went to the garage.

A midsize, silver, luxury sedan—manual transmission, just the way he liked. He placed his bags in the trunk and then took his place in the driver's seat.

Devin turned on the radio, twisting the knobs—talk radio. They were discussing universal health care and the effects of a flat tax. He removed a pair of sunglasses from his suit jacket, placing them on his face. Then he started the engine.

He wanted to get to the hotel a few hours before the meetings began.

"I think we're lost," Hannah said as she fought with the map, its edges rustling as she tried to shake it further open.

Her grandfather laughed. "No," he said, pointing, "we're right where we need to be."

"How do you know?"

"Because," he said, indicating with his finger, "there's the Tower Life building."

John Temple sat in a taxicab, listening to music on his MP3 player, scribbling in the margins of his Bible with a pencil as he read. The driver pointed to the right, saying something. John removed his headphones. "What did you say?"

The driver repeated himself. "That's the Tower Life building." He pointed to a tall art-deco-style building.

John shrugged, uncertain of the significance.

"That's where Eisenhower was stationed when he received the news about the bombing at Pearl Harbor."

John nodded, unmoved, and returned to his Bible.

Architecture really wasn't his thing, but it was the kind of thing that tedious Devin Bathurst was probably interested in.

Devin liked the Tower Life building.

He leaned against the window of his hotel room, staring out across the afternoon skyline of San Antonio. The city was an odd combination of cathedrals and art deco, all boiling with a kind of cutting-edge modernity—a place where the old and the new seemed to clash in a strange kind of beauty.

Somewhere down below it all, near the San Antonio River, was the Alamo, a building that was built as a Catholic mission, only to be used as a woefully inadequate fortress.

Religion and war, he thought. They always seemed like such strange but fitting bedfellows to him.

He held his breath for a moment.

Somehow he felt the two coming together again—here in this very city.

Devin stepped out of the shower, clearing a long path of open mirror as he dragged his hand through the moisture on its slick surface.

He looked into his own eyes, seeing if they betrayed anything. His game face needed to be on tonight—the kind of thing that people couldn't simply see straight through. Whatever happened, he needed to remain calm and placid. The politics were too delicate.

His black suit was laid out on the bed. His shirt was white and crisp, freshly ironed. He dressed leisurely, putting his cuff links in place with an expert twist. A half-Windsor knot came to an effortless close, the knot sliding into place beneath the stiffness of a starched collar that snapped down over the red tie.

Devin looked himself over in the mirror.

Power. He exuded power.

Good, he thought. The last thing he wanted was to betray any kind of weakness—especially in that den of wolves.

John sat on the corner of the bed watching television. It was a movie involving a murder mystery. He looked at his watch. The meetings would begin soon.

Reaching into his duffel bag he removed a brown, suede-leather sport coat—slightly wrinkled. He threw it on and walked to the mirror.

Untucked white button-up shirt, blue jeans, and a sport coat. It was about what he'd wear to church here in the States, or maybe to a club if he were in the mood. Regardless, it was just a meeting.

Feeling restless, he headed down to the lobby for a drink. It was a five-star hotel. Conference hotels were always five-star, a fact insisted upon by the Domani and one that the Ora had no objections to. Most of the Prima wound up staying in nearby motels, but it was all the same in the end. When a group of fifty or so people got together like this, there really wasn't any way to make everyone happy, and nobody minded out-voting the stingy Prima.

Regardless, whenever John was asked to go to one of these annual meetings, the Ora always picked up the tab for him, so he didn't complain.

He was entering the lobby when he saw her. He stopped. He stared.

Trista Brightling. Gray business suit, blonde hair, perfect posture.

She stood at the desk, alone, checking her watch.

John felt a lump in his throat. His hands might have been shaking; he couldn't tell for certain. His pulse quickened and his stomach turned.

He took a breath and moved forward.

Trista sighed, looking at her watch again. Her uncle Morris was supposed to meet her soon. She'd come down to the lobby early with the intention of being on time but now found herself waiting with nothing to do.

She wished she'd brought a book.

Trista scanned the room for Morris again—

"Hello," John said, approaching with his incorrigible swagger. "I didn't know you were going to be here."

Her mood instantly soured.

"What are you doing here, John?" she demanded coolly, trying not to betray her disgust.

"The Ora sent me this year."

"Really?" she said skeptically. "And why is that?"

He shrugged with his typical, infuriating, devil-may-care grin. "I guess they just like me."

She glared. He was reckless, uncontrollable, a rebel without regard for the rules. No one liked John Temple—especially not her. Not since—

"What are you doing right now?" he asked, obviously trying not to give a hint of the invitation that was coming next.

She sighed and looked at the door, hoping desperately that Morris would arrive to save her. "I'm waiting for someone."

John looked at his watch. "Do you have a minute?"

"No," she said, her tone as flat and nonnegotiable as possible.

"Hey," he said with a sickening smirk, "I just wanted to catch up. See how you're doing these days."

"No," she glowered, "not again, John."

"I just—"

She walked away. Uncle Morris would understand.

"Wait," John called after, following, "I just want to talk."

He grabbed her wrist and she spun into him. She glared, sending him every ounce of filthy look she could muster.

"What?" she demanded, openly angry now. "What do you want to talk about? To ask me how business is? To ask how my uncle is? To see what it was like to be an outcast in my own order? To ask what it's like to beg and plead and grovel my way back to decent standing?"

His expression went blank, startled by her sudden change of tone.

"You're an Ora. I'm a Domani. It's that simple," she said, nearly growling. "One of us has to accept that."

"Trista—," he began.

"Not again, John," she declared with all the strength she had. "Not ever again."

He moved his hands to her arms, holding them tightly the way he used to. His expression softened and he looked into her eyes, an expression of mischief and charm. She took a long, deep breath as his thumbs pressed against her biceps.

Then she let her air out and looked into the eyes of the old familiar cad.

"Get over me, John," she said definitively.

His expression seemed almost confused.

"But—?"

"Am I interrupting something?" Morris said from the left.

"No," Trista said coldly, her scathing eyes still burning into those across from her. "Mr. Temple and I are finished."

He nodded, let go of her, and took a step back. John looked at Morris, nodding again. "I'll let you two get to your appointment."

"Thank you," Trista said.

John said his good-byes then walked away.

"Did he bother you?" Morris asked.

"I'm fine."

Morris removed his glasses, breathed on them, then held them up to the light. "Do you still have feelings for him?"

Trista watched as John slipped through the crowd, his suntanned hand swinging loosely at his side, an elephant-hair bracelet around his wrist.

Reckless and free.

"No," she said. "I don't feel anything for him at all."

Chapter 8

To Devin Bathurst there were moments when being a member of the Firstborn felt less like carrying a gift for Christ and more like being a member of the mob. For him this was one of those moments. Of the fifty or so people who showed up at these things, fully half were acting as bodyguards. The others were usually just the richest or most politically ambitious members of the Firstborn. Machiavellians, mostly.

Most five-star hotels had executive meeting rooms. This one had been reserved at the hotel months in advance, and now guards stood at the door. Each order used a different name for their guards—each with the purpose of checking invitations, but they were guards all the same, meant to keep the outside world out of the Firstborn's business and to keep unwelcome members of the same organization from crashing the gates and welcoming themselves in.

He approached from the elevator, walking to the doors. Devin removed the invitation from his jacket pocket, along with a photo ID, holding them both in a single hand as he flashed them at the nearest guard.

"Thank you, Mr. Bathurst," the first said, his nametag indicating him as a member of the Domani.

Devin gave him a nod.

"I need to see your invitation also," another said—Ora. The man took the invitation and the ID, examining them closely.

"You know me," Devin said flatly.

A moment later the guard nodded sheepishly and handed the materials back.

Two down, one to go, he thought. He approached a guard from the Prima. Each order wanted someone at the door checking credentials—partly in the hope that redundancy would promote security, and largely because no one order would trust the others exclusively with security.

He moved through the crowd and into the meeting room, where as many as two dozen members of the Firstborn lingered around the long table, talking. The conversation was mostly polite but always tainted with the discomfort of suspended isolation.

"Devin Bathurst," a voice said from behind.

Devin turned—John Temple. He groaned inwardly.

"What brings you here?" Devin asked genuinely, knowing full well the Ora wouldn't send John on such an important errand.

John approached. "Nobody really wanted to represent the Ora this year, so they dropped it on me."

They shook hands. "So have you done anything useful with your life?"

"I just got back from Central America," John replied, as if it were supposed to be something impressive.

"Do you have a job yet?" Devin ribbed through a faint smile.

"My work is loving the Lord," John said with a smile, "and doing His work all over the world."

Devin nodded. What a crock. John was a bum—a globe-trotting teenager who had never grown out of his wanderlust and inability to commit to anything.

"Well," Devin said, trying not to sound sarcastic, "that sounds very…noble."

John nodded weakly. "How about you? Still making money hand over fist?"

"Business has been good," he admitted, then stopped. Out of the corner of his eye Devin saw something he didn't expect—

Henry Rice stood at the door in a cheap suit, and next to him, looking sheepish and unsure, was his granddaughter—Hannah Rice.

What was she doing here?

"Excuse me," Devin announced as he walked away from John. The unemployed missionary said something, but Devin didn't hear it clearly, nor did he care.

"Mr. Rice, I thought the patriarchs weren't supposed to arrive until later."

Henry shrugged as he turned to him. "I figured I might as well come and sit for the boring parts—makes me more accessible."

Devin nodded. The old man might be crazy, he thought, but you have to respect a man who forgoes the privilege of sitting out the boring parts.

"Ms. Rice," Devin continued, extending a hand to Hannah. She looked surprised. "It's Devin Bathurst, we met—"

"I know," she said with a nod, obviously nervous.

"What brings you to the meeting of the Firstborn?"

"She's with me," Henry interjected.

"Does this mean...?"

"Yes," Henry said, "yes, it does."

How interesting, Devin thought.

A thumping on the microphone caught their attention, and they all turned to face the speaker. Devin watched as John Temple took his place at the front of the room. "This is the Ora's year to perform the opening prayer, so I will be leading us as we seek God through our meeting."

Devin tried not to roll his eyes.

"Please join me," John said, raising a hand and bowing his head.

What a show, Devin thought, glaring, and John began his very long, meandering prayer.

The meetings were never well organized.

They always opened the same way—the state of the orders. Each order would have a member stand and deliver a theoretically brief presentation about what their order's mission statement for the year was and how they had achieved last year's goals.

Devin hated it. It was all politics. Show everyone else what you'd done and what you plan to do and continue to hope that the others would stay out of your way. Justify your turf and hope that the others would see it your way.

One small group of the Ora had done a pretty good job of helping out in a neighborhood in New York once—their presentation was to request continued access to what was theoretically Domani turf for the sake of their mercy mission.

In all truth it was an attempt to keep an eye on the Domani and to keep them from trying to hurt any members of the Ora.

That simple.

A thousand years of mistrust heaped upon mistrust.

The first presentation ended and the lights came up. What should have been a half-hour presentation had taken nearly two full hours. Devin rubbed his eyes.

Someone suggested a break, and a consensus was reached.

Devin didn't care. These meetings were pointless, just a show of power.

Then he felt a tapping on his shoulder.

"Mr. Bathurst," Henry Rice said into his ear, "do you have a moment?"

Devin nodded. The true purpose behind the annual meetings was not to meet in conference rooms and discuss goals and negotiate boundaries—the real purpose was to provide individuals the chance to meet secretly. That was where the real business was done.

After a few moments, Devin followed Henry to a balcony overlooking the river below. The lights of the Riverwalk glowed through the thick vegetation that surrounded the river itself.

"It's a beautiful city," Henry said with a nod.

"Agreed," Devin replied, wondering what they were doing here.

"Mr. Bathurst," Henry began, "please tell me again how you found my granddaughter."

"I was given the moment," he said flatly.

"More specifically?"

"I had a vision of her being killed. I saw the house and was, through time-consuming research, able to piece together the location."

"Did you know it was my granddaughter?"

"No."

"Would you have come for her if you'd known she was related to me?"

Devin stood for a moment. "The doctrine of isolation—"

"Forget that. Would you have come for her—simply because she was a person in need?"

Devin didn't speak for several moments, then nodded. "Yes, sir. I would have helped your granddaughter, simply because it was the right thing to do."

Henry leaned against the railing, heaving a sigh as his body relaxed. "She still has a chance," he said with a nod.

"A chance for what?"

"A normal life."

"Sir?"

Henry shook his head. "Look at us. What do you see, Mr. Bathurst?"

"I'm afraid that I don't follow."

"Are you happy, Mr. Bathurst?"

"I'm not sure…"

"It's a simple question: are you or are you not happy?"

Devin straightened his tie. "It isn't about being happy, and you know that."

"But she still has a chance at it." Henry stood upright, crossing his arms. "When I look at her I see life before all of this—before all the pain and mistrust. You know how painful this life is. And if I can do anything to save her from the pain we've had to experience, then I'll do everything in my power."

Devin shook his head. "But that's not what we are. We weren't called to live simple or cheery lives—the world needs people like us. God called us to do what was right—to make the world a better place—even if it hurts. Even if that means we have to look past our differences."

"You're right," Henry agreed, nodding. "That's why the Firstborn need more like you."

"Thank you, sir."

The older man turned to him. "Do you know what we are, Mr. Bathurst?"

Devin nodded. "We are the descendants of those resurrected at the death of Christ, charged with using our gifts for the betterment of humanity."

Henry shook his head. "No," he said slowly. "After thirty years of walking with the Firstborn I've learned one very important thing—we are not special. We are not better, and we will not necessarily make the world a better place."

"I don't understand."

"Mr. Bathurst, we are people—scared, hurt, and unwilling to look past our differences. We talk about the orders of the Firstborn, but there is no order. We're nothing more than individuals with some gifts, trying desperately to bring some meaning to a nearly incoherent rabble."

Devin stood for a moment. "I'm not certain I follow."

"Mr. Bathurst," Henry said, placing a paternal hand on Devin's shoulder, "we are small creatures with tremendous gifts—but none of that means a thing if we forget where we come from and why we have these gifts."

"Is everything all right?" Devin asked, suddenly concerned.

"I'm afraid that the Firstborn will tear themselves apart, unless a few good men take a stand."

Devin examined the older man's face, trying to read the expression of concern. "What are you talking about?"

"Corruption," Henry said without blinking. "Horrible things are about to happen—members of the Firstborn are about to do horrible things."

"You don't see the future," Devin pointed out.

There was a twinkle in Henry's eye. "When you get to be my age you find out that there are more ways to know what's coming than to be told the future."

"You've heard that someone is planning something?"

"Excuse me," Blake said, approaching from beyond, "the meeting is about to resume."

"Thank you, Blake," Henry said, and his bodyguard moved away.

The older man stuffed a piece of paper in Devin's hand. "Meet me," he said, "tonight." Then he walked away.

Devin looked down at the slip of paper. *Meet me tonight*, it said in sloppy pen script, probably a combination of haste and shaky old hands, *The Riverwalk*. There was a specific location and a time—

Midnight. Tell no one.

Devin folded the slip three times, then tucked it away in his jacket pocket. Whatever had Henry Rice scared involved his granddaughter's kidnapping, which meant it was serious. And if there was one thing that Devin had come to learn about Henry Rice, it was that if *he* was scared, there was good reason to be.

John sat at the table and leafed through a pocket Bible as he waited for the meeting to resume, when he heard Clay Goldstein's voice. He looked up and saw him—bearded and thin, striding in like a celebrity, even signing an autograph for one of the doormen.

John stood and approached Clay. "Clay."

The producer turned around. Dressed in blue jeans and a T-shirt with a sport coat and tennis shoes, he still managed to ooze charisma.

"I thought you weren't coming. What changed?"

Clay smiled. "It's time for a lot of things to change," he said with a cool, nearly sinister smile. He patted John on the shoulder and headed for the podium. Three bodyguards followed.

John shook his head. Something didn't feel right. Nevertheless, the meetings must go on.

He sighed and returned to his seat.

"Good evening," Clay Goldstein said, clapping his hands together at the front of the room and waiting for a few moments as the group reassembled. The projector flared to life on the table, pouring into Clay's eyes. "Tonight I was going to present the Ora's stance on a subject of serious debate—Overseer."

Clay still wasn't used to the presentation software, and it gave him trouble sometimes. He checked the screen as he tapped the spacebar on the computer, making sure his presentation's first slide came up as it was supposed to.

"But instead of talking about Overseer directly, I need to discuss something more urgent. Not just if or when the Firstborn should start pooling their resources, but why."

The slide changed.

The room gasped.

An image: the imam Basam Al Nassar in his car, riddled with bullets.

"This," Clay began, "is why we need Overseer."

Trista Brightling raised her hand from across the room. "I'm confused. What does Overseer have to do with this?"

"Everything," Clay began. "We all see the world differently. The Prima look to the past, the Domani to the future, while the Ora live in the now. What arrives are more than just differences in perspectives but also in motives and methods.

"And that," he said, thrusting a finger in the air, "is exactly why we need Overseer."

A series of images played across the screen.

A copycat killing. Retaliatory attacks. The unrest at Al Nassar's funeral. Civil unrest.

"How many more acts of violence will we sit back and watch before we do something about it?"

There was chatter.

Morris Childs spoke. "What are you getting at?"

Clay leaned forward. "If the Prima can't keep a handle on their people, then we're going to have to do it for them."

The room went quiet with shock.

"That's right. Imam Basam Al Nassar was murdered—shot to death in his own car—by one of the Prima." Clay felt the blood boil in his face. He was angry now—furious.

Henry looked up sharply. "That's not true."

"Do you want me to tell them who?"

"Stop it," Morris Childs insisted, coming to his feet, "both of you!"

"It's not true," Henry said again, face pale.

"He was murdered in cold blood, and the Prima did it!"

Henry Rice stood. "Stop saying that," he demanded, voice agonized.

"Or what?" Clay snarled, bracing himself against the head of the conference table. "You'll have me murdered too? Like my sons?"

The room burst into argument. People stood, voices rising. The meeting had disintegrated into a shouting match.

Devin sat calmly as the table around him boiled over with conflict. He saw Clay Goldstein as his bodyguards grabbed him and pulled him out a side door, the man's face nearly smiling at the havoc.

Morris stood and shouted at the top of his lungs, face red as a dozen others barked back.

Henry Rice grabbed his granddaughter and began pulling her toward the door, getting her away from the argument, with his bodyguard, Blake, forcing a path through the assembly.

Blake shoved John Temple, and the missionary came back swinging.

The arguments were turning into a brawl.

Devin stood, moving to the door with a half dozen others who had the good sense to leave.

He looked at his watch. Whatever Henry Rice had to say had interested him—but now it meant everything.

"What was that about?" Hannah asked, horrified, as her grandfather shoved his keycard into the hotel door lock.

"Stay here," he said, his voice fast and obviously agitated. The door came open, and he nearly pushed her into the room. "And don't let anyone in."

She stared back at him. "Where are you going?"

"I have to meet with someone," he said, looking around nervously. "It's urgent."

John was the last to leave the meeting room.

What had that been about? Screaming? Yelling? Fighting?

He held his aching jaw and groaned. It was time to get some fresh air.

Chapter 9

HENRY RICE STOOD IN the darkened backways of the almost labyrinthine Riverwalk, stone walls lining the river. Moss and lichen clung to the edges of the sidewalk before dropping off into the twinkling water.

He heard footsteps come down a set of nearby stairs. Henry turned.

Oh no, he thought.

Devin moved down the Riverwalk, feet stepping quickly.

The walk was simply rows of outdoor cafés, restaurants, nightclubs, and hotels crowded around the San Antonio River. Lined with lights, buildings, and palm trees, it was like a cross between Venice and Las Vegas.

Every few hundred feet another vintage-looking bridge arched over the water, which glistened with a thousand sparkling lights. Portions of the walk weaved through the river itself, putting water on either side as the street passed overhead on iron-girded bridges.

The walk seemed to stretch on and on, with a raucous night-life boiling out of its innumerable venues. Rows and rows of tables stretched the length of the walk as people talked loudly and ate.

Devin moved through it all, hardly taking note of the things around him, navigating through the swell of human traffic. Henry Rice wanted to talk to him—in secret, and that was going to be interesting if nothing else.

John Temple held his jaw.

Things had always been tense among the Firstborn. Politics, bluster, threats, pretense—but violence? Whatever was happening, the First-born were disintegrating.

He stood in the Rivercenter at the foot of the hotel. At the end of the Riverwalk, a shopping mall surrounded the brightly lit water, a small artificial lake. At the center of the water was a platform where a jazz band played, its rumbling rhythm pulsing through the air.

John listened for several minutes, then heard something else.

It was like a heartbeat, thundering in his ears. It was—

Henry Rice standing in the dark. Someone approaching.

Confrontation.

Anger. Intimidation. The person shoving Henry into a stone wall.

The old man—

Concerned. Appalled. Angry.

Afraid for his life.

John Temple looked around. It was happening. It was all happening right now.

Devin walked at a brisk pace. He needed to get there soon.

Then he felt it in his stomach, a sinking. Something horrible was about to happen. Even without a vision, he knew it in his gut.

He increased his pace. There wasn't much time.

A horn blared as John ran through the intersection, a car slamming on its brakes to keep from hitting him. Tires screeched. His feet hit the sidewalk at the other end of the intersection near a tall modern-art sculpture—the Torch of Friendship, as it was called, red and twisting.

He kept running, shoving through people.

Henry Rice was afraid for his life.

Not soon—*now.*

John hammered at the sidewalk with his feet, driving his legs like a taskmaster. The world dissolved into a rushing blur around him.

"Hey!" somebody shouted as he shoved past rudely.

He could feel where Henry was, not with precision, but a kind of proximity. Close enough to reach him, far enough to be too late.

John surged forward with all his might, spinning around a corner where a set of stairs led down to the Riverwalk below. Down the steps he went, nearly leaping into the thicket of tables and chairs.

Something twisted and tangled in his stomach. He felt sick, like he was in the presence of—

Evil.

Suddenly, the world was gone.

Pain. Fury. Shoving. Struggle. Yelling.

Stone steps—

—fleeing.

Grappling.

Slipping.

The old man's body falling backward.

John grabbed the back of a chair, and its occupant turned, bewildered and disgusted. John clutched his stomach—he could feel it all happening—

Right now.

"Sir, are you all right?" a waiter asked.

John tried to speak, but he could hardly breathe. He stood upright, trying to walk forward. His body tilted, the world swam. It was overwhelming—the knowledge of—

Pain. Fear. Betrayal.

The steps slamming into his back.

His body sliding down.

The sensation of bones—

Cracking.

Breaking.

Body tumbling.

Anguish. Gasping for life.

He looked up.

"Sir?"

His jaw set, his world righted. He plunged into the night.

Devin took calculated steps, clipping along as fast as his feet would take him.

He moved up a set of stairs and down another.

He stopped.

He stared—incredulous.

On the cement at the bottom of the steps lying on his back was Henry Rice, body twisted and broken. Devin rushed to the bottom of the stairs and checked the old man's pulse.

—nothing—

He stood, staring in disbelief, then removed his cell phone from his jacket, dialed, and waited.

"This is the voice mail of Morris Childs. I'm unable to answer my phone, but if you leave a message, I'll call back as soon as possible—*beep.*"

Devin clutched the phone in his hand, dark knuckles whitening. "This is Devin Bathurst. I was supposed to meet with Henry Rice this evening." He took a long breath and looked down at the old man. "He's dead," he said, voice hardening. "He's dead, and I think someone killed him. Get out of San Antonio tonight. I don't know what's happening, but it's serious and I think it's bad. I repeat, get out now!"

He ended the call and searched through his contacts, dialing again.

"Hello?"

"Trista?"

"Devin?"

"I need to talk to Morris. Do you know where he is?"

"He's missing, Devin. I went to his room and he's gone. It looks like someone's been through his things too."

"What?"

"He's gone!" she announced frantically over the phone. "He's gone, and I think someone took him."

Devin gripped the phone tighter and tighter in his hand.

He heard something and turned his head.

John Temple stood at the top of the stairs, staring down at him.

"I have to go, Trista."

"What?"

John Temple turned around without saying a word and began to walk away.

"Get out of San Antonio—tonight. Get Henry's granddaughter out too, if possible, but get out while you still can!"

"But Devin—"

"Do it."

Devin snapped his phone shut and followed after John. He knew something, and Devin wanted to know too. And he would find out what that was—whatever it took.

John slipped through the crowd, fast—a speed walk, moving through the people and the chairs and the tables as fast as a walk would take him.

Did he really just see Henry Rice, dead? And Devin? Could he have killed him? Why?

He was so blind. It was Overseer. Henry was an opponent, everyone knew that, and Devin had been the one to rescue his granddaughter. It was a setup to earn the old man's trust—to put himself in a position to place pressure, and when things had gone wrong he'd lashed out.

And killed him.

But it didn't make sense. Devin wasn't the kind to be given to crimes of passion—or any kind of passion for that matter. He was cold, calculated, and at moments brutal.

And he was following; John could feel it.

It didn't matter now. He didn't want to be alone with Devin Bathurst—not when there was already a dead body involved.

Devin sliced through the crowd, moving expertly, stepping to the left, dodging to the right. He was gaining on his quarry.

Ahead someone stepped in front of John, and it slowed him. Devin capitalized on the moment, surging forward while maintaining a casual pace.

He was close now. Close enough to surge forward and grab his prey, but not yet.

The moment wasn't right. He had to wait until there were no witnesses—

Then he'd grab him.

And it wasn't going to be pleasant.

John could feel Devin drawing closer—a menacing jungle cat stalking its prey.

The police, he thought, he had to reach police. They would protect him for the moment—he hoped.

Up ahead, a close-knit couple held hands, giggled, and traded pecks as they waited at a bank of elevators that led to the street level. The elevator doors opened—

That was his exit.

The petting couple stepped into the elevator and she leaned into him, sharing an intimate moment. He pressed a button and the doors started to close—

John slid to a stop, hitting the button.

Too late—the doors were shut. He moved forward again, turning a corner—

He ran for several moments, then stopped.

A long, dark walkway stretched out in front of him.

No people. No lights—just water and sidewalk.

John turned around.

Devin.

The dark man stood in a dark suit, a silhouette against the glittering lights beyond. A shade in the night, his red tie hanging from his neck like a stripe of blood, fists clenched.

John ran.

Hannah huddled in the corner of her hotel room, eyes fixed on the bolt that locked the latch in place. The lights were all turned out and the curtains pulled. She heard footsteps down the hall and shrank.

How could this have anything to do with God's plans? Distrust, violence, conspiracy? None of this could possibly be God's will. And she was part of it? It couldn't be true. She had plans for her life—this wasn't among them. She didn't want to be part of this—there were things she had dreamed of and planned and perfected in her mind since she was young.

This was not among her plans.

The footsteps outside slowed, moving closer to her door. At the bottom of the door was a gap between the wood and the carpet, a slender ray of light illuminating the breach. Another footstep, and a long, dark shadow fell across the slice of light, obstructing her view into the world beyond.

The footsteps stopped—directly outside of her door.

She held her breath, not wanting to betray any chance that the room had an occupant worth coming for.

Then the steps resumed and the shadow moved.

Hannah let a small sigh loose from her lungs, then shrieked. The room phone—ringing. She caught her breath and lashed out at the receiver, ripping it from its cradle.

"Hello?" she stammered.

"Get out of San Antonio—tonight." The voice was distorted, mechanized.

"What? Who is this?"

"Morris Childs is missing and your grandfather is dead."

"What?" she said again, incredulous. "This isn't funny."

"Get out," the voice said ominously, "while you still can."

"Who—?"

Click.

She sat on the edge of the bed. Alone.

The sound of Devin's leather shoes snapped off the cement walls as he chased after John.

Hands flat like blades, pumping back and forth, chest out, back straight, his feet punching up and down like pistons as the gap slowly but steadily melted between them.

John cut to the right, up a set of steps, and Devin followed, driving up the steps in threes.

Breathing in. Breathing out.

To his left he caught the sight of the old gothic cathedral rising from the ground: the Cathedral of San Fernando, lit from the base like a picture of Frankenstein's monster.

His chase continued. Steady, calculated—enduring.

John would tire soon—and then he'd have him.

John's lungs burned. His legs ached. His body rebelled.

Behind him he could feel Devin coming down on him—like a menacing jungle cat—bleeding off a swell of wrath and anger that John could feel almost palpably. He ran along the street as fast as he could—and saw it ahead—

—the Alamo.

The last stand of others—a last stand for himself. Maybe.

It was a federally protected park, and there would be park rangers nearby to make sure that there weren't any repeats of other disasters that had happened at the Alamo after hours. He had to find one. It was his only chance.

He cut across the street, stepping in front of an SUV. A horn shrieked at him, lights stabbing at his eyes as he looked to the side. He didn't stop. John leaped onto a short wall—some kind of monument—then dashed toward the old mission.

It was small—much smaller than he'd expected from pictures he'd seen.

There were no guards. What was wrong?

He leaped onto the curb, but his foot caught—and he tumbled.

Exhausted, he tried to push himself up but couldn't.

He saw Bathurst approach, slowly, confidently, hands swinging leisurely at his sides. He stopped just short of John and straightened his tie.

Devin stared down at him—then offered a hand. "Are you hurt?" he asked, his tone cryptic.

John stood, dusting himself off. "You're not going to hurt me?"

Devin's eyes narrowed. "Why did you run?"

"Why did you chase me?"

Devin reached out, grabbing John by the bicep, squeezing hard. "Come with me."

Hannah dialed her cell phone frantically. She had to see if it was true—if her grandfather really was dead.

She had to see it—

She jumped, and the sound came again—like a thunderclap against the door. Someone was knocking. Someone knew she was here.

Hannah held, saying nothing, the phone's antenna quavering.

The knocking came again. "Hannah?" the voice called through the door. Whoever it was knew she was here.

"Hannah, I know you're in there. Let me in. We need to talk."

· Her mind raced, eyes squinting through the low light. Against her better judgment she approached the door and released the bolt.

They stood in the dark behind the Alamo, surrounded by trees and water.

"What do you know about Henry Rice?" Devin demanded, studying John's reactions.

"He's dead," John stammered.

"And?"

"That's all I know."

Devin glared. He didn't buy it. "How do you know he's dead?"

John looked confused, then answered the question. "I felt it as it happened."

Devin nodded. It was an honest answer, he knew that much, and he needed a baseline for determining when John was telling the truth.

"What do you think is going to happen next?"

John frowned. "What?" he answered with an abrupt frustration.

"What do you think will happen now that Henry Rice, patriarch of the Prima, is dead?"

The other man considered for a moment, obviously confused.

Good, Devin thought. He needed to see John speculate, to come up with a creative answer—there was always a giveaway when you were making things up—and he needed to see that.

"I don't know," John said. "Maybe the Prima will fall into disorder?"

Devin nodded. "Why were you there?"

"I felt it," John said again, without missing a beat.

Devin studied the other man's face—it was different from his speculative answer. It wasn't a guarantee, but it seemed truthful to him.

They stood in silence for a moment.

"What's happening?" John asked.

"Morris Childs is missing and Henry Rice is dead—what do you think?"

"Is someone trying to take total control of the Firstborn?"

Devin shook his head. "I don't know, but it doesn't look good. In fact—"

John's face went pale as he stared into Devin.

"What is it?" Devin demanded.

"Henry's granddaughter."

"What's wrong?"

John shook his head. "I don't know who attacked Henry Rice," he said, turning to walk away, "but his granddaughter needs our help right now. I think she's in trouble."

Chapter 10

BLAKE!" HANNAH STOOD ASIDE as her grandfather's bodyguard shoved his way into the room. "What's going on? I got a phone call—what can you tell me?"

"You have to come with me," Blake announced brusquely, pulling the door shut behind him. "We need to get out of here. You're in danger."

Hannah clutched at his arm. "Is it true? Grandpa—? Did something happen to him?"

His face turned stony. "Your grandfather has been in an accident," Blake said.

"What kind of accident?" she demanded. "Is he OK? Where is he?"

"We have to go," Blake said, looking her in the eye for the first time since he'd entered, his eyes pained, face determined. "We're leaving the city."

Hannah went for her suitcase, popping the latches. She began trying to stuff things in.

"You don't need that. Leave it," he said, pulling her from the bag.

"But my things. I need…"

"There's no time for that. Every second you stay here is another second you're in danger."

"But," she looked at his hands, confused, "you have your bag—?"

"Essentials," he rebutted, hefting the bag over his shoulder. "Now let's go."

"Where are we going?" she asked.

"To meet your grandfather."

"Where is he?"

"Just follow me."

Devin and John cut through the lobby of the hotel. Even in dress shoes Devin could slice through the foot traffic, cutting to the left and the right, snapping through the spaces between people.

John slammed into someone—a middle-aged man—and the man went down. "Sorry," John shouted in apology.

Devin grabbed his arm. "We don't have time—take me to her."

They ran through the hotel, stopping at the elevator bank.

"The stairs," Devin announced, shoving his way into the stairwell. "They'll be faster."

They pounded up the stairwell. First floor. Second. Third.

Devin was the first into the hall. "Which way to Henry Rice's room?"

John looked around, trying to get his bearings. "This way."

He ran down the hallway, and Devin followed after. A moment later John stopped and pounded on the door.

No answer.

John tried the knob. Locked. He pounded again.

"She's gone," Devin said. "But where?"

John shook his head. "I don't know."

"Then figure it out."

"I—" John began, face white with panic, "I don't know where!"

"That's it," Devin demanded, grabbing John by the wrist, shoving him into the wall. He didn't believe John's story anymore. The chances that John was responsible for Henry Rice's death was as likely as anything, and just as likely that this was all a ploy to get away with it. "No more games," Devin snarled.

"I'm not—"

"What is this, some kind of distraction so you can get away?"

"I—"

He shook John violently. "Is it?"

John's face filled with red blotches as he tried to fight back, glaring back intensely. "Let me go!"

"Why?"

"Let me go or we'll lose them."

"Tell me where they are!"

"It doesn't work like that!" John growled, trying to shove his way loose again. "You know it doesn't work like that."

Devin stopped, stepping back from the other man, and nodded.

It was a gift from God, not a magic wand. One did not simply request to know—one petitioned God for more than what He'd seen fit to give them in the first place.

And it wasn't something you did while you were being slammed into a wall.

He backed away.

"Do what you have to."

John stepped into the middle of the hallway and stood there. He closed his eyes, tilting his head back toward the ceiling. He turned his palms outward, lifting his arms away from his body, and breathed deep.

He began to murmur a prayer under his breath.

"Heavenly Father above—be with me in my hour of need. Build me and guide me. Hold me and lead me. Take me and break me—make me Your own—"

John's eyes snapped open.

He looked into Devin's eyes. "Follow me."

"What's going on?" Hannah asked again. "I don't understand what's happening, and you're trying to scare me. Does this have to do with what happened during the meeting?"

Blake pressed the button for the elevator again.

"People are causing trouble, Hannah, telling lies to discredit members of the Firstborn."

"Who?" she begged out of pain and confusion. "Who are they trying to discredit?"

"Members of the Prima."

There were only so many possibilities of what he could possibly be saying. Only so many people that could— "You?" she asked suddenly, shocked by the possibility. "Someone wants to discredit you?"

He nodded.

She thought back to the meeting—to the images on the screen. "Do they think you're guilty of killing—?"

The doors opened to the lobby.

"Come on," he said again, and took her by the arm. "Now isn't the time."

Devin skipped the last two steps and burst through the stairwell door, following after John.

"There!" John shouted, pointing across the lobby.

There was Hannah, and with her was—

"Blake Jackson?" Devin said, confused as he watched Hannah disappear out the door with him.

Then he felt it—a tremor in his hands—

The blast scattered across the world.

Sirens. Ambulances. Police.

Mangled bodies being rushed from a ruined building.

Smoke rising like a plume.

Men. Women. Children—

—all dead.

Devin snapped back to the moment—and charged across the lobby.

He stopped on the sidewalk, scanning the crowded night street. They were nowhere to be seen.

John burst in front of him, charging into the busy street. A horn blasted. Devin followed, cutting through the street.

The convention center was ahead, tall and squatty—and there was Blake, nearly dragging Hannah, farther between the buildings.

Blake grabbed her by the wrist—she was starting to become a problem.

"Blake! Ow, you're hurting me. You have to tell me what is going on."

"Quiet!"

Blake looked back and saw two figures cross the street. He grabbed her, pulling her hard and fast, but it wasn't fast enough. Devin Bathurst and John Temple were coming down on him fast.

It was too far to plunge ahead with the girl.

They were gaining on him.

He looked to the right—a stone wall. He looked to his left—there was a long drop past the railing leading down into some kind of promenade—rocks and running water flowing down a pathway.

Trapped.

The sounds of feet smacking down on concrete reverberated as they echoed off the walls.

Hannah looked back. "Devin?"

They were close enough that she could recognize them—they were too close.

He plunged his hand into his duffel bag and grabbed what he was looking for—in one swift move he snapped around, leveling the pistol.

"*Stop!*" he shouted.

Hannah moaned in anguish.

They kept coming.

"I've got a gun!" he called through the dark.

They stopped fifteen feet away.

"Back off!" Blake shouted, spit erupting from his mouth.

He looked over John's face—worry and panic. Good.

He looked at Devin—eerie calm. Blake pointed the weapon.

"Stay away!" he shouted to them.

Devin's face remained calm as he turned to John. "I'll stay here; you go get help."

John nodded and began to back away.

Blake shifted his focus—concentrating on the missionary's chest through the iron sights.

John stopped.

Devin relaxed his shoulders and adjusted his shirt cuffs. "It's time to stop running, Blake."

"Stay back!"

"I know you murdered Al Nassar."

"He worked for Hamas!" Blake shouted back. "He recruited suicide bombers in Israel—he was responsible for the deaths of dozens of innocent people! I saw it!"

Devin continued, "And I know you killed Henry Rice."

"What?" Hannah demanded, turning her pained face to Blake.

He looked into her eyes as they began to fill with tears.

"It was an accident!" he shouted. "I wanted to include him, but he wouldn't have it. He found out about Al Nassar and the others. I told him about our plans, but he wanted to stop us."

"Us?" John said. "Who do you mean by us?"

"I know what you're planning, Blake. I've seen it," Devin said with a cold nod. "The bombing. You're going to kill innocent people. Why?"

"To save hundreds more!"

"You don't know that," John interjected.

Blake shook the pistol. "Don't tell me what I do and do not know! It has to be done!"

Devin's eyes narrowed. "You're still just a murderer."

"And what does that make you, you coldhearted thug? I know the things you've done."

"To prevent worse things."

"I'm doing the same thing."

"Killing after the fact isn't the same."

Blake put his finger to the trigger as he strangled the pistol grip. "I was placed in this life to execute God's wrath on Earth."

"And yet your God hates all the same people as you," John replied gravely. "How convenient."

Blake shook, rage overtaking him. "Do you know what it's like? To see what's been done? To see the things that people have done to others? To live with that? Murder or rape? Pictures of dirty back alleys rolling around in your head? Don't tell me you'd do nothing." He pointed at Devin. "Don't tell me you wouldn't kill in the name of justice."

"It's not about justice," John said boldly. "Jesus Christ paid the price of all sins on the cross when—"

"Shut up!" Blake shifted the weapon again. "Real people don't talk like that. You think your pious act sounds good, but it's just a show. Real people know that we live in a real world, and there are a thousand Al Nassars wandering the streets every day." He shook all over. "You can talk about Jesus like you know what you're saying, but what do you do when you have the chance to stop someone?"

Silence.

Blake began to scream. "You don't understand because it's all just a game to you. It's all about an image—Christian chic. But you're not down in the trenches, looking life in the ugly, nasty teeth. It's all academic to you."

John's fists clenched.

"You've never watched mass murder," Blake continued, "in all its gory detail, knowing full well that the man behind it was parading behind his own mask of piety, walking the streets unharmed."

"I felt Henry Rice die!" John shouted back, stepping forward. "I felt his fear and his pain. I felt the betrayal as you shoved him down those stairs. I felt his bones breaking and snapping—and I felt him die!"

Hannah began to writhe in Blake's arms, trying to fight free.

"Stay back!" Blake shouted, finger trembling over the trigger. John continued forward. "I have no problem killing you!"

Devin reached for his cell phone and began dialing.

"Stop!"

Neither ceased.

Blake's mind raced—out of options.

He threw Hannah at John, then turned and ran.

John felt Hannah's thin, young frame slam into him, steadying her before he turned his attention back to Blake.

Blake had a head start and a thirty-foot gap. John surged—then saw Blake swivel and—

BLAM!

A bright yellow flash as the weapon blasted at the night air.

John hit the ground, tumbling to a stop, concrete tearing into his hands and knees and back. He covered his head.

BLAM—BLAM—BLAM!

The sounds of running grew distant. John lifted his head, looking. Blake was gone.

Devin approached Hannah.

She was sitting on the ground, legs twisted beneath her. He knelt near her, checking to see if she was hurt. He took her wrist to check her pulse, but she threw her arms around him and sobbed.

His first reaction was to pull away, but he held there, body rigid. She stuffed her face into his chest, arms holding him tight. He took a hand and placed it on her shoulder, patting as gently as he knew how. She pulled close.

The whole thing made Devin uncomfortable—a nineteen-year-old girl with her arms thrown around him. But her grandfather was dead. He reminded himself that normal social rules had to be suspended. He wanted to say something comforting to her—to tell her that everything was going to be OK, that the life she had lived wasn't over, that she wasn't in danger—

But none of that was true.

Chapter 11

DEVIN STOOD WITH THE others in his hotel room, putting his cell phone to his ear.

"Trista Brightling," she announced from the other end of the line.

"Trista," Devin spoke into his cell phone, "it was Blake Jackson who killed Henry Rice."

"I understand."

"Where are you?"

"I'm getting out of San Antonio, just like everybody else."

"Everybody else?"

"The Firstborn are scattering to the wind, Devin. Clay Goldstein is long gone, and Morris is still missing."

"Do you think someone grabbed him?"

"No one is sticking around to find out. I don't know a single member of the Firstborn who was in that meeting that isn't fleeing the city right now. I don't know what you're still doing in the city."

"Blake is planning something," he said flatly. "I think he's going to set off a bomb somewhere. He said it was necessary."

"Where are you?"

"My hotel room, packing."

"Are you alone?"

"No," he said, looking at the others. "I'm with Henry Rice's grand-daughter and John Temple."

No reply.

"Trista?"

"What's John doing with you?"

"We both found Henry Rice."

"Keep an eye on him," she said, voice brimming with anxiety. "I have to go."

She hung up.

Devin looked at the other two.

"A bombing?" John asked. "Is that what Blake's planning?"

Devin nodded. "I had a vision."

"Where? When?"

Devin shook his head. "There's no way to know for certain."

"We have to get this figured out."

Devin grunted. "There's no 'we' in this. I have to find Morris, and I have to find Blake. This bombing needs to be stopped. Chances are good that both Morris and Blake are still in this city—if I can find one I'll probably find the other, but there isn't much time."

"Do you know where they are?" John asked.

"No, but I'll find them. I assure you." Devin turned to Hannah. "You're not safe. I need to get you someplace where you can stay unseen for a while—or until this scenario has come to completion."

She wilted.

"I'll look after her," John said.

"No," Devin replied, flatly.

"Why not?"

"Do you want the truth?"

"Yes."

"I don't trust you."

"What?" John's face was turning red, fists clenching.

Devin took Hannah by the elbow. "Come with me. I'll see to it that you're safe." He started to lead her out of the room.

"Hey," John exclaimed, stepping in front of the door. "I can handle this."

"I don't have time for this."

"You don't have time to take care of her and find Morris."

Hannah seemed to shrink in the face of the conflict.

"That's the trouble with seeing only the moment," Devin said. "You can't see far enough forward to tell what's coming at you. You can't plan, you can't predict, and you do what seems good at the moment—like seducing Morris's niece."

"I didn't seduce her."

"You destroyed her reputation, John. All because you couldn't see past the moment—and that's why you'll always be reckless."

John growled. "And all you can see is what's coming—what could happen, what might be. You're cold and distant and afraid. All because you can't get your mind off the future—and that's why you'll always be a thug."

Devin blinked then went to push past.

"Wait," John said, thrusting his arm across the doorway, blocking the exit. "You need my help."

"I need good help."

John smirked scathingly. "Right now you know for a fact that a member of the Prima is guilty of murder, assault, and criminal intent in terrorism. The leader of the Ora knew this but said nothing, and the leader of the Domani is missing—which means it's probably an inside job. So let me ask you—who can you trust?"

"I can't trust you—not with my life"—he looked at Hannah—"or hers."

"I'm the only help you've got. I may not be what you want, but I'm here."

"You're absolutely right…" Devin said with a nod.

John began to smile.

"…you aren't the help I want. Now excuse me."

Devin pushed past into the hall, holding Hannah by the arm.

John followed after.

"Where are you going to go? What are you going to do?"

"I told you, they're probably still in the city."

"Do you know that for a fact? Clay's already left town. Blake could have gone anywhere, done anything. You don't know where this mosque is—so how could you possibly have the first clue which way he was going?"

"I'll figure it out."

Devin felt a hand grab his arm.

"You don't have a clue what you're doing. You're so used to seeing things coming that when you miss something you don't know what to do next."

"That's not true."

"Or is it that you can't admit that you don't know what you're doing?"

Devin glared.

John squared up to Devin, looking him in the eye. "It's called hubris. Arrogance. The belief that you can control the future."

Devin held for a moment, staring into the eyes of a rash upstart, brimming with bravado but wanting in brains. But John had a point—he didn't have a plan. He struggled to keep his face calm—to not reveal any of the doubt that surged through him.

John put a hand on Devin's shoulder. "You need to know what's coming—or you're going to miss something big."

He felt himself slip—revealing some portion of his concern.

John's face became serious. "You know what you need to do."

Devin nodded.

Slowly he removed his jacket and loosened his tie, laying both gently across the bed. He unfastened the top two buttons of his shirt and undid his cuff links, setting them gently on the lapels of his resting jacket. The sleeves folded back, held in place by their starchy crispness.

Hannah and John were watching him from the corner of the room.

He lowered, as always, to his knees, hand steadying himself against the carpet—soft to the touch. Back straight, hands clasped, head bowed, eyes closed. Just like his grandmother had taught him. He took in air and held it, releasing it slowly—then let his mind begin to work.

Devin breathed in. Breathed out.

He felt the faith of a man in a foxhole—not a piety fueled by boredom or guilt, but the believing heart of a man staring death in the eye. He muttered his prayer—

"Our Father, who art in heaven, hallowed be thy name. Thy kingdom come, thy will be done, on earth as it is in heaven. Give us this day our daily bread, and forgive us our trespasses as we forgive those who trespass against us. Lead us not unto temptation, but deliver us from evil. For thine is the kingdom and the power and the glory—forever and ever. Amen."

He looked up.

He waited.

Silence.

"Anything?" John asked.

Devin held a moment longer. "No," he said, shaking his head.

He clenched his fists. This was not the way it happened. His shoulders heaved as he began to seethe. His teeth began to grind.

"Why?" he demanded prayerfully under his breath. "Why won't You show me what I need to see?"

Nothing.

His head drooped. It was no use if he was on his own.

He stood, moving to the bed, reaching for his cuff links.

"What is it?" Hannah asked.

"I prayed for foresight—I received none."

"What does that mean?"

"It means try again," John interjected roughly.

"No," Devin said, fighting with his cuff, "it means that God didn't give me a vision—and that means that this is not what God means for me to do."

"So you're just going to quit?" John said, exasperated.

"It's too late."

"What?" John said, visibly angry, as he stepped forward.

Devin stood in the middle of the room, trying to fasten a cuff link with one hand. "It's over. Get out of San Antonio—both of you. Who knows how many people are going to die before this is all finished."

"Are you crazy?" John asked, voice raising.

"No," Devin replied, adjusting his cuff, "I'm being realistic. The Firstborn exist to do what God calls them to. God's not calling me—"

"So you're just going to go home?"

"There are other things to do," Devin said, reaching for the other cuff link. "Maybe you'll realize that when you finally grow up."

John Temple stepped forward, grabbing Devin by the collar.

"Knock it off! Your mentor is missing. The man who killed Hannah's grandfather—*her grandfather*—is out there, and he's planning to kill people. Lots of them. And you want to give up?"

Devin stared back, cold.

"Don't touch me."

John shook Devin's collar with his fists. "You cold, heartless, unfeeling..."

Devin grabbed a wrist and made a sharp movement, and the bedside lamp smashed into the floor, throwing mangled shadows across the walls. John's face slammed into the bedsheets. Devin held him there.

"Stop it!" Hannah shrieked. "Stop it! You're hurting him!"

Devin held for a moment as he thought.

There he stood, restraining an unarmed man, forcing him down, as if he were some kind of schoolyard bully. It wasn't who he was.

He let go.

John stood and backed away, rubbing his wrist.

Devin stood in the middle of the room as the other two stared back, the lamp casting eerie shadows across the walls as it rocked back and forth on the floor.

Everything was wrong—*everything*.

He said nothing—simply trying to find a way to excuse himself and his actions before leaving.

Nothing came to mind.

Hannah stepped forward. "Try again," she pleaded. "If Blake's out there, we have to find him." Her young face softened. "I just want this all to be over so I can *go home*."

Devin looked at his shoes, like a four-year-old caught running in the house. He stood for a moment, looking the girl over. A girl—that was all she was really—a college dropout trying to duck out of her life, hiding from the challenges of the future. She had no idea who she was or where she was going—or even why for that matter. A soccer mom waiting to happen, hoping that suburbia would hide her from whatever difficulty lay in her path.

He could feel her futures churning in his stomach—two lives that could still be. On the one hand was love and happiness, prosperity in a simple and unconcerned life. On the other hand Devin felt her slipping into his world—*duty, anguish, solitude.*

She was scared of everything—and it was written all over her face. She had every reason to be. His life wasn't one of glamour or peace or even happiness. He was one of the Firstborn—if they couldn't bring this to an end now, then her future was lost.

He nodded, then turned his back.

Devin removed the cuff link again and rolled up his sleeve, taking his place, kneeling on the floor once again.

Slowly. Deliberately. Just the way his grandmother had taught him.

He breathed in.

He breathed out.

The Lord's Prayer—the words calming his soul as he muttered them beneath his breath. Then—

Nothing.

Silence.

The ambient creaking of an empty hotel room.

"*Why?*" he demanded quietly, fists tightening into balls, knuckles growing rosy.

Hannah's future twisted in his gut—*Alone. Broken.*

He needed to find Morris. He needed to find Blake. And he needed to find them now, before whatever hope of a future this girl had was lost forever. But the God of the universe—creator of all things—merciful and just—was ignoring him. He was being forgotten, misplaced—disregarded.

Sweat began to form on his brow as his eyes clenched shut.

A sticky bead began to slide down his face—moving across his forehead and down his eyebrow. The droplet stayed.

Then he felt something—not a vision or revelation from God.

A fingertip brushed across his forehead, wiping away the layer of sweat that clung to him. Devin slowly opened his eyes—focusing on the soft shape of—

Hannah.

She knelt down in front of him, touching his face.

"I—" he began, trying to explain that this wasn't necessary—everything was under control.

She hushed him gently, placing a finger to her lips, then took his hands. "I don't want this either, but this needs to be done." She began, voice soft and low, "Our Father, who art in heaven…"

Devin took a breath and joined her, "Hallowed be thy name. Thy kingdom come, thy will be done, on earth as it is in heaven."

The floor shifted, another presence arriving, kneeling down next to both of them, placing a hand on their respective shoulders—his voice joining as they prayed in tandem.

John—

"Give us this day our daily bread and forgive us our trespasses as we forgive those who trespass against us."

Devin felt the rigidity of his body relax and his heart go still—

"And lead us not into temptation, but deliver us from evil. For thine is the kingdom…"

His shoulders lifted—

"And the power…"

His chest felt like it was being torn apart—

"And the glory forever and ever."

Silence.

Quiet and long.

Then he felt it—like his body had been plunged to the ocean floor. The outside world was gone.

Light…

Blinding—

Furious—

Luminous—

…light.

It was vivid—as if he were there—he saw it all…

The past…

Blake, sitting at a workbench, looking over a set of photographs—a mosque—taken from overhead.

He looked over the glossy image, felt-tipped maker in hand, squeaking as he drew pictures on the surface of the photograph. A black cordless phone tucked under his head, pressed to his ear.

"I'm looking at the images of the Islamic Center—it can be done."

A pause.

"There's only one way...it's the only way."

Another pause.

"Everyone will die."

The present...

Blake in the truck—right now—face covered in sweat, driving, fleeing San Antonio. On the phone—"I'm leaving San Antonio right now. Everything is still going to go ahead as planned."

The future...

Tomorrow.

2:35 p.m.

The Islamic Center. Washington DC.

A father in white robes, his son dressed similarly. Walking through the arches—through the pillars, across the opulent carpets, beneath the vaulted ceilings that look like green marble, into the mosque itself.

Barefooted the father and son kneel—pressing their foreheads to the floor with dozens of others—

A blinding blast. A deafening sound. A moment's destruction. A generation's suffering.

Chaos.

Screaming.

Bloody survivors—

A little boy—lying on his face, dead—arm missing.

Sobbing family.

The evening news:

"The world's Islamic community has shown its outrage—"

"Fourteen suicide bombings in Israel today—"

"Iran has declared its outrage against the United States for allowing

this action against such an internationally important location and has
threatened retaliation—"

"*Hundreds now dead…*"

Devin's eyes opened.

"Amen," John said as the three of them looked up at one another.

It was unlike anything Devin had ever seen, heard, or felt before. More powerful, more vivid, more complete than any other revelation that had ever been given. And he could tell from the look in their eyes that Hannah and John had felt it too.

Devin stood.

"Washington DC?" John asked candidly.

He nodded.

"I'm coming with you."

Hannah stood also, voice unsure. "I'll come too."

Devin looked them over. He didn't like it—but something was different.

He nodded. "Washington DC."

Chapter 12

T HE AIRPORT SOUNDED LIKE the whitewater rapids of a mixing river, the hollow squawking of the PA system announcing the current threat level through the noisy discord.

"The current threat level is..." There was a pause as whatever computer that stored the pertinent information shifted from one recording to another. "...yellow."

"Yellow?" John Temple muttered to himself. The one time that he could think of since the inception of the color code that there actually was a threat of a terrorist attack, and it was three shades from red.

John rubbed his eyes. He'd have to sleep on the plane or while they waited to board.

He and Devin were standing in line to buy plane tickets to Washington DC.

Washington DC?

How was all of this happening? It was like a dream where everything was happening too fast. In a matter of hours they would be in the District of Columbia, and then—

What?

Devin turned to him. "Where's Hannah?"

"I don't know. She was just here a second ago."

"Find her," Devin ordered, and continued moving forward in the line.

John stepped out of line and let his eyes drift across the crowd. The girl was nowhere to be seen. He looked around in a full circle. She had been there just a moment ago; where could she have gone? The crowd swarmed in around him, and the world seemed to shrink.

"Uh-oh," he said to himself. Wherever she was, he couldn't lose her. Not here, not now. She was part of this—whatever *this* was.

Then he felt something—from behind a pillar, near a vending machine. It was her.

He approached slowly and stopped. She sat cross-legged on the floor, back to the pillar, head bowed. John could feel the anxiety rising off of her—almost palpable. He sat down next to her. Whatever was bothering her had her deeply shaken.

Silence.

Hannah lifted her head after a few moments and looked at John. "I don't think I can do this," she said firmly as if to herself, shaking her head. She pulled a twitching hand into her chest and held it there.

"I know how you feel," he said with a nod. "That's how I felt the first time I left the country."

Her leg began to shiver and twitch.

"India was my first mission trip ever," he offered. "The food was foreign, the language was foreign—I felt lost. All I wanted was to run back home—to what was familiar. But I stayed."

Hannah tipped her head in his direction. "Why? Why did you stay?"

"Because that's where God called me," he said with a shrug. She looked down at her trembling hand. He reached out, putting his hand on her shivering wrist. "You don't have to do this," he said. "You don't have to go."

Her head turned, and she looked him in the eye.

"Yes, she does," Devin said from the right. "Until this is all over I don't want you out of my sight. Now get some sleep. We leave at six twenty-five in the morning. We'll arrive at one sixteen."

"But the bomb is supposed to go off at two thirty-five, right? Isn't that cutting it a little close?" John asked. "Washington DC can be a tough city to get around in."

"It's the first flight out. Get used to tight schedules. Preventing disaster is always a race against time." Devin reached into a small paper sleeve and removed a slip. "Now, here's your ticket. I even got you a window seat."

Devin sat in first class—the only way he would fly—fingers pressed together in front of his face.

The world was slipping into some kind of madness he'd never felt before. He'd never been as involved of a member of the Domani as he could have been, and now here he was with members of the Ora and Prima on the same plane as he was—and he was picking up the tab.

John was a liability. He would regret bringing him soon enough, he was certain of that. And the girl—she was still just a child, her whole life ahead of her, assuming this whole thing didn't drag her in. She still had a shot at peace—and yet he had her on this plane because of some calling he felt. He was going to destroy the poor girl. Devin tipped his face down and scratched the tip of his nose—a nervous habit. He promised himself that he would only keep the girl involved as long as he had to; then he'd send her on her way to bake cookies and host barbecues—or whatever it was that normal people did.

He went back to work. The sooner he figured this whole thing out, the sooner he could let her go.

Devin tapped on his laptop for a moment or two, bringing up the pictures and information he had saved from the Internet before boarding the plane.

Politically speaking, the location was a nightmare to destroy.

The Islamic Center sat on Embassy Row in Washington DC, established in the 1950s after the funeral of the Turkish ambassador Münir Ertegün. Dozens of Middle Eastern nations had poured money into the building of the mosque—the Saudi Arabian government had made major contributions. The Iranians had donated the expensive carpets, and one Middle Eastern government had even donated the opulent chandelier that hung from beneath the mosque's dome.

The mosque was adorned with flags of all the Arab nations and was controlled by a board of ambassadors. Because it sat on Embassy Row, a stone's throw from dozens of patches of foreign soil, destroying this building would be an international incident.

There had been a controversy in 1983 in which the mosque's imam had been accused of storing weapons and explosives in the basement of the building. As a result, the center was shut down temporarily and the imam banned from the mosque—even arrested on the grounds of disturbing a religious service when he tried to attend months later. The eventual outcome was the unwelcome imam starting an unofficial second service that he held on the mosque's sidewalk every Friday, rain or shine. That would make things crowded and confusing.

It was an extra challenge in preventing this attack—another variable that could cause failure. But failure was something Devin was not known for considering.

If they were going to stop this bombing, they would have to be at the same physical location as the explosive device before the time of its detonation—physics 101. That meant he had to work out exactly how this attack would take place.

He looked at the satellite photos.

There was a car park to the south of the mosque. Blowing out that wall would almost certainly kill a large number of people—but that would require a large amount of planning, and the vehicle would eventually be traced back to the bombers. Blake was too smart for that.

There were also the sewers. Military life had taught Devin about explosives, and what he'd learned was that the best way to use them is to do structural damage—then let gravity do the rest. Explosives beneath the building would knock out the supports and cause the whole thing to collapse on top of the patrons—but that would also take months of planning.

Regardless, if it were that easy to destroy a building on Embassy Row by detonating a van packed with explosives or by breaking into the sewers, then someone would have done it long ago. That was essentially what happened in Oklahoma City, but that was a decade and a half ago—and that was pre-9/11. It wasn't that easy—especially not in Washington DC. Security was tighter these days.

Things were different now—not impossible, but much, much more difficult.

Devin considered a remote-controlled plane for a moment, then reconsidered—even the best remote-controlled planes had only a mile or two worth of range, which meant that they'd have to take off in the middle of the city—which would be noticed.

The other option was to leave an explosive device inside the mosque—potentially with their shoes, which they would be required to take off before entering. The person could exit early, leaving the explosives behind. A detonator rigged to a cellular phone could be activated remotely—but there was a wall between the shoes and the mosque "sanctuary" itself. Cell phone reception might be problem— and a potentially damning variable.

Regardless, there was no feasible way to pack enough explosives in a bag or item to blow through the wall and kill everyone in the next room. As morbid as it was to consider, there was always the problem of people absorbing the blast. Those at the back of the room would die, but those at the front probably would not.

There were security guards out front—potentially to keep out the former imam and his followers—and anyone carrying a satchel large enough to cause that kind of explosion would likely be stopped and their bag checked for exactly that reason.

There was no way to do this and get away.

There was, of course, another way. Unthinkable, but possible.

A person could strap explosives to himself, enter the mosque, go exactly where he needed to for a maximum blast, and set off the explosives—but that would require the bomber to die with the explosives.

These were Christians, and there was no precedent for Christian suicide bombers—

—at least not yet.

Devin's heart raced as he considered the possibility.

But who would do something like that?

Alex Bradley rubbed his temples. He sat in the chair in the dark corner of his hotel and prayed.

"If there is any other way," he uttered prayerfully, "then, Lord, take this cup from me." Sweat slithered down his face, and an unnatural heat overtook him, burning from within. He walked over to his laptop and hit the button, the screen flashing to life. A click with the mouse and he brought up the video file again—the one that he had taped the day before.

It was him—dark hair, strong build, standing in front of an American flag, a Bible in hand. The recorded audio was poor, bouncing off the walls of the basement in which he had shot the video.

"This is a declaration of war—so that the world will understand my actions."

Alex sat back in his seat, tapping a finger to his forehead as he listened to himself bolster himself forward.

"I am a patriot—I love America and I love freedom, but we are under attack. Through means that I do not expect the world to understand, I have been made aware of an impending terrorist attack on U.S. soil—an attack on American children. To prevent this attack it has been decided that the only recourse is a preemptive strike—to hunt down and kill this unknown terrorist in the only place he is guaranteed to be.

"I understand that my actions will not be popular—or well received. It is certain that I will be seen as a villain. I will not be remembered as a hero or a patriot—but those are not my aims. What I seek to do is protect the little children of America from murders—this is my mission—a mission I was given by God Himself.

"The Bible says that to live is Christ and to die is gain. This is my aim—to be crucified with Christ—to protect our great nation, the land of the free and the home of the brave, a nation founded on Christian ideals, with my Christian faith. You see, I do not fear death, because I know that through Christ the price for my sins has been paid and that an eternity in the kingdom of heaven awaits me.

"I know that my actions will not be easy to reconcile—but I assure you, this is the only way. To my mother and father, I want to say thank you for raising me in faith and teaching me the value of patriotism and freedom. To my brother, Michael, I would like to say I'm proud of you—the Marines are lucky to have a man of honor like you. To my late wife, Chloe—who died in the World Trade Center—I love you and I'll see you soon. I love you all.

"May the road rise up to meet you, may the wind be at your back and the sun upon your faces. And may the good Lord bless you and keep you in the palm of His hand—until we meet again."

The video ended, and Alex nodded to himself. This was the only way. The world would not understand—but it was the only way.

He walked to the large, black gym bag in the corner and unzipped it. Alex took one more look at the grayish bricks of C-4 stacked beneath the bag's flap—more than fifteen—enough to wipe them all off the map.

He double-checked the detonator and set it back in the bag, then removed the HK USP .40 pistol his father had given him three years ago, looking it over.

There was no denying it now.

He was going to kill people.

Devin looked at his watch.

"How long until we land?" John leaned over, shirt untucked, sleeves rolled up. Devin resented answering to someone who dressed poorly. Regardless, it was the grown-up version of "Are we there yet?"

"Washington DC is right out the window. We should be landing any minute."

Hannah looked at them from across the aisle—face flushed.

"How long do we have?" John asked.

"A little more than an hour," Devin responded.

"How long is the drive?"

"About thirty minutes."

Hannah stared at them, obviously shaken. "What if we don't make it in time?"

Alex showered.

If he was going to die, he was going to die clean—it was that simple.

He stepped out, shaved, and ran a hand across his smooth face.

Slacks. A dress shirt. A sport coat. He'd look like a workingman coming home from the gym.

He felt the heft of the bag—packed with explosive bricks.

His grandfather, Walter Bradley, had been an explosives expert. When Alex was twelve, his grandfather had decided to unearth a tree stump in the backwoods of Montana. Half a brick placed in a cleft at the base of the stump—that was all. They drove a half mile away and set off the charge. The blast shook the truck even at that distance, and when they returned, there was a hundred-foot crater left where once there had been a stump.

Half a brick.

Alex felt the weight in his shoulder.

More than fifteen full bricks of C-4. It was more than enough.

Devin pushed his way off the plane, checking his watch—forty minutes to go.

He moved up the ramp and into the terminal without looking back.

"Devin, wait," John called from behind. Devin didn't look back. He kept walking. "Wait—we're right behind you."

John came up next to him, Hannah alongside.

"Where are we going?" she asked.

"Car rental."

The rental was silver—midsize, manual transmission. Same as always.

Devin threw his laptop into the back and climbed into the driver's seat. He turned the key. The car came to life. John climbed in next to him, Hannah into the back holding a map.

"Do we have a plan?" Hannah asked.

"As much of a plan as we're going to have," Devin replied.

"So we don't have one?"

"Plans are overrated," John interjected.

Devin looked at Hannah in the rearview mirror. "Our plan is to prevent the bombing of an internationally important mosque filled with innocent people—whatever the cost."

Alex stepped out of the revolving door of his hotel, gym bag in hand, and entered the street.

It was pleasant today. The cold of just a few weeks prior was evaporating, giving way to the first warm-up of the season.

A beautiful day, Alex thought.

He wondered if tomorrow would be as nice—then remembered that there was no tomorrow for him.

The sedan raced across the bridge, gliding over the Potomac River—wide and gray, the car weaving through traffic. They had to get there quickly, but attracting the attention of the police was a guaranteed way to make sure they didn't.

Regardless, there were cars in the way—lots of them. Late lunch hour on a Friday. Just in time for afternoon prayers at the mosque—and to get stuck in traffic.

After ten minutes of driving, Hannah spoke up. "This is Dupont Circle," she said, pointing. A giant roundabout in the heart of DC—the bane of out-of-town drivers.

Devin moved the car into the circle, watching as the back bumper of the car in front of him slowed—red brake lights blinking on.

"What's going on?" John asked, looking around.

"There seems to be some kind of backup."

"Can't we go around it?" Hannah asked.

Devin found her country sensibility charming but unhelpful. "No," he replied.

The car ahead of them inched forward sluggishly, then stopped. A horn blared.

"There was some kind of accident ahead," John said definitively. "This could take awhile."

Devin gripped the steering wheel, squeezing tight. "It could take hours."

His shoulders tensed. Eyes narrowed. Teeth clenched.

His vision blurred and—

The mosque.

Fire.

Smoke.

Screaming.

Smoke rising in thick, gray plumes.

Death.

And a face—a face he knew.

Alex Bradley.

Devin turned to John. "Can you drive a stick?"

"What?"

"Can you drive a car with a manual transmission?"

"Of course. When I was in Kenya all I had was a Land Cruiser with—"

Devin shoved the car door open and stepped into the traffic, a car horn protesting behind him.

"What are you doing?" John demanded.

"You drive. I'll run. If you get out of this before I make it to the mosque, don't bother to stop for me—stop that bomb."

"But I don't even—"

"Do it!"

Devin slammed the car door and slipped through the maze of cars.

Alex slung the bag over his shoulder—it was heavier than he had planned, making the trek a little slower going than he'd hoped.

He knew the path to the mosque—he'd walked there and back every day for a week now, preparing for this moment. The target had probably been there those days, but there was no guarantee—this was the day and time God had given them—a time set for judgment.

Alex thought of his late wife—Chloe. It was her death that had brought him to a deeper faith and Christian walk, a faith that revealed the future to him. A year later he had joined the Domani and as a former marine had slipped directly into their unofficial paramilitary branch.

He'd been sent all over the world to fight the enemies of God. Mission after mission—all successful. He considered that this would be his last. Fitting, he thought.

He looked up and saw the minaret ahead of him—he would be among the last to ever see it standing.

John looked around the sluggish traffic of Dupont Circle—then something moved. The cars began to slip slowly through the net of police and ambulances that lingered at the nearby car accident that had caused the jam.

"We're moving," Hannah said.

John nodded, checking the dash clock. "But we're still not going to make it."

Devin's legs pumped up and down as he bolted toward the mosque—its shape growing bigger on the horizon.

Closer and closer.

Alex moved up the short set of steps, under the arches, toward the courtyard beyond. Thirty feet to go and he'd be at the front door of the mosque.

He didn't acknowledge the security guards ahead, hoping to slip past. "Excuse me, sir," one of them said. "What's in the bag?"

Alex kept moving forward.

"Sir?" another one added.

He felt them closing in on him. One stepped in front of him.

He paused in the middle of the courtyard, the minaret towering overhead, the walls closing in around.

"I'm sorry, sir, but you need to let me see what's inside the bag."

Alex looked at that man's black shoes. "My gym clothes."

"Do you mind if I take a look?"

Alex held his breath. How was he going to get out of this? His mind raced—panic began to overtake him. He stopped—felt the weight of USP .40 hanging from his hip. He'd planned for this.

He looked up—the man was middle-aged, bald, and rotund. A black mustache crossed his face.

"Certainly." He knelt down.

"Where do you work out?"

"Huh?" Alex asked, confused.

"Your gym clothes," the guard said. "Where do you work out?"

His mind raced—he'd rehearsed this contingency. "There's a workout room at my office." He put his hand to the zipper, hoping he could talk his way out of this.

"That must be nice. Now let's see what's in the bag."

Alex dragged the zipper across the top of the bag, the flap opening.

The guard gasped, stepping back.

It was the moment Alex needed.

The pistol snapped forward, blasting the guard in the chest—the man was dead before he hit the ground—thrown back like a rag doll.

Alex swung his torso—pointing at the guard to his left.

The pistol bucked and the man went down—a wound to the stomach.

A lousy shot. Shrieking lifted from the street.

Alex stepped forward as the wounded, bleeding guard reached for his radio, keying it to speak. Alex raised his pistol, looking across the plane of gun metal toward the man's forehead.

The gun went off as something slammed into his side.

The shot went wide, blasting at the stone wall.

Alex hit the ground, the gun going off again. He turned his face, saw his attacker—

Devin Bathurst? How had he gotten involved in this? Devin came at him fast—the man's entire weight slamming into his middle.

Alex came down hard with his fists, trying to fight Devin off of him, ramming a hand into his face—his dark features slick with an instant glistening of sweat. Alex kicked his opponent in the stomach as hard as he could.

His opponent went tumbling, and Alex brought the gun to bear—

Devin was already up, facing him—a fast move grabbed Alex's wrist. The pistol twisted in his hand—Hard. Fast. The ligaments strained as if they would rupture and snap—his hand released and Alex felt the weapon spill from his hand.

Just feet away the wounded guard choked on his blood, screaming with pain.

Devin moved like lightning, snapping under Alex's arm, grabbing him from behind. A hard knee rammed into Alex's back and he ripped around. A swift move and he had Devin in a headlock, jerking him around by his neck.

Their bodies spun in unison, and they tumbled to the floor. Alex's body slammed into the stone, painful and sudden—he could feel the blood vessels just below his skin bursting—big purple and yellow bruises would form shortly.

Alex felt his opponent scramble over him like a jungle cat tearing at the soft underbelly of its prey. He couldn't get his bearings—Devin was behind him, arm around his neck, squeezing tight.

He hacked out a violent cough. A blood choke—standard military combat training.

In a few moments he would pass out—*mission failed.*

He felt Devin's legs swing around his waist from behind, holding him in place while the choke took effect. He threw a swift punch over his shoulder, smashing into the soft skin and hard bone of Devin's face. His opponent hesitated—*good.*

Alex kicked loose, flipping onto his stomach—Devin on his back now.

The pistol was ahead, lying on the floor. He reached for it, clawing at the tile. His fingertips touched the blue steel—

A sharp blow came down hard on the small of Alex's back, and he flattened with a howl. Devin was up—in front of him—Devin's foot kicked the pistol skittering away.

Alex rolled onto his shoulder again as fast as he could, sending a series of wicked pedal kicks into Devin's leg, chest, and shoulder. His opponent recoiled for a moment, and Alex clawed to his feet with every ounce of speed he had.

His face ripped side to side, eyes darting—*the bag.*

He scrambled for it.

Devin felt the air escape from Alex's body as he threw himself into a full-bodied lunge, tackling the other man hard. His elbow hit the stone first, sending a shock wave of splintering pain shooting through his whole left side.

Alex broke free with a vicious chop to Devin's throat—he hacked, trying to catch a breath, vision blurring, stomach turning. The bomber clawed at the gym bag, reaching into the flap.

Devin threw his arm around Alex's neck again, trying to resume his blood choke. Alex came around fast. He saw stars—an elbow plowing into his face like a piston. Devin rolled onto his back, face bleeding, vision blurry.

He looked up, eyes focusing again.

Alex was on his knees, gripping the detonator, a cable running to the bag.

Devin lunged.

The would-be bomber was ready for him. Devin was caught in a swinging motion—his own momentum used against him—and his chest was pinned to the ground.

Devin tried to get up—tried to throw off the weight of the other man. Something long and thin dropped below his chin and pulled tight—the detonator cable strangling him. He felt the cable jerk him upward by the throat, choking him as it did.

The corners of his vision began to go pasty white. He gasped for air. Out of the corner of his eye, through the haze, he saw a hand holding the detonator itself—a detonating button on top and an arming trigger in front.

Devin grabbed the wrist that held the detonator and twisted—fighting with all his strength. A finger pulled the trigger.

A light inside the bag lit up.

—armed—

Devin threw all his weight back, slamming Alex to the ground. He heard the gargled sound of sucking air near his right ear.

The detonator tumbled.

He lunged for it, grabbing at the plastic handle—

A solid kick hit him in the ribs, and Devin rolled away, body flung by the force of the blow.

He lifted his eyes—and saw the bag.

Alex staggered to the detonator, picking it up. He held it. Squeezed the trigger.

"The sword of the Lord and of Israel," he declared, then keyed the detonating button—

—*click*—

Nothing happened.

He keyed it again—

And there was a sound like thunder.

Chapter 13

JOHN DOWNSHIFTED AND PULLED to the side of the street as police cars tore past, flashing red and blue lights. He looked at the clock.

"Are we too late?" Hannah asked.

"I think so."

He looked at the sky—no smoke, no fire. Just police cars.

Maybe it wasn't too late.

Devin watched as Alex Bradley hit the ground, bleeding from his chest.

The wounded security guard held the USP .40 in his hand.

Alex moaned as he lay there. Devin looked down. He held the detonator cable in his hand, yanked from its place in the C-4 bricks. He let go and pushed away. Without the cable connected to the explosives, the detonator had become nothing more than a fancy toy.

Three police officers moved up the steps, weapons drawn—obviously brought by the sound of gunshots.

Devin rolled onto his stomach—hands on the back of his head. Best not to be confused for the shooter when there were cops involved. Someone put handcuffs on him—a precaution.

The mosque doors opened. Hundreds of people, scared and confused, filed out. Devin watched as they paraded by, directed by the police around the bleeding men as EMTs worked to save them.

Then he saw a young man walking with the crowd. He had long, dark curly hair. Blue jeans and a tight T-shirt. Muscular and attractive.

He felt a soreness from his limbs, not from the fight but—

The young man at home. Finishing a bomb.

Meeting with others.

127

An elementary school. Screaming children.

Devin shook his head violently, trying to stop the thoughts, but the images kept coming.

Crying. Shouting.

Teachers murdered. Children massacred.

Blood and rubble.

Devin tried to stand but felt the knee of a police officer jam into his back. This would only last a moment. They would hold him until they had regained control of the situation, then they would take his statement and let him go.

But right here, right now, he was staring a terrorist in the eyes—and he was getting away.

There were police ahead, redirecting traffic.

"What happened?" Hannah asked.

John shook his head. "I don't know. But it doesn't look like a bomb went off."

She looked at the crowd as they moved out of the beautiful mosque. There's so many, she thought.

She'd lived in the city but never in a community with Muslims. It still shocked her to think that there could be so many. Of course there had to be a lot of them—but in America?

It was silly, she knew, but she had grown up in a predominately Christian community. In her mind everyone was still a Christian—or totally godless. To see people—not foreigners or pictures from a magazine—real American citizens walking out of their mosque, practicing a faith she didn't understand—it was staggering.

A husband and wife walked past, not three feet away from her car window. The wife had a scarf over her head, dark green with yellow stripes—she was so beautiful. He was tall and thin, glasses on his face, curly hair and a goatee. He held their baby son as they walked down the street. The baby boy saw her, looked her in the eye, and smiled big, giggling uncontrollably. His body shook as he laughed.

She smiled back.

They were people, real people—not ideas.

Hannah scanned the crowd and saw another set of eyes—deep and handsome. His hair was long and curly, a tight blue T-shirt clinging to his muscular body.

She felt a chill wash over her, and she saw—

The young man in the darkness of his home, building a bomb. Preparing to kill. "Tariq, you must be prepared to martyr yourself for Allah…"

"Turn around," she said.

"What?" John was dumbfounded.

"Turn the car around—that's our guy."

"Who?"

"The guy with the long hair—his name is Tariq." They had to do this. Finish it, and then go home. "Turn the car around."

"I can't—there are police all over the street—"

This was everything she had worked so hard to run from. But now it was staring her in the face.

She opened the car door.

"What are you doing?" John demanded.

Hannah climbed out of the vehicle, John shouting after her.

She slammed the door and began to move—following the man into the crowd.

Tariq Ali moved quickly down the sidewalk.

Dupont Circle was the nearest Metro station. That would take him home.

He looked back at the mosque. Something had happened—shots had been fired. Someone was trying to kill Muslims.

America hated Allah—hated the Quran.

They would learn their lesson soon enough.

Hannah walked, resolute across the Washington DC landscape, through Embassy Row. Tariq walked with a swagger a hundred yards ahead.

She could see him ahead. She couldn't lose him. Do this and go home, she thought, do one more terrible, horrifying thing, then go home to a normal life.

Past a line of embassies she clipped, one after another, her quarry just ahead.

He looked back.

He saw her.

Did he know she was following him?

He kept moving.

Hannah told herself that she would follow until she couldn't anymore—even if that reason were death. It was always a possibility.

Her hands began to shake—but her feet kept moving.

Devin finished his statement and the officer nodded, dismissing him.

As far as the police were concerned, he was just a passerby in the wrong place at the wrong time. The bomber had tried to beat him up, and the wounded security guard shot the bomber—end of story.

He walked to the curb and watched as they loaded ambulances—the guard in one, Alex in the other.

His heart sank. He hadn't known Alex Bradley very well. He knew the poor guy had lost his wife in the 9/11 attacks and had always been a bit of a loner—but the same could be said about Devin. He felt what was coming for Alex—these were his last seventy-two hours on Earth.

Anguish began to well up in him as he considered it—his heart feeling like it was physically sinking—

Then he felt it—Hannah was in danger. She was walking into a trap.

John could feel her as he drove down the street. She was near, very near.

He scanned the street, then saw her—Dupont Circle. She was moving down into the Metro.

"Oh no."

She went down the steps in threes, moving past the advertisements for alcohol and cologne.

A decadent country, she thought. America had degraded into a land of commercial consumerism. Where were the values? Where was the justice? Where was God? Not here, she thought.

The Metro station looked like something from a science-fiction film. The ceiling was tall and vaulted. Mist rising from sweating human bodies lingered in the air—blue light shining in bright, undefined shapes through the haze.

He was ahead—moving down the steps toward the train.

She headed to the turnstile, then realized she didn't have a Metro pass. He must have had one already. Hannah moved to the counter to purchase a pass.

She glanced to her left—she was losing him. There was a whistling shriek as the train approached, screaming to a stop.

She paid, taking her pass.

The doors opened. He was already on the train—the doors would close any minute.

The pass was little more than a ticket. She slipped it into the slot and the turnstile spun, welcoming her to the public transit station. She pressed her way down the escalator toward the man she sought. The crowd grew around her, thick like weeds. "I'm sorry," she announced as she pushed between people. "Excuse me. Sorry." Someone shouted in anger.

The doors were just ahead. They began to slide shut—

Hannah lunged forward, wedging herself between the closing doors. They clamped down on her—

Someone shouted at her to get out of the doors. An electronic system announced to her to do the same.

The doors slid open again and she moved into the Metro car.

There was a snapping sound as the doors finally came together and the train began to move forward.

She sat—then looked up.

A jolt shook her body from her core, sending a shockwave of adrenaline through her limbs. The man, Tariq, was sitting there across from her.

He looked at her. It wasn't a glare or any other look of hostility. It was almost neutral. Something in his eye glinted—almost as if he were attracted to her.

She felt something—a whisper on her spine.

The young man as a boy.

His father—big and jolly, laughing.

Family gatherings.

Food. Warmth. Love. Death.

The little boy sobbing. Tears running down his tiny face.

Pain. Anger. Rage.

Revenge.

Hannah tried to break her gaze with him, but she couldn't. There was pain haunting him. A past filled with grief, loss, and disillusionment. A feeling of being lost and helpless—not knowing his place in the world.

He smiled at her. Then looked at the train floor.

A moment passed and the train stopped, the doors opening. Tariq stood, moving with the crowd, and stepped out. Hannah took a deep breath, her knees jumping, hands quivering. She stood and followed.

The people in the station swirled in a thick swarm. Her eyes moved across the swell of human traffic, trying to pick up on the young man through the shifting maze of human heads, but he was nowhere to be seen.

She'd lost him.

Maybe it was for the best—maybe now she could go home.

Hannah moved toward the escalator. They had done their best—but maybe that was all that could be asked of them. Her part in all of this was over.

She turned around—piercing eyes bore into her.

He was behind her.

Her face snapped forward again, trying not to gasp, trying not to let on that she was watching him.

She stepped off the escalator and through the turnstile, moving with the human crush. Hannah stole a glance back—he was still right behind her.

The crowd moved up the Metro steps toward the afternoon sun.

Hannah stopped, reaching down to her shoe, pretending to tie her laces. Her fingers trembled as they played at her shoes. There was no way for him to stop there without drawing attention to himself.

She looked up.

There he was, caught in an eddy of the churning stream of people, pulling away from her up the stairs.

A moment later the rush had passed, only a few stragglers now moving up the steps. She followed, reaching the top of the steps.

Hannah afforded herself a cautious look—everyone was gone. She began to walk down the street to find a pay phone. As she walked she berated herself—how had she been so silly? He wasn't following her. She was only paranoid because of her kidnapping. He had simply ended up behind her in the crowd—that was all.

Then she looked back—and a hundred yards away saw him following.

John's cell phone chirped.

"Yes?"

"John, it's Bathurst."

"Where are you?"

"I'm still at the Center—I'm running behind."

"What happened?"

"Later—now Hannah's on the move."

"She's following our terrorist."

"You let her out of your sight?" Devin demanded, angrily.

"I couldn't stop her. She—"

"She's in danger."

"What?"

"Find her, John—before it's too late."

Hannah moved through the urban sprawl of Washington DC, trying to remain calm. She caught a glimpse in a car windshield—he was gaining.

He was following her. He must have noticed that she was following him, waited for her at the top of the stairs—and now he was closing in, fast.

She hadn't brought her can of pepper spray. Regardless, the stuff was useless if you didn't hit them directly in the eyes. Her grandfather had taught her that. When she first moved to the city he tried to talk her into getting a concealed carry permit so that she could keep a handgun with her at all times. She'd turned him down. She didn't want a handgun then—

—but she wished she had it now.

Hannah could swear she heard his footsteps now, getting closer.

She looked around, hoping to find something—fast.

There were people on the street—not many, but enough. She could scream at the top of her lungs. But he hadn't done anything yet—and the thought embarrassed her. How ridiculous, she thought. A man was following her—a terrorist—and she didn't want to scream because it was rude to call attention to yourself in public, to make a spectacle of yourself in front of everyone. It wasn't logical—certainly not now, but it was ingrained in her down to her core. It was who she was—more concerned with respecting others than ensuring her own safety.

Forget it, she thought, and went to scream.

The sound caught in her throat like a ball. Her hands were shaking violently, her throat tensing—whatever pinched utterance was trying to come out of her mouth was hardly more than a squeak.

She wanted to scream, but she just couldn't bring herself to complete the act. The air was squeezing out of her lungs. Hannah tried again—all that escaped was an anxious moan erupting from her private little hell.

She'd watched movies all her life with stupid women being chased by people, doing stupid things, ignoring obvious solutions. She'd mocked the screen and held those characters in contempt, but now she was that woman—stupid and doomed.

In the woods she'd done everything Snider had asked her, when Blake held her at gunpoint she didn't fight back, and now she was letting this man gain on her, unhindered.

She needed to scream, to draw attention to herself so he wouldn't try anything, but she couldn't bring herself to do it.

Then she saw the next best thing—a coffee shop to her right.

Hannah pushed the door open, moving into the shop, moving toward the line.

There was a draft behind her as someone opened the door again. She looked back. He was entering into the shop—still following her. Hannah stood in line for a moment as he came closer and closer—too close for comfort.

She stepped out, heading for the back of the store—the ladies' room. She pushed her way in and stopped, staring at the door.

No lock.

She waited—wondering if he had the audacity to enter into the women's restroom.

She watched and waited.

"Help me, God," John uttered audibly, trying to conjure up an image of where Hannah might be.

He shifted gears as he tried to move through Washington DC traffic.

Slow traffic.

So very slow.

One did not simply tear through traffic like an Indy 500 driver when he or she was in the nation's capital. Squealing tires and knocking over trash cans belonged in movies—not the District of Columbia.

There was foul taste in his mouth—something horrid. He gagged, then—

Hannah in a coffee shop, her body relaxing, moving back into the shop.

Looking around.

Him.

John fought the stick, changing lanes without signaling. Someone honked. He could feel her—where she was. She was close enough that he might be able to get to her—but in time?

Hannah clenched her convulsing fists, tightened her chattering teeth, and stepped out of the ladies' room. She looked around—then froze.

He approached, coming straight at her.

Her heart skipped.

"Excuse me," he said to her, "my name is Tariq—Tariq Ali. I was wondering if you would permit me to buy you a cup of coffee."

Hannah stared at him, speechless.

"I saw you on the Metro," he said with a charming smile, his voice betraying only the faintest hint of an accent—European?

There was a moment of awkward silence.

"I figured I'd take a chance."

She tried to say something, but all that came out was a soft, confused noise. He was hitting on her.

His smile wilted slightly as he examined the look of shock on her face. "I'm sorry. I didn't mean to startle you. It must seem creepy for a guy from the subway to do something like this."

She shook her head, trying to think of something to say.

"It just felt like we shared a moment on the subway and"—he held for a moment, a look of embarrassment crossing his handsome features— "when I saw you in here—like I said, I figured I'd take a chance."

Hannah remained speechless.

"Well"—he took a step back—"I won't take any more of your time." He turned to go.

"Wait," she said quickly, words rushing from her mouth. "I'm Hannah," she said with a smile, "Hannah Rice."

She offered a hand.

He took it and smiled. "Hannah? That's a very pretty name."

So handsome.

Blake Jackson looked at his watch.

He sat in front of the television, waiting for the news—the bombing of the Islamic Center in Washington DC.

He was watching one of the major conglomerate networks. Which one didn't matter to Blake; he knew they all got the facts wrong anyway. Right now the most pressing issue in the nation was the president's speech about universal health care.

He glanced at his watch again. Minutes now—that was all.

His eyes lazed down to the bottom of the screen, to the ticker that ran beneath the stories with good pictures. The words "Islamic Center" caught his eye—

Blake read.

A shooting. A thwarted bombing.

He picked up the phone and dialed.

"Yes?"

"We have a problem."

John hit his turn signal, cutting right down an alleyway. His fist clenched the gearshift, slamming the car into gear. It was a straight shot—he could drive fast between the brick buildings, the silver sedan slicing like a blade.

A trash truck backed into his view, and he slammed on the brakes— screaming to a stop. The rearview mirror caught his eye—a trail of burnt rubber chasing after. The truck ambled backward, its repetitive warning beep sounding off pedantically.

John's fist came down hard on the wheel, sending a shock wave of pain through his arm—a string of cursing erupting from his lips. He followed profanity with piety, breaking into prayer—

"Why, God? Why?"

It was like being late to work.

John hadn't held a real job in years, but he remembered the feeling of being late to work—not being able to navigate the labyrinth of the city fast enough. He'd been fired for being repeatedly late on several occasions. But there was no getting fired if he didn't make it in time—this was far more serious.

Hannah's life hung in the balance.

"Lord Jesus Christ, Jehovah God, help me!" his prayer choked out of his mouth, blustering loudly through the car. "Forgive me for using bad words—but *help me!*"

The trash men finished loading the cans, and the truck began plodding forward again, moving out of the way.

He popped the clutch and the vehicle screamed forward, another trail of rubber slicing out behind.

Devin moved down the stairs of the subway, praying for the foresight to find Hannah. His phone buzzed.

"This is Bathurst."

"Where are you?"

He recognized the voice. "Blake?"

"Where are you?"

"DC."

"You disrupted the mission."

"Alex Bradley bombing the mosque? Yes."

"Do you know what you've done?"

"He's dying."

"He was going to die anyway. But now there's a terrorist on the loose."

"We're working on that right now."

"He has to be killed. We have to send a message to these terrorist thugs. We're not afraid."

Devin's jaw set. "Knock it off, Blake. This is serious."

"Find him—and bring him to us."

"No," Devin declared flatly. "How's that for an answer?"

"Pithy, but no good."

"When we find this guy, we're going to turn him over to the proper authorities."

"On what charge? Criminal intent? What evidence do you have? A vision from God? He'll go free—you know that. No one is safe until he's dead."

Devin slid through the crowd, making his way to the nearest subway train. "Still, I have no reason to hand him over to you."

"Really?"

"Listen to me—" The line went dead. "Blake?"

Devin growled to himself and stepped onto the train as his phone buzzed again. He snapped it open: *New Picture Mail.*

Devin pressed the button and glared—

His heart beat fast, his hands clenched, his teeth ground, and his face burned.

There, on his phone, was the image of Morris Childs, bound and gagged, huddled in the corner of a basement.

The phone buzzed in his hand. He answered it.

"What do you want?"

"Give me the terrorist, and you can have Morris. It's that simple."

"You're the one who kidnapped him," Devin hissed quietly into the phone, trying not to attract attention to himself.

"It's more complicated than that—but he is in our custody."

Devin breathed in, calming himself, considering his next words carefully. "I'm going to find you, Blake. Do you understand?"

"You have twenty-four hours to see things my way," Blake replied.

Devin clenched the phone. "In twenty-four hours you are going to be very sorry," he snarled. "Consider yourself threatened."

He punched the button and ended the call.

Chapter 14

T HE COFFEE CUP WAS hot in Hannah's hand, even through the cardboard sleeve.

They'd ordered their drinks. Tariq had paid for both of them,
dropping ten dollars in the barista's tip jar, and then asked her if she
wanted to go for a walk. She followed. The business district melted
away quickly, giving way to drab gray apartments.

"Tell me about yourself, Hannah," he invited warmly.

She shrugged. "What do you want to know?"

"Where are you from?"

"I was born and raised in Colorado," she said, wondering if she
was giving away too much information to a man who was a potential
terrorist. "I went to college in Missouri."

"Kansas City?"

She nodded.

"What did you study?"

She shrugged. "I never decided. I guess I never knew what I wanted
to be when I grew up."

"You weren't looking to the future?"

"No," she replied, shaking her head. "I just wanted things to go back
to the way they were when I was younger."

There was an awkward silence.

She'd shared too much. She'd embarrassed him. Now he was
going to think that she was pathetic and desperate and childish. She
panicked, looking for something to say that would sound interesting
and exciting.

"Are you enjoying your coffee?" he asked, saving her the trouble of
coming up with the next line.

"I'm afraid I enjoy it a little too much sometimes."

"No," he said, laughing, giving her a playful shove. "There's no such thing as enjoying coffee too much."

"I do."

"That's silly."

She took a sip of her latte. "What about you? Where are you from?"

Tariq took a drink. "I was born in Philadelphia."

"Philadelphia? But your accent—?"

"Do I still have it?"

She shrugged. "A little."

"My father studied medicine in the United States, that's when I was born, but then he went back home to Palestine to work as a surgeon in Gaza."

"And you moved with him?"

"Yes—of course."

"How did you get back to the United States?"

"When I was twelve—" Tariq stopped. He took a drink. "After my father passed away, we moved back to the States."

"Philadelphia?"

"San Diego. I moved to Lebanon for college, so I spent three years there. That's when I picked up the accent again."

"What did you study?"

"Oral surgery."

"Really?" she asked, excitedly. "That must be so fascinating."

He nodded. "That was what my father wanted me to do, so that's what I pursued."

"Are you finishing your studies here?"

He shrugged. "I'm not actually in school right now. I took some time off to do some other things."

"Like what?"

"Just stuff."

"No," she said, trying to prod him conversationally. "What have you been working on?"

"I don't want to tell you."

"Why?"

"Because it's—" He shrugged. "People don't understand."

Her heart skipped—he was building explosives, she knew it.

"What have you been doing, Tariq?" her tone was suddenly flat.

He smiled and scratched the back of his head. "I like painting."

She considered. "Like houses?"

"No," he laughed, "paintings—like art."

"Of what?"

He shrugged again. "Everything—landscapes, still life, people—whatever inspires me."

"What inspires you?"

Tariq stopped, nearly shrinking away, face getting rosy. "Beauty," he said with a definitive nod. "Beauty inspires me." His eyes looked at the ground, then moved up again, meeting Hannah's. He reached out, touching a lock of her hair. "People like you inspire me."

Hannah's heart thumped in her chest. She laughed nervously.

"I'm sorry, that was cheesy. You're laughing at me."

She placed a reassuring hand on his arm. "No, I'm just not used to people saying things like that."

They stood in silence for a moment.

"You should be used to it," he said with a nod, "because it's true."

Hannah smiled to herself. This man couldn't be a terrorist. He was young and passionate and full of life—surely he wasn't the one they were looking for. She had to have made some kind of mistake.

"Would you like to see my paintings?" he asked warmly. "My apartment is just around the corner."

Maybe he was the man she was looking for. She didn't know what that meant to her just yet, but she felt that something had culminated here.

She smiled.

"Sure."

"Come on, God!" John shouted at the windshield as he pressed on the gas pedal. "I need something, anything. Show me what she's up to!"

He was speeding—nearly fifteen miles an hour over the speed limit.

"Yes!" he shouted, suddenly convicted about his speed. "I know I'm driving too fast, but this is a desperate situation—just look past that for the moment and help me out!"

Ahead there was a stoplight—green.

He could feel her—nearby, but not certain where.

The light changed—yellow.

"No, no, no, no!" he shouted at the top of his lungs, careening toward the light—he wasn't going to make it.

"I believe in You, Jesus!"

Still yellow—almost there.

"I believe in Jesus, I believe in Jesus!" He shouted his mantra over and over again, pressing hard on the gas.

The car accelerated—blasting through the intersection.

The light changed overhead.

"I believe in Jesus!" he shouted triumphantly, hoping that Devin hadn't been given a vision of that.

"This is my place," Tariq said as they walked in the door.

Hannah looked around. The apartment was starkly furnished with tarps laid across the floor and furniture. In front of a tall row of windows she saw an easel, a white cloth thrown over it.

"May I?" she asked, approaching the easel, pointing at the cloth.

"No, no. Not that one; it's not finished yet."

"Just a peek?" she asked with a giggle.

"I don't—"

She moved the cloth back and looked at the painting.

Hannah gasped. It was a painting of a woman with a shawl over her head. "She's beautiful. Who is she?"

"It's my mother," he said, reaching for a photograph set at the base of the canvas, "when she was twenty. I've been working off of this photograph."

"She's very beautiful."

"Thank you," he said with a nod. "You're right—she is very beautiful. I'm painting it for her."

"You're going to give it to her?"

He nodded. "Yes. A gift. To show her how much I love her."

Hannah looked over the soft face, painted in loving detail. She'd made a mistake. This man was no terrorist; he was a loving son. "That's so sweet." She placed a hand on his arm. "She's very lucky to have you as a son."

"Thank you."

She turned, looking around, and saw more paintings. Beautiful greens covered the canvases with words written in Arabic. The faces of children. Shattered houses. Burning buildings. Weeping mothers. Hannah touched one of them.

"These are so sad."

"There's a lot of sadness in Palestine."

"Why?" Hannah said, looking over the pained images. "Why is there so much sadness?"

"Because Israel is a country of criminals and murderers. They oppress the Palestinians. They bulldoze our homes, kill our children and our fathers."

"Why would they do that?"

"They kill young Palestinian boys so that they won't grow up to become Palestinian men."

Hannah shook her head. She was a Christian—she knew about Israel and the Jews, God's chosen people. "That's not true."

"In 1982 the Israeli government helped Christian militants massacre over three thousand Palestinians. A butchery that lasted nearly two full days. They even provided flares at night so the slaughter could continue. The Israelis knew that men, women, and children were being massacred, but they did nothing to stop it, and even sent fleeing civilians back to be killed."

Hannah shook her head. "Those must have been criminals. They were punished, I'm sure."

"No," Tariq said, shaking his head, "it was at the order of the government to let it all happen. Ariel Sharon was even tried for crimes against humanity—and found not guilty. So they keep on killing our sons."

"That's horrible. It can't be true."

"The Sabra and Chatila massacre. Look it up if you doubt me. It's a disgrace to humanity and the freedom of Palestine."

"Did you—" She stopped. "Have you lost anyone?"

He nodded again, pointing to a painting of a little boy. "This was my brother Abdoo. He was shot in the streets of Rafah. Martyred. He was carrying a white flag, but they shot him in cold blood. And this," he said, pointing to another painting of a young man, "was my older brother Kamal. He wanted to end the oppression and the genocide, so he fought the Israelis. He was captured and executed."

Hannah's eyes began to well.

"That's terrible."

"After they killed my brother, they came to our home. We were eating dinner. The Israeli police took all the men outside—my eldest brother, Djamal, my uncles, and my father. They were placed against a wall and shot."

Tariq looked at the floor, then looked up again. He saw her face and his expression changed to sympathy. "I'm sorry, I'm making you uncomfortable—let's change the subject."

"No," Hannah said, squeezing his shoulder, "it's OK. I'm sorry about your family."

He shook his head. "I want to show you one of my other paintings, not sad ones." Tariq began to move toward the next room. "Stay here; I'll be back in a moment. I have paintings of the Mediterranean coast I'll bring out and show you."

He moved through a doorway and was gone.

Hannah looked around, scanning over the paintings. So much pain. So much hurt. So much agony and misunderstanding.

There was a crawling over her skin—moving from her fingertips up her arms.

Tariq, in this room.

Toiling, hunched over a nearby table, hands toying with wires.

Concentrating. Checking the plans.

A small handle. Explosives—all strung to a vest.

Placing it all in a cabinet at the base of a nearby workbench.

This couldn't be. Not Tariq.

She opened her eyes and looked around. She saw the bench, the cabinet, the reality of them both. Hannah stepped forward, quietly, trying not to make any noise. She inched toward the cabinet, crouching down near it.

The door didn't want to budge, swollen shut. She gave a tug and it opened.

Hannah looked in—reached into the darkness of the space. She stood, holding it in her hands—a vest of explosives bound together beneath packages of washers. Her mouth fell open.

There was a creak in the floorboards.

She turned around.

He was there.

There was a twitch above John's eye, like blood pumping through his forehead. There were no images this time, just a feeling.

Hannah was with *him*; he was angry and desperate.

John felt them—exactly where they were. He worked the clutch and raced forward—not much time now.

"Tariq?" she stammered. "What is this?"

He approached, eyes sharp. "You were following me, weren't you?"

"I—"

His fists wrapped around her biceps, squeezing tight, shaking her hard. "Who sent you?"

"No one. I—"

"Liar! Who sent you?"

"I don't know what you're talking about."

He ripped the vest from her hands, moving to the window, scanning the street below. "Who else is with you?"

"I'm alone," she whimpered.

"Rubbish. Who are you with? The FBI? Homeland Security? Who?" He shook her again.

"No one. I'm with no one."

His eyes became fierce. "Are you wearing a wire?"

"What?"

"A wire. You're bugged, aren't you?"

"No, I—"

"Put your hands on the bench." He shoved her forward, frisking her roughly.

"I told you, I'm not with anyone."

"Shut up!" he shouted.

There was a noise outside the window—a car.

He stopped, moving back to the window, pulling her with him roughly. Hannah looked—a silver sedan parking at the curb. Someone got out.

"John?"

"I knew it!" Tariq shouted. "What is he? Police?"

"He's a friend."

Tariq let go of her, throwing the encumbered vest over his shoulders. "He's a dead man."

John rushed up the steps, leaping—the shock running up his legs, grasping at the stair rail, hands slick with sweat.

Up three flights—maybe another three to go.

He saw everything that was happening.

Another step. Another image.

Hannah.

Tariq.

The vest.

The detonator.

Explosives.

Shaking.

Shouting.

Shoving.

Screaming—"*Help!*"

A *handful of her hair.*

Ripping her to her feet.

John could feel them in his pounding chest. They were close—so close.

The top of the steps.

The door ahead.

He twisted the knob, shoulder slamming into wood.

The chain shattered—the door bursting open.

John stood in the doorway, seething, hair soaked with perspiration. Sweat streamed down his face as he tried to catch his breath.

"*Stop!*" Tariq shouted, whipping around, Hannah clutched by his right arm, detonator in his left hand.

John held.

He couldn't hope to win this. His shoulders sank, weary hands resting on his knees, steadying his breathing.

"I have a bomb!" he shouted. "I'll blow you all to kingdom come if you come any closer!"

It made him mad, but John tried to remain calm and detached. How would Devin handle this?

He breathed slowly, drawing in air through his nostrils.

Help me, God.

John could feel the young man—his thoughts and feelings blossoming like an open book. He felt a cocky smirk cross his features.

"Who are you with?" Tariq demanded, shouting at John.

"Look," John said, spreading his hands diplomatically, "you don't want to set off that bomb—not here."

"I'm going to be a martyr!" he said back, voice becoming calmer. "I will die in jihad."

"But this isn't how you want to do it."

"Don't tell me what I—"

"You don't want to set off a bomb in some random apartment building. You want a quality target."

"I'll blow you up if you come any closer."

"But you don't want to—not here at least. You're willing to tolerate me for the moment in order to get to a better target."

It was true—he could feel it. Tariq didn't want to die like this. He wanted to send a message—to make headlines. This wasn't the way.

Tariq's eyes shifted to the left, eyeing a cabinet. John felt something else.

"Now you're wondering if you can get to your gun in time. But it's hidden behind a box of paints so that no one will find it."

He could feel the anger and frustration welling up in Tariq.

Don't push it, John.

Tariq was getting desperate. He needed hope of getting out of this building and to a quality target, or he'd blow the bomb right here.

A delicate balance.

"Look, Tariq—"

"How do you know my name? Who are you with? Who's been watching me?"

John relaxed his shoulders, moving his eyes to Tariq's chest. He wanted to look at the man, acknowledge him, without challenging him.

"Tariq, you've done nothing wrong. Why don't you take off the vest, and the two of us can sit down and talk—"

"Are they watching the others?"

John stopped. "What others?"

A flash of emotion erupted invisibly from Tariq—he'd betrayed something important. It was like fire and ice, chilling and burning. A feeling slung from Tariq's soul like a dart, desperation overtaking him like a tiger clawing from a cage.

There were more of them—Tariq wasn't in this alone—and he would kill and die to protect them.

John knew he was in trouble—

Hannah felt herself tumble forward as Tariq shoved her.

She hit the floor and looked back to see Tariq ripping a box from a cupboard.

Submachine gun in hand, he pointed it in the direction of John—who threw himself through a door to the right of the apartment's entrance. The tiny submachine gun ripped noisy holes in the far wall—debris raining to the floor.

Smoking cartridges jingled on the floor like bells.

Tariq stood cautiously. He aimed the weapon at the wall and held the trigger.

The patter of gunfire pelted the wall for a brief moment—then stopped.

He turned back to her. The smell of burning sulfur hung in the air—the unmistakable odor of discharged firearms.

Hannah looked at the wall—no sign of John. Was he hit? Bleeding? Dead?

Tariq threw a hooded sweatshirt over his suicide vest and thrust a small pistol in his belt, a spare magazine in his pocket. He grabbed her by the arm. "Come on," he said, dragging her toward the front door, weapon ready.

Tariq snapped his attention to the bathroom door as they passed it. John was on the floor, covered in chunks of drywall. John gave the door a solid kick from the inside, and it slammed shut.

Tariq squeezed the trigger—perforating the wooden door with a spray of bullets.

Click—

Empty.

The weapon clattered to the floor, a curl of white smoke rising from the ejection port.

Tariq seemed to panic. He didn't check to see if John was dead; he simply pulled Hannah into the hall toward the world beyond.

John lifted himself, debris covering him. Wreckage tumbled off him as he stood, drywall slipping off his body like rain, adding to the hazy cloud that already filled the tiny bathroom.

His forehead stung. He touched it with his fingertips—blood. A tile had burst off the wall and struck him.

He staggered into the room, preparing to follow. His eyes scanned the floor quickly. He saw the open cupboard—

—and a handgun—like something from an old-time detective show.

He walked toward the weapon, eyeing it like a rattlesnake. John had never fired a gun in his life or even held one, for that matter. It was rare that he was even near them. They made him nervous.

Reaching down, he touched the metal—it was like a shock wave rippling through his body. Could he shoot it? Could he shoot at a person? Could he kill?

His thoughts shifted to Tariq, moving toward a crowd of innocents, preparing to kill as many as he possibly could.

There was no time to think.

His fingers wrapped around the weapon, ripping it from its place, dashing out the door. They were still in the building. He could catch up with them if he was quick.

His thoughts focused. The elevator—they were in the elevator.

He went for the stairs, pulling out his phone.

Devin rode the subway. His phone buzzed.

"This is Bathurst."

"Devin, it's John—Hannah's with him—our terrorist. He has a bomb, and he's going to set it off wherever he can."

"Do you know where his target is?"

"I don't know, but he isn't going for plan A. I think there's more of them."

"How many?"

"I don't know, but he's desperate. He isn't going to risk giving away the others. He just wants to kill as many Americans as he can while he dies."

"Where are he and Hannah?"

"Close."

"Do you have a plan?"

"I have a gun."

Devin paused. John with a gun? It was almost more frightening than a terrorist with a bomb.

"Where are you?" Devin demanded.

John gave him a street address. "I'm headed for the elevator. I should see them any—"

Gunfire barked into Devin's ear through the phone.

"John!"

Bullets—three of them—pocked the walls as John threw himself back around the corner.

John shoved his arm around the corner, aiming as best he could from cover. He pulled the trigger—it wouldn't budge.

A chunk of wall shattered nearby as he threw himself back around the corner.

He looked at his own gun, examining the mechanisms—the safety. Of course, he knew about those. Near the cylinder there was a switch. He pushed it and it snapped into place, the ridges digging into his thumb.

John threw his upper body around the corner again and fired three times, fast.

The weapon roared in his hand, throwing itself. He wasn't prepared for that. The bullets punched through wallpaper—completely missing. Shooting was harder in real life than it was on TV.

The sounds of return fire cracked back, snapping past. A bullet passed inches from his head as Tariq dragged Hannah back into the elevator with him, using it as cover.

John threw himself back behind the corner, body shaking.

This was insane. Where were the police? Surely someone had to have called this in by now. But this was Washington DC, murder capital of America—gunshots were simply ignored half the time.

"John!" Devin called through the cell phone. "What's going on?"

John leaned out, firing at air. Nothing there.

Standing, he moved into the hall, inching forward, pistol ready.

She huddled in the corner of the elevator watching as Tariq glanced into the hall. He pulled back fast as a gunshot rang out.

Tariq reached into his sweatshirt, pulling out the detonator.

He was desperate. Trapped. It wasn't what he wanted, but he was going to die his way. His thumb reached for the top button—

Something broke in Hannah—tearing from the pattern of everything she'd ever done before. She lifted her leg and sent a strong kick into Tariq's jaw. He fell to the side, then looked at her—confused.

Hannah lunged for his gun. She'd shoot him before she would let that bomb go off.

He grabbed her hair and threw her away, then ducked into the hallway, running.

She came to her knees, and a moment later John came around the corner.

"Are you OK?" He knelt near her.

"Get him," she said fiercely, staring him in the eye. "Just go get him."

John stood slowly, backing away from her, then went down the hall after the bomber.

This couldn't be over soon enough.

Tariq ran down the street as fast as his legs would carry him.

The subway—he had to get to the subway. There were people there, lots of them, in swirling eddies. He could take out dozens martyring himself.

He looked back—the man was chasing after him, two hundred yards back.

His legs thundered as he pushed forward, explosives rattling against his body, hindering his sprint. The Metro station was ahead, the escalators going down below the street.

Tariq looked back again—still being pursued. His head swung back ahead toward the people coming out of the station, and he saw a man, black skin, expensive suit, rising from below. The man's eyes seemed to drill into Tariq as he stepped in front of him.

Tariq didn't stop—he threw his weight into the man, and they went tumbling down the escalator. Steps, lined with grooves, dug into Tariq's side, the man grappling with him.

The world tumbled. Spun. Swirled.

Then went dark.

John raced to the bottom of the escalator toward where Devin and Tariq lay.

"Are you OK?"

Curious onlookers began to swarm.

Devin stood. "I'm fine." He checked Tariq's pulse.

"Is he…?" John didn't finish.

Devin nodded. "He's just unconscious."

A woman approached. "Should I call an ambulance?"

"No," Devin said, lifting one of Tariq's arms over his shoulder, signaling to John to join. "We'll take him."

Chapter 15

DEVIN LOOKED TARIQ OVER, bound and gagged with duct tape, and slammed the car trunk down, shutting him in. He got in the car and looked at Hannah sitting in the passenger's seat.

"Is he safe back there?"

Devin considered; he himself had been locked in a trunk and escaped just a few weeks prior. But Devin hadn't been tied up. "It should hold him for a while. We'll check on him every so often."

He started the car.

"I don't understand," John said again. "Why aren't we turning him over to the police?"

"Blake and his people want him."

"What for?"

"Don't worry about that. They have Morris, and they're willing to make a swap."

They drove in silence for several minutes before they reached the highway.

"Where are we going?" Hannah asked.

"To an old friend."

Devin dialed as he drove down the interstate, placing his hands-free set in his ear. The phone rang for a moment.

"Yes?"

"Blake, I have your terrorist."

"Where is he?"

"Don't worry about that. Where's Morris?"

"He's alive. You'll have him as soon as we have our terrorist."

Devin nodded to himself. "Fair enough."

"We'll give you instructions about where to leave him, and we'll give you Morris when we have our terrorist."

"No," Devin said flatly, "a direct exchange on open ground." There was silence on the other end of the line. "Got it?"

"Fine. We'll call you with specifics."

Devin began to protest, but the line went dead.

This was going to be dangerous. Swapping valuable goods was always dangerous—especially when neither party trusted the other. If they'd grabbed Morris to begin with, then they had a purpose for him before this had ever started. That meant that they wouldn't want to give him up if they didn't have to. And if Devin knew human nature, they wouldn't. They'd show up, shoot Tariq on the spot, and drive away. In all likelihood, Morris wouldn't even be brought to the exchange. But *everything*—a successful exchange, living through the situation at hand, and anything resembling an acceptable outcome—was contingent on having a bigger army.

Devin looked around the car. Hannah was asleep in the passenger's seat, and John was scribbling in his Bible in the back.

They needed allies.

He dialed the phone again.

Someone picked up on the other end. "What do you want?"

"Hello, Saul; it's Devin."

Hannah's eyes fluttered open, seat tipped back, a spring-green world slipping past.

"Where are we?" she asked.

"Pennsylvania," Devin said without shifting his gaze.

"What's in Pennsylvania?"

"An old friend—Saul Mancuso."

"Is he one of the Firstborn?"

"He used to be."

"Used to be? What happened?"

Devin shrugged. "He fell away."

"What do you mean by that?"

"He lost his faith—stopped believing in God. Saul moved to Pennsylvania to get away from the world and its superstitions."

"Wait," John said from the backseat, "we're going to meet one of the Fallen?"

"That's right, John."

Hannah shook her head. "I don't understand. Why would we go to a guy who lost his faith?"

"He's not a true believer—not anymore. That means he's above the politics."

"That's convoluted," John said, shaking his head.

"He's not one of us, so it's highly doubtful that he's one of them. We don't know who we can trust in the Firstborn anymore, so we have to start looking outside of the Firstborn."

Devin hadn't been to the compound in years, but it still felt the same—inhospitable.

There was only one approach, down a long back road. It was nearly unidentifiable from the road and a mile and a half drive from the pavement to the front gate. The last half mile of the drive announced the coming of the compound with signs that read "No Trespassing," among various other unwelcoming warnings.

The trees grew in a wild, thick collection, hanging over the road in a darkening canopy, blotting out the sun overhead. Patches of mist curled through the trees in ominous swirls.

"This is unsettling," John said, peering out the windows.

Devin nodded. "I think that's the idea."

The car stopped at the front gate. It was the only entrance in through the set of double fences crowned with tangles of razor wire. More signs littered the front gate—all warning that trespassers would be shot.

Devin put the car in park, leaning out his open window. He pressed the button to the intercom and looked up at the security camera set atop a post.

"Who is it?"

"It's Bathurst. We're here."

The intercom went dead.

"Saul?"

Silence.

"Professor Mancuso?"

Devin looked at Hannah and John, not certain what to say.

John leaned forward. "How good of a friend is this guy?"

"It's been awhile. Maybe—"

There was a loud buzzing sound as the chain-link gate unlocked.

The intercom crackled to life again. "It's open."

Devin signaled to John, and he exited the car, pushing the gate open, then returned to his place in the backseat, the gate sliding back into place on its own.

Devin drove slowly, glancing around. Not much had changed since his last visit. The "compound" consisted of a half dozen buildings, most decaying, scattered over nearly twenty acres of land, much of which housed expensive landscaping equipment and heaps of scrap. Security cameras were positioned everywhere.

The house was the biggest of the buildings. It was old, Victorian, and covered in a fading wash of yellow paint that flaked away in slivered lateral sweeps. In several sections the paint was completely gone, leaving only the gray tones of old decaying wood paneling. Further out was the second largest building—squatty and gray, consisting of cinder blocks and a tin roof.

Devin pointed. "That's the tactical building," he said.

"What's that?" John asked.

Devin shrugged. "Don't ask." He brought the car to the house and got out. He stood in the open for several minutes, then realized that he wasn't going to be greeted. He moved to the front, opening the ancient screen door with a whining squeal, and knocked on the hardwood door beyond.

Inside there was the sound of dogs barking at the door as someone came forward, their footsteps reverberating through the door. The handle turned and the door opened.

"Devin?"

Devin nodded. "Hello, Carson."

Carson was in his thirties—tough as nails and grubby. He wore a blue plaid shirt with the sleeves rolled up, his face smudged with soot from welding. The man tried to look around Devin at his companions.

"Carson, this is John Temple—"

Carson shook his hand. "Didn't you fool around with Morris Childs's niece?"

John looked away. "Something like that."

"And this," Devin said, motioning, "is Hannah Rice."

Carson shook her hand. "Do you know a Henry…"

"He was my grandfather," she said quickly, cutting him off.

"We're here to see Saul," Devin interjected.

Carson nodded, motioning them in.

They were led through the house, which smelled like wet dog. The walls were sparsely decorated with only a few pictures, mostly of ships. Carson stopped at a nearby door and knocked.

"Yeah?"

"They're here."

There were some disgruntled noises from beyond the door. "Come on in."

The door opened and Devin moved in, the other two following behind.

"I'm going back to work," Carson announced and shut the door behind them.

The room was a library—big with walls covered in books, mostly tattered. The smell of pulpy paper hung in the air. The only window was covered by yellow curtains that diffused the light, filling the room with a dark amber hue.

In the center of the room was a man hunched over a desk, a reading light bent over the text that he scanned intently. His hair was white, his face craggy. He wore thick reading glasses that bounced off the lamp's glow like a set of spotlights. He didn't look up but continued reading.

"Professor Mancuso," Devin said, trying to keep his voice soft.

The older man lifted his right index finger to quiet Devin, tracing the lines of the page with his left. A moment later he finished the page—held for a moment, took a breath, then closed the book, setting it aside. He looked up at them—a dark silhouette accented by two glowing lenses in the black.

"It finally happened, didn't it?" he said, sitting up straight, voice gravelly and harsh. "The Firstborn went too far."

Devin nodded. "Yes, sir. Some of them."

"Which ones?"

"As of yet we still don't know the extent of the conspiracy, but Blake Jackson appears to be running things, and Alex Bradley was involved too."

"Too bad about Alex—I heard about his wife. The news says he tried to blow up a mosque."

"That's true."

"You were the one who stopped him, weren't you?"

"Yes, sir."

"The news said a security guard got him, but when I heard it was Alex I knew only a Firstborn would know how to stop another Firstborn."

"That's correct."

"So," Saul said, standing up and removing the reading glasses from his face, "let's see what you've got going on that makes it so important for you to seek out a crotchety old man like me."

He followed them back through the house, out to the car. Devin held out his keyless remote and clicked.

The trunk popped loudly, swinging upward fast. Devin gestured. "Meet Tariq Ali."

The light hit Tariq's face and he began to thrash, attempting to hit someone.

Saul Mancuso looked in the trunk and nodded. "I see. What'd he do?"

"He was going to set off a suicide bomb in DC."

"Uh-huh. And why didn't you hand him over to the proper authorities?"

"They've got Morris."

"And they want to make a swap?"

"Yes."

"Why?"

"They want to kill him *their way*."

Tariq's eyes grew large.

Saul looked over the detainee. "You go to that swap alone and they'll kill you. It's that simple."

"Wait a minute," John interjected. "Do you really think the First-born are capable of something like that?"

Saul nodded. "Yes, I do. They think that they're God's secret agents on Earth, and that gives them the right to do whatever they please. They're not just capable of it—that's their desire. If trying to blow up an internationally funded religious center wasn't enough to prove that to you, then you're not very bright." He turned to Devin again. "If you plan to go to that swap, you'll need to make sure they behave. So my question is—you and what army?"

Devin shut the trunk. "I was hoping you could help with that."

Saul looked into Devin's eyes, trying to read him. Then he visibly straightened himself.

"OK. We have to prepare for an exchange—and we have some things to find out. Devin, come with me. John, find Carson. He'll show you where to put Tariq. Hannah, see what you can scrounge up in the kitchen. I imagine you're all starved. We'll gather in the house for supper in an hour."

He turned, and Devin followed Saul across the yard to the tactical building. Saul entered a room where a few couches faced an old battered television. A rug was thrown across the floor, covered in grainy dust.

Saul moved to the middle of the room and kicked the floor rug out of the way with his foot, revealing a metal hatch in the floor. He knelt, pulled the hatch open, and signaled Devin to go down into the darkness below.

The steps leading down were steep, nearly vertical. He stepped onto solid floor and looked around. The room was pitch black.

"There should be a switch to your left," Saul said, and Devin groped until his fingers glided over the wide plastic stub.

He gave the industrial switch a push, and a loud popping sound thundered through the darkness as the overhead lights fluttered on, filling the place with a sickly fluorescent glow. His eyes adjusted to the light.

Guns.

Racks and racks of guns lined the tiny room.

Shotguns, rifles, pistols. Boxes of ammunition.

To his right he saw a row of Colt M4 Carbines—the fully automatic little brother to the M16.

Devin moved to the top of the stairs again, looking at Saul, dumbfounded. "Are you preparing for a war?"

"I've been preparing for this." He looked Devin squarely in the face. "You know what you're getting yourself into, son?"

"Yes, sir."

"And you're prepared to see it to the end?"

"Yes, sir."

Saul considered for a moment. "I'll make some phone calls."

Chapter 16

JOHN LOOKED AT TARIQ Ali.

He and Carson had moved the young Palestinian to a room in the tactical building. This was where they would keep him until further notice. Not an ideal option, but it was the best they could do with such short notice.

John had spent nearly thirty minutes in the building, just trying to get some feeling of the young man they'd captured. Anything at all—anything that might tell him what to do next.

He felt nothing.

John stared at Tariq through a metal grating welded in place in the door frame, guarding what now served as a makeshift prison cell. Tariq sat on a chair, saying nothing. John put a hand on the grating and looked at the other man, trying to study his face. For the first time since he'd stepped into the building he could feel something—Tariq was holding something back.

"You said something about the others. What others?" John asked, hoping for some kind of visceral response, some kind of giveaway that he could feel.

Tariq looked away, and John felt a surge of emotion coming from the man—he was definitely hiding something.

"Is something else going to happen? Is there another attack being planned?"

No reply.

After twenty minutes of getting nowhere, John sighed and walked away. Time for a shower. And supper.

The sun was setting when Devin joined Hannah in the kitchen. He'd found a spare room and had slept for several hours, hoping to rejuvenate some of his lost energy. But he still felt exhausted.

Hannah had fried up some hamburgers, a smell that had been strong enough to pull Devin out of bed. She had also found the makings for salad and extra sandwiches. Devin ate with purpose and focus, the way he'd consumed "chow" during basic training all those years ago. He hadn't felt hungry until now. Food was a crutch. But now, with something hot hitting his stomach, he felt like his stomach might never be completely full.

Saul entered midway through their meal. "Including Carson and yourselves, we have fifteen," Saul announced, taking a seat and reaching for a sandwich.

"Good," Devin replied, dabbing at his mouth with a napkin. He considered the numbers—that might even be enough to give them a full advantage.

"The first of them will be arriving tonight—the rest tomorrow." Saul took a bite of his sandwich and chewed vigorously.

"Then the swap will have to take place tomorrow night."

"Exactly."

"And they're all members of the Fallen?"

Saul nodded.

"I suppose that's good. It keeps the likelihood of a breach at a low."

Hannah rolled an apple in her hands. "I don't understand the Fallen," she said. "Who are they exactly?"

Saul wiped his mouth on his sleeve. "The Fallen are members of the Firstborn who have either lost their faith or are sick and tired of the politics—so they don't have anything to do with the Firstborn anymore."

She looked confused. "Is it common for the Firstborn to lose faith?"

The professor shrugged. "It's common for people to get tired of politics and infighting. And when you tell people that they don't have faith unless they play political ball? Well, people lose faith. That simple."

Hannah nodded. "So there's a lot of them?"

"There's only a few thousand of the Firstborn that the orders formally know of. Of those I'd say a quarter of us eventually fall away."

"That many?"

Saul harrumphed. "With the political games that get played every day in this world, the real surprise is that the number isn't higher."

"Do you still have visions?"

"Me?" Saul asked. "Not much. I moved into the middle of nowhere to get away from them."

"But do you still have them?"

"Yes."

"But you don't believe in God?"

Saul Mancuso shook his head. "No, I'm afraid I don't."

"But how do you explain the visions?"

He reached for a bottle of water, twisting off the cap as he gestured. "How do you explain human life?"

"God made it."

"Can you prove that?"

She was quiet for a moment. "You can't prove that He didn't."

"The God of the gaps," he said with a grunt, taking a long pull of water. "If science can't explain it, then obviously God made it."

"Sure."

"Well, then, by your standard the tax code was made by God too," he said sardonically. "There's a lot that people don't understand and that science doesn't have a complete explanation for yet, but that doesn't mean it's supernatural. It just means it's a little bit advanced."

John ambled into the kitchen, his hair still damp from the shower. "I smell burgers." He sniffed appreciatively and pulled up a chair. Hannah handed him the platter of food. "Tariq is secured, all locked up in the tactical building. But I was talking with him—"

Devin glared. "You talked to him? Why?"

"I wanted to know more."

Devin groaned inwardly. Talking to the prisoner was monumentally stupid. Making Tariq think he had a friend would make him cocky and less likely to talk—assuming he knew anything.

"There's more of them," John said. "He has friends, and they're planning something—something really bad."

Saul scratched his chin. "How do you know?"

"It's true," Hannah interjected. "When we were in his apartment, he said something about the others."

"Why didn't you say anything sooner?"

"Look," John said, his voice starting to rise, "a lot has been happening. Anyway, I asked him about it, and he's definitely holding something back."

No one said anything.

John's tone became heated. "Don't you understand? There's still a terrorist attack coming!"

"Well then," Devin said, unbuttoning his cuffs, "that means we have until the swap to learn everything that this guy knows."

Devin pushed away from the table, walking out of the house into the evening chill.

Saul could keep Hannah busy for hours explaining his empiricist perspective on the Firstborn and their abilities. John was busy stuffing his face. Now was his chance to speak to Tariq alone, to undo any damage that blasted John Temple might have done.

Devin entered the tactical building, walking to the makeshift cell door. He unlocked it and moved in, purposeful and fast. Tariq's eyes lifted then looked away in contempt, ignoring Devin's approach.

Devin reached down, grabbing his collar, ripping him up from his seat.

Surprise covered Tariq's face as he was slammed into a nearby wall. "What is wrong with you, man? This is the United States. I have rights!"

Devin held him there, voice soft but fierce. "I am not with the United States government. Do you understand?"

"This is *so* illegal!"

"So is terrorism—a crime the American people are no longer tolerant of."

"Let go of me!"

"Tell me where your friends are."

Tariq's face went calm, glaring haughtily.

Devin looked into the young man's eyes and saw it—the coming terror.

Men in masks—AK-47s.

Children crying—screaming.

Demands.

News cameras.

"...two hundred and fifty schoolchildren murdered..."

Devin's body began to shake as he felt the images come to him.

Tariq's expression remained calm. "I'm prepared to die."

"Good," Devin said, eyes not moving, "because you'll beg for it by the time I'm done with you."

Devin returned to the kitchen, where the others were finishing up their meal. Devin dropped into a chair and seethed.

"The target is an elementary school," Devin said without prelude. "They want to kill children. Morris Childs warned me about this. I can't believe I didn't see it coming. They're targeting children, of all things!"

"That's horrible," Hannah said.

"It's perfect. An elementary school in our nation's capital. It's Virginia Tech, Columbine, September 11, and Beslan all wrapped up into one."

"Beslan?" Hannah asked.

"Don't you follow the news?" Saul asked.

"Sometimes, but—"

"Beslan," Saul announced, cutting her off, "was an attack on an elementary school in Russia in September of 2004."

"Wait, I did hear about that, I think."

"Chechens stormed the school, took everyone hostage. There was a three-day standoff. Ringing any bells?"

"I think I remember now."

Devin crossed his arms. "The Russian special forces, Spetsnaz, tried to talk them down. Something went wrong, and the rebels set off the explosives."

"Something went wrong?" Saul said with a grunt. "They waited

until the eyes of the world were on them, and then they murdered a
school full of children."

"They wanted to negotiate," John interrupted.

"To talk?" Saul snorted. "They had enough explosives to kill everybody in that building and enough guns to fight a war. Do you really
think that was for the purpose of talking?"

"Well—"

"No," Saul interrupted, uncompromisingly, "they went in with the
intention of killing everyone—everyone. They didn't want to talk; they
wanted to make a statement."

Devin nodded. "Just like Blake."

"Yes," Saul said, soberly. "It's the will of every person on Planet
Earth to tell everyone what is theirs."

"What do you mean?" Hannah asked.

"Do you know what a human being is?" Saul asked.

"I don't know what you mean."

"An animal," he said with a grunt. "The world is filled with pred-
ators, and the human animal is weak and lonely and scared. So we
declare what's ours—and hate everything else."

"It's not that simple," John said.

"Yes, it is. When you're born you move into a culture, a belief system,
a paradigm, and it becomes comfortable. We're told that this is the way
things are—then we put it in a box, lock it away, and never consider
it again. It's like a warm blanket in the lonely cold of the cosmos." He
sat in a nearby recliner. "Then somebody comes along and challenges
those things—tries to tear away your warm, comfy blanket, and you
resist, because it's cold out there."

"What does this have to do with—"

"Everything," Saul said, voice hostile. "We fear and hate things that
aren't like us. Sunnis and Shiites, Muslims and Christians, Republicans
and Democrats." He held for a moment, considering. "Prima, Ora, and
Domani." He took a breath. "That's what all this is about—avoiding
and hating people who aren't like us. Refusing to consider the other
side—and condemning those who don't listen to ours."

"But we're Christians," Hannah said. "We don't—"

"Christians don't what? Persecute one another? Hate people who aren't like them? Even those who are of the same faith?" Saul shook his head. "No. I'm afraid that if you are Christian soldiers, then you're the only army on Earth that shoots their own wounded.

"D'Angelo understood something," Saul continued. "The Firstborn cannot get along—won't get along—and they'll kill each other. That's why I knew I had to prepare for the inevitable."

Hannah's face was covered with confusion. "Wait," she said, raising her hand like a fourth grader.

"Yes?"

"Who is D'Angelo?"

Saul leaned back in his chair. "The monk Alessandro D'Angelo lived in Italy in the 1400s."

"Was he a member of the Firstborn?"

"Yes. In fact, he truly is the father of the modern orders. You see, back in those days it was hard for people to understand what the Firstborn were. As I've said, there are a lot of ways to interpret this ability. You think it's a gift from God and I think it's a fluke of nature, but most of medieval Europe thought that it was witchcraft."

"Witchcraft?"

"Yes. Not a divine gift, divination. A mark of the beast—a demon-possessed sorcerer predicting the future. Makes sense if you think about it. There are members of the Firstborn who still think that our gift is satanic."

"That doesn't make any sense."

Saul shrugged. "They still exist. Regardless, the medieval Firstborn were hunted down and tortured in order to discover the whereabouts of anyone else with their abilities. Most were eventually burned at the stake. This went on for nearly one hundred years before the birth of a certain Italian."

"D'Angelo?"

"Correct. Alessandro D'Angelo was an orphan—no known lineage—but when he was fourteen, he discovered that he was one of the Firstborn."

Hannah leaned forward. "Which gift did he have?"

Saul Mancuso leaned forward, voice intense but disimpassioned. "All three."

"What? Were his parents of different orders?"

"No one knows—but what is known is that D'Angelo was the most powerful Firstborn to ever walk the earth. He saw the Firstborn across the world being persecuted, and he called them to Italy."

"How?"

"I said he was the most powerful of all the Firstborn, didn't I?"

She nodded, eyes not moving away from his.

"He hid them in Italy. He was the first to realize that there were three basic gifts—and so he established the orders."

"The Prima, Domani, and Ora?"

"Yes. All Italian names: Prima meaning 'previously,' Domani meaning 'tomorrow,' and Ora meaning 'now.' He established them like monastic orders—with patriarchs at the head of each."

"Like my grandfather?"

"Yes. Men like your grandfather."

"And Morris Childs," Devin added.

"And for a while the orders flourished in secrecy. But the persecutions didn't end. And when a member of the Firstborn was captured, they would often betray the whereabouts of the other Firstborn to save their own lives—but almost always members of the other two orders."

"But," Hannah frowned, incredulous, "why?"

"Because the orders felt loyalty to the people they were most like—and they betrayed those who were different. It's called in-group versus out-group. We blame the plight of a person like us on their circumstances and the plight of someone different on their actions. That simple."

"Then what happened?"

"Those who saved their own skins were hunted down by the friends and families of those whom they betrayed. The orders stopped talking, started hating, and tumbled into violence."

"And that's why there's the doctrine of isolation?"

"Yes."

"And you think that the Firstborn will never be friends?"

He grunted. "Do you think that Israelis and Palestinians will ever be friends?"

"After the things Tariq said?" She shook her head. "No."

"Well, there you have it. They may form shaky truces and smile at one another for a weekend each year, but I doubt anything will ever make them friends." The professor grunted. "Do you think that Devin and John here will ever be friends? Sure, you're all here together out of necessity—but do any of you even trust each other?"

The room was silent for a moment. No one looked at each other.

"Would you risk your necks for each other if you felt you had another option?"

Devin's phone began to buzz in his jacket. "Excuse me," he said, clearing his throat, glad to change the subject. He stood. "I think this is them."

Devin stepped out of the house, surprised his phone got reception this far out—but Saul probably had whatever it took figured out.

"This is Bathurst."

"Do you still have the terrorist?"

"Yes."

"Come to Morris Childs's home in New York—midnight tonight."

"You took over his home?"

"Midnight tonight."

"No," Devin said definitively.

"What?"

"Neutral ground. Tomorrow night. Ten o'clock."

"Tonight, or not at all."

Devin shook his head. "He knows something more. There's another attack coming."

"You're bluffing—trying to buy more time for your muscle to show up."

"I'm trying to buy time so that we can learn where this attack is going to take place—before it's too late."

"Midnight tonight or nothing."

"Their target is an elementary school," Devin said flatly. He waited a moment for it to sink in. "If I have to choose between Morris and an elementary school full of kids, I know which one I'll choose."

There was silence on the other end of the line.

"Give us until tomorrow night—or no deal."

"Fine," Blake spat across the line. "Where?"

"I'll send you the address before the swap."

"No. You'll give me five locations, and I'll choose one. That way you won't have a chance to set up an ambush."

"Likewise."

"Bring the terrorist."

"No. The parcel will be at a separate location of our choosing. The parcel does not go to the exchange point until we have Morris."

"How do we know that you'll follow through and give us our terrorist?"

"Simple. You send a representative to our side and we'll take him to the parcel—he'll phone in a confirmation letting you know that our word is good—but he does not come to the exchange until we have Morris."

"No," Blake said again, continuing to bargain. "We'll do the same with Morris. You send one of your people to confirm that he's OK. Once both parties have made confirmation, we'll bring them to the exchange spot and make the trade—straight across—one for the other. Got it?"

"OK," Devin said firmly, "tomorrow night, ten o'clock. Call me at nine thirty for a list of locations. You'll have ten minutes to choose and call us back. We're in Pennsylvania—Cameron County—I'll tell you that. So be prepared for an exchange there."

"Tomorrow night," Blake agreed. "*Thresher.*"

Devin smiled and turned off the phone.

Chapter 17

J OHN SAT IN THE living room, staring at his hands. He was nervous, which was not something he felt very often. Usually he just felt everything in passing as he moved through the world. But it was all becoming so real so fast, a nearing future that he simply had no clue what to do with.

Saul entered from the next room, taking a seat. "Nervous?"

"A little," John nodded.

"Don't worry. You guys won't be doing this alone. The people I contacted are on their way."

"Who exactly is coming to join us?" he asked. "Are they all Fallen?"

Saul shook his head. "No. There's one active member of the Domani—a woman."

John's heart skittered, and his flesh went cold. "Trista Brightling?"

Saul nodded his head. "You know her?"

John looked away. "Yeah. I used to."

Saul laughed. "Is she the one who got you into so much trouble a few years back?"

John nodded. "I met her during a short-term missions trip—eight weeks in Barcelona, Spain. There was an instant connection. We talked a lot—nothing serious, at least not at first."

"Then it got serious?"

"Yeah."

"Did you know she was Domani?"

He shook his head. "Not at first, but then as time went on I could feel more and more of her—her secrets. I realized that she was Firstborn."

"But you didn't tell her?"

"No. It was stupid, but I loved her. I was going to quit missions work. I even set up a real job working for Goldstein so that I could buy a ring."

"But?" Saul led.

"The last night we were supposed to be there she called her uncle Morris and told him about me. He knew who I was. He told her that I was Ora—our relationship wasn't allowed."

"Don't tell me," Saul said, "you wanted to continue in secret, but she wouldn't have it?"

"I didn't even bother asking," John said. "I left Barcelona that night. Just got on a plane and flew to Thailand. It was more than a year before I came back to the States."

"And you never resolved things with her? Never called, wrote, talked?"

"No," he said, shaking his head.

"Just like the Ora," Saul mused. "No regard for the future and the possible consequences—just the joy of the moment, right?"

"Yeah," John said with another melancholy nod, "but it's all in the past now—and I intend to leave it there."

Hannah was in the kitchen cleaning up. The exterior of the house had a very definite Depression-era look, but the kitchen must have been refurbished in the sixties, given its tacky avocado-green color scheme.

Devin entered. "Well?" she asked.

"The exchange is going to be at ten o'clock tomorrow night."

"Good," Saul said as he and John entered from the next room. "What about location?"

"We give him a list of five. He chooses one."

"Simple enough," Saul agreed. "Pick one location you want and another four you know he'll turn down."

"Maybe," Devin said. "And one more thing."

"What's that?"

"He called me Thresher."

Saul and John stifled disgusted laughs. Hannah turned from her dishes, leaning against the sink, looking them over.

"I don't understand. Who's Thresher?"

Saul shook his head and looked at her. "Remember D'Angelo?"

"Yes."

"Before he died, he started to prophesy."

"Like the Domani?" she asked.

"No—like the prophets of the Old Testament. He was betrayed, and he escaped the trap but was wounded in the process. His companions— a hodge-podge of the few Firstborn from each of the orders that he still felt he could trust—found him. They did what they could for him—but it was too late. It took him a month to die."

"Why then? Why did all his prophecies happen then?"

"Because," John interjected, "he was trapped between this world and the next. He began hemorrhaging visions and prophecies about the future."

"He was delusional," Saul grumbled, "wounded and bleeding— hallucinating. The only reason any of his statements were taken seriously was because of the gifts he had in life."

"Did anyone write down these prophecies?"

"Yes. All of them."

"What happened to them?"

"The Firstborn fought over them—so that they would have D'Angelo's visions for themselves."

"Where are they now?"

Saul shrugged. "All over the world—some lost to antiquity, some buried or hidden. Others were destroyed, and some are hidden in plain sight."

"Regardless," Devin said, "he prophesied repeatedly about one thing—that someone or something called Thresher would bring an end to the Firstborn."

Hannah considered. "And each side is afraid that the other is Thresher?"

"Exactly," Devin said with a nod.

"And so," Saul said with a sigh, "one man's delusion resulted in six hundred years of fear, distrust, and death."

Hannah sat in confusion. "This all happened?"

"Yes," Devin said, "and it's happening again."

Devin looked at his watch—10:00 p.m. "We have exactly twenty-four hours to extract everything Tariq knows about this coming attack—or we lose him."

John shook his head. "I don't like it, but we have to accept the possibility that maybe Morris's life isn't worth this."

"Regardless, we're going to have to try."

Saul nodded. "Agreed."

"Then how do we get information?"

Devin considered how he wanted to respond.

"You don't suggest torture? Do you?"

"If it comes to that."

John stood. "Wait a minute! You don't actually think you're going to torture another human being, do you?"

Saul worked his hands together. "Tariq is a terrorist—a human being, but a terrorist. He has information about a coming terrorist attack against children, and he's not willing to comply. He has forfeited his right to comfort. Do you understand?"

John held, fists balled, eyes darting from one to another. "I can't believe this," he blustered, then stomped from the room.

"Torture is still a last resort," Devin said with a nod.

"Agreed," Saul replied.

"In the meantime we treat this like a hostage situation—he's a hostage-taker holding valuable goods. We shut off his power and heat until he gives us hostages."

"What do you suggest?"

"Take away his clothes and his heat. Don't feed him. Shut off the lights for a while—then drill him with a strobe light. As he starts to give up information, we give him his amenities back."

"You realize this is highly illegal, right?"

Devin nodded. "I don't think we have a choice. He's the only asset we've got."

John sat outside of the makeshift prison cell and looked in. "I need to know what you know. When is this attack going to be? And where?"

Tariq said nothing. He simply lay on the floor, staring at the ceiling.

"Listen, if you don't help me, I think they're going to hurt you."

Tariq heaved a weary sigh as if he'd just been asked a very stupid question. "I'm not afraid of pain or death."

John looked into the young man's unwavering eyes. "Children are going to die," he said angrily. "If you let it happen, then it's the same as if you did it."

The young Palestinian balked. "For every one Israeli that dies, three Palestinians are murdered—even children. Especially children."

John nodded. "I've heard about the violence."

"But do you know it?" Tariq asked pointedly. "Have you ever tasted death?"

"I've felt people die, yes."

The young man seemed to ignore the statement, looking up at the ceiling. "When I was in Palestine, there was a boy in my neighborhood—Omar. We were best friends—I loved him like a brother. We played together every day. We went to school together. We were both just children when the Israeli bulldozers came through our neighborhood, destroying all the houses that the Jews thought might be a threat. Omar's house was bulldozed—wiped from the earth. So he came to live with my family."

"It sounds like you were close."

"I loved him like I loved my own soul—my friend. Then one day we were playing in the street. We'd made guns out of wood—but the Jews didn't stop to make sure—they simply shot him."

John could feel Tariq's heart sag, the sense of loss still weighing down on him after all these years. "I'm sorry about your friend. The Israelis were nervous and—"

"They were murderers. They said, 'Look, a Muslim child with a gun! Good, we have a reason to kill him!'"

"I'm certain that wasn't their thought."

Tariq shook his head. "He was shot in the side—a flesh wound. My father was the surgeon who worked on him. He said that Omar would be just fine."

"He made it?"

"He bled to death six hours later."

John looked at the cement. "I'm sorry about your friend."

"By the time I left Palestine, my father, two brothers, two uncles, and countless friends had all been murdered by the Jews."

"You can't blame the Jews, and you certainly can't blame America."

Tariq sat up on the concrete, setting his arms across his knees. "This isn't about Jews and Christians; this is about Zionism—colonialism, people forcing their way of life on us. In 1948, when Israel began, the Palestinians were swept aside, like dust. They're like the Nazis. They'd have all the Muslims in camps if they could get away with it. All because of this doctrine of Zionism—and we resist it. And it's not just the Jews. America supports this Zionist doctrine as well—so they must be fought also."

"Tariq, this is about children," John pleaded.

"It's about freedom!" Tariq stood. "When people are denied their freedom, they must fight back—and none of the world will support Palestine, so Palestine must fight for itself." He moved toward the grating. "Maybe once America has lost a fraction of the children whom they have killed they will start to see reason!"

John was flabbergasted. "Tariq, do you realize what you're saying? You're talking about murder. Do you really hate humanity that much?"

Tariq threw his hands at the grating. "I love humanity. I love the children of this world." Tears began to flood his eyes. "I have a family and friends and loved ones. I don't want to kill, but we have been given no choice. That's why I must become a martyr."

"Do you really want to die that badly?"

"No!" he shouted, shaking the grate. "I want to live. I want to have a family and friends and peace—but as long as innocent people are being murdered in my homeland, then none of this is possible."

"But you're an American!"

"It's my Muslim brothers and sisters who are being murdered—I can't turn my back on them. The world hates us and wishes to kill us all. They love to make us die—so we learn to love death as much as they love life. Do you understand? You can't murder the willing."

John shook his head. "You can't possibly think that this will bring you freedom."

"But it has. A man who is not afraid to die is free indeed." Tariq glared into John. "Are you afraid to die?"

"No," John said.

"Why?" Tariq demanded.

"Because I know that I'll go to heaven. I'll be with Jesus forever."

Tariq continued his stare, eyes narrowing. "You are afraid to die."

"No, I'm not. I have security in Christ."

"Words. With you everything is a show. You are afraid to die— because you don't really believe what you're saying. You simply decided to become a Christian, like all Americans, and then never had the guts to consider the world from another perspective."

"That's not true," John said, backpedaling. He was being read, just as he did of others so often. Tariq was looking into him, seeing the soft spots, pushing the buttons.

"You settled on a religion—a way of seeing the world—because it was convenient, and you know it. You don't really believe what you claim to believe until you are willing to die for it. So let me ask you— what are you willing to die for?"

John said nothing. He simply walked away.

Chapter 18

IT WAS MORNING.

John sat on the treads of a backhoe, staring into the trees. What Tariq had said the night before shook him.

It was the "golden hour," as his friends in the film industry referred to it. A soft amber haze settled on everything, twinkling through the leaves. None of this was a comfort to John. He rubbed the back of his neck, kneading the flesh, trying to work out the knots. He hadn't slept well on the guest bed, one of many Saul had in his outbuildings.

"I heard you were out here," a female voice said softly.

"Hannah?" He turned.

Trista. His heart seized in his chest—he tried not to let on. "I heard you were coming."

She shrugged. "They have my uncle, and I wanted to help."

John stood, walking to her. She was dressed more casually than usual—designer blue jeans and a burgundy sweater—he was used to seeing her in a skirt. Her features were commanding, yet feminine as ever, not a hair was out of place—her posture was perfect. "Did Saul call you?"

"He made a call asking if I had any leads regarding Morris's whereabouts."

"Do you?" John asked.

"No. But when I found out what was going on here I wanted to be part of it."

"Did you come from New York?"

She nodded.

John put his hands in his pockets. "I'm sorry I tried to talk to you in San Antonio. It was tacky."

She shook her head, eyes apologetic. "None of that matters now. You're working to help my uncle—that's all that matters."

"Doing this wasn't my idea."

"But you're still here." Her eyes dropped. She reached out, taking John's hand by the fingertips, lifting her eyes again. "Thank you."

"No problem."

Her eyes wandered again. "I'm sorry for barging in on you like this. You wanted to be alone, didn't you?"

"No," he said, cradling her hand in his own, drawing it to his chest.

She looked up at him, breath laboring, eyes softening. "John, I—"

He leaned in to kiss her.

Her expression soured. "What are you doing?" she demanded, pushing away. "John, I thought you understood. We can't do this. It would never work." She backed away slowly, shaking her head. "I'm sorry if I gave you the wrong impression. I shouldn't have come out here."

She walked away, leaving John hanging his head.

Looking over their tiny army late afternoon, Devin waited for Saul to explain the situation.

In total, there were fifteen of them in the living room—four First-born and eleven Fallen men. Women lost faith and left the Firstborn as well, but the stereotype was men, and that was precisely what Saul had found: ten angry men, the bitterness that came from years of coercion and manipulation rising to their faces now.

Of course there were many more Fallen whom Saul knew and had contact with. But not all of them could be helpful. Not all of them could have made it in time. But these men—these especially angry, dedicated men—were the people whom Devin would have to rely upon.

Saul stood at the front of the room. "All right," he said gruffly. "Doubtless you're all up to speed, but I'll recap.

"Thursday night at the annual conclave in San Antonio it was discovered that Blake Jackson was planning to destroy a major mosque in Washington DC. While that attempt was thwarted, his target, a

Palestinian and would-be terrorist, Tariq Ali, was apprehended by Mr. Bathurst and his companions.

"Jackson also made apparent that he has kidnapped and is holding Morris Childs—patriarch of the Domani. With the recent death of Henry Rice, patriarch of the Prima, Morris's death would certainly plunge the Firstborn into chaos, and that will be bad for all of us."

There was chattered agreement.

"It's time for us to tell the Firstborn what they needed to hear back when we all left—that they're not always right. They are not perfect, and they can't push people around."

A swell of agreement rose into the air.

"Blake Jackson called us Thresher." There were groans and growls. "I say that if he considers us Thresher, then that's exactly what we'll be." A round of applause shook the room. "Now, we have some preparing to do." He turned to Devin and nodded for him to begin.

"We're down to five locations," Devin said, pointing to the map, "here, here, and here. All are good locations. We'll give them ten minutes to decide—which will provide them with enough time that they won't back out of the deal but not enough time to plan an ambush."

The room of Fallen listened intently as Devin continued—sleeves of his dress shirt rolled to his elbows, top button undone. He felt under-dressed for a briefing, but he was getting tired.

"I've been over all of this several times before, but I'll say it all again: I want you all carrying weapons. We hopefully won't need them, but it should be a deterrent if they decide to try something. I also want you in body armor. There are bulletproof vests with the weapons—be sure to have one." He stopped for a moment, looking over their faces. "Do you all understand?"

It was serious. Devin knew that. The danger was real, and the people here stood a good chance of getting shot if something went wrong. He wanted them to know that, and from the looks on their faces it appeared the message was sinking in.

"We'll be breaking down into three teams—one small team to stay here and monitor the confirmation made by Blake's man, one team to drive him there and back, one team to stay at the drop in a show of force, and someone to make the confirmation. John?"

"Yes?"

"I want you to keep an eye on Blake's man when he comes to make his confirmation."

John nodded. "OK."

"This is a big responsibility; are you sure you can handle it?"

John nodded again. Devin knew that John was more likely to act on instinct than think something through. Normally it was what he disliked about John Temple, but in this situation it was exactly what they needed.

"Mr. Bathurst?" a female voice asked.

"Ms. Brightling?"

Trista stood in the corner, but even that couldn't seem to keep her presence from flooding the room. "I'd like to join John in that duty."

John was overcome by obvious surprise.

"Why?" Devin asked. He didn't like the two of them together.

"I don't have military or police training like a lot of these men do. I doubt I'd be much use at the exchange—either for looking menacing or shooting back if it comes to that."

Devin nodded. "Fine. You can stay here with John and Hannah."

The meeting adjourned and the room cleared. Devin gathered the maps and the papers.

"Devin?"

He looked up. "Yes?"

It was Hannah, arms crossed, face pained. "Thank you for keeping me here."

"I don't want you near danger—I've already put you too close to these things already."

"It's just that..." She hesitated. The expression on her face seemed so tortured, almost like guilt. "My grandfather died trying to stop Blake—I think I should probably help."

"No," he said definitively. Every moment she was closer to this whole thing the further she'd be dragged into this dark and violent world. He considered telling her that she still had a shot at a future, but he held off. She was young—she'd fight him out of pure youthful indiscretion. "You're staying here and that's final. Understood?"

She nodded, relief plain on her face. Whatever emotions of guilt and duty she had been experiencing were beginning to subside—and that, Devin told himself, was good.

"Relax while you can," he ordered, giving her a terse nod. "Get some rest."

Devin strode out of the house, gearing himself up for confrontation. He approached Tariq's makeshift cell and opened a door. Devin stood in the threshold, stance wide, hands clasped in front of him.

Tariq huddled in the corner in his boxer shorts under blazing bright lights, sweat dripping off of him.

Devin adjusted his collar. They'd put a half dozen space heaters in the hall to make Tariq's cell unbearably hot.

"Are you ready to tell me what I need to know?" Devin asked, taking a step into the cell, shoes clipping on the cement floor.

No reply. Tariq remained huddled in the corner, unmoving.

"Do you want water? I would be more than happy to provide you with water in exchange for some information—a sign of good faith."

Tariq's head lifted, slick and sweaty. He pushed himself up with an arm until he was standing. "Do you want to kill me?" he asked, taking a step toward Devin. "Then kill me. I'm not afraid to die."

It still amazed Devin—the young man was strong, good-looking, intelligent, almost no accent. Under other circumstances he'd have befriended him.

Devin took a seat in the hallway and stared at the young man. It was a waiting game now. See who would crack first. Making prisoners stand in the corner without rest had proven to be a highly successful method of gaining information in other circumstances. They didn't have the time to wait for that, but he could still wait for the kid to crack. He would eventually.

Devin found a book—a grimy paperback novel about the Napoleonic war—and placed a chair in the hallway, taking a bottle of water from a nearby compact fridge. He sat, appearing as casual as possible.

"You look hot," he said in Tariq's direction.

Tariq didn't respond. Only the belabored rising and falling of the young man's rib cage indicated to Devin that Tariq was even still breathing.

"There are bottles of cold water in the refrigerator right here. Let me know when you want one. I'd be happy to discuss a trade."

Devin took a sip of the ice-cold water. It tasted like the plastic bottle it was kept in, something that canteen usage had allowed him to grow accustomed to, but he made as much of a show of it as he could without breaking from his usually calm demeanor. He wanted Tariq thirsty—and as far as the kid was concerned, the contents of Devin's bottle was the purest chilled water on the planet: melted ice from the peaks of the French Alps.

Tariq's shoulders heaved under the onslaught of unbearable heat, skin slick with an oily sheen of dripping sweat. Tariq didn't budge.

Devin opened the novel in his hands and began to read.

He was halfway though the novel before he began to worry. Time slunk along. Tariq didn't move. The novel was tedious, filled with sketchy facts, unnecessary detail, and nauseating melodrama. Just the kind of thing Professor Saul Mancuso would read.

Devin closed the book, then looked at his watch—less than an hour until the exchange. Not even sixty minutes to learn everything he could from this young man before he'd have to trade him.

Anger overcame Devin. He'd wasted his time trying to be humanitarian with a man who had no respect for the idea. Now his time was nearly up. He'd squandered what chances he'd had to capitalize on this moment by giving this obstinate punk the chance to do the right thing—something he obviously wasn't going to do on his own.

"Mr. Ali," Devin said, standing, his voice as solid and commanding as he knew it could be, "look at me."

Tariq turned his head, looking over at Devin, acknowledging his presence with an attitude of contempt.

"Mr. Ali, I'm done with you. You are a member of a terrorist cell whose aim is to kill children—I will gain information from you. Do you understand?"

Tariq glared for a moment, then turned around, walked back to his corner, and curled into a ball.

Devin took a step back, then turned, walked out of the cell, and shut the barred door.

"Fine," he said to himself. "We do it the hard way."

John was moving through the hall when he looked up and saw Trista from behind. Hair up, shoulders back.

"I don't understand," John said, approaching Trista from behind. She stopped, obviously holding her breath. "Why did you request to work with me?"

She hung her head—clearing her throat as her face turned toward him slightly. "I have my reasons, John. You don't have to read into everything."

He stepped up next to her, circling in front. Her eyes were turned away from him. His hand raised to her chin, fingertips gently drawing her face toward him. Trista's eyes lifted to meet his, surprisingly wide.

Blue. Her eyes were blue. He'd nearly forgotten that.

He could feel a shock to his lungs, like he'd been dropped in a pool of frozen water. "You talk like you don't even know me," he said with a twinge of tremble in his voice.

Trista didn't seem to breathe for a moment. She cleared her throat and seemed to instantly transform, breathing normal, face business-like. Trista reached up, removing John's fingertips from her chin. "I thought I knew you," she said with a flat nod, "but you lied to me, John Temple. You put me at the center of a scandal that ruined my reputation. Then you left me hanging while you hid in Asia."

He was quiet for a moment. "Do you remember the time we took the train into the mountains in Barcelona and got lost?"

Her frosty look stayed for a moment, then broke as she let out a small embarrassed laugh. She looked away, nervously chewing a fingernail.

"We were supposed to be gone for three hours," John said warmly, leaning closer. "Four wrong trains, and we nearly made it to France."

She tried to hide her smile. "You're supposed to be the traveler."

"Hey," John said, feeling an impish smile on his face, "it was your idea."

"But you," she said, smiling as she jabbed a sharp fingernail into his chest, "were supposed to be navigating."

"We spent eight hours on trains that day—nonstop." John looked at his feet, suddenly feeling exposed. He lifted his head, looking her in the eyes with every ounce of boldness he could summon. "I think it may be my favorite memory."

Trista took a step back, crossing her arms, trying to regain some of her seriousness. "Of us?" she asked.

John didn't blink. "Ever."

Trista remained silent for a moment, expression enigmatic and pensive. She nodded after a few moments. "I remember that day too."

He looked at the wall, examining the cinder block walls, nodding.

Silence.

John scratched the back of his head. "I loved you; you know that, right?"

Trista's warmth evaporated, her jaw setting, expression scathing. "Don't say that, John. It's not fair."

"I did love you," John insisted, putting a hand on her arm.

She pushed the hand aside and took another step back. "Don't lie to me and then tell me you love me, John. It was never meant to be," she said, turning and walking away, "and that just hurts too much."

"Wait," John called after her. "Trista?"

She didn't look back.

A power drill. Three speeds. Reversible, with a forest of bits waiting to be locked into place.

The plastic case came open with a snap, and Devin lifted the device from its nest. He gave the trigger a pull—a shrieking buzz, the bit's grooves blurring like a twister, the pistol grip shivering mechanically in his hand.

Good, it worked.

He let go of the trigger and released the bit from its place. His fingertips slid over the collection, touching them each in turn.

That one.

A spade bit, used for drilling holes through walls—a wide bit with a spike protruding from its flat middle. It looked menacing—good. It would also be effective, and that was equally good.

It would punch a hole through the back of a man's kneecap.

"What are you doing?" a voice asked from behind. He looked back and saw John Temple standing there. The man saw the drill in his hands—eyes suddenly startled.

"Tariq is going to talk. It's simple mathematics. Hurt a man badly enough and he'll tell you everything you want to hear."

"Even if it's not the truth?"

"There's more to it than that," Devin replied, adjusting the bit.

"How?" John growled. "How could it possibly be more complicated?"

Devin looked down at the drill in his hand. He shook his head. This would never work. They would never be able to return Tariq to society—they'd have to kill him.

His phone buzzed in his pocket.

He set the drill down and snapped the phone open. John watched him intently. "This is Bathurst."

"It's nine thirty," Blake's voice announced. "What are the locations?"

Devin moved to the nearby table, picked up a list of locations, and read them off. "You have ten minutes to make your choice. Agreed?"

"Agreed."

"Good."

He hung up and stepped into the next room. "We'll have a location in ten minutes."

The room remained quiet.

"It's time to get ready, people."

John stood at the doorway of the outbuilding, light spilling out behind him into the dark of night. Saul approached and stood next to him.

John shook his head. "I just walked in on Bathurst. He had a drill. He was going to use it on Tariq—luckily his phone rang and he didn't have a chance to use it."

Saul nodded.

"What a heartless thug," John spat.

"No," Saul said, shaking his head. "He is what he is, and you can't understand it any more than he understands you."

"I'm not deranged."

Saul considered for a moment. "Would you shoot a man if he was going to kill a child?"

"Yes."

"Then what would you do to save a hundred children?"

John sat in silence. "Are you saying he was right?"

"I'm saying he was willing to do what you weren't—what needed to be done. The world needs people like him."

"I don't know—"

"And you stopped him, because you are his conscience—and people like him need people like you—despite the fact that he doesn't want to hear that."

"Is that your point?"

Saul shrugged. "I'm just an old man with too much time on his hands. I've read too many books and lost too many friends—what do I know? But if you ask me—the world needs everyone."

"Even the people we don't like?"

"Especially the people we don't like."

Chapter 19

M4 CARBINES DISLODGED FROM their racks, clutched by the hands of the Fallen.

Weapons loaded.

Actions cracked.

Body armor strapped into place.

"OK, people," Devin said, standing at the front of the room, "are you ready?"

A collective shout.

"Bow your heads."

Many faces dipped in reverence—others simply remained silent out of respect.

"Heavenly Father, be with us tonight as we go to face an enemy that seeks to destroy. We ask that You be with us. Lord, give us the strength to stand our ground and to fulfill Your will. In Your holy name—"

"Amen." The word thundered in chorus.

Minutes later they were leaving. Vehicles were loaded in twos and threes. Engines revved and headlights flashed on.

Devin stood with Trista in the dark of the outdoors. He turned to her.

"Keep an eye on Temple when he gets back—don't let him do anything irrational."

"Understood."

"Good."

As Devin climbed into the driver's seat, his phone buzzed. "This is Bathurst."

"We've decided on a location."

"Where?"

"Location two."

"Understood. We'll meet you there."

"And one more thing."

"What's that?"

"I want Hannah to be the one to make the confirmation on Morris."

Devin's heart dropped. "No," he said flatly. "I won't let you pull her any deeper into this. She still has a chance at a life outside of all of this."

"That's not your choice, Bathurst. Tell her to do it and see if she does the right thing."

"Fine," Devin replied with a snarl. "I'll ask her."

"Good."

He stepped out of the car and walked to the armory in the tactical building.

"Why me?" she asked, mind racing. "Why would they want me to confirm that Morris Childs is alive?" Her chest began to tighten—her heart speeding. "It doesn't make sense. I don't even know him." Her mind filled with all of the possibilities—of shooting and violence—more trauma as she fought for her life.

"They don't think you're a threat. You won't try anything." Devin looked away.

Her hands began to shake and twitch, adrenaline flooding her system, the edges of her vision going gray. "I don't want to do this," she stammered.

"I won't make you," Devin replied.

Hannah shook her head, looking out the window to the vehicles beyond. "Why?" she asked. "Why should I be special?" She heaved a sigh, body still shuddering. "Everyone else is going—why should I escape this?"

For the first time ever Devin Bathurst looked torn to her—as if some part of him disagreed with the other. For once she saw pain and anguish crossing his features as his strong facade weakened.

"I've seen your future," he said blandly, trying to sound unaffected.

"You don't have to be one of us. You can still live a normal life. You can get married and live in a big house in the suburbs and spend the rest of your life in relative comfort. But if you come any deeper into this world, I'm afraid you won't be able to get back out."

She listened to his words, taking them in. What if she really had a chance to have comfort—to belong? Could she pass that up?

Hannah looked down—her whole life spreading out before her. She could choose comfort—because that was the natural choice. Or she could choose pain and service—but why?

"What if this is what God's calling me to do?" she asked quietly. "What if this is what I was made to do?"

Devin nodded. "Then you'll ask God—because I won't make you do this." He took a step back. "We have to go now."

No more time. No more future to plan for, no more present to indulge in. There was only this choice—one that she would have to live with for the rest of her life.

Devin nodded again. "I'm getting in the car. I'll let Blake know you're not coming." Then he walked away, closing the door behind him.

Hannah stared at the door, body trembling. She had never been good at praying—she'd tried the traditions of formula and the free-flowing personal prayers, but she'd never found a rhythm to praying that she especially liked. All she could do was fill her mind with the dazzling blur of panic and fear that flooded out of her heart in directed chaos.

Was this what God was asking of her? Was this what she was made for? Could she trade her happiness to fulfill her purpose?

The room was silent.

Could she ever be happy without fulfilling her purpose?

Devin climbed in to the driver's seat of the car and dialed the phone.

"Yes?" Blake replied.

"Hannah won't be doing the confirmation."

"No deal."

"We already have someone else."

"I said Hannah Rice—you give me Hannah Rice—got it?"

"I'm afraid that won't work," Devin replied.

"Then this exchange isn't going to work."

Devin held his anger in. "Blake—you have to understand—"

The car door opened and Hannah climbed into the passenger's seat. She looked Devin in the eye—young, foolish, resolute.

"I'm going," was all that she said. She reached for her seat belt.

"Bathurst?" Blake demanded over the phone.

"Hannah's with me now. She'll do the confirmation. We'll be right there."

Devin snapped the phone shut and slipped the vehicle into drive.

The cars moved down the road in a convoy, like a stream of ants gathering into their hill. Taillights slipped into the darkness and headlights washed the pavement with light.

A left turn—dirt roads.

Billows of dust lifted in the darkness, splaying out from the grinding of the tires as they tumbled and turned over the road.

Almost there.

Devin Bathurst looked out the window of the sedan at location two. It was an empty field in the middle of nowhere. There were no lights. Good; they'd beaten Blake's crew to the exchange. They would have control of the ground—

He hoped.

The cars stopped in a row behind him. He got out and looked around. Devin had drilled the plan into them. They took their places behind their vehicles, using them as cover as they waited for the incoming enemy.

The night air was cool and smelled of dewy sweetness. It was hard to believe that just a few weeks ago he'd been knee-deep in snow at the epicenter of a spring blizzard, and yet here, half a continent away, it felt like early summer.

He popped the trunk, donned his bulletproof vest over his dress shirt, scooped up an M4, and threw the sling over his shoulder. He had considered putting on combat fatigues for convenience, but this was a business meeting. The bulletproof vest and the gun would explain that he was serious, but keeping a dress shirt and slacks made him look reasonable—a delicate balance to strike while staring a dangerous enemy in the teeth.

Hannah stepped up next to him, wrapping her arms around herself for warmth. "Are they coming?"

"They should be here any minute." He reached into the trunk and handed her a vest. She strapped it on. His eyes lingered on her for a moment until she looked at him.

"Is everything OK?" she asked.

Devin steeled himself, then nodded. "I am," he said. "I have to be."

Five minutes—five agonizing minutes—passed before they saw the first of the headlights loping over the curvature of the terrain.

"Here they come," Devin announced, and light spilled over them.

The first vehicle looked like an SUV or truck, but it was impossible to make it out with the blinding lights boring into their eyes. It stopped a hundred yards away. A second vehicle joined the phalanx, followed by a third, a fourth, and a fifth. They left their engines running, rumbling in the night.

The parade continued for several minutes, the sounds of car doors opening and slamming shut—boots on dirt. They couldn't see a thing—just headlights. Fifteen sets of headlights.

John turned his head to Devin. "I think we're outnumbered."

Devin nodded, analytical. "Maybe we are—or maybe we're only supposed to think we are."

The bright cascade of light that sliced through the night was broken by the silhouettes of five figures walking toward them.

Devin nodded. "That's our cue."

They stepped forward into the brightness, squinting as they tried to make out the shapes. A moment later they arrived almost halfway between the two lines of vehicles—ten feet from one another.

Blake Jackson stood in the middle of the group, wearing a thick down coat over a bulletproof vest, flanked by two men on either side—both sets wearing SWAT gear, one set blue, the other set brown camouflage.

"Bathurst," Blake said through the dark, "glad to see you could make it yourself."

"Likewise."

"And you brought the girl as your representative."

"I see you brought friends."

Blake nodded. "Domani Paramilitary and Prima Militia. I even have members of the Ora Strike Force—compliments of Clay Goldstein."

"The Ora Strike Force is a joke," Devin replied definitively.

"It doesn't matter—I still have all the power of the Firstborn on my side."

"How did you get Goldstein on your side?" Devin asked.

"Overseer—it's been passed."

"And you're the new leader of the Firstborn?"

"Interim—until we find someone else."

John balked. "And by interim you mean indefinitely?"

"Watch it," Blake warned.

"How did you get the Domani and the Prima to agree?"

"Morris Childs is missing and Henry Rice is dead—it wasn't hard to do."

"And they agreed to come after me?"

Blake nodded. "You're holding and protecting a terrorist."

"*You* are a terrorist."

Blake said nothing. He simply motioned to one of the Domani Paramilitary and removed his helmet and gun, stepping forward. "Brock will be performing our confirmation."

John Temple came alongside Brock. The man was four inches taller than John and noticeably bigger. He looked like he'd played college football or something—dark hair and blue eyes.

This was the man John would be responsible for. Devin hoped he was up for it.

Hannah looked at Devin, almost concerned. He nodded at her, and she moved toward Blake and his men.

"At your request Hannah will be performing our confirmation."

"Good," Blake said with a nod. "Then let's get started."

Hannah stepped forward, face turning back to Devin—one last look at something resembling sanity before the plunge.

Her eyes still dazzled by the headlights, she was met just ahead of the vehicles by a group of three men who looked like soldiers. One approached with a black cloth bag.

"We're going to have to put this over your head," he announced over the rumble of the engines.

She eyed him skeptically, trying not to shake.

"It's for your own safety."

Then he reached out with the bag, lifting it over her head—

And her whole world was plunged into darkness.

Once again, Hannah tumbled through the disorienting tumult of sensory deprivation. They drove for who knew how long; she tried to count the passing seconds, but her thoughts froze up in fear.

Suddenly the SUV stopped, and they pulled her out. She groped hopelessly at her world.

"Are we there?" she asked.

"No—just changing vehicles."

"Why?"

"A precaution."

They frisked her a second time, loaded her in another vehicle, and continued the drive—deeper into the darkness.

John looked in the rearview mirror as he drove from the exchange spot, thoughts of being ambushed on the way back to the compound filling his mind. He took a long, slow breath and looked at the man in the backseat. Brock sat perfectly still, blindfold over his eyes.

John reached for the car radio, turning it on. "What kind of music do you like?" he called to the back.

Brock grunted. "What do you listen to?"

"Mostly worship music."

"Why?" Brock laughed.

"Because I like it."

"Whatever," he scoffed. "It's your business."

John felt awkward. He turned the radio to a classical station and continued driving. After what felt like an eternity, he arrived back at the compound. There was a long buzz as he pressed the button at the gate.

Trista spoke through the intercom. "Who is it?"

"It's John," he said as he looked up into the camera positioned near the floodlight.

"Come on in."

There was a buzz, and John got out of the car, moving to the fence, pushing the gate away, driving toward the building where they held the terrorist.

Darkness—that was all Hannah could see, a shroud covering her head. They had switched cars again. Maybe she was back in her original vehicle. They were driving in circles now, trying to confuse her—making sure that she couldn't find her way back.

It was like being kidnapped all over again—that same living hell—moving, seeing, and knowing only at the whim of another. She was completely dependent upon them. Her body shook, but she didn't struggle—passive acceptance was what she'd heard it called, the act of giving in to the will of another and not fighting back.

The car stopped—another exchange?

"We're here," the driver announced.

Someone opened her door, letting her out. They guided her by the arm, moving her across wet ground—they were outside; that was something to go on. The darkness of her world was accented by a glow of light filtering in through her head covering.

The bag slipped off of her head.

She was inside a big canvas tent the size of someone's living room, and at the center of the room was a chair—and a man dressed in black, his own head covered as hers had been. A soldier reached out, removing the black bag—

Morris Childs.

He lifted his eyes and made a relieved noise. "Have you come for me?"

She nodded, removing a cell phone from her pocket. "We're making a trade right now."

"Good."

She held up the phone and took a photo of the two of them together. Then she sent it to Devin.

John let Brock out of the car, searching him again—no weapons, no wire, no tracking devices. He almost let him continue, but this was too important to let anything slip. John checked him a third time just to be sure.

John couldn't find a thing.

He led the bigger man by the arm, taking him into the tactical building, moving into the sickly light toward the makeshift cell.

Trista approached. "Are you ready?" she asked, coming up alongside John.

He nodded nervously as she moved alongside Brock, much closer to him than John was comfortable with, fearing Brock might grab her. They brushed against one another—then separated.

Inside the cell Tariq was sitting in the corner, clutching his knees. John reached up and removed the blindfold from Brock's face.

Brock looked at Tariq, then John and Trista. "Is that him?"

John nodded. That was the bitter young man who had decided tragically to heap his pain upon the world—now being sentenced to an equally bitter and unjust fate. "That's him," John said.

Brock nodded. "Good."

John watched as Brock reached into his pocket—presumably to remove the cell phone he'd put there, but when his hand lifted there was something different—

A gun—

The weapon snapped upward, leveling at Tariq through the grating. John couldn't see it, couldn't feel it—but it was happening. Brock was going to kill Tariq now—and they'd never have to give up Morris.

The moment took over, with everything happening fast.

He threw his weight into Brock's arm, sending his arm swinging wide.

The blasting of a cannon reverberated through the room.

Trista screamed.

Brock shoved back, trying to aim. John grabbed his wrist—wrestling for the pistol, another blast stabbing at the quiet of the room.

John howled—Brock jerking his hand in an unnatural twist. John crumpled to his knees. A savage kick and he went sprawling back—hit the cement hard.

John eyes focused through the pain—Brock was aiming at Tariq once more. John lashed out. A merciless kick to his opponent's knee. Brock doubled, clutching his leg.

John was on his feet—faster than even he expected. He grabbed at the handgun—wrestled with Brock's brawny grip. The gun swung wildly. Trista was ahead of them—shouting loudly, the gun waving in her direction—

The weapon discharged.

John screamed in horror.

The bullet burst off the far wall in a cloud of concrete—missing her by inches.

John's elbow came down on Brock's gun hand, blowing a hole in the floor. John sank his teeth into Brock's skin—clamping down with ferocity. The gun hit the floor.

Something went wrong. A fist plowed into John's stomach and the air ripped from his lungs. A sickening pain boiled through his body, shaking him to the core—he felt like he might die—and landed him on his knees.

A set of meaty hands grabbed John by the collar, lifting him to his feet.

Civility left him and he screamed, lashing out with every ounce of malice he could call up. His attacks were brutal. Brock brushed them all aside, grabbing his throat with an iron clamp of a hand, shaking him like a rag doll.

John's back slammed onto a nearby table—the air escaping him— moist salty sweat bleeding from his pores. Blood boiled in John's ears—his heart thundering in his lobes. He was in a fight for his life—

And he was losing.

John's hands searched blindly across the tabletop and found something hard—he swung at Brock's head and broke free.

He hit the floor—battered and abused. He looked up—Brock was bearing down on him fast. A kick to John's stomach—air screaming from his lungs.

Another kick to the stomach. John screamed without air—a sickly sucking from the pit of his bowels.

"Stop it!" Trista shouted as if he might listen to her. "You're going to kill him!"

Brock didn't reply—he kicked again, then waited.

John lifted to his hands and knees trying to crawl away—a big, fleshy hand grasped the back of John's sopping head, sinewy fingers curling around his hair, clutching a handful of sticky-wet follicles. It felt like the back of his head was being torn off as the brawny arm lifted him to his feet.

John moaned in agony—turning—throwing a punch at Brock's middle. The fist bounced off Kevlar body armor.

A blur of motion and John felt himself rammed into a cement wall—shoulder blades slamming hard.

Brock lifted a fist, and it balled in front of John's eyes. He tried to break loose, shaking his whole body in futility. John took the fist and his sight blurred—blinded by pain.

"Stop!" Trista shouted again.

The brawny fingers wrapped around John's throat—squeezing with intent.

"Brock, listen to me!"

He glared viciously into John's eyes. The picture of Brock's angry, aggressive, violent face choking him to death dipped further and further out of focus. John could feel himself dying—

BLAM!

A bullet hole exploded on the wall—the sound of a brass casing bouncing in a twinkling jingle off the concrete floor. Brock turned his head—his grip relaxing slightly.

Trista stood in the middle of the room holding Brock's pistol expertly, the weapon leveled at the man's head, her voice steely. "Brock, let him go."

Brock's hands released and John hit the floor as he stepped away—moving toward Trista.

"Give me the gun," Brock said.

John watched from the floor, battered and fatigued, unable to get up or help or move.

"No." Her voice was firm but accented with a tremolo of fear.

"Give it to me!" He was angry now.

John lifted himself slowly, body hunched as he tried to move forward. Every bit of his body screamed out against him, trying to stop him from moving—

"Give me the gun!" he shouted again.

"No, Brock—"

He twisted her hand—a quick blow to the side of Trista's face—

The pistol dropped.

Anger flared in John and he stood—dizzy and beaten—hands reaching for Brock's shoulders. He grabbed, ripping the big man back. Brock wasn't expecting it.

They hit the ground.

The pistol clattered to the floor. Brock clawed for the pistol—fingers touching it.

The gun went sliding—Trista kicking at it hard. The weapon spun across the floor, hitting the wall.

Brock turned his attention to John, grabbing him by the throat again—squeezing hard. John's vision blurred—filling with red and white blotches as air and blood were cut off from his head. The big man's teeth bared, snarling, shoulders hunching over him.

John tried to fight back—coughing and choking. Brock was killing him—there on the cement floor. His body went tense, trying to ward off death. The big man's fingers curled tighter and tighter—

Thunder cracked and Brock screamed, grabbing at his arm. A bullet wound gaped from his bicep.

He stood, turning to Trista. "You shot me!" he blustered, incredulously.

"Don't come any closer—"

"I should—" He took an ominous step toward her.

She fired until the gun was empty.

Devin looked at his watch. He'd received the photo from Hannah. But what about John? He should have sent confirmation by now—it was that simple.

"Is something wrong?" Carson asked.

"I hope not."

The rumble of engines was all anyone at the exchange point had heard for minutes on end. Devin tried not to reveal his anxiety, but something was wrong.

At last his phone buzzed, and he removed it from his pocket.

"This is Bathurst."

"It's John."

"Temple, what's wrong?"

"They never intended to give up Morris. Brock snuck a weapon in somehow—he tried to kill Tariq."

"Where's Brock now?"

There was a momentary pause. "Trista took care of it."

Devin looked up, eyeing the bright lights across the field, wondering how much firepower was behind that veil of lights.

"Devin, it's a trap—get out of there, now!"

Devin nodded and ended the call. He turned to Carson. "Get ready to run—it's a trap."

"What?"

"Do it."

Devin went back to his phone.

Hannah looked Morris over—he didn't look mistreated, not like she had been when she had been kidnapped.

They'd left her alone with him in the tent for a moment. It seemed unwise, but they had enough firepower that it didn't appear to bother them.

Her phone vibrated. A text message from Devin: *Trap. Get out now.*

Her heart skipped. This wasn't possible.

She looked around, scanning the tent, then leaned close to Morris, reaching for his bindings. "Mr. Childs."

"Yes?"

"It's a trap. This whole thing is a trap—we have to get out of here."

He looked her over, appearing more confused than scared. "What makes you think it's a trap?"

"I just got a message. Something must have happened."

"Oh," he said, hesitantly. "Are you sure this is a good idea?"

"We have to do something," she said.

He considered for a moment, then nodded.

"What's the best way out of here?"

Morris took a long, deep breath and looked at her with pained eyes. "I'm sorry, Ms. Rice. I truly am, but I'm afraid that we can't do this."

"Escape?"

He nodded.

"Why?"

"Because," he said, almost apologetically, "this is my operation."

Her mind raced. "What?"

"I'm the one who saw the coming attack in Washington DC, and I'm the one who contacted Blake to stop it."

"But you were kidnapped!"

He nodded. "For the sake of appearance I created the illusion of my abduction."

"To shift blame?"

"Until I was certain that I could gain the kind of support I needed."

"Overseer?"

"Yes," he said with a paternal nod. "I needed something to shock the Firstborn into action—to get them to unite under one leader. That was the only way to fight the evils of this world."

She stepped back. Everything that she was afraid of—everything that Devin Bathurst had feared for her—was coming true.

"You have to understand," he said, his voice grandfatherly and soothing, "I was doing it for the good of America—for the Firstborn."

She shook her head, trying to get him out of her thoughts.

"I'm a patriot," he said. "Do you know what people like that terrorist want to do to America?"

She couldn't believe what she was hearing.

Morris spoke softly, approaching her. "I had a friend in the World Trade Center. His name was Neil. We went to college together—we even went to Vietnam together. He was in a different place than I was, but we still kept in touch. Then one morning I woke up to hear what those murderers had done."

It all sounded so similar to what she'd heard from Tariq. Another sob story—another holy crusade to destroy a faceless enemy.

"I can't let you do this," she said, shaking her head.

He put a hand on her arm. "What could you possibly do to stop me?"

She looked him in the eyes—then shoved him. He wasn't expecting it. The older man stumbled back, hitting the dirt.

Hannah ran out the tent entrance, past a guard. "Stop!" he shouted, grabbing her wrist. As if by instinct she swung out with her arm, her elbow connected with his eye, and the man went back, letting go of her wrist.

She melted into the night, ducking between the SUVs that were parked outside, then pressing forward, fleeing from the site. Hannah stole a glance back—the guard was slow, weighed down by heavy gear.

Car doors slammed behind her as soldiers climbed into idling vehicles, engines roaring. The road was ahead. Lights ignited, and the

SUVs raced in. She threw her body into a run, arms pumping, legs burning as she sprinted forward.

The SUVs gained, careening past. One came to a skidding stop, peeling out in front of her. She looked back—soldiers in pursuit.

Surrounded. Cut off. Trapped.

She reached for her phone, dialing frantically as they climbed out of the hulking vehicles.

"Yes?" Devin answered, obviously shaken.

"It's Morris Childs," she shouted into the phone, soldiers reaching for her. "He's behind everything. Blake is working for him."

"Morris?"

"Yes, he's—"

A militiaman grabbed at the phone, ripping it from her hand, throwing her to the ground.

"What?" Devin's voice squeaked from the phone's speaker five feet away. "What's happening? Where are you?"

A soldier's heavy boot came down hard on the phone, and it went silent.

"What are they doing?" Blake asked, looking through a set of binoculars. Devin and his people were climbing into their vehicles, as if they were about to leave.

A nearby militiaman snapped a phone shut and turned to Blake.

"That was Morris. The girl knows. I don't know how, but she knows."

Blake turned his attention to the exiting force. "Stop them."

Devin was reaching for the door handle of the silver sedan when the rear window exploded.

Muzzle flashes erupted from behind the headlights—a dozen or so guns. There were sudden blotches of light that called out intermittently across the field, heralded by the distant bark of gunfire.

"Fall back!" he shouted at the top of his lungs. "Everybody get out of here!"

Chunks of grass and dirt burst from the ground, weapons fire snapping past in a violent torrent of rushing air.

Devin hit the ground, nestled his assault rifle against his shoulder, snapped the safety off, and opened fire.

Single-round burst. The bullets hammered through the air in sharp concussion. The headlights, he thought. Shoot out the headlights—it was their one big advantage. Five rounds in rapid succession and a headlight burst.

The ground in front of him began to boil with impacting lead.

A round struck the ground in front of him, not three feet away. The billow of dirt and debris washed over him, chunks of soil cascading into his eyes.

They weren't going to win this fight.

The first of the cars were starting to fall out, driving away. All Devin could do was cover the retreat.

He reached for the selector switch—fully automatic.

The bullets were getting closer.

Devin rolled on his side, away from his former position, the ground festering with bullet strikes. He came to his stomach—peered down the iron sights—and held the trigger.

A string of blustering gunfire clattered from his weapon, ejecting a stream of hot brass. A collection of rounds pounded into the side of the car above him with a chorus of hacking smacks.

He stood, turned toward the vehicle, threw himself over the hood, slid across it, and dropped below on the other side. A bullet cut across the surface of the hood, leaving a scar. Devin threw the door open and twisted the key—the car came to life.

Throwing the vehicle into gear he stomped the gas and began to speed away.

The headlights winked on and Devin fought the vehicle—

Ahead were no less than a dozen Domani Paramilitary and Prima Militia, weapons raised. He gunned the engine and the sedan shot forward, swerving around them.

This was madness.

Bullets pattered against the back of the car, shooting out the remaining chunks of the rear window, as he raced away from the exchange ground—two SUVs following.

He looked in the rearview mirror. The SUVs were coming down on him hard, one nearing his back bumper, headlights stabbing through the empty space where the rear windshield used to be.

Devin slammed the clutch, ripping at the gears. They were in a car chase and there was one rule—whoever makes the first mistake loses. He drew air into his lungs, slowing his heart rate.

The glow of his headlights cut a swath through the darkness, illuminating the dirt road ahead. Whatever was coming, he had to react fast.

The speedometer climbed upward, rising across the horizon of numbers—faster and faster.

Seventy-five miles per hour. On the highway it was normal—on a dirt road it was suicide.

He came over a hill, stabbing the brake with his heel. One solid press to the pedal, then another—quick bursts would slow him but keep him in control as the vehicle plunged down the long, steep slope.

The SUVs came over the hill too fast, one sliding to a stop—nearly going off the road.

The second came up fast. Someone leaned out the window—assault rifle in hand.

Gunfire raked the vehicle, punching through the roof, blasting the passenger seat to chunks of drifting material, hanging in the air like dust. Bits of padding and metal rods were all that remained.

Devin hadn't planned for this.

A solid slam rocked the back bumper of his car.

His mind raced—everything was unraveling—his thoughts couldn't get past the moment. He fought to relax, trying to keep his car on the road.

A second slam—and he drifted to the right, the SUV coming alongside, gunman hanging out the window. Too close—the gunner wouldn't miss.

He slammed on the brakes, and the SUV rocketed forward—racing past, sliding fast across the dirt road.

Devin nosed the car to the right onto another road and gunned the engine, leaving the SUV behind.

The silence was broken only for a moment by the sound of the handgun dropping to the concrete floor.

John stood in the tactical building, silent, Trista next to him.

The sweet, mechanical scent of gun oil, sulfur, and smoke whispered through his nostrils.

Brock lay on the floor in front of them, body laid out, his shoulder blades propped against the wall, head hanging forward—limp—like a hollowed-out melon. The once gray wall was covered in a thick, globular spray of red—blood and brain matter—all in varying shades and consistencies.

Brock's body lay there, not moving.

A man. A civilian. A Christian. A full life cut short.

The body didn't move. Legs splayed, palms up, skin white. John wondered how much the body weighed—a collection of tightly packed flesh and bones and muscles, none of which were capable of assisting in the move—if that was even what needed to be done.

John wanted to say something, but the silence persisted—empty and long.

He felt cold all over, his stomach twisting inside.

Something warm touched his hand—fingers, soft and feminine, interlacing with his own. He turned his head to Trista and looked into her eyes. She stared at him for a moment, then reached out with her spare hand, dabbing at his face with her thumb like his mother used to do. She wiped something away that felt like sweat, then looked at her fingers—

—blood.

John touched his own face, examining his fingertips—examining Brock's blood.

What had they become?

Chapter 20

MOST OF THE FALLEN team made it back to the tactical building before Devin. Nearly thirty minutes after everyone else had arrived Devin entered the planning area, throwing the door open loudly. He moved to the table and seethed.

No one spoke.

His breathing became more infuriated.

"What happened out there?" he demanded after several minutes.

"There were more of them," Carson said with a shrug. "And they had us outflanked. They must have snuck up around us while we were waiting."

"Why? As a precaution?" Devin snarled. "No. It was a trap, and they were there before we were."

The room remained silent.

"They knew we were coming—they had a team in place before we ever got there." Devin took another breath, calming himself. "Casualties?"

"A few minor wounds," Saul said with a nod, "but for the most part everyone seems to be OK. But nearly half are still out in the field."

"Doing what?" Devin asked.

"Maxwell and Danny are pinned down in an abandoned outbuilding about ten miles from here," one of the Fallen, a man named Benson, said from a folding chair near the wall.

Devin nodded. "Someone needs to go pick them up."

"Cory and Michael are already on the way," Benson continued.

"Good. How long until they get there?"

"Five minutes, maybe."

"Good. Let me know when they arrive."

Devin left and turned into the room next door. There he sat alone on the lumpy couch, facing the blank TV. He rubbed his temples, working his thoughts.

Things had gone so wrong. Horribly wrong. This wasn't the way things were meant to be. The Firstborn were supposed to be agents of God on Earth, not warring factions. But Blake had done it; he was Overseer of the Firstborn now—a genuine coup. The Firstborn would never be the same, not with him in power.

Someone had known the location where they would be. Someone knew where Maxwell and Danny were—and that reinforcements were coming. It was possible that Blake and his people had seen it—they were Firstborn, after all, but there was another possibility, one more chilling.

Maybe there was a traitor among them.

And Morris, he thought. Hannah had insisted that Morris was behind it all.

Of course he was. He was the one who had first warned about the attack—he was the one who had organized this whole thing.

—the head of the serpent.

Trista must have suspected something. Maybe that was why she was helping them now. Or maybe she was the traitor.

He considered the possibility for a moment, but it just didn't seem to make sense.

"Devin," John said, standing in the doorway.

"Yes?"

"There's a problem."

He followed John back to the planning area, where a speakerphone sat in the middle of the table. All the Fallen gathered around.

"We got to the outbuilding," a voice crackled over the phone through an exceptionally weak signal. "Maxwell and Danny were dead. It was a trap. They knew we were coming. There was a firefight—I'm pretty hurt, and Michael is missing."

"Slow down," Devin said in the calm voice he had. "Can you get back to the compound?"

"I think I'm being followed. I don't want to lead them back to—"

The sentence was cut short—blistering gunfire pattering across the line, the sounds of tumbling impact reverberated through the speakers—crunching distortion spilling out from the phone at the center of the table.

"Cory?" Devin asked, voice strained.

No reply, only gunfire.

"*Cory!*"

Then the shooting stopped and the line went dead.

No one spoke. Awkward silence hung like a veil.

A grating dial tone rose from the phone, reverberating throughout the room. Everyone stared at the squawking receiver as if something would magically change.

Saul reached out, turning off the phone, and the room went completely silent. No one spoke for the better part of a minute. Devin was the first to speak, and only one word came out of his mouth: "Morris," he said, face hard.

In a slow cascade every eye in the room lifted, looking at Devin.

He looked back, studying their faces. He was about to make a statement that would change his life, one that would undo everything that had defined him since he had first entered into the world of the Firstborn.

"We have to kill Morris," he said definitively.

No one replied at first.

Saul was first to speak after a few awkward moments. "What will that accomplish?"

"I received a call from Hannah before she was grabbed. This whole scheme, from the very beginning, was Morris's. He was the one who saw the terrorist attack coming; he masterminded the mosque bombing, brought in Blake—and saw to it that he became Overseer."

"And you think that killing Morris will solve everything?"

"Cut off the serpent's head," Devin said with a nod.

"There's still Blake."

"We may have to take care of him eventually, but for now Morris will have to do."

There were nods, some hesitant, others emphatic, but it was the prevailing understanding that Morris was the cause of it all—and had to go. Even Trista Brightling, his own niece, was nodding her head.

Saul nodded, then looked at Devin. "Let's get to work on a plan."

John watched her. Maybe it was habit or compulsion. Maybe there was something dysfunctional about him.

Trista stood, nodding as they considered all of the possible places that Morris could be—the properties where he was most likely to be, the protection he was likely to have, all of it.

As the discussion slipped into redundancy, he heard her whisper, "I need to get some air," to someone nearby, and then slip out of the room. She didn't usually tire of these kinds of meetings the way he did. Was it Brock? How did it feel to her—to know she had killed a man? To know her own uncle was behind all this?

He thought of her, alone outside, wrestling with it all. She needed someone. And that someone was going to have to be him. John moved to the door and stepped out.

He saw her standing less than twenty feet from the tactical building's door.

"Trista," John said softly, "are you OK?"

She turned around, looking back at him through the darkness of night. "I was just getting some fresh air." She sounded flustered.

"Do you need to talk?"

She didn't reply.

John moved closer. "Does it bother you what they're planning to do to your uncle?"

Trista wrapped her arms around herself, hugging her elbows close. She gave a small nod.

"I don't like it either," he said, putting a hand on her shoulder—

—*her shoulder*. He'd forgotten the way it felt, the electricity that coursed through his tendons when he touched her there.

She put a hand on his, gently pushing off his touch as she rolled her shoulder away.

John put his hands in his pockets, trying to pretend that nothing had happened. "Come on," he said with gentle insistence, "they're going to need you inside."

Devin braced himself against the table.

"Here's what I couldn't figure out," Saul whispered musingly, leaning close. "How did Brock get a gun in here? He was checked three times, and yet he still got a weapon past John."

"Don't ask my opinion about John Temple," Devin grumbled.

"So I looked at the gun."

"What about it?"

"It's one of mine from the arsenal."

Devin lifted his eyes, looking at Saul, then scanned the room to see if anyone else had heard. "Why did you wait until now to mention this?"

"Because there are only two possibilities—either we have a complete incompetent—"

"Enter John Temple."

"Knock it off," Saul insisted. "John's more capable than you give him credit for. He made some stupid mistakes, but in the end all he did was embarrass himself—let the politics go."

Devin touched his fingertips to his forehead, "What's the other possibility?"

"That we have a saboteur. A mole. A spy."

"Do you think John—?"

"He may be brash, but he's loyal. That leaves one other person."

Devin looked at Saul, then looked away. He didn't want to consider it. But he had to.

His head swung up as John came through the door, holding it for Trista. The room went silent—all heads turning to stare.

"Where were you?" Devin asked.

"I was getting Trista," John said.

"No," Devin continued, looking past John, "you, Ms. Brightling, where have you been?"

She frowned, slightly defensive. "I had to use the restroom, then I was getting some air. That's all."

"May I see your phone?"

Trista looked startled. "My phone?"

"Did you make any calls?"

Her mouth hung slack. "What are you suggesting?" She looked to John, eyes darting all over his face. "John, help me. You know I was just getting some air."

John looked back at Devin. "She's telling the truth. I was with her."

"The whole time she was out there?"

John's face firmed up. "Yes," he said, "I was with her the whole time she was out there."

"Then you won't mind if I look at her phone, right?"

He frowned. "That's not necessary, really."

"It's just a precaution."

"Devin, I don't think—"

Devin moved toward them fast, reaching for Trista's purse.

"Devin!" John shouted, trying to step in front of Trista. "Listen to me. You have got to trust her."

Devin grabbed John's collar and shoved him into the nearest wall. "I will trust her—once she shows me her phone."

"John," Trista began, voice strained.

"She doesn't have to show you anything."

Devin's nostrils flared, eyes narrowing as he glared long and deep into John, fists pressing hard into John's chest, pinning him in place. Devin's attention turned back to the woman. "Hand your phone to Saul."

"Trista!" John shouted, trying to break loose.

Trista complied, walking toward Saul, handing him her phone. The professor took the device, holding it in one hand, punching buttons with his thumb. "Call history," he announced, examining the tiny glowing screen. "Your last call ended less than five minutes ago—a call to Blake Jackson."

Trista didn't argue; she simply looked down. "I'm sorry," she whispered.

"I count ten calls," Saul continued. "She's been calling him regularly since she got here."

Devin let go of John and turned toward Trista, marching toward her fast.

"Devin, I'm sorry. I was trying to—"

He grabbed her roughly by the wrists. "You're a traitor!" he shouted, shaking her hard. "You've betrayed us all!"

"Stop it!" John shouted, moving to her defense. "Let her go!"

"What did you tell them?" Devin demanded. "What do they know?"

"*Devin!*" John shouted again, putting a hand on Devin's shoulder. Three nearby men grabbed John, arms wrapping around him as they pulled him away.

Devin continued his shaking. "What do they know?" he barked, spit arching from his mouth like venom, his nose nearly touching her own.

"They know everything," she cried. "They knew where you'd be. They knew your positions, how many of you there were. I told them everything."

Devin straightened, voice calm. "I should kill you," he said with an icy indifference. "Where are they operating from?"

"Morris Childs's home, in New York," she stammered, her voice trying to stay calm, "Get out of here!"

"What?"

"Leave. They know about the compound. They know where you are. And they're coming *now.*"

Devin snapped into action. "Move everything we need," Devin ordered, pointing to a nearby collection of firearms. "I want everything out of here in twenty minutes."

Bodies flooded through the room, all trying to find the items they were responsible for. It would only take a few more minutes at this rate, then they would be gone, leaving Saul's compound behind. They'd have to find a new base of operations, but that was manageable—being overrun was not.

Saul Mancuso walked up to Devin, hands in his pockets. "Let me know if there's anything I can do to help."

Devin waved a hand absently. "Just get whatever you need. I'll make sure we have everything else to keep this operation moving."

"I'm not going with you," Saul announced without prelude.

Devin stopped, turning to his old friend. "What?"

"Devin, I'm getting too old for this kind of thing. I'm no use in a fight, and I'll only slow you all down."

"Absolutely not," Devin replied, firm in resolve. "You're coming with us, and that's final."

Saul cleared his throat, putting a hand on Devin's shoulder. "We don't have time to argue about this; do you understand?"

"Professor, I—"

"I'll be in my study. That way, when they ask me which way you all went, or what I saw, I won't be able to tell them—no matter how persuasive they are."

Devin grabbed the older man's arm, squeezing hard as he leaned close, whispering with intensity, "I won't allow this. You are coming with us. I'm not interested in arguing with you."

Saul removed Devin's hand. "You of all people should know the value of distributing misinformation. And you know that no one can do a better job than me."

"Saul," Devin growled, "I'm not going to argue with you about this."

Saul shook his head. "Have you ever been able to change my mind, Mr. Bathurst?"

Devin stared for a moment, nodded in understanding.

"Hurry up," Saul said. "You're wasting time you don't have."

Devin watched as Dr. Saul Mancuso turned around and walked out of the tactical building, knowing it would probably be the last time he ever saw the man.

Carson patrolled along the fence, watching for anything unusual, eyes peering through the darkness. There was a snapping sound in the distance. He crouched slightly, drawing his M4 Carbine to his shoulder, keying the safety with one smooth motion.

Carson took a long deep breath, his aim steadying. His ears strained to hear anything unusual—but only caught the sound of spring peepers in the night air.

He squinted, trying to focus on the world beyond—swells of mist rolling through the bluish light of the moon. His body turned slowly, side to side, like a turret, weapon pointing into the distance. Nothing fell into his slowly swinging sights, at least nothing he could see—probably just his imagination.

He stood, taking a step back—then looked to his left.

Domani Paramilitary—assault shotguns in hand, slipping quietly across the property. One looked up—they'd seen him.

Carson lifted the weapon, selected his first target on instinct, squeezed the trigger—

Devin stood in the tactical building, one hand propped against the table, the other running across the top of his head. He stared at a map, trying to see if there was something he had missed. Members of the Fallen scurried around him, jamming weapons and equipment into bags and boxes.

A sharp sound cut the relative quiet.

Automatic gunfire called out through the night outside—then was silenced with an orchestra of shotgun blasts.

"Everybody get out of here!"

A Domani Paramilitary squad of four moved through the tall wild grass, slick with night dew—one of a half dozen teams.

The squad was one. They were not individuals—they were one coherent whole, sharing thought and motion—their movements a precisely executed maneuver, moving in a tight diamond, bristling with shotguns.

First objective: the main house—a reasonable place to find the most targets.

They "stacked," lining up to the left of the door. The leader moved up close to the hinges—waiting—the other three packing in tightly behind, each man pressing his kneecap tightly into the cleft of the knee in front of him. Shoulders pressed together, weapons down—like a tightly coiled spring waiting to burst.

The leader tried the knob, checking it softly—locked. He signaled silently.

The third man in the stack fell out, moving in front of the door, ejecting one of his shells, replacing it with buckshot. He lifted the SPAS twelve-gauge, muzzle hovering near the wooden door just between the knob and the frame—right over the lock itself.

He waited a moment—

The stack leader jammed his knee back into the man behind him, who did the same in turn. The jerk of the knee went snapping through the stack like a shock wave—

The shotgun blast slammed into the wood, splintering a chunk of door from its place—the door hanging slack on its hinges.

The knee jerk was instantaneous—the final man in the stack replying with a return snap. A whiplash of energy rushed to the front as the spring of men burst forward—the last man ramming ahead—sending the stack crashing through the door like a bulldozer.

The breaching man was last in, weapon raised high and to the rear, looking overhead in case of an elevated position.

To the right of the team a hostile moved down a staircase—he saw them, screamed an alarm. His voice was drowned out by a shotgun blast. He hit the wall, then lay on the landing—moaning in agony, clutching his side. One of the team moved in to subdue.

"Clear," a team member shouted.

Down the hall, around the corner, and into the kitchen—two men caught off guard. A chorus of shotgun blasts sent the first sprawling into the refrigerator, the door swinging open, spilling its loose contents.

The second hostile went for his gun. The first slug hit him in the chest—ramming into the man's armored vest. A round took him in the arm and he howled, grabbing at the stinging appendage. The leader of the breaching team approached—bringing down the butt of his SPAS on the man's neck—the folding stock ramming hard.

The man dropped.

"Clear," the leader declared.

Professor Saul Mancuso sat in his study, flipping through the pages of an ancient text. He heard the barking of weapons throughout the house—they would come for him soon.

His eyes scanned the page, then stopped.

Outside the door in the hall beyond he heard a floorboard creak—he'd been meaning to fix it for fifteen years now. He knew its sound intimately.

They were in the hall.

He set the text back in its folder and stood, placing his hands behind his head. He would go quietly.

The door exploded inward—soldiers spilling in.

He went to open his mouth—

But was silenced by shotguns staring him in the face.

John Temple threw himself to the floor of the tactical building, the sounds of battle singing all around outside in a treacherous opera of weapons fire.

"The lights!" Devin—the only other person in the room—shouted, pointing.

John's mind crashed—what was going on? The shock of it all sent him into a tailspin as the world crumbled around him.

"The lights!" Devin screamed again, his finger pointing to the switch near the door.

John ran for the door, the heel of his hand coming down on the switch, plunging the room into darkness—the world outside the window blazing bright in the moonlight by comparison. Motion outside the window caught his eye—a group of four militiamen moved toward the building, weapons ready, extinguished flashlights fixed to the fore end of the shotguns.

He reached for the doorknob, twisting the lock. Maybe that would hold them a minute longer. He rushed back to Devin. "What do we do?" he demanded in panic.

"What did you see?"

"Soldiers—four of them."

They looked back out the window, flashlights coming on outside—light crisscrossing through the barred windows.

John felt Devin's hand clutch his arm. "Come on."

Trista Brightling looked over at the other prisoner—Tariq. They'd thrown her in the cell with him when they'd discovered she was a traitor. He wasn't threatening. He simply sat quietly in the corner looking sad.

Outside she heard the guns.

They were coming for her.

But maybe they wouldn't be able to get to her in time—maybe John would show up and take her hostage. She'd have no choice but to stay a prisoner. It was an unspeakable option—but she couldn't stop thinking about it.

The door squealed open and Trista stood. Militiamen flooded in, light burning into her eyes.

"Halt!" someone shouted.

"It's me!" she shouted back. "Trista Brightling."

A hand clutched her throat from behind—Tariq.

"Get away!" he screamed, intense and obviously afraid. "Get away from the door!"

"Let her go!" a militiaman shouted. Tariq clutched her tighter.

Trista's self-defense training kicked in—sending an elbow to Tariq's face. She broke away. A volley of blasts crashed into Tariq's body—throwing him back.

He twitched for a moment—then stopped.

"Are you OK?" a militiaman asked.

Trista put a hand to her chest, trying to slow the beating of her heart. She nodded, gathering her thoughts, then knelt in front of Tariq.

A fat bulging bruise was already forming on his forehead, bulbous and purple lined with sickly yellow. She touched his neck.

"He's dead."

Devin listened, intent on the noises overhead. The last of the militiamen left the armory, shutting the door behind—an odd gesture but probably force of habit.

He looked back at John, the man's face flush with anxiety.

They stood in the underground armory a few moments longer, then pushed the overhead hatch up, sending it back with a weighty thud.

Outside there were still smatterings of intermittent gunfire playing out a drama of call and response—like a deadly game of Marco Polo.

Devin moved to the top of the steps and held, looking around to be sure. He stood, moving toward the window—he looked.

Two militiamen not five feet away, backs turned, talking.

Devin dropped, looking back. John was climbing out of the hatch. He motioned John back. This was no time to go taking chances by indulging curiosities.

There had to be a way out. But nothing was coming to mind.

Blake sat in the front passenger seat of the SUV as they approached the compound.

A member of the Ora Strike Force stood at the gate waiting for them to arrive—shoving the chain-link gate out of the way as they approached. The compound was theirs, completely overrun.

A moment later they pulled up to the holding area—about ten hostiles on their knees handcuffed behind the back, heads down. Guards stood around them in a circle making sure they didn't try anything.

They were all alive, shot with rubber bullets—an invention used frequently for crowd control. Rubber slugs would strike a target, knock them down, even incapacitate them, all without killing the target—assuming, of course, that one was not hit in the head. They needed to be taken alive—even if he didn't know how much longer he wanted to keep them that way.

The SUV stopped and Blake climbed out, looking them over. His eyes moved from figure to figure, taking their faces into account. "Where's Bathurst?" he asked after a moment.

One of the Domani Paramilitary scanned the prisoners. "It looks like he's not here."

"Find him," Blake ordered calmly. "Nobody lets their guard down until Devin Bathurst is found. If he's around here, he needs to be found."

A stack of troops began to move out.

"And one more thing," Blake added. "With Devin, shoot to kill."

Chapter 21

JOHN STOOD IN THE corner of the arsenal room. They'd retreated back into it when they realized they were surrounded.

"What next?" John asked, trying to make sense of the situation.

Devin stood beneath the hatch overhead, face turned up, listening intently for the sounds of approaching soldiers.

"Devin?"

He turned to John, throwing him a harsh look, hushing him fiercely. "Quiet."

"What are we going to do?"

"We wait them out, then get away from here."

"And then what?"

Devin looked John over, face sober. "I'm following through with my plans."

John held for a moment, thoughts reaching. "What plans?"

Devin turned back. "I'm going to find Morris Childs."

"And?"

"I'm going to kill him," Devin announced, unapologetic.

The ghostly fluorescent tubes hummed overhead, giving off an occasional ticking sound.

John nodded, trying not to clench his fists. "You really think that will fix everything?"

Devin nodded. "Yes," he said with an eerie calm, "I do."

"But," John began, frustrated, "he's been like a father to you."

"More than a father," Devin announced with a huff. "He's the only person I've got."

"Then why?" John shouted, stepping in toward Devin.

"Because this has to stop," Devin announced, stepping back.

"Not like this it doesn't. Not with more death."

"This is exactly how it needs to end," Devin spat. "You're just too weak to accept that."

"It's not weakness," John blustered, grabbing Devin's shoulders, trying to implore with him. "We're becoming weaker all the time!"

"What are you talking about?"

"Think about it," John beseeched. "When was the last time you had a vision? We've been surrounded by danger for hours. We've been shot at, ambushed, betrayed—and we never saw what was happening, never saw it coming. Think about it, Devin; our gifts aren't getting stronger. They're getting weaker!"

"*Hmm*," Devin uttered, almost sarcastically, "what are you saying? That God has forsaken us?"

"I'm saying we've forsaken each other—which means we have forsaken God."

"I don't believe this—"

"What do you believe?" John demanded, shaking Devin as hard as he could. "Do you honestly believe that fighting the Firstborn will make the world a better place?"

"Morris Childs isn't one of us, not anymore."

John felt his body sag, his mouth open, shoulders heaving with anxiety, eyes darting from one stern feature to another. "Do you hear what you're saying?"

"John, listen to me, you have to—"

"*No*, you listen to *me*! There are terrorists out there, and they're going to kill children. Children, Devin! And you want to murder Morris Childs?" He shook his head in weary sorrow. "There are people out there who want to kill us, people with complaints and legitimate pain, because they think that somehow it will make things better—just like you want to kill Morris Childs."

"We'll fight them when the time comes—"

"When the time comes? What time do you think this is? How can we fight an enemy when we're so busy fighting each other?"

Devin broke away, trying to walk off. "I've heard enough."

"You haven't heard a thing I've said!"

"Keep it down, will you? You're going to bring Blake's people down on us."

John grabbed at Devin's arm. "They're people, Devin."

"Blake's soldiers?"

"Blake's soldiers, the Fallen, everybody!" John's face burned with anger. "Sunnis and Shiites, Christians and Muslims, Domani, Prima, and Ora. We're all people trying to make it in life."

"And some people have to be stopped."

"Fine," John growled, hand squeezing around Devin's bicep.

"What are you doing?"

"I'm stopping you before you do something that can't be undone."

Devin shoved John back, getting ready to strike, then stopped. He lifted a hushing finger.

John paused. "What is it?"

Overhead there was a sound—nothing much, just a simple shock wave as the weight of something came down on the concrete overhead. The sound came again, and again in a slow, predictable rhythm—

Boots, walking across the floor above.

They were back, checking the building.

Devin reached out, killing the lights.

"Devin?" John whispered.

He reached out, grabbing John by the face, a hand clutched over his mouth.

"*Shhh!*" Devin spat.

Silence.

Long, deafening silence.

Then the boots continued, moving toward—

The hatch.

John took a long breath, held it. He didn't even want his lungs to make a sound. Not here, not now.

The boots stopped. Stayed.

A click. A creak. The hatch began to open—

The slam of the door striking concrete thundered through the underground arsenal.

They were trapped like rats. Nowhere to go. No escape to be seen. The darkness was all they had—a thin veil of darkness that wrapped itself around them, blocking them from the prying eyes of the intruding force.

A flashlight snapped on from outside the hatch—the blade of light cutting through the protective blanket of darkness.

John felt naked as his covering was slashed to ribbons by the unwelcome light.

The beam remained static for a moment, granules of dust and chipping paint fluttering downward, defining the contours of the radiant shaft that probed into their hiding place.

Then the light shifted—no longer a static force of nature, but a living thing, clawing into their refuge, its slow travel across the floor cutting deeper and deeper into their haven.

They pushed back, away from the intruding rays as best they could, feet trying to get away from the probing spotlight that crept and slithered across the floor.

John's body wanted to gasp—an involuntary response, like a knee jumping under the tapping of a doctor's hammer. His heart beat fast. His mind raced.

He knew what was happening. His body wanted to survive and was preparing to fight a tiger—but he couldn't.

Adrenaline flooded his system, pupils dilated, heart rate thundered, pumping blood through his pounding heart, oxygenating his muscles. His lungs expanded to draw in more air for his blood—a swelling vacuum that would draw into it whatever oxygen it could—a gasp that would give him away, leading to death or capture.

He drew air in through his nostrils, slow and steady. Not fast enough—his body shuddered as his muscles took over in desperation, dragging air into his lungs.

A warbling, panic-stricken swarm of air filled his chest, warm and refreshing—

The beam stopped.

The soldiers talked among themselves—voices incoherent.

Then the light turned away from the gap above. Only incidental flashes drizzled from overhead.

John heaved a sigh—

Devin's hand grabbed his shoulder, throwing him around the corner of a metal gun rack, slamming John to the floor.

A boot came down on the top step. Then another.

The light returned—not from overhead anymore, but slicing laterally across the landscape of the armory, the blade cutting a swath through the darkness, painting the wall with the mangled outline of the rack's shadow, waving side to side as the beam scanned across the room.

John felt like a turtle stranded on its back, its shell made useless—a predator tearing into his soft, unprotected underbelly.

He turned to look at Devin—

Gone.

He peered through the crisscrossing metal of the rack toward the blistering bead of light that flooded the room, its master veiled by the brightness. The boots continued their descent—another step further down.

Then he saw Devin, creeping up alongside the stairs from the other side, hidden in shadows, directly beneath the flashlight. In his hand Devin held something he hadn't had before, something he must have just picked up here in the armory. What was it?

—a combat knife, wide and long with jagged teeth for serrations along the back.

Devin was about to kill…*one of his own.*

"Hey," a voice shouted loudly from above, "everything's been checked twice. We're packing everybody up and getting out of here, so hurry up."

"OK," the flashlight man replied, "just a second."

"Is there anything down there? Because we need to go."

A momentary pause.

"No," the flashlight man announced, then flicked off the light, plunging the room back into its warm cloak of black. "There's nothing down here." The boots moved up the stairs, and a moment later the hatch came slamming back down.

A moment of silence. Total darkness. Then a loud *click* from across the room. A single yellow bulb, encased in a round plastic cage, came on. A backup light that hung in the corner. Dimmer than the overhead fluorescents, but better for staying hidden.

John watched as Devin walked from his place near the power strip where he'd turned on the lights and approached a metal cabinet, opening it and removing something that captured his full attention.

"What is that?" John asked.

Devin glanced up. "HK Mark 23 pistol." He twisted a thick black cylinder into the muzzle of the weapon. "And this is a homemade silencer. Illegal, like most of the collection down here, but effective." Then he began to walk toward the steps.

John stood, marching after Devin. He got close, grabbing at a shoulder.

"Wait a minute." No response. "Bathurst, wait!"

Devin spun into John's right hook—fist striking hard. He came back again fast, face confused—then angry.

John felt a hand grab him, trying to throw him away. He held on—if he was going down, Devin was going with him—the concrete's surface slamming into him.

The world exploded with lights and globs of color as the pain whipped through his body. John shoved upward, pushing away from the floor. Devin came at him from the right.

A hand grabbed the back of his neck—

John unleashed the full fury of his body into Devin's side, but his opponent sidestepped, shoving him down by the scruff of his neck.

A sharp-toed shoe hit the back of John's knee, and as he went down he felt a hand, like a blade, slam hard into his side.

John lay on the floor for a moment, staring upward through blurry eyes.

He choked. Hacked. Coughed. Then felt his aching chest heave and fall as his body clawed for air.

"Are you finished?" Devin demanded.

John looked up at Devin, looming like a tower. He reached out, grabbing at the other man's ankle. "Devin," he moaned, hacking painfully, "what are you doing?"

"This needs to be done," Devin replied, voice lowering as he started to walk away. "I'm sorry. It's not what any of us want—but it's what we all need."

John's body collapsed, rolling onto his back. "Need," he said to himself. "It took me a long time to realize it, but the world needs people like you, Devin Bathurst." Devin stopped. "We need people who see the world in black and white, who know what needs to be done in order to deal with the problem at hand. People who see a solution...and can execute it with resolve, even when it's not pretty."

"Especially when it's not pretty."

"That's right. The world needs people who can do the terrible, unspeakable things," John said from his back, studying the contours of the ceiling overhead, "but not today." His eyes lazed over the imperfections, eyes moving over each and every bump that swelled and retreated from the level plane of the cement above. "Today," he said slowly, "the world needs us to forgive—because if we can't forgive each other, then how can we ever love each other?"

Devin remained silent, holding at the steps.

"And if we can't love the people who are supposed to be our friends, then how can we ever love anybody else? If we can't love the world, then what right do we have to save it?" John swallowed hard, still recovering from his ordeal. "And if we can't love the world, then how can we ever love our enemies? And if we can't love them, then what did Christ die for?"

John rolled to his side, rising to his knees. He looked Devin over. "If we aren't doing this out of love, then why are we doing any of this at all?"

He kept his eyes on Devin, looking into his profile set against the distant glow of the dim light. "You know what the right thing to do is."

Devin remained silent for a moment, cold and unmoving. "There are things that need to be done."

Then Devin turned away and disappeared up the steps.

John knelt on the cement, staring at the dark, cold floor. His body ached. His joints whined. His brain, overwhelmed, seemed to shut down. He stayed there, kneeling, staring at the floor. How long, he couldn't say, but it felt like hours.

Suddenly he moved, placing his clenched fists behind his head, face turning to the ceiling.

He took a moment and let his feelings slip away. John was a man of feelings, and the world needed people like him—but right now the world needed him to think in straight lines, from the problem to the solution and back again.

"God," he said as unassumingly as he knew how, "I've made mistakes. We've all made horrible mistakes." He breathed a lungful of dewy night air. "I feel my guilt—but I need You more than I need my guilt. Take it away from me." He began to seethe, the passion of his prayer welling up inside. "Take every inexcusable thing and rip it to shreds—I don't want it; I want You!" His fists began to beat his chest. "The world doesn't need me, God. Not really. The world needs You. I need You, and tonight I need You more than ever."

His hands fell gently at his sides, knuckles brushing the rough concrete.

"Give me what I need so that I can do Your will."

Then he felt it—a stabbing in his side—

A man in an abandoned building. Weapons. Explosives. Prayer. Preparing for his attack—in the morning—

John's eyes snapped open.

"Thank You."

John stood, moving from his place on the floor. He felt rejuvenated now, body loose. He moved up the steps and looked around in the darkened tactical building. All quiet.

On the wall there was a panel of keys, hanging from hooks—one set missing. Devin must have taken one of the cars already.

He stepped out of the building, set of keys in hand, moving with purpose toward the row of parked vehicles, punching the keyless entry as he walked until a set of headlights winked on. He moved toward the car—a broken headlight cover, but the bulb wasn't broken and there were no bullet holes. It wouldn't attract too much attention.

Three minutes later he was headed toward the highway—to Washington DC.

Chapter 22

THE DRIVE WAS LONG, even longer with the blindfold on. Her captors insisted that the drive was only four hours, but it felt like an eternity.

Hannah had been led from the SUV by the arm, taken into a house, up a flight of steps, and shoved into a room.

They hadn't tied her up, so removing the blindfold itself was easy. She looked around. A guest bedroom—red walls, green sheets. The place had a rustic quality to it. She tried the doorknob—locked. She continued scanning the room.

At the far end of the room she saw a window and the dark world beyond.

She held for a moment, listening for the sounds of approaching footsteps, wondering if they could hear her movements.

A step toward the window—a string of chatter came to life just beyond the door. She stopped, waiting for the sounds to pass, then took another step forward.

A creaking floorboard.

She lifted her foot, and the board relaxed back into place with a long squeaking whine. A grimace crossed her face.

Another step—almost at the window. Then she was there. She looked down.

Down below, three armed guards stood in a loose circle, talking with one another. One held a large Rottweiler on a leash. The big dog looked up at her, its green eyes flashing in the light of the window. An alarming roar broke the night air as the creature barked through jagged teeth set within its frothing mouth.

The guards looked up—one shining a flashlight.

Hannah backed away from the window, nearly falling over—the floorboards protesting under her heels.

She sat on the bed and thought.

She'd been detained before—in the snowy countryside, in the city, and now here, wherever here was. The first time it had been horrifying—kidnapped for no apparent reason—but the next time she'd been detained by an angry young man she felt sympathy for. Each time she grew stronger—slightly more so than the time before. Now she felt defiance bubbling up inside her.

This was what Devin had warned her about—the way she was becoming comfortable with atrocity inflicted upon her.

Someone worked a key in the lock.

Hannah looked around for whatever she could find, anything hard enough to knock a man flat—a telephone, a drawer, or a chair. Her eyes fell on a lamp and she lunged for it, reaching for the cord in the wall. Unplugging it would plunge the room into darkness—she'd use that to her advantage.

She was in this world now.

"Hello, Ms. Rice," Morris said as he snapped on the overhead light.

Too slow. She held.

"Mr. Childs?"

"Yes," Morris said. She could feel him approaching from behind. The door was closed behind him and locked with the clicking of a key from the hall.

Morris placed a hand on her shoulder. "How do you feel? Have you been mistreated?"

She felt his hand, warm and endearing—like her grandfather. Then her thoughts returned to who he was and what he'd done. She shrugged his hand away, turning to face him as she stood.

Hannah looked deep into the older man's eyes, glaring. She said nothing.

Morris looked her over for the moment, features softening as a realization came to him—her glare breaking through his exterior.

"I'm sorry about all of this," he said with a nod. "I'm trying to justify my actions—there are simply things I must do."

Her mind swam—here she stood in the presence of the man who had cut into her life, thrust her into this dark world of hatred and mistrust, and she couldn't think of anything to say. A string of insults and fury came to mind, but all at the level of a third grader.

"Why'd you do it?" she asked, wondering where the words had come from.

"Do what?"

Her thoughts worked. It was an unexpected question, even for her. She wanted to know what she meant too. "Why did you do all of this?" she asked, looking him over. "Why did you tear the Firstborn apart?"

His features sank. "I'm trying to save the Firstborn," he replied, looking somber and misunderstood. He nodded to himself as he looked at the floor and then lifted his face to her. "Are you familiar with Alessandro D'Angelo?"

"The monk who brought the Firstborn together," she said with a nod.

"Are you familiar with his prophecies?"

"Like Thresher?"

"Yes," he said with a warm nod, voice low and sagelike. Morris looked her over, examining her reaction, trying to determine something— but what?

"Come with me," he said, and motioned her to the door.

A moment later they were moving through the big house, the halls littered with soldiers. Morris waved a hand in an understated gesture. "This is my home. My wife isn't here at the moment—I sent her to stay with our eldest daughter until all of this is resolved."

He led her to a door on the ground floor and turned the knob. She looked down into the basement below—dark and foreboding.

"What's down there?"

"Come with me," he said tenderly, reaching out with a hand. "I'll show you."

They descended the stairs, Hannah going first. "This is the old wine cellar," he said as the cool air permeated her body, licking at her flesh. "Wine hasn't been kept down here in years, but it still serves a very important purpose."

Morris reached out, flipping a switch. A solitary light bulb snapped on, dangling from a low-hanging wire over an old wooden table. "Have a seat." He waved at an empty chair and Hannah took it.

She watched from the table as Morris walked to a large safe in the corner of the room, twisting the knob with a clattering twirl. Three spins then he stopped, reaching for the heavy metal handle, pushing it down.

A solid metallic slam reverberated through the entirety of the basement as the mechanism drew the thick bar out of place. The door yawned open—the safe filled with darkness.

She watched as Morris reached his hand into the shadows and removed something—a file.

He returned to the table and sat at the corner adjacent to Hannah. She examined the file as he carefully opened it. Inside was a folded piece of parchment, brown and faded from the years.

Morris's face seemed to light up as he looked at the scrap. "Six hundred years old," he said. "We wanted to keep it in a plastic bag, but the chemical composition of plastic will eat through a document this old."

"What is it?"

He smiled. "This is one of the prophesies of D'Angelo, written on this very parchment six hundred years ago—telling us of ourselves right now."

Her eyes wandered over it. Six hundred years old—a piece of history.

"Here," he said, reaching for her hand, taking it gently, "touch it." Morris placed her hand on the parchment.

Real people had written on this—people with hopes and dreams and families had scrawled out the letters and drawn the ornate embellishments that covered its surface. Someone else's hands had touched this, and now she was touching it also. She was reaching out to the past—and the past was reaching back. Her mouth spread into a smile.

"You feel it, don't you?"

She nodded.

"The power of prophecy—you're reaching out to the future and the future is reaching back."

"What does it say?"

He took the folder and removed a photocopy of the parchment and another sheet. "This is a copy of the original text in Italian, and this is an English translation." He cleared his throat and read, "'When the little children are threatened with Saracen hands in the capital of the world's greatest nation, the Firstborn will face Thresher from within. Those who follow Thresher will destroy the Firstborn as agents of evil, but those who stand firm in the truth, completely destroying evil, will see God.'"

She nodded. "Who are you following?"

"I'm here to see evil destroyed. Not allowed to thrive."

Hannah shook her head. "But Devin...?"

"Devin was never meant to get involved. But he captured an agent of evil...and allowed him to live. He harbored and protected that which should have been destroyed without hesitation."

"But," she stammered, "Tariq? A person? Destroyed? How is that doing good?"

"I understand your dilemma," Morris agreed, paternally, "but he wanted to kill children. Specifically targeting innocents. How is that not evil?"

Hannah considered for a moment. "But you and Blake wanted to kill innocent people at that mosque too. How is that not evil?"

Morris leaned close, "Evil has thrived because it has been *allowed* to. Someone must stand up and do what must be done. And D'Angelo predicted it all—that those who allowed evil to thrive would be destroyed. The compound has been raided, and everyone who tried to stop this important action have been captured. Who do you think is being blessed by God?"

Hannah's body relaxed, fingertips gliding along the edge of the parchment. She breathed in the cool, damp air of the cellar. "It's all happening," she muttered. "It's all happening right now."

"Yes," he said. "Everything D'Angelo said would happen is coming true."

"Have his other prophecies come true?"

"Yes," he said, "all of them."

She sat quietly.

"That's why I had to do what I did," Morris implored. "The truth of the Firstborn is to honor God on Earth—to protect the innocent and the weak. I had to stand fast in that truth or Thresher would have overtaken us all—destroying the Firstborn. That's why we have to destroy the evil—completely."

"That's why you want to kill Tariq?"

"That's why it must be done. If the evil is allowed to flourish, then—" He stopped and looked away. Then he turned his eyes on her, challenging. "Have you ever tried honing your ability?" he asked.

Hannah shook her head. "I don't think I understand."

"Did your grandfather ever teach you how to use your ability as a Firstborn?"

"Is that possible?"

Morris leaned in toward her. "Do you know why I became the leader of the Domani?"

"No."

"Because I became the most powerful of the forward-seers."

"But how?"

He leaned closer still, his voice a whisper. "Because I could see."

"See what? I'm confused."

"You know where our gift comes from, right?"

"God."

"Yes. He shows us what needs to be seen so that His will can be done on Earth. We see the world outside of time."

"Outside of time?"

"Yes," he said with a nod, "time is a container that holds humanity, not unlike a fleshly body. It's a vehicle that carries us forward. But when we are needed, God shows us the world outside of the confines of space and time."

Hannah nodded, trying to understand.

"You see, when we don't see clearly enough, there's only one recourse as a member of the Firstborn—to ask God for more."

"And He shows us more."

Morris shook his head. "Not always. Sometimes He remains silent."

"Why?" she asked, certain her brow was furrowing.

"So that we will reach out."

"To what?"

Morris looked her over, considering for a moment. "Close your eyes."

She looked him over for a moment, then complied. Her eyes drifted shut, darkness overtaking her.

A world of black.

"Now think of something from your past," Morris said, his voice coming from some disconnected place, the tones humming off the cellar walls.

Her mind searched for something to dwell on—her grandfather. She saw his face, gray and warm. He smiled at her.

"Now reach out," Morris said.

"What?" Hannah said, eyelids lifting.

"Keep your eyes closed. Reach out…with your soul."

"How?" she asked, totally uncertain.

"Do you know what eternity is?"

"I guess so."

"It's the world free of time. Touch eternity."

Her thoughts went dark. "I don't know what you're talking about."

She felt a hand touch hers. "Listen to what I say. Your body takes up only a fraction of this room. One room in one house on one continent. Seven billion people live on this tiny planet—one planet in an entire solar system. One star in millions that make up a galaxy. One galaxy in thousands—all in an endless expanse of space that goes on and on without fathomable measure. And it's all simply a fraction of eternity."

Hannah's heart rate picked up as she considered how small she really was.

"It's all the work of an eternal God," he said softly. "He's reaching out to you—simply…reach back."

She felt her body shudder, her thoughts numb. Hannah's mind flooded with thoughts of her grandfather.

Thoughts from her childhood.

Her adolescence.

His home.

His words.

His murder.

Hannah felt herself trying to claw away from the thoughts in her mind—but some other part of her was still reaching out.

Blake and her grandfather.

Anger.

Shouting.

Shoving.

Tumbling. Down. Down. Down.

Blake seething, panicking.

Then she saw something else—something that confused her, unsettled her—a sensation of sickness coming over her.

A figure—not a man, something else.

Like a man but drenched in shadow.

Blake did not acknowledge the form.

It simply whispered in Blake's ear—compelling him to—

Something.

Hannah's thoughts broke and she looked up at Morris.

"You saw something," he said with a nod.

"Yes," she replied.

"Reach out," he said again, "and He'll reach back."

Chapter 23

T WAS NEARLY DAWN.

A soft glow was just starting to creep over the horizon, the darkness becoming more penetrable.

Devin Bathurst rubbed his eyes. He was wide-awake, but his eyes itched. He imagined the stressed blood vessels that crisscrossed over the surface of his eyes bulging with the strain of overwork, their outer walls pressing against the interior of his eyelids, teasing the soft flesh. It felt like sand.

He was almost there.

He'd driven the rest of the night, from Pennsylvania to upstate New York.

Morris Childs's house was less than ten minutes away. He needed to get there before dawn—his operation would go more smoothly under the cover of darkness. Devin glanced at the green glowing numbers on the dashboard clock. Just after 4:00 a.m. He had a few more hours of darkness—he hoped.

By the time he glanced at the clock again, his ten minutes had passed, and he could see the familiar turns leading up to Morris Childs's house. He parked the car along the side of the road and walked toward the edge of the outside fence.

The house was big, nearly four thousand square feet, a luxury Morris had afforded himself after years of successful business practice.

Devin stood at the outside edge of the house, looking through the fence. There were probably half a dozen guards patrolling around outside. It was like a movie. But Devin knew the odds better than that. One did not simply march into a place like this when he wasn't welcome.

If this were a film, he'd have snuck up behind a patrolling guard, dealt a swift karate chop to the back of the neck, dropped the man like a sack of potatoes, taken the man's uniform, and slipped in.

But this was real life.

If you try to sneak up on a guard and he spots you, there is no second chance. He radios for help, and where there had been one, there would now be five—and in real life people don't shoot for dramatic effect. Every bullet is meant to kill.

This was stupid, he thought. A ridiculous thought that wouldn't work. It was hopeless to think that he'd get in. But the future of the Firstborn was at stake. He had to end Overseer—

—and that meant dealing with Morris Childs.

There was only one thing left that Devin knew to do.

Devin draped his black sport coat over a branch and rolled up his sleeves. He dropped to his knees in the soggy dirt, back straight, hands clasped—the way his grandmother had taught him to pray. His breath came in and went out, his body relaxing, joints easing.

"Our Father, who art in heaven, hallowed be thy name."

It wasn't a complicated prayer, the simplest of all—and the most routine of any ever learned, and yet it meant the world.

"Thy kingdom come, thy will be done, on earth as it is in heaven. Give us this day our daily bread, and forgive us our trespasses..."

Devin's voiced stopped. He was beseeching God to help him break into another man's property—to trespass literally.

"As we forgive those who trespass against us..."

He thought of John's words.

His lips stopped, unable to continue.

"Hey," a voice announced, a flood of light washing suddenly across the landscape from behind, "what are you doing here?"

Devin lifted his hands slowly, a sign of surrender. He lifted his body up to his feet and turned around, staring into the flashlight. "My name is Devin Alexander Bathurst. I'm here to see Morris Childs."

"Bathurst?" the guard said. "Somebody said you were dead."

"No."

The flashlight flicked off and the guard approached. "I'm Shawn," he announced, thrusting out a hand.

Devin looked down, confused, then shook the hand. "Are you a member of the Domani?"

"Prima, but Henry Rice told me what you did for his granddaughter. That was pretty gutsy."

Devin nodded. "Thank you."

Shawn scratched the back of his head, adjusting the SPAS twelve-gauge slung across his chest. "Look, if Blake knew you were alive, he'd see to it that it was temporary. I'm supposed to shoot you on sight if I see you, but I don't want to. I know who you are and what you've done. I've always respected you. So, just make it easy on both of us and get lost for a little while, OK?" Shawn grimaced. "Put your head down. Find someplace to hide for a couple of weeks. This whole thing will have blown over by then, right?"

"No," Devin replied flatly.

Shawn shook his head. "I'm not saying I agree with them, but they really will kill you if they catch you."

"Then I guess I'll have to deal with that."

Shawn balked. "What are you doing here, anyway?"

"As I said, I'm here to see Morris Childs."

The guard shook his head. "That's not a good idea. These people want you dead."

"Do you?"

A scoff. "No, I don't want you dead, but Blake's Overseer now. We do what he says."

"Why?"

"Authority placed on Earth by God. We don't question that."

Devin was silent for a moment, speechless. Could this man really think that it was the will of God to simply do what he was told—to ignore the tiny voice inside of him that made him think that maybe this was a bad idea?

After a moment he spoke. "You really won't question Blake, will you?"

"Nobody likes a naysayer."

Devin shook his head as he considered the words he was to say. "The world needs people who are different from us, who disagree with us. We have to consider that they may be right."

Shawn blinked. "Why?"

"Because it keeps us humble. It's not comfortable, but holiness and comfort don't live in the same place."

Shawn took a moment to digest this new information, then opened his mouth to speak. "Look, as far as I'm concerned, I never saw you. If you leave now, then nobody ever has to know you were here. OK?"

"Groupthink," Devin said with a scoff.

"What?"

"Groupthink is when people stop challenging the way things are being done. It becomes easier to go along and get along than to stand up and consider if any of this should actually be done."

Shawn looked thoughtful. "What about the leaders? They take a stand, don't they?"

"Oh, sure. They make up their minds and punish those who disagree. Soon all of the discontents scatter or shut their mouths. The system thinks that it's impervious—that it cannot fail. Underlings lie to their superiors, telling them that nothing is wrong, that everything is under control, and the system continues without regard for the chinks in its own armor—until the day something goes wrong."

"And then?"

"Pride comes before a fall."

Crickets chirped through the night air. Neither spoke for several moments.

Devin spoke, "I need your help."

Shawn ambled across the lawn, looking back at the trees as he moved. His eyes shifted forward again, toward the other guard. Domani Paramilitary. He didn't know the man—most of them didn't know each other. Most were still reeling from the thought that they were now expected to start trusting one another—or at least trust that Overseer knew what he was doing when he threw them all together. The man was patrolling near the side of the house, looking bored.

"Hey," Shawn announced loudly across the grass, drawing the other guard's attention.

The other man raised a gloved finger to his lips, exasperation covering his face. "Quiet," he hushed back. "There are people sleeping."

"Sorry."

"It's OK," the guard replied, rubbing at his drooping eyelids. "What do you need?"

"There's something I think you should take a look at."

The Domani man looked around. "Can it wait?"

"Just come with me."

The guard opened his mouth to protest, then shrugged. "All right."

Shawn led the guard toward the trees...away from the house.

Devin watched as Shawn led the guard away from his position, leaving the entire side of the house unpatrolled for a moment.

He'd been studying the movements of the guards. They weren't precise, or clockwork of any kind, but they were regular. It would be only a few minutes before the next guard came around the corner.

A brief window of opportunity.

Shawn and the guard were out of sight.

He moved. His black shoes nearly slipped as he moved his way across the wet grass. The house was getting closer by the moment, the structure looming over him. He stopped, dropping to a knee, cringing at the thought of yet another grass stain on his dress pants. Devin dropped to his chest and looked around—no guard yet.

His attention snapped to the left—perched on the wall, maybe twelve inches from the roof, was a set of floodlights, big, bulging, and domed. Like bug eyes, staring down at him.

They were connected to a motion sensor. Step into the field, and the entire side of the house would erupt with a splash of light. Devin had been to the house enough times to remember the light and how bright it got when the children ran underneath it at parties. It would draw the attention of more than one guard, and there he'd be—naked, vulnerable, and unwelcome.

He checked his watch, noting the time. He had to move fast—but not so fast that he would trigger the motion sensor.

Sensors like these were tricky. He'd experimented with them when he was younger, trying to figure out what their tolerances were. A cat running by was more than enough to trigger the light, but grass swaying in the breeze was not. Motion could pass through the field—if it was slow enough.

Devin began to tip onto his side, rolling slowly, body parallel to the side of the house. He made it from his chest to his back.

No light.

He completed the roll, body controlled as he inched from his back to his chest. Devin checked his watch. Not much time.

Slowly. Pedantically. Painstakingly. He continued moving toward the house.

He inched forward with each turn, holding his breath, hoping he wasn't moving too quickly. There was a cracking sound—

He stopped. It was the kind of sound the light made as the circuit completed, snapping to life.

He waited.

No light.

Devin swiveled his head, examining the area. He was getting closer now—soon he'd be under the arc of the motion sensor—close enough to disregard the speed of his movements.

The sound came again. He held, waiting.

Nothing.

The sound repeated again. The thoughts coalesced in his mind. The sound wasn't coming from the wall of the house—it was bouncing off the wall, distorting his perceptions. It was coming from the trees—the sound of crunching branches. Shawn and his temporarily distracted guard were returning.

He had to hurry.

Devin rolled to his stomach, face in the grass, and began to crawl as fast as he could—body tense and controlled, trying not to move too quickly—but trying not to get caught. His fingers dug into the wet blades and dirt, dragging himself forward in tight precision. Sweat trickled down his face, mixed with dark soil.

The crunching foliage grew louder. Maybe Shawn was stomping to warn him.

The conversation floated across the lawn. The distracted guard sounded upset by the interruption to his work as he moved back to his patrol.

Hand over agonizingly slow hand—Devin shimmied across the turf.

The voices erupted from the trees, close now. Soon they would see him.

Out of time.

He rolled again, fast, body tumbling across the sod. Devin surged, throwing his weight forward toward what he saw just ahead—

The light flashed on.

Shawn threw his attention to the left.

The light.

The game was up. There was no more cover of darkness to—

"What was that?" the other guard asked.

"I ..." Shawn began, trying to think of something fast to explain the situation.

The guard shrugged. "Must have been a cat."

Shawn paused. "What?" He looked to the wall. There was no one there. "Yeah," he mused, "a cat or...something."

Devin listened as the sounds of rustling Kevlar moved away. He held fast in the window well for a moment in the same position that he'd landed in—his silenced HK pistol digging into the small of his back.

Through the window he could see Morris's workout room. He checked the edges of the window—no alarm.

Devin began to work.

That alarm clock rings like a resounding trumpet or clanging brass, Morris Childs thought as his arthritic hand reached for the squawking machine and slapped down on the button.

The table lamp came on with a click, warming his quiet corner of the room with dim light. He groaned, body weak and tired.

He'd spent too much time inside these last few days as the Firstborn changed and grew around him. His feet touched the cold hardwood floor, and he winced in his lethargy, feet probing for his slippers. A foot found the closest of the two and slipped into the woolen glove. Morris reached down, his slick, silk pajamas swishing past their interweaving folds. A hand found the other slipper, and he tucked his foot into it. His hand reached onto the bedside table, fishing blindly through his nearsightedness, then his fingertips touched what they were searching for.

Morris donned his glasses, eyes acclimating to the warm burn of the lamp's yellow glow. Then he stood, slowly. He groaned, a hand touching his lower back. His knees felt like blocks of wood being dragged across pavement as they worked to straighten.

The older gentleman walked to the bathroom at the other end of the room. He moaned as he carried his creaking body the short distance, shutting the door behind.

He'd been young once—invincible. Flying jets in Vietnam had made him cocky—it was a stereotype that pilots were cocky, but he'd learned a long time ago that most stereotypes were the product of some kind of truth. Back in those days he'd done stupid, brash things for the sake of salving bravado. In those days he'd thought he'd gotten away with his exploits—and in a sense he had. Then one day all the debts he owed his body came due, and his joints froze like ice.

It had been a long time since his cocky youth, but he carried it with him, like a chain around his neck. All he'd seen was the moment—he could never see through the haze of what was in the here and now to see the consequences that lived beyond. It was when he came home to discover that his first wife, Olivia, had left him that he found something more important than drinking and carousing for the moment's fun.

Three weeks home and he was a broken man. He'd heard it said that when a man reaches the end of his rope, he finds God—Morris quickly came to agree with this. When he crawled out of his stupor he found religion. A man approached him on the street—a member of the Firstborn who had been led to him.

A lot had happened since then.

So many choices, so many difficult decisions.

The Firstborn had never trusted one another—but he'd watched as they splintered, drifting further and further apart in an age of terrorism. He had to do something. No one else could—at least that's what he told himself for the millionth time as he washed his hands in the sink, looking at his face in the mirror.

The face he saw was old.

And tired.

He blinked at the old man in the mirror. He was running out of time. The previous fall he'd had his third heart attack, and if he was going to leave a legacy, he had to do it now, before it was too late. Uniting the Firstborn was to be his last act.

Morris opened the medicine cabinet, squinting as he checked the labels on the bottles. The child safety cap took him a moment to get open, then burst off in his arthritic hand, spilling pills into the sink. He groaned and began to scoop the tiny tablets back into their cylinder, keeping one in his palm. After replacing the bottle, he shut the cabinet.

There was that face again. Old and tired.

He stared for a moment, then threw his head back, swallowing his heart medicine.

Morris then entered the walk-in closet, the hangers squealing as he pushed them across the rod.

He stopped. There was a sound coming from the other room—

Running water?

Morris stepped out of the closet, the day's clothes in hand. He tossed the garments on the bed and took a seat. Then he stopped. On the chair in front of him he saw something—its form shimmering in the dark light of the predawn world. The form was familiar to him—

HK Mark 23—a homemade silencer fashioned to the muzzle.

Morris felt the blood drain from his body. He hadn't put that there. It wasn't there when he'd gone to the closet. What was happening? What was going on?

Something caught his eyes. Light beneath the bathroom door—where he had been just minutes before. Wedges of dark formed by the silhouette of feet beyond.

The knob turned.

Morris knew to shout for help, but he felt it catch in his chest.

Another heart attack?

The door opened and a man stepped out—tall and strong. Dark slacks, black shoes, a pink dress shirt, the top buttons undone, sleeves folded back—a crimson towel thrown over his shoulder.

"Devin," he uttered, voice trembling.

Devin Bathurst stood in the doorway to the small bathroom, a bowl in hand that Morris recognized from the kitchen. The trespasser reached into the bowl, and there was a swishing of liquid. Devin's hand lifted from the bowl, his fist crushing something—a washcloth. Cascades of dribbling water tumbled from between Devin's fingers, wringing from the cloth, gushing from his iron clutch.

Morris looked at the gun, then back at Devin, washcloth in hand. The old man nodded. "You're going to kill me," he said slowly, the thought only now becoming real to him.

The floorboards wailed as Devin's heavy shoe came down on them, moving forward in elegant strides. He came within three feet of Morris and stopped. Devin remained silent.

"I understand," Morris said with an accepting nod. He thought of trying to fight back. There had been a time when he would have won. But those days were gone. He thought of screaming for help, but that wouldn't save his life. Something in his heart sagged. He had done horrible things. Necessary, perhaps, but he had organized the Firstborn for the sake of killing. He had seen to it that Blake had become Overseer, and the man had used his power to destroy.

Morris took a long, slow breath. In all truth, he deserved to die. And he knew it.

He nodded at Devin. "This is what you think you have to do."

Devin knelt, setting down the bowl of water and the towel.

"That's not enough water to clean up the mess you'll make," Morris announced with a kind of morbid helpfulness. His wife loved the hardwood floor. She'd refused to let him replace it all these years. Blood—his blood, no less—would be too much for her. "You'll need more water."

Devin stood. "If I need more I'll get more." Then he picked up the pistol. "Morris Childs," he said firmly, "you have single-handedly conspired against the leaders of the Firstborn to bring them under your control. You have put yourself in league with murderers, thieves, and hypocrites."

"I was trying to unite the Firstborn," he stammered. "I was doing what I thought was best."

"You are a terrorist, a kidnapper, a conspirator, a murderer, and a fraud." Devin stood for a moment, pistol hanging in a gentle grip at his side. "You deserve to die."

Morris shook his head. "Devin, I don't expect you to understand. I did what I had to do."

Devin Bathurst nodded in the shallow light. Like the angel of death, Morris thought.

"I'm simply doing what I must do also."

Morris closed his eyes. "Then do it," he said softly.

He could hear Devin as he knelt again, setting the pistol aside, hand reaching once again into the swishing bowl of water. Morris felt the strong hands reach for his slippers, removing them one at a time, the towel sliding into place below them. The pads of his feet rested on the soft, fluffy fabric, and he felt his right foot be placed in the large bowl.

The water was warm—pleasant and soothing. He felt the sopping washcloth run across his foot, rough and warm.

He worked in silence, washing Morris Childs's feet. The cloth moved along the outsides of his feet and along the arches, between his toes and across his heels. And when Devin Bathurst was finished, he stood.

Morris looked up at him. "Devin, I…"

Devin pressed the button on the side of the pistol, and the magazine dropped out into his waiting hand. He pulled the slide back, sending a single tube of brass hopping into the air—the mechanism locking back as the unspent round hit the floor with a heavy thud. Devin tossed the empty pistol and its magazine on to the bed.

And without speaking he walked to the door.

"Wait," Morris called as Devin's hand touched the knob. "Why did you come here?"

"Because I realized that even though we are at war with each other, you're not my real enemy."

"Devin, I…"

He didn't turn around. "If we can't even love each other…" he said, pain in his voice, "then what do we stand for?"

Morris heard the knob begin to turn.

"I miss God," the older man announced.

Devin looked back.

"I miss God," he said again, "before the politics and the pain. I miss knowing my place and my purpose."

Devin simply nodded. "Me too." Then walked out the door.

Devin stepped into the hall. It was over, and he knew it.

Blake stood in the middle of the hallway, two guards with him. One of them was Shawn. Blake looked confused at first, maybe even surprised, then he nodded to the guards, pointing at Devin. "Please take Mr. Bathurst."

Shawn stepped forward, lifting his eyes at the last moment. Devin held the gaze until the guard looked away again.

"I'm sorry," Shawn muttered, taking hold of Devin's elbow, "I…"

"I understand."

Chapter 24

THE CAR GLIDED SOFTLY across the asphalt, rolling to a stop.

John looked around. It was a kind of pull in his chest as his feelings drew him nearer and nearer to where he was meant to be. He'd driven through the neighborhoods of brick homes and sloping grass lawns through narrow, twisting streets, but now he was drawing closer to the center of the living beast that was the District of Columbia.

John had considered going into real estate when he was searching for a real job. It made sense to him, the way a neighborhood lived, grew, and died. Behind him were the vibrant, living areas, where money flowed through metropolitan channels like blood through veins. But as he drew closer to where his heart was pulling him, he could see the ragged, dying edges of the organism—a place where life had left and only survival remained.

Where once there had been a vibrant, living community there was despair. For whatever reason people had left the area—perhaps it had grown unfashionable, or people who had lived outside of their means had fallen prey to foreclosure, but life had left and gone somewhere else. There were no new buyers to fill the void, and so property prices dropped...and dropped, until it was cheap enough that the most desperate facets of society could afford to live there.

The result was a section of city where poverty and desperation were the defining characteristics. John had often been told that where there's smoke there's fire, and had often said that where there's desperation there is despair.

He knew that drugs moved into these places, trapping people. With drugs came violence. With violence came lower property values, which attracted slumlords. Slowly, what had been a community would decay into the remains of a dying neighborhood: a thing that was known as the ghetto.

John had worked missions in the inner city—perhaps that was why he understood real estate and property value—but it still didn't keep him from being nervous as he rolled through the increasingly unwelcoming streets.

Where once there had been manicured lawns and crisply painted houses he now saw decaying structures, flaking paint, and overgrown yards. Young men walked by in groups, like pack animals, heavy coats sagging to one side or another, weighed down by heavy objects stored within. One of them eyed John, an obvious outsider, and the car he was driving.

Reaching out nonchalantly he keyed the rocker switch on the door's armrest. The locks snapped down with a sharp mechanical thud. The group stopped and stared, eyeing the vehicle as John rolled through the stop sign.

He wasn't given to mistrust toward people, but this pushed his tolerances.

Another block, and the world was looking more deserted. His eyes wandered to the sides, then came forward again: a little boy moving through the crosswalk. John would have rolled through, but he saw the boy moving slowly, a heavy, clear plastic backpack slung over his shoulder. The boy, no more than six, looked up and made eye contact.

He felt it in his stomach: a kind of nausea.

Men drawing together.

Explosives unpacking.

Weapons cracking open.

Bags filling with instruments of death.

John touched his forehead, an oily sheath of sweat wiped away, leaving a glistening sheen on his fingertips. It was all happening right now.

The boy moved to the end of the crosswalk, and John stepped on the gas pedal.

No more time.

Disgusting, he thought.

Ibrahim set the wad of cash on the counter, paying for his cup of coffee. The man working the morning shift at the convenience store simply nodded, muttering something, then handed the young man a receipt.

Ibrahim nodded, thankfully, then stepped out into the morning chill. He took a sip from his tall Styrofoam cup, sucking the hot beverage through the narrow lip of the lid. Even with the elaborate blue and brown design on the outside of the cup, it was still just cheap, tacky coffee. The "cappuccino" from a corner store always tasted horrible to him. It was sweet, thick, and for lack of a better word, gooey. It was as if someone didn't have the time or patience for creamer and had added butter out of desperation.

Disgusting.

But it was warm and caffeinated, and at this early hour it was hardly worth his time to complain. He was out a dollar and seventy-six cents, and while he would probably throw the latter half of the cup away, the first half was what he needed to wake up.

Ibrahim looked across the street toward the building.

Today was the day, the day his years of thought and passion would finally pay off. His dreams and aspirations would finally come into fruition. Raised in the dregs of an Arab ghetto himself, he was used to the layout of the neighborhood, but with his Yale training in engineering and political science, he knew what was really at stake here.

It was a visit to Mecca that had taught him the plight of the Middle East and the corruption of the Zionists. He knew full well that the world wouldn't understand, but living a life of lucrative and gainful employment wasn't going to make the world a better place.

For God, he thought. For Allah he would right the wrong thinking of others.

Today was the day, long waited for, like a wedding at the end of seemingly endless engagement, and yet he somehow felt nothing.

He sipped his disgustingly sweet coffee and stared at the building. Crisp air slipped into his nostrils. It would be his last morning. Nothing would stop that now.

Then he saw the car, rolling into place at the safe house across the street.

One of the others? No, it was someone else. The stranger stepped out of the vehicle.

Something was wrong.

This was it.

John's heart stopped as he looked up at the building.

There was no getting around it. He knew this place with his heart. The building looked like an old store that might have been converted into an apartment building. It was red brick, four stories tall, and covered in lewd twists of black spray paint and vibrant messages bursting off the walls in pastel bubble letters. The doors and windows were boarded up, most of them covered in the mangled overgrowth of color.

A sign, hardly visible beneath an artist's handiwork, read: "For Lease." Rust ate at the corners of the heavy sheet metal announcement, betraying the time it had spent hanging there, unheeded. Whatever the place had been before, it was empty now and in total disrepair. There were no obvious signs of any kind of tenant.

He stepped out of the car and sent the door swinging shut with a hard shove. John looked around. No one was looking, except perhaps the young man across the street sipping his coffee. John moved toward the building and down the side.

The wall seemed blank, except for a sloping ramp to accommodate those who might have had a wheelchair. An oddity, but an understandable feature. John moved up the slanting walkway and stopped at the door, reaching for the cold, metal handle. His thumb pushed down on the chilly handle—

The latch gave way.

His heart stopped. The door was unlocked.

He placed his ear against the cold metal and listened.

Nothing. He pulled gently with his body weight, drawing at the door. It gave way, gliding toward him.

John looked into the darkness, giving his eyes a moment to adjust— then stepped into the black beyond.

Ibrahim took a deep breath, then another draw of coffee, watching as the stranger stepped through the side entrance into the building.

This was a problem.

After another casual sip of the oily brew, he tossed the rest of the container into a nearby trash can, overflowing with wadded newspapers and stained paper napkins. He moved across the street.

The last day of his life had officially begun.

Dust hung in the air.

The place was a mess. Dirt and grime were everywhere. The smell of mildew blurred with the scent of rotting wood. Where there was still wallpaper, it peeled from the walls. Where there was still carpet, there were ratty holes with exposed floorboards beneath.

John stepped carefully.

A floorboard squeaked. He paused, trying not to make noise. Above, maybe a floor or so higher, he could hear chattering voices and the sounds of chair legs scraping across linoleum. He held his breath as he stepped, his leather boots coming down gently on the soggy, decomposing boards beneath his heel.

A shriek.

He threw his back against the wall, sending a thumping noise through the frame of the building as his eyes shot down to the floor—a giant screaming rat, the size of a healthy kitten, shot across the hall toward a yawning hole on the far wall. Its tail slurped into the darkness like a noodle in the lips of a ten-year-old boy—then was gone.

The voices upstairs went silent for a moment.

John stayed.

He could feel their demeanor—curious but not startled. Why? He took a breath and concentrated his thoughts on the source of his gifts—

—the cross.

They weren't worried because there was something else going on.

Someone was supposed to be in the building. There was someone else who hadn't arrived yet.

"Ibrahim?" a voice shouted down the stairs.

His voice caught in his throat, choking at him. Did he have the guts to reply?

He grunted a reply of some kind.

"Get up here," the voice announced again. "We're going to pray."

John put a hand to his chest and moved toward the stairs, ambling up the squealing, splintering steps. He stopped at the top and looked at the door, a small gap where it had been left ajar.

His eyes squinted as he moved toward the gap, trying to see in.

A figure moved by his view and then passed by. Like a parting curtain the passing body revealed what lay beyond.

A table, strewn with plastic and wires, bricks of white and bags of screws. An automatic rifle hung from the back of a chair by its strap.

There were three of them in there. He could feel it.

John took a step back.

This was a bad idea. He shouldn't have come. He couldn't take on three of them. This was ridiculous. It was time to call the police.

He turned around and moved down the stairs as quickly as his feet would carry him. At the bottom of the steps he took one last look upward, then looked back—

He stopped. A man glared at him—handsome, young, and muscular.

John darted forward—shoving his weight past the other man, ramming by.

A sinewy fist grabbed John by the arm, an open hand slamming into his back between the shoulder blades. His body spun, then hit the drywall. The soft material caved as John's shoulder punched through the wall.

The man lunged at him, and John threw himself from the wall, his arm, covered in soggy white powder, sweeping out in a vicious swing.

The young man took the blow to the face, snapping back fast.

John turned to flee and felt the sharp strike of a booted heel connect with the small of his back, sending him sprawling forward. A hand grabbed his ankle and John kicked back, trying to fight free, flipping onto his back.

His eyes lifted. The other three stood at the bottom of the steps, staring. One had a pistol.

The man reached down, taking John by the hair.

"Who are you?"

Chapter 25

BLAKE STOOD IN THE hall as they threw Devin into the space below the stairs and slammed the door shut. They'd removed the light-bulb from the ceiling to make sure that he'd remain in the dark. That was important. Devin Bathurst was smart, tough, and tenacious. Superman, no—but well worth keeping in darkness.

Devin stood in the shadows, upper body illuminated by the ambient light of the hall. Blake gave him a nod, then motioned for the nearby guards to shut the heavy oak door.

"Put a towel at the bottom of the door to keep out the light from the hall. And I want three people here at all times." Blake reached into his pocket and removed a skeleton key, twisting it in the old-fashioned lock. All the doors were antique Victorian doors that Morris Childs's wife apparently couldn't live without—a lucky break that had simply saved them all the trouble of changing the interior locks.

He held up the skeleton key. "And I'll hang on to this."

He stomped away.

Blake liked the feeling of his boots stomping on the floor, the way he watched the other Firstborn scatter to the corners of a room and silence the whispered chatter. He liked that he felt tired, the weight of the office bearing down on his shoulders. He was Overseer now, and that meant he couldn't be wrong. It was exhausting, but he liked the feeling.

At last, the Firstborn were all under one flag—and he was their weary captain.

"Blake."

He turned, looking down the hall. Morris Childs stood there, fully dressed now, arms crossed.

"What are you doing with Devin?"

Blake let his eyes wander across the walls as he considered what he was going to say. There were a thousand things he could say, but there would be only one that was right in his mind. He was Overseer; Morris would have to wait for him to speak.

"I'm making sure he doesn't cause any more trouble." He turned to walk away.

"Blake?"

He stopped, letting out an audible groan, hoping it sent the message. "Yes?" He looked back.

"I was wondering if you might have a word with me in my office."

Blake examined Morris for a moment, then let his eyes drift lazily toward the men who stood at the door where Devin was held. They all looked away. He didn't feel it was appropriate for Morris to question him like this—not in front of the others. The task of Overseer was difficult enough without...

"I only need a few minutes."

Blake cleared his throat and nodded, following the older man into his office. The door creaked, then clicked shut.

"How can I help you, Morris?"

Morris took a long breath, moving toward his desk. He sat on the edge.

Blake considered how much he disliked Morris's informality around him.

"What are you doing, Mr. Jackson?"

"I'm unifying the Firstborn."

"I mean, what are you doing with Mr. Bathurst?"

Blake considered for a moment, then nodded. "Look, you should know sooner or later. Devin is a traitor to everything that we stand for."

"What do we stand for?"

"Unity."

"What about virtue?" Morris asked, his tone smacking of flippancy.

"Unity is a virtue."

"What about love?"

Blake heaved a sigh, hoping that Morris would get off his back.

"Devin is opposition to Overseer—that means he's in opposition to God. We have to make sure this ends here."

"What are you talking about?"

"We're trying to save lives here…and all he cares about is what the idiot Temple has to say."

"I'm not certain he's wrong."

Blake let his head tip to the side, trying his best to convey the incredulity that was bubbling up inside. "We were trying to stop a terrorist attack!"

Morris looked down. "And did we act like terrorists ourselves?"

"That's ridiculous."

"No," Morris replied. "We were so convinced that we were right. What if we were wrong?"

"What did he say to you?" Blake snapped.

"Nothing. I just started to think—what if we were wrong? Sometimes it's good to keep people around who disagree with us."

"No," Blake said definitively, "no, that's not right. That's absolutely wrong."

"Just listen to what I have to say…"

"No," Blake snapped, annoyed. "I'm not listening to any more of this. If you want to disagree, that's fine—but you keep it to yourself. Got it?"

"I don't think—"

"I'm Overseer," Blake said flatly, taking a step toward Morris, "and I don't like your tone."

A look of sudden shock and realization crossed the older man's face.

"I'm done with Bathurst. Tomorrow I'm going to take everybody out, and they're going to see what happens when you defy God." Blake turned on his heel and moved to the door.

"What are you going to do?"

"I'm going to make him choose," he announced, reaching for the knob, "and then everybody is going to see him accept the consequences."

"Blake Jackson," Morris announced, as if scolding a small child.

Blake turned back. "No," he announced flatly. "I decide around here. Got it?"

Then he left the room, locking the door shut behind him.

Dr. Saul Mancuso sat in the garage, watching the shadowy forms of guards move past the glossy gray windows.

Ten men sat around him. The Fallen, as they were called—but they were the most elevated men here, as far as he could tell.

He grunted to himself. Half the men in the room had lost their faith in God because of hypocrisy; the other half had left because they were fed up with the politics. He'd been saying it for years: religion was dangerous. And now Blake and his unquestioning cronies were proving him right.

Saul leaned against the wall, waiting for morning.

The pale glow of dawn felt empty somehow. And lonely.

He heaved a sigh. Ten years ago he would have prayed. That would always take the edge off of the bad parts of life. And now it was such a bitter pill. He coughed into his hand to hide the audible sigh that was coming. Academia was his religion now. At least there they used facts as a basis for crucifying you.

Hannah sat in the room, staring at the locked door. After her talk with Morris she'd slept some, but it wasn't much at all, not enough to be well rested.

She stood as she heard the approaching footfalls and the sound of a heavy body stopping at the door. Something twisted in the lock, and the door floated open. Blake stood in the door, looking her over.

Hannah sat, drawing back into her seat.

"Are you OK?" he asked, dipping his head.

She looked at her feet.

"Look…" He broke off for a moment, then stepped into the room, closing the door behind him. "I want you to know that I don't want you to get hurt. OK?"

She nodded, still refusing him eye contact.

He took a seat on the bed near her, trying to lean close. Her gaze drifted to the wallpaper.

"The Firstborn are fracturing," he said in a soft, low voice, "and I don't want you to get hurt."

No reply.

"I can't guarantee you'll be safe unless you're on the right side."

She looked at him, feeling a frosty gaze lift off her face. Hannah wanted to yell, to scream, to tell him he was a despot and traitor, a power-mad lunatic who had lost sight of everything good about the Firstborn. Her eyes tipped down toward the floor.

"Are you on my side?"

She didn't say anything.

"Hannah," he demanded, "can I count on you?"

"I…" she began, then broke off. "I had a chance to have a normal life. I could have lived in a nice neighborhood with children and a future." She laughed, weakly. "I could have been one of the church ladies that all the other women look up to."

He took her wrists in his big, ragged hands, the sinew closing gently. "You can still have it," he said softly. "I can make sure that you never have to get pulled into the dangers of the Firstborn—but you'll have to stay near me. I can't do it unless you're willing to make it very clear to everyone that you're on the right side. Do you understand?"

She looked up at him. "No, Blake," she said softly. "I just…don't think I can."

"You have to choose, Hannah. Yes, you could have had a normal life, but you're neck-deep in this thing now, and the only chance you have to keep from becoming a lonely, embittered, pathetic wreck like Devin Bathurst is to let me protect you from all the bad things in this world."

Hannah looked him over. He was dead serious.

"I'll see to it that you're sent to the best college with a nice place to stay—a big house all to yourself—with friends nearby. You could have a car and nice clothes and money to spend. And when you finally find a guy that's good enough for you, I'll make sure you have the biggest wedding a girl could hope for—and a big house to share your life with him in."

He put a hand on her shoulder.

"Right now you're standing in the middle of a violent, dangerous, and tumultuous world where everything and everyone you love can be ripped from you in a moment. Tomorrow I can make all of that go away and give you the life you deserve, but today you have to make a stand." His tone was somehow sincere and commanding. "Will you stand with me?"

"I…"

"Don't answer. Just think about it."

Then he stood and left.

Chapter 26

JOHN TEMPLE SAT IN the kitchen chair, a hand zip-tied to the radiator. The slotted contraption was cold, obviously inactive for quite some time. Whatever this place was, it was falling apart.

The men stood in a huddle ten feet ahead of him, chattering in a foreign language of some kind. He could feel their motives—using a foreign tongue to keep their conversation private. But he could feel it all.

There were four of them. They were well dressed—upper middle class.

There was an argument about what to do with John. They chattered quickly, interrupting one another. Every once in a while the one named Ibrahim would look back at John, scanning him.

The leader was named Hassan—John had caught that much—and despite his calm demeanor, he was frothing with anxiety. He was nervous, and his thoughts kept bending toward how best to kill their unwelcome guest.

John took long, deep breaths as they chattered, trying to reach some consensus about how best to get rid of him... and when.

One of them, a big man he'd heard called Jean-Paul, looked at his watch and announced his thoughts.

"...Tariq..."

It was one of the few words John actually understood with his ears. They wanted to know where the fifth member of their party was. It was 6:00 a.m., and Tariq still hadn't arrived. Eight thirty was zero hour, Jean-Paul announced in something other than English. Something must have happened to Tariq.

Four heads turned to John in unison.

He stared back.

They said nothing.

"Where's Tariq?" Hassan asked, brushing a fleck of debris from the arm of his gray suit jacket.

John wanted to scream. His pulse snapped forward a beat, his veins crackling as he tried to keep his fingertips from trembling. His eyes didn't move from the men. The one named Jean-Paul took a step to the left to gain a better vantage.

Four sets of eyes probed John's features.

Hassan examined the thin piece of debris, holding it between his thumb and forefinger. "Where is he?"

John felt the muscles in his abdomen tighten, holding his bladder at bay.

Hassan, handsome and well groomed, stepped toward John. The man scratched the back of his head casually as he approached, then squatted down in front of John, reaching onto the table where they had placed all of their captive's things. He picked through the wallet, staring at one of the cards held in the slender plastic sleeve.

"Jonathan Eric Temple?" he asked, reading from the driver's license.

"I know what you're planning to do," John said, shaking his head.

"Born July 15?"

"Don't do this."

"You're an organ donor," Hassan said with a nod. "I'm impressed."

"They're children."

"There are children in Palestine too. Are American children somehow more special than the schoolchildren murdered with bullets bought with American dollars?"

John's mind wandered for a moment, trying not to get drawn too deeply into the moment. He had to fight the urge, or he would strangle in the immediacy of it all. Think about the future, he said to himself. Somewhere in the tangle of thoughts a prayer tried to form itself.

"Do you believe in God, Mr. Temple?"

"Yes," he announced, voice cracking slightly, "and He loves you."

A heavy smack sent John's face whipping to the side.

"Don't preach at me, Christian." Hassan's voice was sharp and his words stinging in their sincerity. "Where's Tariq? Why is he late? Are there more of you? Where are they?"

John glared, defiant.

"My entire mission could be at risk," Hassan said gently, as if teaching a young boy to fish. "One of my holy warriors is missing, and I'm looking into the face of a man who has been snooping in my safe house." The squatting man examined his manicured fingernails. "What do you think I should do?"

John let out an exasperated sigh, eyes drifting to the side.

A sharp cracking sound brought John's eyes forward again, responding to the snap of Hassan's fingers. "We serve the same God, Christian. Do you know that? Why are you trying to block the plans of our God?"

"My God doesn't murder children."

"Yes?" Hassan said, as if surprised. "Exodus—the angel of death, sent by your God, slays all the firstborn of Egypt. Jericho—your God commands the Jews to slaughter all the citizens—women *and children*—as well as all the inhabitants of the Promised Land."

"That was different."

"How? No different. Your God killed children because He knew the power of that message. He knew the only way to turn Pharaoh's heart was to strike deep into it. It was the murder of innocent children that has awoken the sleeping lion of our wrath. It will be children who bring America to its senses."

John shook his head. "What do you hope to accomplish?"

Hassan put a hand on John's shoulder. "Do you know why the Middle East is a slave to the demand for Western oil?"

No reply.

"Because the caliphate, the Islamic world, will not stand together. They have grown cowardly and complacent with Western decadence. Cigarettes. Movies. Depictions of women as objects of sexual desire. The glorification of alcohol. The people of the Middle East have lost sight of Sharia—the laws of God. They will not stand together—and so they have become slaves to the West."

"And how will killing children fix that? Revenge?"

Hassan stood. "When America has been sufficiently angered, it will plunge once again into the heart of the Middle East—and then the Muslim world will be forced to unite."

John Temple felt his heart rate slow. For the first time he understood it—the feeling he was drawing from this man. It was like little boys playing soldiers—only these little boys were used to death and thought nothing of it. They were prepared to die, just like little boys dying in a game of cops and robbers, throwing themselves to the ground in spasms, enjoying the attention of their flailing appendages as they hit the floor.

He smirked.

"Is something funny?" Hassan asked casually.

John shook his head. "No."

"Really?" Hassan stood, thumbs thrust through his belt loops, striking a pose like a fashion model.

In a flash the suited man's hand struck the table, snatching something—

A knife.

Hassan swept the blade past John's face, reaching for his wrist. The blade slipped between the hard plastic of the zip tie and the soft flesh of John's hand.

A quick jerk and the plastic popped loose.

John cradled his hand, squeezing the place where the double-edged blade had slit him.

Hassan walked away, moving back toward the men behind him. He looked back at John. "Get up."

John cradled his hand. He didn't move.

Hassan leaned close to Ibrahim and whispered something in his ear. The man nodded and moved away. John hadn't heard it and was too focused on the pain to feel it. Hassan looked at him again.

"Get up, Mr. Temple."

He remained seated.

Hassan nodded. Then stepped forward.

Three big steps and he was on John, towering over him like a colossus.

John's world spun as the heel of an expensive shoe slammed into his chest. He went sprawling back, air fleeing from his lungs as he was flung and ripping from his chest as his back hit the floor.

He stared at the ceiling—cracked and yellowed from time, black blotches outlining islands of water damage.

The sounds of footfalls rippled through the floorboards as the three of them approached him. Someone grabbed his ankle.

John kicked.

A toe connected with his side.

Hands reached for him, groping at anything they could grab—ankles, wrists, biceps, hair. He felt them pull in tandem across the floor, a splintering board slicing into his leg. John tried to fight, but he felt his form glide across the wood, dragging toward some ill fate.

Halfway out the room.

A hand came loose, and he took a swing at someone—a weak hit at best.

A retaliatory strike.

The doorway.

John's hand scrambled across the wooden frame, grasping at the edges. The lip of the frame seared into his flesh, cutting hard. They threw their weight into the pull, but his grasp held, fingers throbbing.

A heel crushed into his fingertips, and his grip came loose, his body tumbling across the bathroom floor—a loose tile cutting at his arm.

He was bleeding.

Body aching. Muscles tingling.

He heard the sound of squeaking metal and a throaty gurgle in unused pipes. His eyes lifted as Ibrahim continued twisting the valve on the bathtub faucet. A husky grumble coughed from the valve—then a quick spurt of dirty water came hacking from the ancient, unused pipes.

Hands grabbed his shoulders, heaving him upward, shoulders slamming into the heavy metal rim of the old claw-foot tub. A bay of windows covered in decaying newspapers shed the only light into the room, filling it with a nauseating shade of amber.

They forced his body back, his head thrusting beneath the spout. A splash of frigid, dirty water hit his face.

One last squeak and the valve opened wide, the faucet belching out a heavy gush. Water filled his mouth. His nose. His eyes. The taste of rust, caulk, and decay filled his mouth, cheeks bulging from the pressure.

A sharp punch to the diaphragm, and his lungs sucked for air—

Flecks of copper piping tumbled down the back of his throat, ejecting out as fast as he coughed them out.

Panic overtook him.

He was going to drown. He was going to die. His lungs were going to burst.

Strong hands yanked him from beneath the rushing flow, and he hit the black and white tile floor with his face.

John didn't try to get up. He choked. Gagged. Sobbed. His muscles were weary and his eyes burned.

Hassan knelt down next to him, removing his jacket and rolling up the sleeves.

"We have time, Mr. Temple," he said with a nod, lifting his head by a fistful of sopping hair. "You're going to tell me everything I want to know."

Chapter 27

THE SUV BUMPED DOWN the back roads, the dappled spring greenery of upstate New York rolling past. Hannah's eyes relaxed as she stared out the window, letting it all blur together. She hadn't slept well, and she still wasn't fully awake. Her eyes lifted toward the front seat. "Where are we going?"

Blake turned his head from his place in the passenger's seat, looking back at her. "We're going somewhere private so we can talk with Mr. Bathurst."

"Where is he?"

"He's in one of the other vehicles."

"How many are there?"

"Vehicles?"

"Yes."

"Enough for everyone."

"Everyone?"

"Yes. I want everybody to see this."

Hannah sank back into her seat and let her eyes fall lazily back toward the passing world beyond the glass. Fifteen minutes passed in silence before the SUV rolled off the back road, through the trees. A moment later they stopped, the driver climbing out.

She reached for her seat belt.

"Hannah?"

She looked up at Blake, who was nearly turned around in the seat in front of her. It was just the two of them in the vehicle now. "I need you to do me a favor—something that will help both of us."

"What is it?" she asked cautiously.

He heaved a sigh, scratching his chin. "If we're going to let you off the hook for helping Bathurst, then I need you to show everybody that you've changed sides."

"I..."

"And it needs to be a pretty bold statement."

"Blake." She looked his face over. "This isn't..."

He pushed his jacket to the side, reaching to his hip. There was a snapping noise, and he brought his hand back, holding a pistol.

Hannah didn't know the name of the weapon, but she'd seen them in movies about World War II—a classic American model. Blake turned the weapon, holding it by the barrel, extending the grip to her.

"Colt 1911," he announced, "forty caliber, seven rounds plus one in the pipe."

She looked the gunmetal over, examining the rough texture of tiny raised pyramids that checked the back of the grip. Her voice was small. "What are you asking me to do?"

"I'm sorry," he said, shaking his head, "but if Devin Bathurst refuses my offer, I'm going to have to make an example of him. If I'm going to protect you, then you're the one who's going to have to do it. Got it?"

Blake reached for the door handle, beginning his slide from his seat.

"Blake," she stammered, "I don't think I can."

He stopped, staring out the car door, then looked back at her. "Then pray Devin sees reason."

Devin Bathurst climbed out of the SUV's trunk, hands bound behind his back, two guards pointing weapons at his chest.

"This way," one of them announced.

He stepped forward and saw the collection of people, all standing in a wooded clearing. Armed guards—Domani Paramilitary, Prima Militia, Ora Strike Force, all surrounding the Fallen who stood, ragged and defeated, in a small cluster.

The two escorting guards shoved Devin in front of the gathering of people, and he stared back at them. He recognized most of the faces—all of the Fallen, including Dr. Saul Mancuso, who crossed his arms, defiantly glaring at the guards around him. To the far right stood Morris Childs, a look of concern crossing his features, with his niece, Trista Brightling, standing next to him.

"Devin Alexander Bathurst," Blake announced, approaching from the left, standing at the edge of the small crowd, "do you know why you're here?"

Devin took a breath and put his shoulders back.

"Do you?" Blake asked again.

Devin said nothing.

"You're here because you have knowingly and deliberately defied the office of Overseer—a position created by God. You have engaged in conspiracy against the Firstborn and engaged in deliberate sedition. Do you acknowledge these charges?"

Devin wanted his hands to be free. He wanted to step forward and deck the cocky punk. Instead, he said nothing.

"I'm prepared to pardon you, Mr. Bathurst. I just need to know whose side you're on. Are you with us?"

Devin's muscles tightened. His face began to grimace. "No," he said flatly. "I'm not with you."

"Mr. Bathurst," Blake began, his voice rising, his tone straining, "I don't think you understand what you're saying. If you don't give up your childish defiance of God, then you are going to be judged by God."

"There's a difference between you and God."

"I know the truth—which you defy."

"Is there a chance you're wrong?"

"That's ridiculous."

"What if you're wrong and are just too stubborn to admit it? What then? How many people have to suffer to feed your ego and your intellectual comfort? How many people—"

"That's enough, Mr. Bathurst!" Blake shouted.

"No," Devin announced again, "we're all different."

"But we're united!"

"Under one man—one way of thinking and seeing."

"Mr. Bathurst!"

"If we approach each other with smug arrogance, then how can we ever love each other?"

"You have a lot of nerve," Blake started.

Then Devin felt it—a glistening up his spine, like a thousand tiny spider legs. That old familiar feeling.

The future.

John Temple. A bathroom. Lights snapping off and on.

Chaos.

Water. Plunging beneath the surface—back to air, then down into the darkness again.

Screaming. Frustration. Video camera.

The hacksaw. John's neck. The arm rocking back and forth. Dirty water filling with blood.

Crimson swirls.

Devin looked up at Blake as the man finished saying something with a growl.

Blake stopped.

Silence.

A bird chirped in the woods.

"Who cares?" Devin asked.

"Excuse me?"

"Who cares if either one of us is right or wrong? If one way of seeing is better than another?"

The crowd stared.

"If we can't even love each other—then what do we stand for?"

Blake was silent.

Devin held for a moment. They were all looking at him now. "Who cares if we take care of the people who are like us, who agree with us? Everybody does that. Even dictators take care of their friends. But if we can't love the people who are different from us—respect them for who they are and how they see the world—then how are we any better than killers ourselves?"

The crowd remained silent. At the far right Morris Childs nodded, smiling.

"There are things here that are far more important than our stubborn pride. There's a world out there that has to be dealt with—even if we don't agree on how, we still have to be there for each other."

"Mr. Bathurst," Blake growled.

Devin turned his back and dropped to his knees, the way his grandmother had taught him. His wrists were bound, so he couldn't clasp his hands in front of him, but his head bowed, eyes closed.

And he began to pray.

Hannah watched as Devin lowered his head.

The way he had in San Antonio—the prayer of a lone man.

Blake turned to her, face snapping her direction. He grabbed her arm. "Hannah—it's time. You have to be the one to do this. You have to make sure everyone knows what happens if they defy God."

She felt him lead her to the front of the small crowd and push her forward. Hannah stood there, pistol in hand.

"Mr. Bathurst," Blake began again, "because of your repeated refusal to admit your failings and your constant defiance to the office of Overseer, you have been judged."

Blake turned to the others.

"I want everyone to know that this is what happens when you defy God."

He turned to Hannah, motioning her toward Devin.

She looked down at the firearm in her hand, turning it over. She held her place.

Blake stepped forward. "What is it?" he whispered in her ear.

"I can't do it."

He gripped her shoulder hard. "You have to. There's no other way."

She shook her head. "I won't."

"Hannah Rice, do this and it will be the last thing you ever have to do for me. After this you will never have to be part of the Firstborn again—but we have to show these people that you've earned it." He patted her on the shoulder. "Now do it."

He took a step away from her toward the crowd.

She looked down at Devin. He had to know what was going on—yet he remained calm.

"No," Hannah said with a small voice.

Blake stopped. "What?"

Her eyes lifted, staring him in the face. "I said no. I won't do it."

"Hannah Rice—do not defy me!"

"I'm sorry, Blake."

"Hannah, do it!"

"No!" she said flatly.

The world stared in disbelief. She felt a small tremor run through her chest. This wasn't her.

"I'm ordering you as Overseer—"

"Do not make me choose between you and God—because you will lose. I don't care if you can offer me comfort and simplicity—that's not what I was made for."

"I was appointed by God. This is His judgment on Devin Bathurst."

She stepped forward, took Blake's hand, and pressed the firearm into his palm. "If you're so sure you know the mind of God, then you're going to have to shoot Devin Bathurst yourself." Hannah turned around and stepped toward Devin. "And that means you'll have to shoot me too."

Hannah knelt down to Devin's right and bowed her head, folding her hands in front of her.

Morris Childs watched as Blake stood, seething. It was obvious—Blake's plan wasn't working.

His panicked face looked into the watching crowd. The whole point of this expedition was to send a message—but the message being conveyed was one of weakness.

Blake began shouting at the crowd, trying to explain why he was going to have to do this. Morris simply watched the back of Devin's head. The young man was like a son to him—a son he had betrayed, plotted against, and deceived, but a son nonetheless.

Blake turned toward Devin, lifting the pistol, angling at the back of the man's dark head. Morris felt it—a tingling on his tongue, almost a sour taste—

The gun going off.

The round exploding from the muzzle.

The hole punched through the back of Devin's head.

The body, slumped forward, weeping blood.

The future—seconds away.

Morris stepped forward, saying nothing. Blake must have heard him. He turned, pistol in hand.

"What are you doing?"

Morris felt a hand press into his chest, blocking his way. He eyed his spot next to Devin.

"I'm standing where I belong," Morris said with a nod, and shoved past.

"I won't let you do this!" Blake shouted.

Morris shook his head and continued walking. "I don't follow you."

Behind him Morris heard Blake moving, shifting. A mechanism clicking.

Then he heard something else—

The gunshot exploded through the silent air of the forest clearing.

Blake watched as Morris Childs went sprawling forward, back arching, arms flailing, chest striking the dirt.

Dust rose in a cloud.

The body lay still.

The sound of the echoing gunshot rolled through the trees.

Blake looked down at the pistol in his hand—smoke curling from the hot barrel and ejection port, rising like steam. He looked back at the gathered crowd. They stared at him in disbelief. Trista Brightling rushed forward, kneeling at her uncle's side, checking him, making panic-stricken noises.

"How much are you willing to sacrifice for the truth?" Blake asked. "As Overseer, these are the choices I have to make."

They stared back at him, faces souring.

"I had no choice. He didn't leave me any other option."

Trista stood, looking at the blood on her hands. "He's dead," she announced.

Blake held. Morris Childs, leader of the Domani, was dead. The finality of it all sank in.

Trista Brightling wiped her hands on the back of Morris's shirt and walked away from Blake—

He swung the weapon toward her. "Don't do it," he announced.

Trista glared at him for a moment, then turned her back. She stopped next to Devin and put a hand on his shoulder. She knelt, bowing her head.

Blake squeezed the grip of the weapon, stepped forward, and raised the pistol, the muzzle hovering at the back of her skull, nearly touching her blonde hair. His hand shook.

Something caught him off guard in the corner of his eye.

Dr. Saul Mancuso stepped past them to the left of the praying line, kneeling just in front of Devin Bathurst.

Blake stepped away and turned around. Three of the Fallen were walking toward him. He lifted his weapon. "Go back," he ordered.

The three men ignored him, taking their place with the others, kneeling.

"Get up," he snarled. "Get up, now!"

No reply.

Another of the Fallen took his place.

"I'm warning you!"

Blake looked back at the soldiers who stood with the Fallen. "Stop them," he said harshly. "That's an order!"

The one named Shawn stared back, then unslung his weapon, setting it on the ground—and stepped forward.

"If you do this," Blake shouted, "you will never be welcome among the Firstborn again."

Shawn knelt with the others.

Blake looked back—the others were following, all setting down their weapons as they moved toward the growing mass of kneeling bodies.

And then Blake came to the realization—

He was the only one still standing.

Devin's eyes were pressed shut, beads of sweat on his face.

The Lord's Prayer.

He felt himself relax. It didn't matter if he lived or died. John needed him. Small children, targeted for murder, needed him.

He felt Dr. Saul Mancuso's hand reach out, touching him on the shoulder. Devin's head lifted, looking at the older man, examining his face as he prayed.

"What are you doing here, Saul? You don't even believe in God anymore."

"Shut up," Mancuso replied.

Devin smiled inwardly and let his head bow again.

They were all together—dozens of them, united in faith, praying as one. Different perspectives, different lives, different goals. All together.

And then he felt it—

As his head dropped to its lowest point his world stopped.

He could feel it all—he felt the others around him—they could all feel it—from the beginning.

Blake murdering the imam—

Bullets. Glass. Blood.

Disposing of the weapon—someone, drenched in shadow, whispering in the man's ear.

He saw the shadowy figure in San Antonio, moving from one to another, whispering in ears—distrust mounting and growing. Henry Rice—

Falling. Breaking. Dying.

The figure covered in shadow, watching.

Washington DC, Pennsylvania—

Shouting. Hitting. Gunfire.

The shadowy figure moving from one to another, pitting them against each other.

John Temple, in Washington DC. A building.

Across the street. Through the doors. Up the stairs. Into the bathroom. Screaming, straining, fighting. Water bursting from the tub in sprays.

Four of them. Weapons. Explosives. Video cameras. Recording their final message.

The future—

The hacksaw. The blood. John's lifeless body.

The elementary school. Stepping through the front doors. Murder. Bullets tearing through bystanders.

Hundreds of children in a gymnasium.

A standoff. News vans. The world watching. Afternoon.

The explosion.

An aerial view of the school—the walls blown out, glass shattered. Ratty debris spread across the street, turning grass to soot. Smoke rising in a tall tower of black.

The mangled corpses of small children.

More violence. More blood. More death.

Devin lifted his head. They had all felt it. They knew exactly where to go. They knew exactly what to do.

Chapter 28

J OHN'S HEAD PLUNGED INTO the dark, swirling water—his vision filling with the murky ruddiness of rust and dirt, bubbles flashing before his eyes. His hair ripped back and he came up gasping—

Then plunged beneath again.

He'd held back what he knew about Tariq and the Firstborn out of stubbornness—but now he was ready for it to be over. He hadn't had a full breath in what felt like hours. His body was preparing to collapse.

The hand that held his hair let go again as they traded the duty again.

His body leaned against the lip of the tub as he hacked and sobbed.

Hassan knelt next to him again. "Are you ready to tell me what happened to Tariq?"

John groaned in exhaustion and misery. Behind him he heard as they began to pour a bag of ice into the full tub.

His eyes stung. His ears rung. His muscles ached. He was ready for it to be over.

John closed his eyes and reached out with one last prayer—

And suddenly he felt it.

"Hang on, Temple. We're coming."

They were coming for him.

He wasn't going to make it that long. They would kill him first. But if he could stall them long enough, it might all mean something. If he could delay these men, keep them here, then the others stood a chance—just a chance—of stopping them here—

Maybe.

Hassan looked John in the eye. "Are you ready to tell me what I need to know?"

John balked with what little strength he had, a gurgling sound sputtering from his lips. His weak voice muttered, "Not a chance."

A thick hand grabbed his hair.

Dying quickly could be easy, he thought. But he had to make it last…

Devin walked back to the SUV; some had stood, most were still kneeling. All were experiencing some kind of emotional release. A few were crying.

Blake stood in the middle of it all, pistol in hand, a confused look on his face. No one tried to subdue him. He approached Devin. "What's going on? What happened?"

Devin opened the SUV door, looking for the keys. "John found the terrorist cell."

"Tariq's dead."

"There are more of them—and they still plan on carrying out the attack."

Blake's mouth opened and hung there. "But how come none of us saw that?"

"When was the last time you had a vision?"

"I don't know, a few days. Maybe more."

"Through all of this you haven't seen a thing?"

"No. Why?"

"We're being blocked by our own blindness." Devin realized the keys weren't in the vehicle. He looked back at the milling crowd. "Thresher isn't a man—"

"What? Then who is it?"

"Thresher is Satan himself," Devin announced, walking away. "We've been turned against each other."

Blake remained silent, setting his pistol down on the hood of the SUV absentmindedly. He followed after Devin. "What are you going to do?"

"We have to find John. They're going to kill him…and then they're going to murder a lot of children."

"Where are they?"

"Washington DC."

Blake came up alongside Devin. "You can't drive that far. You'll never make it in time." He put a hand on Devin's arm, keeping him from leaving. "Let me help, Bathurst."

Devin turned. How like a bully. Play to the crowd. Do what makes yourself look powerful and tough, but when the power shifts, you immediately change sides.

"Do you have a plan?"

Trista leaned against the SUV, hugging her elbows close to her body. Her uncle dead…murdered. Children in danger. Terrorists. And John.

She banished the thought from her mind. He was reckless, foolish, immature. If he got hurt, it would no doubt be sad—but this went beyond sadness. Something deeper didn't want him to get hurt. There was a concern one felt for others simply as other humans, and then there was something more. Not just the outrage of a crime committed against another, but the sense of impending traumatic loss. As if a piece of her soul was being ripped away from her. Something she could never have back and could never live without.

She shook her head. How ridiculous. How naïve. How childish.

"It's Morris's plane," Blake said, talking to the small group gathering around him, just a few feet away. "I'm certified to fly. I can have us there in time. But only four of us will fit in the plane."

"Four?" someone asked. "What do you plan to do with just four people?"

"We can try," Devin announced. "So now we have to decide—besides Blake and I, who else is going?"

Trista felt a kind of involuntary twitch. She turned toward them. She stepped forward.

"I'm going," she stated loudly.

A dozen heads turned to look at her.

Blake shook his head. "Ms. Brightling, I would hardly say that you're—"

"I'm going," she said flatly.

"It's John Temple we're talking about here."

The world seemed distant. Her body shuddered. She touched the corner of her eye, brushing away something wet.

"He'd do it for me."

The group remained quiet.

"I'm going too," another voice announced.

Hannah Rice stood at the edge of the group.

"Hannah," Devin said, shaking his head, "are you sure you want to—"

"I wasn't made for a life of comfort. None of us were." She shrugged. "It's time for me to do this."

Devin considered for a moment. "OK," he said.

"I don't believe this," Blake balked. "I know it's not politically correct to say, but combat is no place for women—no offense, ladies."

Trista felt Devin's gaze drill into her. There was something probing about the way he looked at her, as if to ask if John were still important to her. She tried to speak back through her own gaze, using her face as if to say she felt nothing for the young man—that he was nothing more than a faded artifact of her distant past.

Her eyes must have said something different. Devin let a small smile form at the corner of his mouth. Devin didn't make a habit of smiling. He looked at Hannah. And nodded.

"The ladies are coming with us. The future looks optimal with them along."

Blake didn't protest. He simply stared, then nodded.

Devin looked at two of the nearby guards. "We're going to need guns."

The floor was littered with droplets of water, polluted with granules of rust and debris. Cubes of ice scattered across the floor like scattered blocks left by playing children. The black and white tiles of the bathroom floor were sprinkled with dust and drywall. An amber

hue washed over everything, tinted by the color of faded newspapers
fastened in front of the windows.

John lay curled in the corner.

How long had he been here?

How long since the message of hope first entered his mind?

Long, he thought. Too long.

He lay on the floor, nearly in the fetal position, body shaking from
pain and cold. His lungs convulsed with a violent spasm in his chest.
Droplets of water trickled down his lips, the bitter taste of copper
sliding along with them.

They were through the doorway. Standing. Talking. Arguing.

This was how it went. First boldness in bullying. Then failure to
achieve. Then panic.

John was not well known for his foresight, but he knew what came
next—

Murder.

All it took was for one of them to panic—to worry. Death always
seemed like a quick fix. That thinking had always made suicide
popular.

John didn't understand the words, but he understood the thoughts.
Hassan wanted him alive—for now. As long as there was information
to be had, Hassan wanted to try to gain it—the big man, Jean-Paul,
agreed. The one called Ibrahim was advocating violence—painful
death. The fourth, one simply called Ali, stood aside.

John rolled on to his back. In the next room men were arguing about
when to kill him. It was still a new experience for him. Something in
him wanted to laugh. He still wasn't used to this kind of thing. John
rolled on to his side again, reaching out to pull himself across the floor
into a more comfortable position.

Jean-Paul looked up and saw John. He shoved past the others, moving
fast. The big man dealt John a fast, brutal kick. Then he turned around,
walked back into the hall, and slammed the door behind him.

All that was left was the sickly glow of amber light.

Devin sat in the passenger seat of the small aircraft, watching the world pass beneath him.

One plane. One pilot. Three passengers. One duffel bag—contents: four assault rifles, four pistols, and more than a hundred rounds of ammunition.

Devin looked at his watch.

It was all taking too long. They had to get to John before—

He didn't even like the man.

There was more to this than one man. But somehow he still felt responsible. Maybe he would have liked John Temple in a different life, if he'd simply been Devin's shoe salesman, or waiter—or even just a friend. But there were politics involved.

Devin touched a fingertip to his bowing forehead.

They'd been turned against each other. Their single greatest source of strength was their unity, and they'd allowed themselves—for hundreds of years—to be torn apart.

He felt the future.

The screaming. The thrashing. The water. The blood.

Devin clenched his fist in frustration. They had to make it to John in time.

Hassan sat at the table, eyes wandering over the slick gray fabric of his expensive suit.

A beautiful weave, he thought.

Too much time had been spent on the American. They'd wasted nearly two and a half hours trying to get answers that weren't going to come.

The mission should have begun already, but they were still trying to find out what had happened to Tariq. Every moment they spent here was another moment they might be found.

Maybe they were under surveillance.

Maybe the operation was already in jeopardy.

Maybe it wasn't.

Perhaps the smug young man really didn't know anything, in which case he was no longer of any use.

"Ibrahim," Hassan said calmly.

"Yes?"

"Get the video camera. I want to record it when we cut off the American's head."

The plane hit the runway with a squeal, the tires dragging across the black asphalt.

"Will the car be ready for us?" Blake asked.

Devin nodded. He had made sure the rental would be ready when they landed. It would be easier that way.

Five minutes later they were out of the plane, four figures moving across the runway in the morning light. Their destination would take some time to get to. He could feel it. For the first time in his life Devin Bathurst could feel exactly what was happening right then.

The morning air tickled his skin. The sun warmed his face. And the dangers pulled him forward.

The duffel bag, filled with weapons, dropped into the trunk, and the hatch slammed shut. Devin climbed into the driver's seat and turned the key. Midsize sedan. Manual transmission. Silver.

If he was going to drive toward the valley of the shadow of death, then he was going in style.

John lay on the floor.

The doorknob turned slowly, squealing. Light sliced in through the widening gap as the door opened. His eyes—accustomed to the dark—stung under the flood of new light.

Feet entered, wreathed in an angelic glow that hugged the blurry outline of an expensive dress shoe. A shadow fell across him, salving his eyes from the bitter sting of the blazing light—a moment of relief, soured by the knowledge of its source.

Hassan.

The man stood over him, watching with a kind of predatory hunger.

John tried to pull himself up, tried to fight his way to his feet.

A harsh kick sent him back to the floor.

Ali, the fourth man, entered. Three rough kicks in rapid succession. John went limp. Zip ties clasped around his wrists, holding him in place.

Ibrahim entered. A tripod. A digital camera.

The big man—Jean-Paul. He had something in his hand.

A hacksaw.

John tried to back away.

Jean-Paul stopped.

Hassan knelt. "There are things we want you to say for the camera. Do you understand?"

John snarled through the blood and rusty water that drizzled from his lips. Droplets sprayed from his mouth.

"One last time. What happened to Tariq?"

John let his eyes droop. They were going to kill him. All that was left was to buy time.

"He's dead."

Hassan nodded. "I don't mourn him. He died as a martyr. To mourn him would disgrace his memory."

"They're coming," John said defiantly.

"Excuse me?"

"There are more of us. And they're coming here to stop you."

"Then we'll simply have to move quickly. There is a subway station less than a block from here. Our target is only a few stops away. And even if they catch up with us before then, we are more than capable of setting off our explosives in the trains themselves—killing hundreds."

"That's not your target."

"But a potent message, no less."

"They're going to stop you."

Hassan laughed. "Really? And you can tell the future?"

John laughed in return. "No, that's Devin's job."

"And who is Devin?"

"A man you don't want to meet."

Hassan nodded. "Then I'll make sure that I don't." He motioned for Jean-Paul, then pointed to Ibrahim. "Start the camera."

The man with the hacksaw approached.

"They're almost here," John said, realizing it himself as if for the first time.

Hassan balked. "That's ridiculous." He pointed at Jean-Paul, motioning the man to perform his task.

The big man moved forward, grabbing John by the hair, pulling it back hard, thrusting his chin into the air, exposing his neck.

John looked forward, into the eyes of the man in front of him.

Death was all he saw.

The desire to cause death. To experience death. To die.

He remembered what Tariq had said—that they loved to die as much as others loved to live.

How unfortunate.

Jean-Paul placed the sharp, fanglike teeth of the hacksaw against the left side of John's neck and pushed forward—

Skin split, tearing apart in a slicing line.

Pain shot through his body—no—not pain—the warm sensation of cutting flesh, then the terrifying feeling of dead skin hanging from his neck to either side of the bleeding divide.

Blood sprayed from the laceration.

Screaming was all that John heard.

His own horrified screams.

Hassan watched as the saw made its first stroke through the soft flesh of John Temple's neck, slicing through skin toward the blood-rich artery beyond.

"Hey!" Ibrahim called from the other room.

The screaming stopped with the cutting. Jean-Paul approached, coming to Hassan's side.

Ibrahim came running from the window in the next room.

"There's someone here. Four of them."

"Get the guns!" Hassan shouted.

Canvas came off of the stack of weapons. AK-47s with massive drum magazines carrying a hundred rounds each. UZIs. Grenades. Bullets. All meant to keep the police back when they took control of the school—but now they would be more practical.

Jihad—more than just the closer devotion to the path of God that so many holy men spoke of, but an actual holy battle in which they would strike down their foes before moving on to the fury ahead of them.

Hassan nearly smiled to himself.

So these were the people who had come to stop them. His father had fought in Afghanistan against the Soviets as one of the Mujahedin. He himself had hoped to fight one last battle himself before the end.

They would shoot their way out. Kill the four trespassers, go to their target, and execute their mission.

They would win this battle too. They were better armed—and they were ready.

Chapter 29

THIS WAS THE PLACE. Devin felt it. Rundown. Beat up. But the place nonetheless.

This is where it all had to happen. This was the time when it all would end.

They pulled into the alley, away from prying eyes. The vehicle stopped. Each stepped out of the car. The trunk snapped open, and he pulled out the duffel bag. Devin handed a pistol to Hannah. She looked it over.

"Is this the only way?"

Devin reached into the bag and removed a UMP .45 submachine gun, a rugged piece of equipment with a folding stock and a blocky front end, accented by grooves along the top of its frame. "You're welcome to stay in the car if you feel it would be better."

Hannah didn't speak. She simply reached for a magazine, jamming it into the base of the grip, then donned a Kevlar vest.

Devin led them—a party of four—down the alley. There was a wheelchair ramp at the back of the building leading up to a graffiti-ridden door. Devin moved to the hatch, giving it a small tug.

It moved.

The door was unlocked and open. He turned to the others. "Stay close to me," he said as reassuringly as he could. "Keep your head down and your eyes open."

They nodded with him.

Trista looked scared but determined. Hannah held her weapon with confidence but showed obvious signs of fear. Blake, however, simply looked ready to kill.

"Remember—incoming fire has the right of way. Don't play in the traffic. Your job is to support me. Do what I say and don't panic. Got it?"

Nervous nods.

"Good."

He opened the door and entered cautiously.

The first floor was dark. A long hallway with rooms to either side. A set of stairs at the far end with a glow of light pouring down from above.

Devin moved forward slowly. Carefully.

The hall was dark. Dank with soggy floorboards. The smell of mold hanging in the air. The decaying steps just ahead.

Overhead they heard the sound of feet moving across the creaking floorboards. Strings of dust and chalk slipped from the ceiling above.

Devin stopped. The others held behind him.

He felt it coming.

The grenade tumbling down the old, corroding steps. The sounds of the metallic casing bouncing down by threes, pin-wheeling, twisting on an elliptical axis, offset by the grenade's blocklike fuse.

Devin stared. It hadn't happened—

—yet.

"Get back!" he shouted, pushing backward, and then he heard the explosive start to tumble.

Everything began to happen fast.

Trista hit the floor, falling into place next to Hannah as she was shoved into a nearby room by Devin.

The grenade exploded with a deafening bang.

The sounds of twirling shrapnel buzzed through the air like killer bees, pattering against the walls like rain. A cloud of thick, brown dust rolled through the hall. Chunks of plaster tumbled from the ceiling.

Trista watched as Devin was up in a flash, across the hall in another room, body pressed against the wall, squatting low. His shoulders pivoted, torso spinning out into the hallway, weapon ready.

An explosion of gunfire—brass spewing from the chattering mechanism—the ejector door snapping back and forth like a piston.

Devin disappeared through the dust, thunderous gunfire following behind.

A thousand pinpricks of gun chatter ripped at the door frame, filling it with holes the size of Trista's fist. Chunks of wood did cartwheels through the air as the wood—old and black—was chopped to bits.

Why had she come? What had she been thinking? These people meant to kill her, not just scare her off. These people wanted them all dead. She threw her arms over her head.

Someone down the hall shouted something in Arabic. Another person shouted back. Something tumbled over the top of her—Hannah, thrusting her upper body into the hall.

Hannah squeezed the trigger—

The weapon chugged like a freight train, roaring out a chorus of bullets. On and on with an unrelenting spray of bullets.

The rifle's action snapped open, pinned in place—

—*click*—

"*Grenade!*" Blake's voice hollered through the drift of tumbling dust.

Hannah stood, racing at Trista—slamming her weight into Trista's body, covering her.

What had gotten into this girl?

The explosion was only loud for a second—a piercing snap and then a stinging jab to the ear, like ice picks stabbing for her brain. The shock wave pushed them forward—a section of wall blowing inward, disintegrating. Dust filled the room instantly.

The violent exchange continued without them in the hall.

Hannah was standing, hacking. She pressed the release on the side of her weapon, and the magazine slipped out, falling to the floor with a thud. She reached for Trista—

"Come on!"

Trista stood, looking Hannah in the eye. This was a new creature.

Three stray rounds came popping through the wall, sending bits of confetti spraying from one side of the room to another, leaving a group of distantly placed holes on the far wall.

They shrieked in unison.

A sudden thought of John entered her mind.

Trista gripped her weapon, ducking toward the chunk of blasted wall. She lifted the butt of the weapon and knocked a hanging slab of drywall from its place. She jammed the muzzle of her submachine gun between the severed wires and splintered two-by-fours, squeezing down on the trigger.

The weapon snarled.

John heard the gunfire. It was all going on downstairs—maybe two floors below.

His body ached. He clutched the side of his bleeding neck. The door hung open.

They'd left him alone.

He pushed himself up with his spare arm. Pain sliced up his side. He gripped the side of the freezing bathtub, squeezing with all his might. His body lifted.

Shouts, screams, and gunfire wafted up to his ears from below.

His feet came into place beneath him, and he walked into the next room.

He tried to focus. His vision was blurred, one eye nearly swollen shut. John steadied himself against the table, letting his eyes lift.

A swath of canvas—beneath it lay a stockpile of weapons.

His hand reached out, almost instinctively, and clutched the first thing he could find—a pistol.

It was unlike him—but these were desperate moments.

Somewhere in the back of his mind he fought a theological debate about violence and war and the thought of turning the other cheek—a time and a season for all things under the sun.

He snapped the safety to the off position.

If ever there were a time to kill, then this was it.

Devin watched as the shooter retreated up the stairs again. Whoever they were, they were blind firing at best. With the dust there was no chance of him hitting anything—but he was effectively cutting off that approach.

Something caught his attention to the right—another hallway— another set of steps. There was another way up, which meant there was another way down also. He had to plug the hole.

The dust in the hall was beginning to clear. Trista and Hannah stood on the opposing side. Trista braced herself against the battered wall, firing madly.

"You two!" He jammed a finger at them.

Hannah looked up.

"Cover the stairs!" he shouted through the din, pointing. Hannah nodded, leaning into the hall under Trista.

Devin stepped into the hall as Hannah started shooting. He plunged through the dust, charging toward the second set of steps.

"What are you doing?" Blake demanded.

Devin looked back—Blake. Even now he couldn't stand the thought of not being in charge—of taking a supporting role, even when he was needed elsewhere.

But now wasn't the time to debate the role of leaders.

"Keep up!"

Hassan scrambled, pulling back from the steps. They had a foothold downstairs; it had to be broken. He pointed to Ibrahim.

"Another grenade," he shouted in his native tongue.

Ibrahim pulled the pin, counted, tossed it down the stairs.

Whoever was downstairs let out a long, heavy burst of suppressing fire. They were simply shooting at air. Amateurs. But they were holding the stairs.

"Ibrahim."

"Eh?" The young man looked back at him.

"Get downstairs. Use the back way. Cut them off from behind."

Ibrahim stood, rushing to the next room.

An exchange of fire. Ibrahim back-pedaled fast, rushing toward

Hassan. "Too late!" The door slammed shut behind—bullets instantly blowing holes through the wood.

Not good. They were outmaneuvering them. Hassan spun, falling to his backside, sitting on the floor, holding the AK-47 out in front, spraying a raucous volley of rounds at the doorway—raking the surrounding wall with bullets.

The weapon tried to leap from his hands. Bucking. Kicking. Raising off target. He fought the rifle down, the muzzle flashes obstructing his already stuttering view.

A line of bullet holes pierced at the wall into the room beyond.

"GOD IS GREATEST!" he screamed.

The far wall frothed with bursting holes, sending splashes of faded wallpaper bursting into the room in a thick cloud. The door was fraying—falling from its hinges.

Devin cut left, throwing himself down behind a dusty, withered couch. Somewhere to the right Blake slammed his back into a wall behind some kind of countertop.

The burst ended. Devin fell to his shoulder at the left end of the couch, opening fire, punching holes through the barricading door. Blake must have joined the fray also—a string of holes, in a steadily rising line, streaked across the wall from the right.

A second volley replied—two shooters this time, dozens of rounds.

The wall perforated. Pictures fell from the wall and an old clock exploded.

Windows shattered beyond the boards that kept out the light. A giant cardboard box began to disintegrate. Plumes of paper drifted through the air in a cloud.

Blake was resorting to his pistol, sending return rounds through the plaster.

A bullet punched a hole through the wall, streaking past Devin's face to the sound of a zipper pulled too fast.

He reloaded and returned fire.

John stumbled through the hall. The world was blurring. Tipping. Undulating beneath his feet like a wave.

He fell, gripping the edge of a window frame. His shirt was soaked in blood, running from his neck. His hand clenched the wound, applying pressure.

He had to get downstairs. He could feel them—Devin, Hannah... *Trista.*

John gripped the pistol and pushed himself up.

Hassan pulled himself behind cover.

The wall they were shooting through was coming down in chunks.

They were surrounded. They were cut off. Something deep inside him told him that this was not a battle they would win as easily as he'd thought.

If he could get to the explosives and out to the subway, he could get to a target. He wouldn't be able to kill as many as he had hoped—but the message would still be profound.

Ibrahim shouted in frustration at the other end of the room, firing madly at the wall. A deafening chain of bullets erupted in the action, lancing out at the wall. Then the gun snapped to a stop—

Empty.

Ibrahim was clawing at a nearby table for another magazine.

Hassan looked back at the wall.

Then something strange happened. For a split second all the gunfire stopped. There was no shooting. No explosions. No shouting. For a split second there was—

Silence.

The sound of a single stray bullet punched through the wall, sending a shower of debris through the air.

Hassan was looking down, reaching for his pistol, when he heard Ibrahim gasp. The edge of a gurgle ran at the front of the choking wheeze. Hassan threw his attention to the other man—

Ibrahim stood in the middle of the room, weapon tumbling from his hands—a bright red puncture wound glowing with crimson in the man's right side, clasped beneath tightly clenched fists.

He watched as Ibrahim looked back at him with a look of shock and confusion, sucking air from an obvious lung wound—

Then fell.

He stared. The body didn't move. Didn't breathe. The pool of red began to spread across the floor.

Hassan turned back to the wall, raising his weapon. He screamed as he let loose a rapid succession of rounds.

Then he stood. He had to get upstairs.

There was only one thing left to do.

Trista was working the action on her weapon, trying to jam another magazine into place.

"I'm out," Hannah announced, dropping her assault rifle, reaching for the pistol at her side.

They heard screaming. Someone coming down the steps—fast.

Trista couldn't get the magazine to go in properly. She fought the angle.

"Stay here," Hannah shouted over the shooting.

"What?" Trista looked up and saw Hannah throw herself into the hall, firing with the pistol—

There was a clatter of explosive shots, and something hit Hannah—she clutched her side. She tumbled back. Her body hit the floor.

Trista stared. Shocked. Confused.

The footsteps continued down the stairs.

"Trista," Hannah murmured.

Trista fought the weapon.

The footfalls were off the steps now. On the concrete. Headed their way. Ten feet. Five feet. A cracking sound as the weapon cocked.

"Trista!" Hannah murmured again, near frantic.

Trista adjusted her weapon, shoving the magazine into place. It slipped into position with a snug click.

"*Trista!*" Hannah screamed.

Trista didn't look. She simply threw her arm into the hall, weapon in hand, firing blindly.

The weapon sounded like a long roll of thunder echoing down the hallway, the jingle of brass following in a twinkling downpour.

The gun went quiet.

Something hit the floor.

Trista looked into the hall where Hannah lay clutching her side. Hannah tried to prop herself up on an elbow.

"Are you OK?"

"The vest took the hit," she replied, mostly shocked.

"What happened to the shooter?"

Hannah pointed toward her feet. Trista stood, craning her head into the hall.

Not two feet from Hannah lay a corpse, weapon in hand.

Trista thought she was going to be sick.

They must have hit one. The amount of fire had slowed considerably—the density lessening.

Devin checked his UMP—empty. He reached for his pistol. He stood, moving to the room beyond. Blake stood and followed after.

Devin moved toward the doorway, pistol raised, locked in place, aiming straight ahead. He edged toward the frame and in one fast move turned into the room.

A lone man was running out the far door, pistol in hand.

An exchange of fire. The sound of each pistol's blasts merged with the sounds of the other. A bullet landed in the door frame, sending a cloud of sharp splinters ripping through the air. Devin gripped his cheek and dropped to the floor. The other man fled.

Blake shoved his way over Devin, making chase.

"Blake!" he shouted after. "Wait!"

Too late. Blake was trying to catch up with the lone gunman.

Devin looked around. His pistol was on the floor to the left. He must have dropped it. Devin grabbed his weapon and tore after Blake.

Through the doorway. A set of stairs to the right. He dashed up the steps to the sounds of running just ahead.

Shouting. Gunfire.

His shoulder hit the door that hung ajar, throwing it open. His pistol came to bear.

An empty room. He moved down the hallway, to the right, and into another room. Empty also.

Something was familiar about this place. A table sat in the middle of the room. Canvas covered a stockpile of ammunition and explosives.

Devin heard another outburst of screams and gunfire a floor above. He turned to go toward it, then something caught his eye—

The bathroom.

He recognized the place. It was where they had kept John.

Devin stepped toward it. This was where the beheading was supposed to take place.

He noticed a small puddle of blood on the floor, mixing with the thin film of water that covered the tile. Devin moved forward, into the bathroom. Overhead the light flickered off and on. A sickly amber glow filled the room.

This was the kind of place nightmares were made of.

A tripod stood in the corner, a camera perched on it. Devin walked toward it, mind racing. If they'd killed John, they'd have recorded it. He had to see. His hand reached for the power switch, flicking it to VCR mode, snapping the viewfinder into place. Devin's stomach turned at the thought of what he might see.

Then he heard something in the next room.

Heavy footsteps, near the table, scooping up metallic objects—ammunition.

The view screen flashed blue, sounding off a joyful ping to announce its activation.

The person in the next room stopped, jamming a magazine into their weapon.

They were curious.

Footsteps approached, cautiously, to the side to stay out of the line of fire.

Devin thought about throwing himself into the doorway, firing wildly. His better judgment stayed his hand.

The barrel of an AK assault rifle peeked through the doorway, waist height, flagging the position of the incoming individual.

A mistake.

Devin capitalized, his foot lifting high, slamming into the front end of the weapon. The gun went off, sending a bluster of gunfire into the far wall. The gun hand recovered, trying to swing back into position. Another kick. The gun pinned against the frame.

The rifle went off like thunder—the muzzle flash flickered in the dimness, bullets ripped at the wall. The porcelain toilet exploded. The room blossomed with shards of white. The pipe burst, sending a torrential spray of water blasting through the room. Water touched one of the fluorescent bulbs overhead, and it exploded in a downpour of sparks.

Devin leaped forward, pistol blasting—the shot sent wide by a swinging fist.

The big man lunged into him. Thin by proportion, but a foot taller. Long curly hair. Scruffy mustache.

Devin took a blow to the face.

His world spun in the tumult of water and sparks, the only remaining light flickering like a strobe.

Devin's foot slipped on the wet floor, and he went hurtling backward. A solid kick sent the pistol from his hand, sliding behind the destroyed toilet. He flipped to his front and onto his hands and knees to push his way up in the swirling inch of water.

Brawny hands grabbed the back of his shirt.

Devin felt himself being lifted, then plunged beneath the surface of the bathtub's water.

Bitter cold water.

Chunks of ice floated around his ears.

The hands pulled him back—then dunked him again.

Devin held his breath. The hands pulled him back again.

He moved with the force of the pull, throwing his head back. The hard bone in the back of his skull connected with the man's face, and he stumbled back, clutching his nose. Blood slicked the tumbling drops of water that clattered to the floor.

Devin spun and kicked at the back of the guy's knee. The big man recovered fast. Devin punched hard, striking the already bloody face.

The man's head snapped back—whiplashed by the force of the punch. Long curly strands snapped backward, water cascading from them.

Three vicious blows. Rapid succession. The big man began to buckle from the onslaught.

Devin felt brawny hands grab his collar—his body was shoved back, slamming into the wall, forming a crater in the plaster. An ancient calendar—open to July of 1972—fell from the wall.

Devin punched again.

The man stumbled back.

Another blow. And another. And another.

A heavy fist took Devin across the cheek. Strong fingers curled around his neck. His body shifted hard as his weight was thrown against the sink, hitting it with his hip. The wind escaped him. The man focused on Devin's throat, squeezing.

A swift blow from each side landed hard on the sides of the big man's head. He let go with his strangling hand. An elbow to the man's forehead—the terrorist's skull connected with the medicine cabinet. The glass mirror fractured with a caving smash, the glass giving way in a spider-webbing crater.

Pills, bottles, and toiletries spilled from the shelves into the sink.

The big man shoved Devin back, and he fell against the claw-foot bathtub, his head hitting the hard metal. He howled in pain.

Devin tumbled to the tile floor, rolling to his chest. He looked up.

The terrorist was in the doorway—AK-47 in hand.

The weapon was leveled at Devin's chest.

The gunman aimed deliberately.

Devin knew what was coming next.

The sounds of gunfire bounced off the walls, echoing through the bathroom.

The bullets punched through the newspapers, shattering the glass, shredding the amber-hued coverings.

The world went still.

Devin braced himself against the bathtub as he watched the man drop to the floor.

Where once had stood the big man now stood another figure—

John Temple, pistol in hand—battered and bloody.

Devin stood, moving toward the other man.

"Are you OK?"

John looked down at the weapon, an expression of horror on his face. He dropped the pistol on the floor—stumbling against the door frame, propping himself up.

Devin looked at the body, then looked back at John.

A realization struck him that he didn't want to admit. He looked at the other man.

"You saved my life."

John looked into Devin's face, the ruddiness leaving his cheeks.

"I know," he said soberly. He put a hand on Devin's shoulder. "I know," he said again.

Then Devin felt it—a gnawing in his stomach.

He pulled John's arm over his shoulder.

"We have to get out of here."

Blake came around the corner, weapon raised high. The fourth and final floor. Nowhere else to run.

He saw a man standing there, stacking explosives into a briefcase.

The window was open to the left. The fire escape clung to the side of the building just outside. The man still intended to carry out his plan.

Blake raised his weapon. His finger moved to the trigger. The sights drifted over the man's chest.

Then he felt it.

Something warm in his chest.

His name is Hassan.

A beautiful woman.

A valiant pursuit.

Young love.

A beautiful wife.

A husband.

School.

A doctor.

The arrival of his first child.

Hassan crying with pride and joy.

A father.

Three children.

A family.

Love.

Violence.

His children killed before his eyes.

His wife dying in his arms.

Pain. Anguish. Fury.

Bloodshed.

Blake looked at the man and saw himself.

No separation. Just two men.

Hassan's eyes lifted.

Blake's weapon lowered.

He wanted to hold the man, to let him sob and weep on his shoulder. So much pain. So much loss.

Blake didn't want this man to die. He didn't want to kill him. He saw the world through this man's eyes—and it was bitter.

Hassan looked at Blake, eyes following the weapon as it lowered. Something softened in the man's eyes. Hassan clutched something in his fist—cylindrical—a detonator?

Then he said something. Loud. Strong. Unwavering. Sincere in belief.

"ALLAHU AKBAR!"

God is the greatest.

Chapter 30

SUNDAY AN EXPLOSION WENT off in an abandoned building in Washington DC." Devin Bathurst fastened a gray tie around his neck, listening to the radio as he prepared for his meeting. "While there are no eyewitness accounts available at this time, preliminary findings indicate that it was the headquarters of a terrorist cell working out of the District of Columbia."

Devin examined the tie in the mirror, removed it, and reached for another, the hotel shower dripping in the background.

"The blast completely destroyed the top floor of the building, causing the eventual collapse of the building. Currently it is believed that the explosive devices that were being built there went off accidentally, killing the occupants of the building. The FBI and Department of Homeland Security have not been forthcoming with additional details. While sifting through the wreckage, the FBI and the Department of Homeland Security both have stated that the remains of five individuals have been found. Three of them have now been identified by dental records, and so far all three have been confirmed to have had ties with Middle Eastern terrorist organizations."

Devin looked at the assortment of ties he'd laid across the bed. None of them were right. His eye was caught by a yellow tie with blue stripes that had been given to him as a gift. He suddenly imagined John Temple wearing it—exactly the kind of thing he would wear.

He thought about what was going to have to be said to these people. The things that needed to be done. Reckless things.

Devin reached for the yellow and blue tie.

"Today we have Allen Feinstein, a representative from the FBI with us. Allen, tell me about what the FBI and the Department of Homeland Security have found so far."

"Well, there are a lot of things I'm not allowed to talk about, but

I can say that as of yet we are still piecing together what did happen, and at this point there is still a lot of speculation. And I'm guessing personally that we will probably never know exactly what happened in Washington DC this last Sunday, but I think I speak for everyone who has been involved in this investigation, that we are all very lucky and very blessed that things happened the way they did, instead of the alternative."

Devin fastened his tie in a double Windsor knot and turned off the radio. He had a meeting to get to.

A group of children scurried in circles around the jungle gym, moving as quickly as their fledgling legs would take them across the sand.

All were safe. None were harmed.

Laughing. Smiling. Living.

John Temple sat on the park bench watching, elbows resting on his knees, fingers clasped casually. High-pitched shrieks of joy lifted from the children's play as they carried on without care for the dangers that daily passed them by.

He smiled at them. So small. So reckless. So free.

They were what he had spent these last days fighting and bleeding for—children. The legacy of the past. The joy of the present. The hope of the future.

Someone sat down next to him.

"Trista?"

"Devin told me you were here," she said. She wore a blue sweater and faded blue jeans. Her hair was down, and a single blonde strand fluttered across her face. "How's your neck?"

"Seventeen stitches," he said, touching the puffy pad on the side of his neck, the swelling bruises on his face throbbing. "I'm going to be fine."

John looked back at the children, a single giddy squeal rising from the gaggle. He cleared his throat. "I heard you were going to be leaving the country." He looked at her and she nodded.

"I figured it would be good to get away from everything for a while."

John nodded. "Where do you plan on going?"

"South America."

"How long are you going to be gone?"

"Awhile. I can't say for certain when I'll be back."

"When do you leave?" John gulped, trying to keep his voice from cracking.

"Tonight," she said firmly. "This is something I have to do. I plan to do some missions work. Get back to what I love." They were quiet for a moment. "Besides, I haven't left the country since you and…" She stopped, her face turning to him with a pained expression. "John," she began hesitantly, "there's something I wanted to discuss with you."

John nodded empathetically.

"These last few days we've spent some time together—"

"I know"—he shook his head—"I know."

"Really?"

"I've done a lot of thinking," he said slowly. "I was wrong to pursue you when I knew you weren't available. I was wrong to walk away without an explanation, and I was wrong to bother you now."

"Oh," she replied.

"It's taken me a long time to realize it, but I was wrong. I should have left you alone."

"I—"

"Everybody was right—it's time for me to move on." He stood, looking her in the eye. "I won't bother you anymore." He remained for a moment, fighting back a tear. "Thank you," he said, looking at the grass, "for being something special to me. It's been an honor to have my heart broken by you." He gave an awkward nod. "Good-bye."

He turned and walked away.

"Wait," she called after him. "Where are you going?"

He stopped, looking back at her, now standing. "Devin said he wanted me to wait for him outside the meeting. He didn't say why."

She didn't seem to care about her question anymore. She stood, looking at him. "Will I see you…when I get back?"

"If you'd like that."

She gave a small nod. "I would."

He smiled.

"OK."

Devin Bathurst stood at the front of the room, looking out. The top representatives from each of the orders had come. The richest, the most political, the most ambitious, all trying to use this meeting as some sort of leverage in the wake of everything that had gone wrong. In theory they had come to Colorado to finish the business they had begun in San Antonio. But these were the people who still thought this was all a game—the ones who had missed everything that had happened these last few days.

"We failed," Devin said flatly. "We failed to stand together. We let perspective get in the way of truth—and we let it divide us. Good men made poor choices and paid dearly for their mistakes."

They stared at him—twenty-five men and women from three different orders, spread around the long conference table. None of them so much as blinked.

"We alienated each other. We shunned the Fallen. We let politics get in the way of something bigger." He looked the room over. "Shame on us."

Someone at the far end of the table raised his hand—Vincent Sobel, in a pressed Italian suit and perfect hair, as always.

"Yes?"

"In the wake of Blake Jackson's...untimely passing, I would like to nominate Devin Bathurst to be our new Overseer."

There were nods.

"Agreed," said a middle-aged woman representing the Prima. "I second the motion."

Sounds of approval filled the room.

"I say we put it to a vote," Vincent Sobel announced as he stood, opening his hands to the room. Approving noises. "All in favor say 'aye.'"

A chorus of voices.

"All opposed?" he continued.

Silence.

"The 'ayes' have it then," Vincent said with a nod, smiling.

There was happy chatter.

"Congratulations, Mr. Bathurst," Vincent said with a polished smile, turning his attention to Devin. "It looks like you're our new Overseer."

Devin looked down at a knot in the table's wood, focusing on it for a moment, then looked back.

"Politely," he said with his typical composure, "I'm afraid that I'm going to have to decline."

"What?" Vincent asked, genuinely surprised. He let out a nervous laugh.

Sounds of concern filled the room.

"I'm afraid," Devin began, "that I'm not the right man for the job."

"But," Vincent replied, trying and failing to conceal his overwhelming embarrassment, "Everybody loves you. You're the future of the Firstborn."

"No," Devin said firmly. "You want me because I don't challenge the way things are. You, Vincent, want me specifically because you think you know how to manipulate me politically."

"Hey!" Vincent protested, face flushed with the anger that rose from underneath his glossy exterior.

Devin continued. "I don't challenge the way things are done. I maintain the status quo, and sometimes that's good. But right now what we need is someone a little tougher to love. Someone a little more reckless. Someone less aware of how to play the politics and more likely to actually act out of his conscience."

"What are you suggesting?" Vincent demanded, leaning forward.

Devin smiled. "I hereby nominate John Temple as Overseer."

A collective gasp filled the room.

"You must be joking!" Vincent said, throwing a pen as he collapsed back into his seat.

The other representatives joined in Vincent's angry protest.

"I am not joking," Devin announced, signaling the more than two dozen protestors to quiet down. "If it weren't for that man I might have spent my whole life thinking I couldn't possibly be wrong."

"I can't believe you're serious," Vincent groaned, shaking his head.

None of these people, save Devin and Hannah, had been there when Morris died, when they had stood together. None of them had seen the man John Temple had proved himself to be. They were exactly the people who needed a wake-up call, exactly the people who needed to lose control over everything they had.

"I second the motion," a voice said from the far end of the table.

All heads turned.

Hannah Rice.

Vincent Sobel leaned across the table toward her. "You can't possibly—"

"He's the man this organization needs." Wearing a gray pantsuit, she stood tall and alert. "John Temple has proven himself to be a man of courage and character."

"Ms. Rice," Vincent said firmly, "I'm going to have to ask you to rescind your motion."

She shook her head. "No," she said, and took her seat.

"Look," Vincent said, voice filled with disgust, "no one here knows him like I do. No offense to John, but he's brash, he's reckless, he has no sense of duty or dependability. He hasn't had a real job in years. I've had to babysit him for Clay ever since the whole Trista Brightling incident…"

Devin balked, reaching for a nearby Bible that sat idly on the table. He lifted it and flung the book across the tabletop. The leather cover glided across the table and came to a slow stop. "Read it," he said flatly. "Love your enemies and love each other. It's that simple."

Devin began to walk for the door as the room spilled over with protest.

"Devin," Vincent announced as he stood, "we want *you* as Overseer!"

"Fine," Devin replied, loosening his tie, "I accept."

Sighs filled the room.

"My first order is to announce John Temple as my successor—and to step down."

Devin stepped out of the room, leaving the sounds of shouting behind him.

Devin moved into the hall.

John stood in the hall, looking very uncomfortable in a tie. "What's going on in there? What did you say?"

"Thank you for meeting me here," Devin said, patting the young man on the shoulder. "You're our new Overseer."

"*What?*" John blurted. "How am I supposed to—?"

Devin laughed. "Do what you can to bring them together—then dismantle the office. God needs to be in control of this, not us."

John shook his head in confusion. "Why don't you do this?"

"Because I'm not the right man for the job. The world needs people like me—but not for this. I'm a political animal. No matter how hard I want to make things better, I'd only keep things political. What these people need is to have their world turned on its ear."

"That's reckless."

"I know," Devin said with a nod, "but that's your area of expertise." He looked at the door. "Now get in there and make your inaugural address."

"Devin, I—"

"Don't say anything. Just—"

John threw his arms around Devin, pulling him close in a manly bear hug. Devin was startled for a moment, then put his arms around John, giving him a squeeze.

"I'll pray for you," Devin said.

"Good," John said, stepping back, face panicked, "because I'm going to need it."

Devin nodded, then let go and walked down the hall.

Behind him he could hear the doors of the conference room opening. John was entering the room as Overseer.

Their world would never be the same again.

Devin reached for his car keys, fishing them out of his pocket. He approached the rental car.

Midsize. Manual transmission. Sedan.

—blue.

He unlocked the door and looked at the setting sun.

Things were changing. For the first time in half a millennia the Firstborn were coming together—being forced to face all of their many differences—and their single similarity.

Blake. Overseer. Terrorists. Perhaps that was all drawing to a strangely melancholy close. But they were talking, whether they liked it or not. This wasn't the end.

Then he felt it with his whole body—the future.

This was just the beginning.

Acknowledgments

I WOULD LIKE TO THANK the following:

Allan Cecil: I couldn't have done this without you. More than anyone, you helped me write this book.

Mom: For all the encouragement and support over the years. I'm a proud mama's boy.

Dad: For believing in me. I can't put into words how much that means to me.

Karen Dyke: For being my helping friend and encouragement during the writing process.

Jeff Gerke: For ALL the help. I owe you a huge debt of gratitude I can't hope to repay.

Debbie Marrie: For acquiring an unknown like me and giving me a chance.

Lori Vanden Bosch: For making the editing process such a blast.

Dr. James Keaten: For introducing me to behavioral orientations and intrafaith dialogue—and all our long conversations.

Dr. Thomas Endres: For not kicking me out of your office when I needed to talk.

Russel Garrett: The strongest man alive.

Lee Vary: For the helpful ideas that got me through in a pinch.

Jessica Barnes: For being an awesome friend and answering my questions.

Greyson: My brother and friend. A real-life Devin Bathurst.

Squirt: I love you, sis.

And everyone else who saw me through this process that I didn't have room to mention. I love you all.

FREE NEWSLETTERS
TO HELP EMPOWER YOUR LIFE

Why subscribe today?

☐ **DELIVERED DIRECTLY TO YOU.** All you have to do is open your inbox and read.

☐ **EXCLUSIVE CONTENT.** We cover the news overlooked by the mainstream press.

☐ **STAY CURRENT.** Find the latest court rulings, revivals, and cultural trends.

☐ **UPDATE OTHERS.** Easy to forward to friends and family with the click of your mouse.

CHOOSE THE E-NEWSLETTER THAT INTERESTS YOU MOST:

- Christian news
- Daily devotionals
- Spiritual empowerment
- And much, much more

SIGN UP AT: **http://freenewsletters.charismamag.com**

8178